MAHIMATA

BOOK 2 OF ASIANA

RATI MEHROTRA

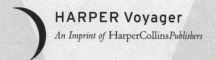

HARPER Voyager
An Imprint of HarperCollinsPublishers

MAHIMATA. Copyright © 2019 by Rati Mehrotra. All rights reserved. Printed in the United States of America. No part of this book may be used or reproduced in any manner whatsoever without written permission except in the case of brief quotations embodied in critical articles and reviews. For information, address HarperCollins Publishers, 195 Broadway, New York, NY 10007.

HarperCollins books may be purchased for educational, business, or sales promotional use. For information, please email the Special Markets Department at SPsales@harpercollins.com.

Harper Voyager and design are trademarks of HarperCollins Publishers LLC.

FIRST EDITION

Designed by Michelle Crowe
Lotus ornament by teamplay/Shutterstock, Inc.
Map illustration by Amy Goh

Library of Congress Cataloging-in-Publication Data has been applied for.

ISBN 978-0-06-256455-9

19 20 21 22 23   LSC   10 9 8 7 6 5 4 3 2 1

ALSO BY RATI MEHROTRA

Markswoman

Mahimata

Praise for *Markswoman*

"Well-developed characters and intriguing worldbuilding . . . will keep readers engrossed in this fast-paced, enchanting postapocalyptic fantasy debut."

—*Library Journal* (starred review)

"An utterly remarkable world with female assassins and telepathic blades; I adored this book."

—*New York Times* bestselling author Julie Kagawa

"Mehrotra's page-turning debut concocts a solid fantasy world with a strong heroine. Readers will look forward to the next in the series."

—*Booklist*

"*Markswoman* gives us a heroine as principled as she is fierce, a gifted outcast who is forced to navigate the maze of treachery at the heart of a unique and finely drawn world."

—A. J. Hartley, author of *Steeplejack*

"*Markswoman* is unputdownable. Rati Mehrotra paints a vivid world filled with compelling characters, awesome knives, and all the thrilling adventure and drama you could want."

—Sarah Beth Durst, award-winning author
of the Queens of Renthia series

"*Markswoman* is a breathlessly paced postapocalyptic fantasy with a highly original setting and characters you can't help but love (and hate)."

—Beth Cato, author of *Breath of Earth* and *The Clockwork Dagger*

ACKNOWLEDGMENTS

This is the book of my heart. Yet it would not exist without the help of several amazing and talented people.

First and foremost, I must thank my editors at Harper Voyager, Priyanka Krishnan and David Pomerico, for guiding this little craft to safety. Thanks also to designer Damonza and art director Jeanne Reina for the lovely cover and to the entire team at Harper Voyager for all their hard work in making this book possible.

My deep gratitude to my agent, Mary C. Moore of Kimberley Cameron & Associates, for being my beta reader, advocate, and advisor.

Thanks to all the friends and fellow writers who read and critique my work: Charlotte, Ariella, Phoebe, Kari, and Vanessa. The writerly life would be very isolating if I did not have you.

Much love to my parents, grandmother, and sister for their enthusiasm for and encouragement of my creative pursuits.

Lastly, thanks to you, dear reader, for sharing this journey with me. I hope we meet again.

CONTENTS

Map   IX

The Five Orders of Peace   XI

PART I

 1: *The Only Worthwhile Penance*   3
 2: *Samsarandev*   11
 3: *The Dark of His Mind*   19
 4: *The True Successor*   25
 5: *Igiziyar*   38
 6: *Wolf's Kiss*   49
 7: *Menadin*   59
 8: *Doors and Dreams*   68
 9: *Up the Holy Mountain*   74
10: *Amaderan*   83

PART II

11: *The Council of Ferghana*   95
12: *The Funerary Chamber*   104

13: *Nineth*   115

14: *In the Cavern*   121

15: *The Seeing Stone*   127

16: *Message from Kai Tau*   133

17: *Two Worlds*   140

18: *The Apprentice Smith*   150

19: *The Door to Kunlun Shan*   159

20: *Time Outside Time*   166

21: *The Beast in the Forest*   172

22: *A Duel and a Theft*   181

23: *The Secret of the Sahirus*   190

PART III

24: *The Temple of Valavan*   205

25: *A Burial and a Promise*   216

26: *The Land of the Living*   226

27: *Return to Ferghana*   230

28: *An Unexpected Ally*   240

29: *The Battle of the Wolves*   254

30: *The Gun in His Hand*   263

31: *The Name of the Blade*   270

32: *After the Blood*   278

PART IV

33: *A Friend's Fury*   293

34: *Together, Alone*   305

35: *To Forge Kalishium*   314

36: *Council of War*   326

37: *A Vision from the Past*   331

38: *Reunions*   346

39: *An Hour of Peace*   355

40: *Someone to Fear*   362

41: *The Ride to Jethwa*   370

42: *The Battle of the Thar*   385

43: *Behind the Lines*   399

44: *The Shape of a Man*   405

45: *Ice Mother*   421

46: *The Cost of Victory*   438

47: *Into the Dark*   446

Acknowledgments   459

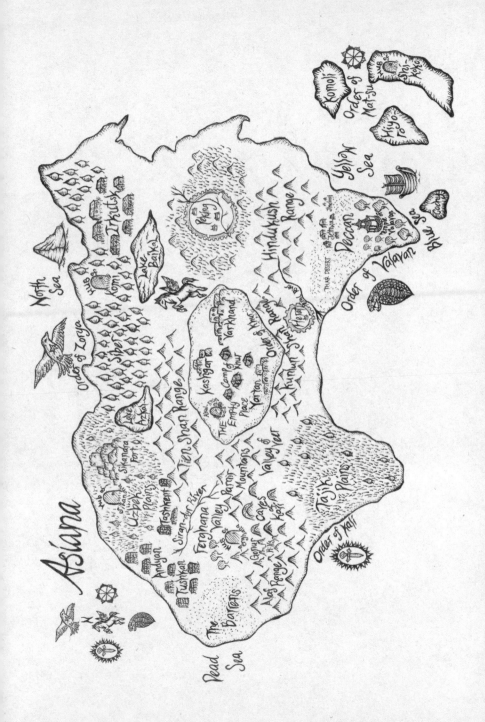

THE FIVE ORDERS
OF PEACE

THE ORDER OF KALI

The oldest Order of Peace in Asiana, its jurisdiction extends from the Pamir Mountains in the east to the Barrens in the west, and Tashkent in the north to the Tajik Plains in the south. The Order dwells in the caves of Kali, discovered by Lin Maya, the first Markswoman of Asiana, in the year 85 of the Kanun. Their symbol is an inverted katari encircled by a ring of fire. Fierce devotees of the Goddess Kali, they burn their dead on funeral pyres, consigning the ashes to sacred urns along with the katari of the deceased.

THE ORDER OF VALAVAN

The second-oldest Order of Peace, it is also the largest. It holds sway over the Deccan peninsula, the most densely populated part of Asiana. Valavian boundaries stretch from Peking in the north to the island of Cochy in the south. The Order dwells in an ancient temple: a step pyramid with nine platforms, each symbolizing a level of enlightenment. Their symbol is a striking cobra, signifying their lethal combat skills. The Valavians practice sky burial, leaving their dead on the roof of the temple for vultures to pick clean.

THE ORDER OF ZORYA

Northern Asiana, ruled by the Zoryans, is a land of taiga, permafrost, cold lakes, and fast rivers. Sparsely inhabited by humans, it is rumored to teem with wyr-wolves. The biggest town in the Zoryan jurisdiction is Irkutsk on Lake Baikal. The symbol of the Order is a soaring white falcon with a star on its breast. True to their symbol, the Zoryans do not stay in one place long, but move with the seasons, across the ice, through the forest, and along the windswept coast. They drag their deceased on sleds to the North Sea, leaving them to float away on ice floes, their kataris tied to their hands.

THE ORDER OF MAT-SU

Rarely seen on the mainland apart from the annual clan assembly, the Order of Mat-su rules the islands of the Yellow Sea, of which the main ones are Komoli, Hiyoro, and Shikoko. They scorn the use of force, and their kataris are mostly for ceremonial purposes. The Mat-su symbol is the eight-spoked wheel of life. They believe in reincarnation and do not mourn the passing of any of their number, choosing instead to hold festive gatherings to celebrate death, no matter how it comes. They speak in riddles, giving them a reputation for wisdom among the islanders and for affectation among the mainlanders.

THE ORDER OF KHUR

The only Order of Peace in Asiana composed of men, it was founded by Zibalik, the first Marksman of Asiana, in the year 240 of the Kanun. Zibalik trained with both the Order of Kali and the Order of Zorya before establishing the camp of Khur in the heart of the desolate Empty Place—protected by miles of cold desert in every direction. Unlike the other Orders, Marksmen stop using their clan names once they swear allegiance to Khur. The symbol of the Order is the winged horse, signifying strength, courage, and freedom. Marksmen bury their dead with their kataris in a grove at the edge of their camp—a cluster of tents in the shelter of a massive dune.

MAHIMATA

PART I

From *The Oral Traditions of the Order of Kali* by Navroz Lan of the Order of Kali

In the beginning there was darkness without thought or form. Then out of the supreme night came a dream of light and life that created ripples in the dark. Time came out of its trance and Kali took form, black-limbed and four-armed. She began to dance, faster and wilder, until the ripples became waves, and the waves became music that rose and crashed on the uttermost reaches of Kali's thought.

Like bubbles from a sea, the first gods—Brahma, Vishnu, and Shiva—rose from the waves of Kali's dance. Brahma, the god of creation, plucked a lotus from Vishnu's navel and divided it into three parts. One part he flung below him, and that became the Earth. One part he flung above him, and that became Amaderan. The third part he flung into the outermost reaches of the universe, and this became the skies and the heavens full of stars.

But it is the Goddess Kali we worship—she who dances freely and from whose dance are woven all things of the beginning. Kali the dark one, who came before light itself, before time itself. From her womb we were all born, and to her we will return in the end.

CHAPTER I

THE ONLY
WORTHWHILE PENANCE

The cold desert that festered in the heart of Asiana, hundreds of miles from any lake or river, had many names. It was called the Desert of No Return, the Sea of Death, or simply the Empty Place. Every year it crept forward, invading villages and killing life. Those who lived in the oasis towns of Kashgar, Yarkhand, and Yartan took care to travel in large, well-stocked caravans, skirting its borders. Even then, lives were lost, entire caravans vanishing into the maw of sudden, savage sandstorms.

In the middle of the desert, twenty miles from Tezbasti, the nearest village, a vast dune curved to the north and east. On the lee side of this dune, against all expectation, was a cluster of tents: the home of the Order of Khur.

The sun sank to the horizon, casting a fiery glow on the little settlement. Somewhere, a camel coughed, a sound that was swallowed by the rising wind.

In the lamp-lit interior of the Maji-khan's tent argued two men: one young and lean, the other massive and gray-bearded. Both wore identical grim expressions.

"You don't know what you're asking." Barkav, the head of the Order of Khur, paced the carpeted length of his spacious tent. "If you wished for a penance, you should have come to me. This is just self-indulgence."

Rustan forced himself to stay calm. He had known this was not going to be easy. No one, not even the Maji-khan of Khur, could understand why he needed to go away. "Father," he began, his voice even but resolute, "being a Marksman means everything to me. *Everything.* This life is all I know, and giving it up is not just a penance. It is the only worthwhile penance. Not forever," he hastened to add, seeing the stormy expression on the Maji-khan's face, "but long enough for me to atone. I took the life of an innocent man."

"You're still blaming yourself for that?" Barkav asked in disbelief. "You acted on *my* orders."

Barkav had sent Rustan to the village of Tezbasti to take down a mark, a man convicted by the elders of the Kushan clan council of murdering his own father. Except that the poor man was innocent; he had been framed by the village's corrupt council.

"I know," said Rustan. "But it was my blade. *My* katari." They had been over this many times, and his anger and guilt over the fatal error had not lessened. If anything, the need to understand himself and come to terms with what he had done was sharper than ever.

Rustan was a Marksman, one of the few men in Asiana bonded to a telepathic kalishium blade—kalishium, that could look into the heart of its keeper and know the truth.

But his katari had not warned him. *I am innocent*, the man had cried. And Rustan had not believed him.

He could not stay with the Order any longer; to do so would be to put himself and others at risk.

"I could command you not to go," said Barkav. "I could put you under guard."

"You could also kill me, Father," said Rustan quietly. "But you will not."

Barkav glared at him, and Rustan tried to meet his eyes without flinching. He knew the Maji-khan would not force him to stay against his will.

"That's not all, is it?" said Barkav in a rough voice. "There's something else. What are you not telling me?"

Rustan swallowed. Now for the hardest part. He had inadvertently confessed his feelings for Kyra to Samant, the Master of Meditation, but he had told no one else. He tried his best not to think about her, the Markswoman who had tumbled out of the Akal-shin door one day and into his heart. It was against the law, the Kanun of Ture-asa, for a Marksman to give in to desire. He had fought against his attraction to Kyra with all he had before realizing how futile his efforts were. One day, in Kashgar, they had kissed. It had felt like a moment of rightness in a world gone wrong. Three days later, Kyra almost died during a duel with Tamsyn Turani, the Hand of Kali.

No matter what the Maji-khan thought of him, Barkav was entitled to the truth. Rustan owed him this much.

"I made a vow," said Rustan. "When Kyra lay dying on the floor of Sikandra Hall, Tamsyn's blade buried in her flesh, I made a pact with . . . with whoever holds the strings we dance on."

"And what was your vow, Marksman?"

Rustan closed his eyes. "Let her live, and I'll not ask for more. I will leave Khur, empty-handed as a beggar."

It came back then, the wave of helpless terror that had washed over him when Tamsyn's blade found its mark in Kyra. She had fallen to the floor, blood seeping from her wound, and he had fought against his fear and willed her to live—and she had opened her eyes. Tamsyn had vanished, as if her existence had been burned away. There was some greater power at work in all this; even if there was not, Rustan still had an oath to fulfill.

Barkav exhaled. For a time, there was silence between them. When the Maji-khan spoke again, he sounded tired. "I have long known how you felt about the Markswoman. But I did not expect you to behave like Shurik."

"I'm not like Shurik," snapped Rustan, anger sharpening his tone. "Please, Father, don't compare us."

Infatuated with Kyra, his friend Shurik had broken the law and used Compulsion to try to make her flee with him from Kashgar. Rustan had caught them just in time and helped Kyra free herself from Shurik's bonds. Rustan had been sickened by Shurik's abuse of the Mental Arts. He had not acted out of love, but selfishness, and Kyra almost paid the price for it.

He thought perhaps Shurik understood this now. The elders had made him give up his blade and meditate from sunup to sundown ever since. Rustan saw him sometimes, stumbling back to his tent after dark, an emaciated shadow of his former cheerful self. He had tried to talk to him once, against the elders' orders, but Shurik shied away from him. Rustan had left him alone after that. The Maji-khan would decide when his punishment was complete; Rustan hoped it would be while Shurik was still alive.

"I know you are not like him," said Barkav. "That is why I expected more. War is coming to Asiana. Kai Tau is forging weapons and amassing an army. We'll need every Marksman we have."

Rustan's stomach twisted. Kai Tau, the leader of the outlaw Tau clan, possessed a dozen kalashiks that he had stolen from the Arikkens several years ago. The guns were a vile legacy of the Great War, and nothing could stand against them. Armed with the deadly weapons, Kai Tau had led the slaughter of the clan of Veer: Kyra's clan. She was the only one who had survived the carnage, and she had sworn to avenge her family. If there was going to be a battle, she was sure to be at the forefront of it.

"Have you heard from Elder Ishtul?" asked Rustan. Barkav had sent the blademaster of Khur to the Thar Desert to spy on the Taus.

"Not yet," said Barkav. "But I've had reports from the Order of Valavan. I've heard rumors of the terror Kai Tau inspires in people. There are even stories that claim he is no longer quite human. Look at this." He retrieved a rolled-up parchment from the top of the wooden trunk that doubled as his desk and tossed it to Rustan.

Rustan caught and unfurled it, frowning.

"It is testimony," said Barkav, before Rustan could ask. "An account from someone who escaped the Taus."

Rustan scanned the bleak words with increasing horror:

My name is Rajes Lubali. I was born in the year 835 of the Kanun in the village of Dhakari, in the central Thar. I am nineteen years old. When the Taus invaded my village, we had some warning from one of our lookouts. We hid the children and the elderly, and the rest of us surrendered without a fight. The Taus made us kneel in the village square with our hands tied behind our backs. They picked some of the men and women—those who were young and strong—and took them away. I was not chosen, I think because I am small and weak from a childhood illness.

We were all afraid of what would happen to those who had been taken away. But we were also relieved not to be chosen. We thought the Taus had got what they wanted and would leave our village. But then a huge man with a monstrous face came forward. He did not walk like a man but was hunched like a beast. Seeing him struck fear in all of us, and some began to cry. "Look at me," he commanded. "Behold your true king before you die." His voice was like many voices speaking together, and we were forced to obey him.

He raised his arms and I saw the barrels of two kalashiks. I realized we were going to be killed. I fell forward as the first shots rang out. Bodies dropped over and around me—among them my parents, sister, aunt, and cousin. I lay beneath the bodies, not moving. One of the guards walked around us, shooting into the bodies. Every second I thought that I would die. But by a miracle, I survived. Late that night, long after the Taus had gone, I crept out. All around me were the dead. I checked for survivors, but no one else was left alive.

Rustan knew from what Kyra had told him that this was chillingly similar to what had happened to her family. Barkav took the parchment back from him. "You see the evil we're up against?" he said. "We have very little time to prepare ourselves. Kai Tau aims to destroy the Orders and set himself up as undisputed king of Asiana. The Taus will bring chaos and darkness to our land. Will you leave now, in this critical hour, instead of standing with us?"

Rustan bowed his head. How easy it would be to lie, to assure his Maji-khan that he would return in the blink of an eye, that he would not abandon his companions in the fight against the murderous outlaws. The truth was much harder.

"Father, I—I cannot tell you that this isn't difficult for me. It sickens me to think of leaving. Especially after reading that testimony. But I *must* go into exile. I will return when my penance is complete. And I do not know how long that will take."

Barkav's face hardened. "I see," he said, his voice like flint. "In that case, you will relinquish your blade before you go."

Shock, ice-cold, flooded Rustan's veins. For a moment, he forgot to breathe. He fought against the sensation of drowning and summoned his inner calm. The Maji-khan was asking him to give up his katari, the weapon he was bonded to, the weapon he'd been born to wield.

And yet, wasn't that the *real* punishment? To be divided from himself, to leave a part of his soul behind.

Silently, he withdrew the slim, double-edged katari from its plain leather sheath and touched the silvery blue blade. He ran his fingers along the smooth grip and stopped at the wooden cross guard, engraved with the symbol of the winged horse. The katari had been his constant companion since the bonding ceremony ten years ago. He could feel its presence like a soft thrum in a room at the back of his mind. What would it be like to have that room silenced?

If he thought about it, he would not be able to do it. Rustan slid the blade back into its scabbard and held it out.

Barkav grasped it and at once a gap opened up within Rustan, a chasm between two halves of himself. He tore his gaze away from the katari in Barkav's hand, trembling with the effort to not reach out and snatch it back.

"I can give you another penance," said Barkav, watching him. He could not quite mask the concern in his eyes. "If you wish, you will be switched day and night for a year. Only, don't leave Khur. Don't give up your blade. That way lies madness."

"I have my mother's blade," said Rustan, his throat dry. "The one that Kyra left in my safekeeping. It will keep me sane." *I hope.*

Barkav watched him awhile longer. "Go then," he said finally, his voice resigned. "May whatever you find be worth the price you pay."

Rustan bowed and slowly left the Maji-khan's tent, one dragging step at a time. The farther he went from his blade, the sharper the agony of separation, until he could barely stay upright.

His penance had begun.

CHAPTER 2

SAMSARANDEV

Kyra woke cold and in pain. The candle had burned down, leaving her in the complete darkness of her cell. She sat up, wincing, and touched the bandage beneath her right breast. Damp again. She would have to ask Elena to change it.

Why would the wound not heal? Kyra could feel every suture that Navroz Lan, the eldest of the elders of Kali, had stitched to close it. Her chest hurt as if she carried live coals within; Tamsyn's blade had missed her lungs and heart but torn open the muscles of her chest wall. "Rest," Eldest had advised, "and all will be well."

Kyra was tired of resting. How long since her duel with Tamsyn in the Hall of Sikandra? A month? Two months? A year had ended, and another had begun. But time lost its meaning in the winter gloom of the caves of Kali. Outside, the Ferghana Valley lay buried in snow—a world of ghostly black and white that yielded nothing. Spring was a distant dream.

She hauled herself up, suppressing a groan. No one rushed to her; Elena must have gone to her own cell to sleep.

No matter, she would go out. Perhaps the cold wind would drive away the remnants of the dreams she'd had. Dreams of doors, blood spilled, and lives brutally cut short. Dreams of a man whose face was hidden from her, but whom she knew with cold certainty was Kai Tau, the butcher of her clan. *He waits for you, all these long years, to free him from the evil he has done. Not until you kill him will he know any rest.* So Astinsai, the seer and katari mistress of Khur, had told her. The old woman was one of the few people alive who could forge kataris from the kalishium that the Ones had left behind when they went back to the stars. Perhaps that was where her power came from—the power to see truths veiled from others.

Kyra pulled a cloak around her shoulders and stumbled out of the cell, guided by the light of a sconce in the corridor. She inched her way along the passage until she arrived at the vast, torch-lit cavern that formed the heart of the caves of Kali. All the sacred rites were held in this immense, light-filled space. On the walls danced Kali the demon-slayer, brandishing her elongated sword. In the middle was the raised central slab where pupils lay for the ceremony that marked their transition from apprentice to Markswoman. It seemed but a short while ago that Kyra herself had lain on it while the elders surrounded her, murmuring blessings. She had seen a vision of Tara then, the maternal aspect of the Goddess Kali: a blue-skinned four-armed woman with a garland of skulls around her neck, wearing a wolfskin skirt. The same vision had come to her when she lay bleeding in the Hall of Sikandra, Tamsyn's blade draining her of life.

Her throat tightened at the memory, and she reached for the

katari that hung in a scabbard around her neck. Calm warmth emanated from it, and Kyra relaxed. She was going to be all right. She had to believe that.

She made for the tunnel that led out of the caves but hesitated. What if Ria Farad was on guard duty tonight? Her ears were sharper than a vixen's. She would make Kyra go back to her cell, perhaps even wake one of the elders to make sure that Kyra obeyed. But Kyra didn't want to lie down again. She was sick of her bed, sick of this restlessness that allowed her no peace.

Her gaze went to the private passage that led to the Mahimata's cell—the cell that would now be empty.

Mother, I miss you so much.

She needed to see Shirin Mam again. She cast a quick glance over her shoulder and ducked into the corridor, hoping none of the elders were up and about. Torches mounted on the wall to her right threw a wavering light on the portraits that hung opposite: each of the Mahimatas who had ruled the Order of Kali since it was founded more than seven hundred years ago. Kyra limped along, ignoring the throbbing in her chest, until she reached the last portrait.

Shirin Mam.

The pain of her wound receded. Kyra reached forward and brushed her fingertips against the cool hardness of the panel.

"Why did you die?" she whispered. Her whisper echoed down the passage—*why, why, why.*

Because it was time.

Kyra started. The voice of her teacher, silent for so long, filled her with longing and sadness. Shirin Mam was dead. Nothing could change that. She would never teach another class, choose a novice, or train a new Markswoman. There was no one left for Kyra to call *Mother.* There never would be again.

Stay alive, Rustan had told her, but there were times in the past few weeks when she wished she had not. Returning to the Order of Kali had not been the homecoming she'd yearned for. Everything felt wrong. The duel with Tamsyn had not brought her peace. It had accomplished nothing except to fill the Ferghana Valley with rumors of witchcraft and black magic.

And her dear friend Nineth was gone, vanished from the caves of Kali. Tamsyn had claimed to have killed her, to have *starved* her to death. Nineth of the crumpled robes and cheerful smile, who loved good things to eat and hated being alone.

It was her fault, whatever had happened to Nineth. If she hadn't taken off with Shirin Mam's blade, if Nineth had not tried to follow her, if, if, if . . .

Kyra turned away from Shirin Mam's smiling face. The Mahimata's cell was dark. Why had no one thought to light a candle in it? Just because Shirin Mam was dead did not mean there should be no light in her cell. She would give the novices an earful tomorrow.

She went inside and felt for the candelabra on Shirin Mam's massive oak desk, then scrabbled around in a drawer until she found the stubs of three candles. She returned to the passage, sweating and trembling with the exertion, and lit the candles with the help of a torch. Then she inserted them carefully in the candelabra and stepped back into the cell.

In the flickering light, Kyra could see Tamsyn had left no mark of her hateful presence in this place; it was Shirin Mam's still, from the ebony chest in the corner to the piles of aging, yellowed books and scrolls on the shelves. It gladdened her, which was absurd. It was not as though either woman would ever come back to this room.

She placed the candelabra on the desk and frowned. A single

item rested on its surface, and it was a curious one: a slim, rectangular package tied with string. She picked it up, turning it over in her hands. It felt like a sheaf of parchment wrapped in linen. A letter of some sort? But there was nothing written on the package, no name to indicate who it was for. Had it been left by Shirin Mam or Tamsyn? Why had no one opened it?

It can be opened only by you.

Kyra dropped the package in shock. After a moment, she managed a smile, even as her pulse raced. "Keep doing that, Mother," she murmured, "even if it stops my heart each time."

She traced the linen with her fingertips. Did this package contain the answers to some of her questions? It was naive, but she had long clung to the hope that Shirin Mam might have left explanations or instructions, a safeguard in case of her untimely death.

Kyra's skin prickled with excitement. With shaking hands, she withdrew her katari and sliced open the strings that held the package together.

Two letters slipped out. She laid them on the candlelit desk and read the names written in Shirin Mam's elegant hand.

The first: *Rustan*.

The second: *Kyra*.

Kyra picked up the letter addressed to Rustan and fingered it, resisting the impulse to tear it open. Resisting the emotions that threatened to choke her.

She missed him with an ache that was sharper, deeper than the wound from Tamsyn's blade. She also hated him for stirring these feelings in her, for not being there when she woke at last in her cell after weeks of being trapped in a fevered delirium.

But why should he be there? His place was with his Order.

Even had he wanted to, the elders of Khur would not have allowed him to come to her.

Not that he would have wanted to.

She swallowed the lump in her throat and turned her attention back to the letter. It was bulky, tied with jute string. She burned to know what it said. At least she now had a good excuse to find him. She would throw the letter in his face and punch him in the jaw. No, she would be cold and polite. He would thank her for the letter, and she would thank him for practicing katari-play with her in preparation for the duel with Tamsyn. Then she would turn around to leave and he would say: *Wait, Kyra.* But she wouldn't wait, she'd walk away from there, leaving him pleading and desperate.

She shook her head, almost laughing at her foolishness. She was back where she belonged, and so was he. She was not going to Khur. There was no point in thinking about it.

Kyra picked up the other letter. With some trepidation—and not a small degree of anticipation—she slit it open.

A single piece of parchment fell out. She gazed at it, frustration churning and building within her until she thought she would explode.

Nothing of help was written on the page, no warm words of guidance, or even sharp ones of admonishment. Instead, there was just an ink drawing. It was a strange picture, vaguely familiar. A woman with rippling black hair held a long, slim blade over the bent heads of a row of kneeling men and women. Kyra gritted her teeth. Trust Shirin Mam to leave her with a riddle. She wanted to tear the parchment into tiny bits and fling them at Shirin Mam's beatific portrait.

She studied the drawing again. The image reminded her of something she had seen once before. But where?

The answer came to Kyra in a flash. This was one of the symbols she had seen in *Anant-kal*, the world beyond time. After her death, Shirin Mam had summoned Kyra there and given her a last lesson in words of power—words in the ancient tongue that could, when spoken correctly, shape reality to Kyra's will. They had walked down a vast hall studded with carved pillars. *Commit the images on the pillars to memory*, Shirin Mam had told her, *and the words associated with them will come to mind.*

The word of power associated with this image was . . .

"*Samsarandev.*"

It fell from her lips before she realized she had said it. In an instant, the candles flickered out. Darkness pressed in around her, and then she felt a weight on her head, as of a heavy crown. She stifled a scream, remembering that this was how it had been in *Anant-kal* too, when she had practiced this word of power. Breathing shallowly, she focused her thoughts. If she could tether herself to the present, she could return to it.

The Mahimata's cell. The candles on the desk. The letters, one for me and one for Rustan.

Kyra returned to the candlelit cell, bent double and gasping with effort. Her wound throbbed with each beat of her heart. She straightened up, trying to slow her pulse. Nothing moved except the shadows on the walls. Everything was as it had been.

No, not quite. The parchment with the ink drawing had disappeared from Shirin Mam's desk. All that remained was a smear of ash, a whiff of smoke.

Kyra leaned against the desk. The tearing pain in her chest sharpened and she suddenly felt faint. Now would be a good time to return to her cell. She picked up the letter for Rustan and tucked it into her pocket, then made her way back down the passage, staggering against the wall, concentrating all her energy on staying upright.

But in the central cavern, she stumbled to a stop. The four elders of Kali stood in a row, waiting. When they saw her, they bowed deeply.

It was only then she realized the enormity of what she'd done.

CHAPTER 3

THE DARK OF HIS MIND

He was a Marksman. No, he was not. He had a blade. No, he did not.

Rustan hummed, trying to block out the voices in his mind. They had started their clamoring as soon as he rode out of Khur on his camel, Basil. He had to exert every ounce of self-control to quiet them. It was worst in his unguarded moments: when he was thinking of Kyra, or—like now—trying to sleep.

Above Rustan stretched the dark bowl of the desert sky, pricked with stars. He was alone in the heart of the Empty Place, many miles from the nearest oasis.

He leaned back against Basil's flank, the sand cold and soft beneath him. It had seemed like a good idea to stop and rest for a while. If only he could sleep for a few hours without dreams of any kind: dreams of Kyra, dreams of his katari . . .

As if he had willed it, his katari was suddenly in his hand. Rustan jerked up and gaped at the familiar old leather scabbard.

Fingers trembling, he withdrew the blade from its sheath. It winked and shone in the muted starlight.

He laughed out loud, the sound echoing around the dunes, as he caressed the smooth grip. It had returned to him. And by all that was holy, he would never give it up again.

But as he held it, the blade began to change. Cracks appeared on its surface, dark threads of malevolence spreading along the edges.

No, it was not possible. Kalishium, the alien metal with which the blades of all kataris were forged, was unchangeable, immutable.

The cracks deepened, and the blade broke apart in his hand. The shards crumbled to dust, and the dust blew away in the wind.

Rustan leaped to his feet and scrabbled at the air. Tears burned his eyes.

The voices in his mind rose to an unbearable shriek:

He was a Marksman. No, he was not. He had a blade. No, he did not. He was alive. No, he was not.

Rustan dropped to his knees and pressed his hands to his head. This time there was no controlling them. The voices had taken over his mind, and he had to fight not to scream, not to give in to panic, to madness.

He crawled to his knapsack and groped for the black scabbard he had concealed within it. Yes, there it was. Shirin Mam's blade. He clutched it to his chest, rocking back and forth. The voices slowly faded, and he exhaled, wiping the sweat from his brow with an unsteady hand.

His mother's katari was a talisman, a gift of light in the dark insanity of the world, one he did not deserve. But it had passed from Kyra's guardianship to his own, and he would not relinquish it to anyone. Not until it made its will known.

Meanwhile, he would be grateful it was keeping him alive.

He wrapped himself in a blanket and leaned back once more against Basil's warm flank. He closed his eyes, but sleep did not come, despite his exhaustion. He breathed deep and slow, trying to relax, focusing on the comforting weight of the ancient katari against his chest.

You will have need of me before you are done.

He had met his mother only once, nearly fifteen years ago, and he remembered the wintry morning with the sharp, painful clarity such memories often acquire. He had been summoned to the courtyard of the fort of Chinoor to meet a visitor. He had grown up in the fort, in the heartland of the Pusht clan that dominated the western foothills of the Hindukush, playing with other children whom he called "cousins." He'd always known that he was adopted. It had never mattered, until that day.

He had walked to the courtyard in the bitter dawn, when icicles hung from the eaves and snow crunched underfoot. The visitor stood cloaked and hooded in the middle of the space, under the bare branches of an ash tree.

He had come up to her, puzzled and shy and shivering, and made some sort of greeting. She had answered in kind, then thrown back her hood and clasped his hand. When they touched, he had known at once who she was. Perhaps she told him in some way without words.

At first Rustan was too stunned to take it in, to understand what she was saying. "I am so happy to see you," she'd said, smiling with a warmth and an affection that had pierced him to his core. "But you must be ready to leave. The Maji-khan of

Khur will come for you soon, and then our paths may not cross again."

When he found his voice, it had been to weep, to question why she had left him. She gazed back at him with calm eyes and explained that she had done the right thing and one day he would see that it was so. She wore her serenity like armor that nothing could cut through, not his shouting, not his pleas. She said, quite simply, that she loved him. She leaned down to kiss his cheek, her breath warm on his skin. He turned away from her, silent and full of hate.

"One day," she said, "I will acknowledge you to the world." Then she was gone, back to the horse waiting outside.

Mother, I don't hate you anymore.

Such a foolish thing, anger. It had kept him away from the only woman who could have answered the questions that haunted him. Now it was too late.

Rustan fell at last into a troubled and restless sleep. When he woke the next day, his mouth was dry and his tongue swollen. The harsh glare of the sun pierced the leafless branches of the dead, dry trees beneath which he had curled up. All around, the heat rose in shimmering waves from the sands. He took a few careful swallows from the waterskin tied to Basil's saddle and got to his feet, trying to get his bearings.

To the north was Khur, the home he had left behind. To the east and west lay the open desert, though he would come upon oasis towns sooner or later in both directions.

To the south were the blurred outlines of the distant Kunlun Shan Range. Far, impossibly far. If he hadn't known of them, he would have thought them a mirage, a trick of the desert light. He had never traveled south before and knew of no oasis town that lay in this direction.

Penance was not about taking the easiest route. Rustan took another swallow from the depleted waterskin and made up his mind. He would go south to Kunlun Shan.

The next day, his water ran out. Desperate, he stopped Basil by one of the thick, spiny plants that dotted the landscape and cut off its top with his mother's blade. He chewed the pulp, careful not to swallow, while trying to suck out all the moisture he could find before spitting it out.

He repeated the exercise until his mouth was on fire from the acid taste of the thorny plant. It did nothing to quench his thirst.

That night, there was a firestorm that lasted well over an hour, brilliant streaks of white light radiating out from the sky until his wondering eyes ached from watching. A part of Rustan's mind, the part that was untouched by the heat, the wind, and the raging thirst, thought that it was worth dying to have seen this. The words of an old, unknown song drifted through his mind:

> He will ride through a firestorm
> And crawl over icy stones,
> Bleeding from wounds unseen,
> Stumbling in the dark of his mind.
> That is how we will find him,
> Broken, to be renewed;
> Forgotten, to be remembered;
> Dead, to be reborn.

It didn't make any sense. Dimly, he wondered if he was becoming delirious.

Time passed, but he no longer counted the hours, no longer

shaded his eyes against the sun to see how far the mountains were. In any case, his eyes could no longer be trusted. The landscape was endlessly bleak, the night relentlessly cold. He paused whenever they came across plants of any kind and tried to get what moisture and sustenance he could from them. His parched mouth no longer remembered the cool, delicious taste of fresh water. Even Basil flagged, his humps collapsed in the heat and drought.

It was in this state that, five days later, they arrived at the oasis town of Igiziyar, at the southern border of the Desert of No Return.

CHAPTER 4

THE TRUE SUCCESSOR

A week had passed since Kyra had spoken the word of power she found in Shirin Mam's cell. Every morning since then, Navroz Lan and Felda Seshur had come to pay their "respects" and ask her when she wanted the ceremony. Each time, Kyra had managed to deflect them. It was like a horrible sort of dance—one that she knew would have to stop soon. She was running out of excuses, even to herself. Running out of time.

Now here they were again, looming over her bed, black-robed and formidable as ever. "Greetings, Elders," Kyra said politely, sitting up. "I am still in pain, but I should be able to take up my duties soon."

Navroz Lan crossed her arms, gazing at Kyra out of gimlet eyes. "You have been saying that for the past week," she said. "Not," she added, "that we don't sympathize. But you are merely delaying the inevitable."

Kyra suppressed a grimace. The tall, white-haired elder may

not have been the Mahimata, but her word carried almost as much weight. She was the healer of the Order of Kali and the eldest of them all. She had even taught Shirin Mam once. It was hard to evade her and impossible to fool her. Not for long, anyway.

"What you want from me is incredible," Kyra said at last. "Consider my experience. Consider my *age*."

"Believe me, we have considered," said Navroz drily. "But Shirin Mam has made her will known. I would have thought you would be the last to turn away from your responsibilities."

"*My* responsibilities?" Kyra drew up the blanket around her, knowing even as she spoke that she was giving in to anger, something she had tried hard not to do since her return to the caves of Kali. "What about yours, Eldest? How could you have elected Tamsyn to be the Mahimata of Kali? Did you not *sense* the evil within her? And how could Nineth have vanished from these caves? You owed her your protection." Kyra's eyes burned at the thought of her friend and what she must have gone through at the malevolent hands of Tamsyn.

Navroz did not respond, although a spasm of pain crossed her face, there and gone in an instant. It was Felda who spoke, Felda the mathematician, who had always been Kyra's favorite teacher apart from Shirin Mam, despite her gruff manner.

"In this we are all culpable," she said somberly. "Tamsyn was too powerful for us to disobey her. And at first, it seemed like the right thing to do. The Hand of Kali usually succeeds the Mahimata in the event of a sudden death. And we did try to find Nineth. We searched for days, but we could not sense her bond with her katari."

"We—I—made mistakes," said Navroz, her voice ragged. "I admit it. But there is only one way to move, and that is forward.

You must accept your new role so the Order can continue functioning as it is meant to. So we can *stabilize* the valley."

"I still can't believe Shirin Mam meant for me to open that letter," muttered Kyra.

"You do believe it; you just wish you didn't," said Navroz. "I am disappointed, Kyra. I had thought your vow to avenge your clan more important to you than life itself. Perhaps I have misjudged you."

She threw Kyra a cold look and turned to leave. Felda shot Kyra a sympathetic glance.

They were at the door when Kyra spoke. She knew the elders were skilled in the art of manipulation, and yet, she couldn't let Eldest's remark go unchallenged. "Wait," she said.

Navroz paused with one hand on the smooth gray stone of the wall.

"What has my vow got to do with"—Kyra swallowed and made herself say it—"with my being Shirin Mam's successor?"

"Everything," said Navroz. "Kai Tau has amassed an army and all but declared war on the Orders of Asiana. The clans of Ferghana are filled with doubt and fear, especially after your duel with Tamsyn and her strange disappearance. We have lost two Mahimatas in quick succession. We need to present a strong and united front to the clans as well as the Orders. Innocent people are dying in the Thar Desert while we quibble about what Shirin Mam might have meant."

She softened her tone. "I know it is hard for you to understand. It is hard for us too. Less than a year ago, you were but an apprentice yourself. But you have come a long way since then. This is what I believe: you and you alone are the true successor of Shirin Mam. She has marked you twice. Once with her blade, when it chose you as its guardian, and the second time with her word of power that bound us to you. It is time to leave your cell and accept who you must become."

There was no adequate response to this, so Kyra remained silent.

After a moment, Navroz nodded to Felda, and together the two elders left her cell.

Why had she done it? *Why?* And was there any way she could undo what she'd done? The word of power could not be unsaid, but perhaps another word existed, a word to counter it. She would have to return to *Anant-kal* to find out. Kyra pressed her palms to her forehead. If she only had someone to confide in, someone wiser than herself whom she could trust.

But since Shirin Mam's death, there had never been anyone else. There was only herself and her limited grasp of the right thing to do in every circumstance.

"Is there anything you need?" said a hesitant voice.

Elena was standing at the mouth of her cell, holding a cup in her hand.

"Yes, please," said Kyra, relaxing at once when she saw who it was. "Your company."

Elena was the one person who was always welcome, even though the sight of her pricked Kyra with guilt. Nineth and Elena had been her closest friends for years. Yet she had fled from the caves of Kali, leaving them behind to face Tamsyn's wrath. And though Kyra knew the elders had likely done their best to keep the two girls safe, it hadn't been good enough.

Elena entered and knelt beside her, tossing one of her long black plaits over her shoulder. "Try this," she said, setting down the cup. "My latest concoction: willow bark, turmeric, and winter cherry. It should help with the pain. If nothing else, it will help you sleep at night."

"Thank you," said Kyra gratefully. "It would be good to sleep and even better not to dream."

Elena tilted her head, a question in her eyes.

"I dream of *him*," said Kyra reluctantly. "Kai Tau. Sometimes, I see him killing people. Other times I am dueling him. Either way, they are dark images—bloodstained and hard to forget." She did not add that the dreams ended as often with her death as with his.

"One day you will confront him," said Elena. "Isn't that what Shirin Mam told you?"

Kyra nodded. "The day is drawing closer. Goddess, I wish she was still alive."

She isn't, but you are.

Kyra blinked, but Elena's face betrayed nothing except fatigue. The dark circles under her eyes said she had slept little in the past month, and the way her green apprentice robe hung loosely on her petite frame said that she wasn't eating as she should. Navroz had mentioned that Elena had stayed up several nights by Kyra's bedside, watching over her.

I do not deserve you.

Elena gave her a sharp look. "Drink," she said, jerking her chin toward the cup. "Tell me if it does you any good."

Kyra obediently picked up the cup and took a sip of the yellow-green liquid. It was awful in taste, viscous and bitter, and she coughed as she swallowed it down. "Oh yes, it does do me good," she said. "Anytime I'm in pain, I just have to think, *oh no, I'll have to drink Elena's horrible medicine*, and I shall be miraculously cured." She laughed at her own joke, but Elena didn't join in.

After a pause, Kyra cleared her throat. There were things that needed to be said, and she had to make a start or the gulf that had opened up between them would eventually become impassable. "So, um, what did it feel like?" she asked.

"Are you asking me how I felt when you rode off with Shirin Mam's blade?" said Elena, her voice hard. "Or when Tamsyn called us to her cell for questioning? Or when Nineth disappeared without a trace? Or maybe you want to know how I felt when the elders emerged from the Ferghana Hub carrying your bleeding body?"

"Actually," muttered Kyra, shame stealing through her, "I was wondering how it felt when I spoke the word of power."

A shadow passed over Elena's face and she looked away.

Kyra reached forward and gripped her friend's hand. She'd been so caught up in her own pain and fear that she hadn't given enough thought to what Elena was going through. "I'm so sorry, Elena. Please forgive me. I didn't plan any of this."

"What did you *think* would happen when you left?" demanded Elena, shaking off Kyra's hand. "Tamsyn declared you a renegade. No one could be caught talking or even thinking about you. She interrogated Nineth and me several times, together and separately." She bit her lip. "Nineth was in tears the second time."

Kyra closed her eyes. "I am sorry," she said again, her voice small. *Feeling* small. "I had no choice. Once I picked up Shirin Mam's blade, I only knew I had to get away from Tamsyn."

"There is always a choice, and for every choice there are consequences," said Elena. "We bore the brunt of it while you were off traipsing through the desert." She paused and her voice lost some of its hard edge. "Oh, don't look at me like that. I'm just happy you're alive. But things got bad when you left, and worse after Nineth vanished. She missed you so much. She kept talking about how you got away, and how it must have been a door that you used. And she was right. I wonder all the time if she managed to find the same Hub that you did."

Kyra stared at the remains of the liquid in her cup. She didn't wish the experience of the Hub she had found on anyone, even a desperate Nineth. She had seen visions there, and lost time, and believed she was going mad. "I hope she found another means of escape," Kyra said finally. "I am sure she's alive somewhere— and she's going to come back."

She hadn't told anyone how Tamsyn had gloated about starving Nineth to death, at first because she refused to believe it herself and then because Tamsyn's blade had told her something else. Nineth had starved, but she hadn't died.

But then, where was she? Nineth was terrified of wyr-wolves, so she wouldn't have gone very far from the caves on her own, which made it unlikely she'd found the secret Hub. On the other hand, if Nineth hadn't found it, then why could the elders not sense her through her blade?

Navroz was right about one thing. It was time for Kyra to leave her cell.

She threw off her blanket, gasping as the ache in her chest flared anew. She pressed her lips together, determined not to cry out. Elena watched, concern in her eyes. At last, when she had the pain under control, Kyra asked, "Why will it not heal? Do you really think it has something to do with Tamsyn's blade?"

"You know I do," said Elena. "I can't understand why you won't give it to Eldest."

They both looked at the katari that lay in one corner of the cell, candlelight flickering over the black metal scabbard. Elena had been against Kyra keeping it in her cell, because it would delay the healing of her wound, and Navroz had agreed. Both had teamed up to persuade Kyra to give up the katari so it could be deposited in the funerary chamber.

But Kyra had refused. She would not let Tamsyn's blade out of her sight. She had won it fairly, she told them, and it belonged to her.

What she did not tell them was that she remembered the feel of the blade in her flesh, and with that memory, she was able to access a bit of Tamsyn's skill and knowledge. She knew now, for instance, that Tamsyn had lied about killing Nineth simply to hurt her. The bond created by the wound endured because of the presence of her enemy's weapon—a powerful link, but also a painful one.

"No one can *make* you do anything anymore, can they?" said Elena, when Kyra did not respond. "What did the elders tell you about the word of power you used?"

"You know them," said Kyra, glad of the change in topic. "They don't say anything unless it suits their purpose. All they told me was that they woke from a dream in which I was the Mahimata of Kali, and the dream had to be made real."

"It was more than that," said Elena. "It was like you *commanded* us to acknowledge you as the Mahimata. As we belong to the Order of Kali, so too do we belong to you." She paused, looking troubled.

"What are you not telling me?" asked Kyra, suspicious.

Elena raked her fingers through her hair, ruffling the normally neat plaits. "Baliya and Selene have gone. They left yesterday."

Kyra gripped the edge of her bed, pain forgotten. Baliya and Selene had been in Tamsyn's inner circle of favorites. She had known they felt sorrow and anger about Tamsyn's defeat at her hands. But she had not expected them to leave the Order. The

Markswomen of Kali were so few to begin with; they couldn't afford to lose any of their precious number.

"What about Akassa?" Arrogant and beautiful Akassa had been one of Tamsyn's favorites too.

Elena's mouth twisted in a grimace. "Akassa's still here," she said. "But she's been confined to her cell. She failed her first mark; can you imagine what she's going through? Tamsyn sent her to take down a woman who had killed her baby, just before the Sikandra Fort assembly. But Akassa wasn't able to do it. Tamsyn was furious. She would have taken Akassa's blade, but Mumuksu persuaded her not to. The elders don't really know what to do with her. I'm afraid for her, Kyra. I tried to talk to her while the elders were away in Sikandra, but she wouldn't listen to me."

Kyra took a deep, steadying breath. First Shirin Mam, then Nineth and Tamsyn, and now Baliya and Selene. That left just twenty-eight Markswomen, two apprentices, and four novices. Was she going to lose Akassa too? Who else would leave, rather than give their loyalty to someone they still considered an apprentice? Never mind that she had defeated Tamsyn Turani in single combat. The Order of Kali would diminish and fade, all because of her.

No, she could not let that happen. Kyra struggled to her feet. Elena scrambled up and caught hold of her arm, alarm on her face. "Where are you going?"

"To have a chat with Akassa," said Kyra. "Tell Navroz that I agree to have the ceremony tonight." Had there been any doubt in the elders' minds that this was what she would agree to do at last?

She left her cell and walked down the passage. At the opening of the central cavern, she paused. She had been hoping it would be empty. But a small group of Markswomen sat on the floor, clustered around Mumuksu Chan, the Mistress of Meditation. The weather must have driven them in. Kyra could hear the wind howling outside.

"The no-mind of Tatsam-virag cannot be approached without mastery of the third level of meditation," said Mumuksu. "Close your eyes and count your breaths; let us practice . . ."

An icy gust blew into the cavern, and the torchlight flickered. When Mumuksu caught sight of Kyra, her voice faltered. As if on cue, all the Markswomen turned around and stared.

Silence, but for the whistling wind.

Kyra's cheeks burned. She willed herself to walk straight ahead, despite the physical effort this cost her. She would not let them see the slightest weakness.

She bowed to Mumuksu, and Mumuksu bowed back, relief on her face. She continued her lecture and the Markswomen turned their attention back to the intricacies of third-level meditation, although Kyra could feel them sneaking glances at her as she crossed the cavern to the passage that led to Akassa's cell. She didn't blame them. She would have been consumed with curiosity too if an upstart young Markswoman had uttered a word of power that had catapulted her into the top position of the Order.

Why had she stayed in her cell for so long, hiding like a thief? She should have come out among them a week ago, when she first spoke aloud that stupid word. She could have done something to try to prevent Selene and Baliya from leaving the Order; sworn them to an oath perhaps, or even just talked with them.

Kyra gritted her teeth and calmed herself. She had no one to blame but herself. And Shirin Mam, who was so inconveniently dead.

She ducked into a narrow passage that broadened as it climbed upward. A single torch on the wall showed the steps hewn out of the rock floor. Kyra took her time, climbing with care. One misstep was all it took to slip and break your neck.

She stopped outside Akassa's cell. The steps continued, winding up into the heart of the hill.

It was utterly dark inside the chamber. Why did Akassa not light a candle?

"They won't let me have a light," came a brittle voice. "I am to reflect in the darkness, as a penance."

Kyra stifled a gasp. Akassa had sensed her, had known what she was thinking without even looking at her face. That was advanced Mental Arts for someone who was still an apprentice.

She went back down the stairs a little way, unhooked the lone torch from the wall, and carried it back to the cell. Akassa sat cross-legged on the floor, katari in hand. She shrank back from the light, covering her eyes. Kyra held aloft the torch and studied the apprentice. She smelled unwashed and her hair was a wild tangle.

No one failed the first mark. It hadn't happened in decades. The Mahimata always knew when a girl was ready. Except that Tamsyn had *not* known, merely hoped. Kyra remembered how close she had come to missing her own mark and felt a stab of pity for Akassa.

Akassa lowered her hands. "Why have you come here? To gloat over me? Your victory is complete."

"Go to the kitchen," said Kyra. "Ask Tarshana for some warm water to wash yourself."

"Why?" A mocking tone entered Akassa's voice. "Can't stand to see me like this, can you?" She laughed, a thin, high sound that made Kyra want to shut her ears.

"No Markswoman of mine is going to a ceremony looking like one of Kali's demons," said Kyra. "You clean up or you clear out. Choose."

Akassa's mouth snapped shut. For a moment, her eyes burned with hope and Kyra caught a glimpse of the proud young woman she'd been.

Then the hope died and Akassa's head dropped. "I failed my first mark," she whispered.

"I almost failed mine too," said Kyra. "Tell me what happened."

Akassa did not respond. The torchlight danced about her face, not illuminating it so much as throwing it in shadow. Let her take her time. She would speak eventually. Kyra leaned against the wall and counted the seconds. Thank the Goddess for Elena's new concoction; it had dulled the pain, or she would have collapsed by now. *Talk to me*, thought Kyra. *Trust me.*

At last, Akassa stirred. "I couldn't do it. It didn't feel right. She begged me to put her out of her misery. Instead, I walked away. The Ashkin elders were shocked."

"Your first mark was a woman of the Ashkin clan?"

"Yes. In the village of Thuskjal, just beyond the hills of Gonur. The woman had been convicted of suffocating her own baby. She confessed as much to the village council. She said she didn't know what came over her. The baby was only three months old." Akassa began to cry—dry, hacking sobs that brought no relief.

Kyra leaned the torch against the wall and knelt beside her. She clasped Akassa's shoulders. "Listen to me. If it didn't feel right, then maybe it wasn't right. What was it that stopped you? Doubt of her guilt?"

"Oh, she killed the baby all right," said Akassa. "But it was a madness that possessed her and then passed. She was full of remorse and grief. She wanted to die. Perhaps that is why I could not bring myself to do it." She wiped her face with a sleeve. "I thought Tamsyn would stab me."

Kyra could well imagine Tamsyn's reaction to Akassa's failure. "What became of the woman?" she asked.

"Tamsyn sent Selene to execute her." The bitterness in Akassa's voice was palpable. "All that I accomplished was to prolong the woman's miserable life by one day."

Kyra exhaled.

She did not disagree with Akassa that something felt wrong about this mark. There had to be another way for people like that, people who were sick of mind and didn't know what they were doing. It was a dilemma; the Orders were bound to execute those who took an innocent life, but maybe there were some cases where execution was *not* the right answer. Perhaps Navroz could even have healed this woman. She would have to talk to Eldest about it.

The gong boomed, a distant reminder that somewhere below them, classes were in progress.

"It's Felda's class," said Kyra, making her voice brisk, "and you know how she hates it when students are late. You don't want to be doing derivations during mealtime, do you? Hurry and get cleaned up. Your penance is over."

Akassa's face became ashen. "No, please. I can't face them. Elena's the only one who hasn't treated me like an outcast."

"If I can face them, then so can you," said Kyra. "If anyone says anything, tell them you've been ordered back to your classes by the Mahimata of Kali."

"It's true then," said Akassa in wonder. "You will have the ceremony tonight."

"Yes," said Kyra. *There is always a choice*, Elena had said. But there wasn't, not for this. "Will you attend?"

"By my blade I will." Akassa paused and said softly, "*Mother*."

CHAPTER 5

IGIZIYAR

Water. No mirage this time. The stone walls of the communal well gleamed in the sun where someone had spilled water from a bucket. Rustan slid off Basil's back, his head pounding. He staggered toward the well and pushed his way to the head of the line.

"Hey," shouted someone. "Wait your turn like everyone else."

Rustan hauled up the bucket and took a few swallows before someone snatched it from his hands. He wiped his mouth and straightened up, holding the metal arch of the well for support. He had drunk enough—not too much, not too fast. At least he wasn't going to black out now.

A burly man stood scowling beside him, fists balled up. "Who do you think you are, pushing me like that?"

"I beg your pardon," said Rustan, his voice hoarse. "It has been several days since I drank real water. My caravan was attacked by bandits and I lost my goods." He hated the lie and the necessity of it. But he wouldn't use the Mental Arts, not unless he had no other choice.

The man relaxed his stance. "That's terrible luck. I'm a trader myself and if I lost my goods—well, no point going back home empty-handed, is there?"

"No," agreed Rustan. "Which is why I may stay here for a bit. I still have some coin. Can you direct me to a decent guesthouse?"

"You can stay at the Khan Kerawan in eastern Igiziyar," said the man. "You can't miss it; it's the biggest building in town. Eighty rooms, but I reckon they might be full seeing as how we've been flooded with refugees. *And* it's market week."

"Refugees?" Rustan frowned.

"They're pouring out of the Thar Desert like flies. Some took the Jhelmil door before it was overrun by outlaws, but I think others have crossed the mountains on foot to get to safety." He shook his head. "Those poor people. I've heard terrible stories. A devil-king is loose in the Thar, killing men, women, even children. What are the Orders doing, I'd like to know."

Rustan's stomach clenched. Just a few days' travel from Khur and already the looming war seemed closer, much more real than it had in the Maji-khan's tent.

"You'll see some of them at the Khan Kerawan," the man continued. "I think Nursat, the proprietor, has opened his doors to them, no questions asked."

"That's very kind of him," said Rustan. "How much does he normally charge, do you know?"

"Just one silver sitari and six bronze hikkis a day. That includes two meals, a pallet to sleep on, plus water and shelter for your animals," said the man. "Best deal in Igiziyar, although kumiss, candles, and fodder are extra. So is washing."

Rustan bowed. "Thank you, my friend. I wish you good trading."

He returned to his camel, managing to stay upright. No one gave him a second look. Good. A Marksman without his katari was no Marksman at all. A spasm of pain racked his chest at the thought of his blade; he leaned his head against Basil until it passed.

The Khan Kerawan was a sprawling, two-story affair wrapped around an open courtyard that was packed with people and animals: camels, goats, horses, sheep. Traders laughed, shouted, talked, and argued. A woman drew water from a well in the middle of the courtyard. In one corner, beneath a large and colorful awning, food was being served. The spicy aroma made Rustan's mouth water. A line of people waited their turn, carrying plates and bowls of all shapes and sizes. Some of them certainly looked the part of refugees: thin and travel-worn and weary-eyed. A few had bundles on their backs; others clutched the hands of little children as if they would never let go.

A small, scruffy boy lounged near the gate; he took Basil in hand, grinning when Rustan tossed him a bronze coin. Another boy ran up to escort him inside.

Rustan followed his guide across the noisy and crowded courtyard to a small room at the other end. A tall, dark-skinned man in a white robe rose from behind a desk piled with heaps of ink-scrawled papers and bowed in greeting.

"Welcome to Khan Kerawan. I am Nursat. What can I do for you?"

"I'd like room and board for two nights, please," said Rustan. He placed three silver coins on the proprietor's desk.

Nursat stroked his beard. "Unfortunately, all our rooms are taken this week. You may have heard of the refugees from the Thar Desert. Some of them are five to a room meant for two. Some are sleeping in the open or in animal stalls."

"Please," said Rustan, unable to keep the exhaustion from his voice. "I have traveled for many days without food or fresh water. Two nights of rest, and I will be on my way."

"And what way is that?" asked Nursat. "It's dangerous traveling on your own in these times. Perhaps I can find you some company."

"I don't need company," said Rustan, reluctantly lacing his voice with a hint of the Inner Speech. "I just need a room." He didn't want to use the Inner Speech any more than necessary, but it wouldn't do to have people getting curious about him.

Nursat's eyes glazed. "Yes, of course. I do keep one or two rooms empty for emergencies. Follow me."

He led Rustan through a door behind his desk and up a flight of rickety stairs to the second floor. A gallery lined with doors ran the length of the building on all four sides. Nursat unlocked one of these, ushered Rustan into a tiny room, and told him to come down for a meal when he had rested and washed. Rustan thanked him and bolted the door after Nursat departed.

Turning slowly, he took stock of the room. It was more than adequate for his needs; there was a bunk, a washbasin, even a window that looked out onto the gallery and let in some light.

He drank from a pitcher, long and deep, before collapsing on the bunk. The sun still burned behind his eyelids, as if he had never left the desert. As if the desert was in him. It was an odd sensation, like being displaced in space and time. As if he were not really there at all.

At last he slept, dreaming he'd left his katari in the desert. He stumbled up and down shifting sand dunes, pausing now and then to dig frantically with his hands, but he could not find it. Once something glinted in the sun, and he ran toward it with renewed hope and energy. He dropped to his knees and dug with desperation, but it was not his blade he found—it was a skull. A human skull, bleached in the sun. Smooth and familiar to the touch, it belonged to someone he knew.

Rustan jerked awake, heart racing. It took several minutes for the vision to dissipate. He rose from the bunk and rubbed his eyes. Hours had passed, and it was dusk. He felt dirty and disoriented. His limbs ached, and the image of the skull lingered at the back of his mind. Whose had it been? Not Kyra's. His own, perhaps. Dying in the Empty Place would be an easy way to go. The coward's way.

He washed the worst of the sand from his hair and face and changed into a clean brown robe—an unmarked robe, without the symbol of Khur, as befit his state of exile. He hung his mother's scabbard around his neck, concealed beneath the robe, and went down for a meal.

The Khan Kerawan was even more crowded at night than it had been during the day. Perhaps it appeared that way because almost everyone had moved indoors; the evening meal was being served in a long room just off the courtyard. A small fire blazed in one corner, and several little tables had been drawn close to it. At one table, a group of men were playing dice. At another, two oldsters frowned over a battered chessboard. Outside, a group of people gathered around a larger fire.

A servingman showed Rustan to a table in a far corner where a couple had just finished their meal and gave it a halfhearted swipe with a bit of rag.

"You're in luck," said a familiar voice behind him. "It's mutton tonight."

Rustan turned to see his host, Nursat. "I don't eat meat," he said, smiling.

Nursat's eyebrows shot up. "Kumiss?" he asked.

"No thanks," said Rustan. He nodded to the servingman. "Tea will be fine."

The servingman left and Nursat wandered away to speak with a group of merchants. But Rustan could sense the sharpness of the man's curiosity, and it made him uneasy. So what if he didn't want meat or spirits? It didn't mean he belonged to an Order of Peace.

Then the servingman brought him a plate of food, and he forgot all about his unease. There was a vegetable stew from which the meat clearly had been removed just for him, and thick pieces of bread with goat cheese and onions. He ate with relish, dipping the bread in the stew, enjoying the flavor and feel of real food in his mouth.

A day of rest, and he would continue south to the mountains. Tomorrow he would visit the market and provision himself. He would also have to arrange for Basil to be cared for by a local herder; his camel could not follow where he was going.

"Your tea." Nursat's voice interrupted his thoughts. He grinned and held out a pot. "I like to serve my special cardamom tea to special guests. And something tells me you are not an ordinary traveler." He poured a cup out for Rustan. "Are you going to Kunlun Shan?"

Rustan almost dropped his cup. He fixed Nursat with a piercing stare. He wasn't as strong in the Mental Arts as some of the other Marksmen; without his own blade, his powers were even weaker. But he could make the man talk, if he chose.

Nursat dropped his eyes, visibly unnerved by the pressure of Rustan's gaze, and backed away, nearly colliding with a serving-woman behind him.

Rustan resumed his meal, but his appetite was gone. How had his host guessed his true destination? He would have to find out before he left Igiziyar.

⚘

The next morning, Rustan went in search of a camel herder to look after Basil for the next few months. He found a tall, white-turbaned man who looked competent enough, and parted with twenty silver sitaris—almost enough to buy a new camel in these parts. The man's eyes widened as he counted the coins, but he asked no questions. Rustan gave Basil's neck an affectionate pat, and then the man bowed and led his camel away. Rustan watched them go, tightness in his chest. *I will come back for you*, he thought to Basil. *I promise*.

He wandered through the maze of alleyways in the heart of Igiziyar, glad of the anonymity afforded by the noise and bustle. The town was a hive of activity, lying as it did within sight of the Kunlun Shan Range, along the southern trade route between the lands east and west of the desert. Rustan had taken care to conceal his mother's katari and veil the lower part of his face, but he doubted whether in the hubbub anyone would have noticed even an unsheathed blade.

At last he arrived at the market on the outer edge of town, where camel caravans stretched as far as the eye could see. White-robed traders hurried to and fro, arguing with their drivers, and bargaining with locals for fodder and water rights. Hundreds of men and women clad in all the colors of the rainbow sat beneath a vast canopy, their wares displayed in front of them. Everything imaginable was being sold, from goats and donkeys to spices and sandalwood.

The sellers were a diverse lot: fresh-faced young girls with fragrant bunches of dried herbs, scowling grandmothers with strips of worked leather, bare-chested men polishing knives that glinted in the sun, and old men squatting beside open sacks of grain. Merchants from the east displayed red and green bolts of silk, and traders from beyond the Kunlun Shan Range sat behind clumps of scoured yellow wool. The sellers cracked jokes with their customers and argued over rates, chasing away little boys trying to make off with a sweet bun or a hot kebab.

Rustan bought dates, dried cheese, nuts, and raisins, and stuffed them into his knapsack. He bought naans too, unable to resist the aroma of the freshly baked flatbread. Satisfied with his purchases, he returned to the guesthouse to rest. At dawn he would leave Igiziyar and continue his journey to the mountains.

At dinner that night a brawl broke out in the Khan Kerawan. A beefy man who had drunk far too much kumiss began to rant at one of the Thar refugees who had ventured inside to get food for the rest of her family. "Go back to where you came from!" he shouted. "We don't want your kind here." He kicked over a couple of tables for emphasis, scattering the diners.

Rustan's hands itched to grab the bigot by the neck and plunge his red, puffy face into a bucket of cold water. But Nursat turned out to be surprisingly good at this sort of thing himself. He made short work of the beefy man, tossing him out of the room with an injunction never to darken his door again. A couple of Nursat's friends followed to make sure the man left the premises and did not bother the refugees huddled around the fire in the courtyard.

"You have powerful muscles," said Rustan, as Nursat passed his table.

Nursat smiled. "I've been throwing out drunks for the last thirty years. It's fine exercise."

"Thirty years?" said Rustan in surprise. "I wouldn't have thought you were much over forty yourself."

"Forty-five," said Nursat. "The guesthouse belonged to my father before me, and I've worked here since I was a boy." He looked over to where the servingmen and -women were setting the tables to rights and the diners were drifting back to their chairs.

"You must have seen a lot of people pass through on their way to Kunlun Shan," said Rustan.

Nursat narrowed his eyes. "I had better get back to work," he said, and started to move away, remembering, perhaps, how Rustan had reacted to his first mention of the mountain range.

"Why don't you sit down with me for a minute and share my tea?" said Rustan, a touch of the Inner Speech in his voice. "Do you good to rest a bit before getting back to work."

Nursat obeyed, looking a little surprised at himself.

Rustan beckoned a servingwoman and obtained a clean cup for Nursat. "Tell me about the people who go to Kunlun Shan," he said, pouring out the tea.

Nursat accepted the cup and took a sip. "Not much to tell," he said. "There used to be at least two or three a year, when I was a boy. Then they became fewer and fewer. It is now over twenty years since I have seen a seeker pass through Igiziyar."

"A seeker?" Rustan frowned.

"Everyone who journeys to the mountains is searching for something," said Nursat. "My granduncle went to Kunlun Shan, looking for the secret way up the mountains to the Sahirus.

He never came back. He must have died, like the rest of them. Villagers find bodies on the slopes sometimes, frozen stiff as boards, or washed down with the summer melt into the valley of the Green Jade River. Sometimes the bodies are mutilated or missing limbs. We don't know why."

Rustan gripped the table. Of course. Kunlun Shan, sky-ladder to the heavens, was rumored to be the abode of the mystical and reclusive Sahiru sect that belonged to no clan, gave tithe to no Order, and claimed that the Ones spoke to them in their dreams. He had heard tales of them from storytellers, but until now, he had not realized that he was seeking them out. It was a moment of clarity, a gift from a stranger.

"What made you think I was one of the seekers?" he asked.

"You are not a merchant or a trader. You abstain from liquor and meat. Besides . . ." Nursat hesitated.

Rustan leaned forward. "Yes?"

"You remind me of the last seeker that passed this way. It was over two decades ago, but I remember it like yesterday."

"Who was that man, do you know?" asked Rustan.

"He called himself Rubathar, and we never saw him after that one evening. He was a strange one. He had no money; we wouldn't have taken his coin anyway. He asked us riddles and to all who answered correctly, he told them how long they would live." His face grew grim. "May I never know such a night again."

Rustan stared at the man in some astonishment. "That's . . . incredible," he said. "Foretelling death is an exceedingly rare gift. Perhaps he was merely guessing? Or pretending to have the gift?"

Nursat shook his head. "I didn't believe it at first, but then I saw them die one by one, just as he foretold."

Rustan didn't ask him the obvious question; he already knew the answer. How hard it must be to live when you knew just how many precious days you had left.

"Would you like to forget?" he asked. "I can help you, if you wish."

"Some things are just the price you pay," said Nursat. "I'll carry on paying, because it's worth it, knowing what I do." He rose. "And now, if you will excuse me, I must attend to my other guests."

Rustan inclined his head and watched him leave. Such an ordinary man and such valuable information he had imparted. This was the nature of knowledge; you had to be ready to find it anywhere, without prejudice and without judgment.

The other nature of knowledge was that it led to ever more questions. Did the Sahirus really exist, or were they just another tall tale from the olden days? And if they did exist, could they lighten the burden on his heart? Could they show him a way to be a Marksman without enduring constant guilt and doubt?

And who was this man that Rustan reminded Nursat of, with his dubious gift? No Marksman, of that he was certain. He had been the last seeker to come this way until Rustan himself. What had become of him?

CHAPTER 6

WOLF'S KISS

The wind had quieted as dusk deepened into night. Snow fell outside the caves, soft and heavy. It was a full-moon night—a night for hunting wyr-wolves. But Kyra had asked for the ceremony and there was no question of delaying it any longer. The elders scrambled to make things ready, banishing everyone from the central cavern except the novices, who were put to work cleaning the floor and replenishing the torches on the walls. Mumuksu went down to the funerary chamber and returned with a large package wrapped in cloth that she refused to let anyone else touch.

Kyra sat in her cell, resting. She had taken a large dose of Elena's pain reliever, awful-tasting as it was, in preparation for the night ahead. It wouldn't do to keel over in the middle of the ceremony.

Less than a year had passed since her initiation as a Markswoman. Yet Shirin Mam had marked her as her successor.

What had the Mahimata seen in her that no one else could? The only distinctive talent Kyra knew she possessed was the ability to enter *Anant-kal*. But such a talent was not necessary for someone to lead the Order.

Shirin Mam could have passed on her knowledge of words of power to someone else, Navroz or Mumuksu, for instance. Someone with age, strength, and wisdom, who was familiar with the inter-clan politics of the valley. Someone who could command respect without lifting a finger. All things that would be much more difficult for Kyra.

She closed her eyes, trying to slow her thoughts. The mind was a house with countless rooms and endless doors. She walked along the corridors, away from the questions and memories that haunted her. The ache of those who had gone mingled with the ache of more recent wounds, but she moved past them, going deeper into herself, the way Shirin Mam had taught her.

By the time the gong sounded, Kyra had retreated to a place of calm within. She surfaced reluctantly, holding on to an image of still water and reflected moonlight. She withdrew her katari from its scabbard and held it against her heart. It was time.

They were all waiting for her in the cavern, sitting on the wooden benches that surrounded the raised central slab. Everyone was present, even the novices. Akassa sat next to Elena, her hair brushed, her face scrubbed and defiant. The four elders stood next to the slab in the middle.

When Kyra entered the cavern, Chintil Maya, the Mistress of Hatha-kala, gestured to the seated Markswomen. Everyone rose and bowed. A sense of unreality took hold of Kyra. *It's a dream*, she thought. *I'll wake up and Shirin Mam will still be alive, and none of this will have happened.*

"Today we make our vows to the new Mahimata, and she

makes her vows to us," said Navroz. "The form that this ceremony takes depends on the will of the Goddess. When Shirin Mam was initiated, the gong sounded of itself, so loud that it drove us out of the cavern. When Tamsyn took her place, the torches guttered out, plunging us into darkness."

Kyra started. She had not heard these stories before. Of course, she had never attended a ceremony in which a new Mahimata was anointed to lead the Order. She had run away when Tamsyn was declared the Mahimata, using a secret Transport Hub in the hills of Gonur.

Navroz bowed, pressing her palms together. "Kali, divine Mother, you have spoken into our hearts and told us what must be. Your mask falls today on the face of the youngest Markswoman of our Order. Protect and guide her, that she may protect and guide us."

She knelt and laid her katari at Kyra's feet. "I yield my blade, my heart, and my life."

Kyra stared at her bent, white head in shock. This was *Eldest*, who had caught her nodding off during a history lesson, who had despaired of her mastering the simplest healing remedies, who had held and comforted her when Shirin Mam died. Who, despite everything, now vowed to follow Kyra to the death. Kyra's eyes stung. *Thank you for your trust*, she thought. *I will never let you down.*

Navroz retrieved her weapon and rose, making way for the others. One by one, the elders knelt and repeated the phrase: *I yield my blade, my heart, and my life*. And as they did, desire grew fierce within her to rise above her own petty wounds of flesh and spirit and deserve the title of Mahimata.

The Markswomen followed the elders, then Elena and Akassa, and last of all, the four little novices. Kyra stood rigid, holding her emotions in check. She felt the weight of their oaths settle on her, a burden she would carry all her life. Was this how Shirin Mam had felt?

When they were done, the Markswomen, apprentices, and novices returned to their seats. The elders continued to stand, gazing at her expectantly.

Kyra's mouth was dry. She had to say or do something. But what could she possibly give them in return for their oaths?

At last she walked to the slab, raised her right arm, and brought down her katari in a quick slash. Blood dripped down her forearm and onto the stone: red drops on pure white. She turned to the dumbstruck elders.

"I swear by my blood, with all my power and every breath, I will be worthy of your oaths."

There was utter silence in the cavern. Kyra thought she could feel the individual pulse of each of the women who had sworn to her reverberating within her.

Mumuksu cleared her throat and stepped forward. In her hand was the cloth-wrapped package she had fetched from the funerary chamber. "This passes to you, from now until your death. It has not been used in decades. But one day you may have need of it."

Kyra accepted the package, mystified. It was hard and heavy, with sharp edges. She glanced up at Navroz, who nodded: *You may open it*. She peeled away the outer layers of linen and stopped short. The inner layer was beautiful—shimmering green silk, like the one Rustan had bought for her in Kashgar. Rustan, who had kissed her once, making the whole world disappear. A sudden, sharp pain twisted her insides. For a moment, she could not breathe.

Then she was back in control, stripping away the green silk

to reveal at last the fearsome visage within: a wooden mask of the Goddess Kali in her warrior aspect. The skin was ebony, the tongue long and red, the fangs white and elongated. On her forehead gleamed the third, terrible eye of destruction.

Was she supposed to wear this? The expressions of the elders revealed nothing. Kyra brought the mask up to her face and fastened the jute strings behind her head. The elders gasped and took a step back. She regarded them through the dark holes of Kali's eyes, puzzled. What were they afraid of? It was just her beneath the mask.

The bone-chilling howl of a wyr-wolf shattered the silence. Another joined it, and another. It sounded as if there was a pack just outside the caves.

Ria Farad ran toward the crawlway that led out of the cavern, but jerked back as Chintil's voice rang out, sharp and commanding:

"Stop. We must complete the ceremony before we do anything else."

"But . . . the horses!" cried Ria.

"Will have to wait," said Navroz. "Kyra, step forward."

Kyra removed the mask and laid it on the slab. The four elders raised their blades and slashed her brown robe so that it fell in pieces at her feet. She stood before them, her flesh turning cold, as Navroz lifted up the thick black robe in her arms.

"This belonged to Shirin Mam." Were those tears glimmering in Eldest's eyes? "Wear it well."

Kyra held her arms out for the robe and let the elders help her into it. The robe was warm against her skin, as though it had just been worn by someone else. Navroz wrapped and tied it around her, and Mumuksu corded her katari to her waist.

And it was done. Kyra was now the Mahimata of the Order of Kali.

⚛

As soon as the ceremony was over, Ria began barking orders, telling the novices to fetch their woolen cloaks and saddle the horses.

"Not you, Kyra," cried Navroz, but Kyra ignored her. She was not missing out on this, a wyr-wolf hunt on the night of her ceremony.

The snow-covered clearing outside the caves was a jumble of tracks. Ria bent to study them before making for the paddocks. "There are at least seven of them," she called out.

"What were they doing near the caves?" Kyra panted, trying to keep up with Ria and ignore the searing pain in her chest. It had flared up the instant she started running.

"Perhaps the snow and wind confused them. Or perhaps they were chasing some animal."

But Kyra could tell that Ria didn't believe that. Snow and wind didn't confuse wyr-wolves. They had an uncanny sense of direction that had little to do with sight or hearing. And no matter how juicy the prey, they wouldn't be reckless enough to follow it to the caves of Kali. Too many wyr-wolves had died by kalishium blades for them to make such a mistake.

They reached the paddocks. Close at Kyra's heels were Chintil, Felda, Sandi, Tonar, and Akassa. Akassa's face was filled with grim determination. She had jumped at the chance to go with them, desperate to prove herself.

Sandi lit a lamp. The horses were skittish; they would have heard the howls and known the wyr-wolves were nearby. Kyra had a hard time saddling Rinna. She stroked the mare's neck, whispering soothing words.

Ria was the first out of the paddocks, racing away on her powerful roan mare. The rest fanned out behind her. Clouds scudded across the dark sky; now and then the moon revealed itself, bathing the valley in ghostly light.

The horses galloped, swift and sure-footed, kicking up snow behind them. Kyra's heart sank as she realized that Ria was leading them to the walnut forest southwest of the caves; it was far easier to face the wolves on open ground. At least there would be little underbrush in the forest; the villagers cleared it every autumn before harvesting the nuts.

As the trees thickened, cutting off the moonlight, Ria reined in her mare. Everyone clustered around her.

"We'll walk in single file on the main path that cuts through the forest," said Ria. "I will lead and Elder Chintil will take the rear. Remember: we stay close and stay on the path, no matter what. The Inner Speech only influences the wyr-wolves when we speak together; individually, we cannot hope to touch their minds."

"Do you sense where they are?" asked Chintil.

"They are in the forest, Elder, but I cannot tell exactly where." Ria glanced at Kyra. "Tamsyn would have known."

Kyra snorted. "Tamsyn enjoyed killing wyr-wolves, but she did not have your ability to track them, nor your gift for concealment."

Ria gave a noncommittal grunt. Kyra wondered if she wished Tamsyn was still around. The Mistress of Mental Arts had taken down more wyr-wolves than all the rest of them put together, except Ria.

They walked deeper into the forest in single file, with Ria

leading and the two elders at the rear, where they were most vulnerable. Kyra was between Akassa and Chintil. The wind rose, whispering through the trees, blowing snow from the branches. Ice crackled beneath the horses' hooves. A deep exhaustion took hold of her. Shirin Mam's black robes no longer felt warm against her skin. She longed to be back in her cell, wrapped in her rugs, cradling a cup of hot tea in her hands.

Akassa let out a yell. "Over there! I saw something move."

"Wait!" shouted Kyra. But the apprentice spurred her horse around and veered off to the right. She was soon lost in the shadows between the trees.

"Fool girl." Ria turned her horse around. "Wait for us, Kyra!"

But Kyra had already moved, urging Rinna on in the direction Akassa had taken, hoping the apprentice was all right. Branches whipped her face and she cursed and ducked. Akassa had ridden in a couple of hunts; she should have known better than to take off on her own. Kyra could hear the sound of hooves pounding the forest floor just ahead. She should be able to catch up with Akassa quickly enough.

But the minutes passed, and Kyra's sense of foreboding increased. Soon, she could no longer hear Akassa's horse. The trees seemed to close in around her.

As she slowed Rinna and weaved through the dense forest, Kyra became aware of two things: first, the voices of the Markswomen behind her had faded, as if they had taken another direction. Second, there were shapes in the darkness, flowing on either side of her.

Rinna bucked and snorted in terror. Kyra tightened her grip on the reins and risked a quick glance to her left and right. But it was too dark to see anything.

Then the moon sailed out from behind the clouds, bathing

the snow in silver light, and Kyra saw them as clear as day: two massive beasts loping behind the trees to her left, keeping pace with her.

Fear crept like ice through her veins. Where was Akassa? Where were the others? She wanted to turn Rinna around, but she was no longer sure of the direction in which she was going. Were the wyr-wolves following her, or was she following them?

The trees began to thin, and Kyra could have wept with relief. They were heading out of the forest. If she could gain open ground, she could at least try to make it back to the caves.

Rinna cantered into a clearing. Then she stopped so suddenly that Kyra was thrown over her head, too taken aback to even scream as she fell. She hit the snow hard and lay stunned on her back, staring up dazedly at the moon, now coin-bright in the sky. Every square inch of her body felt as if it had been pummelled, her chest as if it had been stabbed afresh. Snow blew over her hair and cheeks, cold and soft, and from somewhere, far in the distance, came an inhuman laugh. She wanted, in that moment, to disappear, to melt into the snow and swirl away on the wind. To not have to get up and face whatever it was that stood before her.

Stay alive, Kyra.

Rustan's words. They had brought her back from the brink of death in the Hall of Sikandra.

Kyra struggled to her feet, groaning with effort.

Rinna was gone. Despite the cold, Kyra began to sweat. She had no chance against the wyr-wolves without her horse, but still, she drew her blade and advanced farther into the clearing: a vast space surrounded by tall, bare trees that formed a tight, dark wall.

When she reached the middle, she stopped. In front of her, a pair of golden eyes gleamed through the lattice of trees. Another pair, and then another. Huge, lupine shapes materialized out of the shadows—nightmares made real. Kyra swung around and blinked in shock. There were so *many* of them. She trembled and the katari almost slipped from her hand.

One of the wyr-wolves detached itself from the sheltering darkness and padded toward her. It was enormous, almost up to her shoulders, with a thick gray mane and a white streak on its ridged forehead. The beast stopped a few feet from her. A forked tongue flicked over curving fangs that glinted in the moonlight.

Kyra willed herself not to faint. She tightened her grip on the katari and dropped into the jigo-huari stance.

The wyr-wolf reared onto its hind legs, turned its snout to the sky, and howled: a drawn-out, mind-numbing wail that echoed through the clearing.

Kyra stumbled back, ears ringing, dizzy with pain. Her feet sank into a deep drift of snow and she fell, crying out as her left foot twisted beneath her.

The hulking beast loomed above her, blotting out the moonlight. One huge paw came down on the hand that held the katari, hard enough for Kyra to feel the pressure in her wrist, but not enough to injure it. The wyr-wolf lowered its massive head until its muzzle was just a few inches from her face, its golden yellow eyes boring into hers. Kyra could not breathe; the smell of its musty fur was overpowering. She tried to use the Inner Speech, but no words came to her.

The wyr-wolf opened its maw, revealing the rows of elongated fangs that made it such a perfect killing machine.

No. I'll not die like this! Kyra tried to move, but her limbs had gone numb.

The wyr-wolf's tongue darted out.

CHAPTER 7

MENADIN

The sun shone bright in a deep blue sky. Stiff, green heath grass prickled her palms. Crouched on her hands and knees near the edge of a cliff, Kyra's first, frantic thought was that the wyr-wolf had sent her through the door of death.

A huge, silver disc drifted across her vision, and she sprang to her feet, her pulse quickening. She was in *Anant-kal*, the world as perceived by their kataris. The world beyond time. The place Shirin Mam had taught her how to enter before the Mahimata had died.

Kyra glanced down past the cliff's edge. A depthless chasm yawned below her, spanned by a long, narrow bridge. Across the gap, a vast city glittered in the sun. Tall towers and white domes, glass and metal reflecting the light so strongly that it hurt the eyes to look at them. A beautiful city, devoid of life. Just the same as she remembered.

Hope flared within her. Perhaps Shirin Mam had drawn her

to *Anant-kal* again, this time to rescue her from wyr-wolves. Kyra swallowed as she recalled the dripping maw of the beast that had pinned her to the ground with its paw.

A flash of movement at the other end of the gossamer-thin bridge caught her eye. Shirin Mam? *Yes.* Kyra scrambled down the rocks to the bridge and ran across, her excitement mounting. But when she reached the other side, no one was in sight.

A broad road lined with brilliant purple bougainvillea stretched out before her, leading into the city. Kyra walked down the road, trying to remember which one of the sky-touching towers she had seen Shirin Mam enter the last time.

"Looking for someone?"

Kyra's stomach clenched at the unfamiliar voice, and she whirled around.

A tall, powerfully built young man stood behind her. He was light-eyed and shaggy-haired, naked but for a rag tied around his waist.

Kyra stepped back, trying to slow her heartbeat. Too late, she remembered Shirin Mam's cryptic warning: *Beware of* Anant-kal. *We are not the only ones who walk here.*

"Who are you?" she demanded, wishing she had her katari. Without it, she felt small and defenseless.

The man grinned, revealing a line of elongated white teeth. He made an elaborate bow. "Menadin Vulon at your service. May the moon shine bright on our meeting."

Moon? Kyra frowned. The man was oddly familiar, with his animal grace, his amber yellow eyes, and that mane of hair . . .

A sly look crossed his face and his tongue flicked out: a *forked* tongue.

"No," she whispered. "It can't be . . ." Shock coursed through her, robbing her of speech.

"Did you like my kiss?" he said with a smirk.

Goddess help me. Kyra held up her hands against the abomination. "Go away," she stuttered. "Get away from me."

Menadin threw his head back and laughed, a deep-throated sound that was more like a growl. "We have waited for you many years, Kyra Veer."

Kyra spun and ran toward the city.

Between the rows of immaculate towers she flew, turning unexpected corners and dashing into side streets. She came across a sparkling pond, glittering jewellike in the sun, and waded through it, hoping to throw the creature off her scent. Beyond the water was a walled garden, and there she took shelter. She sank to the grass and buried her head in her knees, willing herself to stop shaking.

"It's a beautiful place, is it not?"

Oh no. Kyra raised her head in despair. Menadin stood before her, leaning against the trunk of a twisted tree. He didn't even seem winded.

He pointed to the scarlet flowers near her feet. "Be careful. They bite."

Kyra withdrew her feet. Menadin grinned again, displaying the rows of overlong teeth, the bestial tongue.

"What do you want? And what are you?" Kyra asked, striving to keep her voice calm.

"You would like the history of our race in one sitting?" said Menadin. "It is not as simple as that."

Kyra wrapped her arms around herself. The beast could talk; it could be reasoned with. She *would* escape. "You drew me here, didn't you?" she asked.

"It is a power we have always possessed," said Menadin. "Wyr-wolf venom can be used to transpose someone to Wyr-mandil.

As long as they have the ability to bond with kalishium, like you do."

"Wyr-mandil?"

"In our tongue, 'mandil' means home." Menadin waved his arms in a gesture that encompassed the city. "This is our home—at least, the only home where we walk as humans."

With a jolt, Kyra remembered the story that Aram of the Order of Khur had told her one night as they journeyed across the Empty Place to Kashgar. He had said that wyr-wolves had talked to Zibalik, the founder of Khur, in his dreams, and saved his life. It was Zibalik who had named the creatures wyr-wolves, recognizing them as half-human.

At the time, Kyra had dismissed the tale as pure myth and the men of Khur a credulous bunch to believe that wyr-wolves were anything but dangerous beasts to be put down.

Menadin lounged against the tree, twisting a bit of grass in his fingers. He exuded an aura of power and confidence. When he kept his mouth closed, anyone would think him human.

"Why—" Kyra began, but Menadin interrupted.

"The question is mine. Why do you kill us? Does it give you pleasure?"

"Of course not." Kyra stood, letting anger take over and push fear away. "It is our duty. Wyr-wolves are a plague on the people of Ferghana. When you take the sheep and horses of the nomads, you take away their only means of survival. Some folk have given up trying; they've lost too much, and they're scared of losing more. So they sell what remains and come down to the valley to work in farms. You're destroying a way of life as old as the hills.

"But the worst, the very worst, is when you take humans. Every child that goes missing is a hole in the heart of our people and a mark of shame for our Order. You have bled us too long. For this alone, I will not rest until I clean the valley of every wyr-wolf that infests it." She stopped, panting. Why was she even talking to this creature? She should leave; perhaps if she concentrated hard enough she could return to the forest, find Rinna, and make her way back home.

Menadin was quiet for a moment. Then he raised his head and something in his eyes made Kyra flinch.

"How easy it is to blame the 'other.' Every winter we starve, as game gets ever scarcer. The wild sheep, boars, and deer that used to be so plentiful in the valley and the hills are now hardly to be seen. Your people multiply and mine decline. Are we to be blamed for now and then plucking a fat sheep to feed our young ones?"

"What about *our* young ones?" asked Kyra sharply. "Does a sheep not fill your belly, that you must feed on human flesh too?"

Menadin took a quick step forward so that he towered over her, his face contorted in a snarl. "I have never once tasted human flesh. I might make an exception with you, though."

"It will be the last thing you do, *dog*," Kyra snapped, standing her ground, although every nerve in her screamed to back away, to put some distance between herself and this wolf-man.

"Such spirit," murmured Menadin, "and such a slender neck. I could break it with two fingers."

Kyra's hands flew to her throat. "You can't touch me," she said, hoping against hope that she was correct. "Not in *Anant-kal*. We aren't really here."

"No?" Quick as lightning, Menadin lunged forward and gripped her hair. "Perhaps I can demonstrate how wrong you are."

Kyra screwed her eyes shut, trying to overcome her panic and revulsion. What was happening? Shirin Mam had said that nothing was present in *Anant-kal*, not in the physical sense, anyway. So why could she feel his fingers in her hair, his fetid breath on her cheeks? She struggled to free herself from him, but he laughed, and a feeling of utter helplessness swept over her.

You are only powerless if you think yourself to be. Remember who you are.

Shirin Mam's voice cut clear as a bell through the jangling discord of her mind.

I am a Markswoman—more, I am the Mahimata of Kali, Kyra told herself. *The most powerful woman in Ferghana. Time to teach this dog his place.*

Kyra breathed in and out, seeking the calm at the core of her being. She sank into the second-level meditative trance, and *Anant-kal* vanished.

She was in a dark tunnel, a limbo. The light of her katari burned bright at the other end, her bridge back to her body, her world.

Come, I have need of you.

Then the weapon was in her hand, the slim blade glowing green fire.

She returned to *Anant-kal* to find Menadin's fangs against her neck. Without hesitation, she brought her blade up and slashed his back.

Menadin stumbled and fell. The look of surprise on his face was almost comical.

"You will not touch me again," said Kyra. "Next time, my katari will find your heart and stop it."

Menadin picked himself up. To her amazement, he smiled. "Good. You begin to discover your power."

Kyra's feeling of triumph evaporated. Menadin didn't appear to be hurt at all. She glanced at her blade, quiescent now. It felt real enough in her hand.

"Don't you understand?" said Menadin. "The influence you have on this world depends on how strongly you are present in it. Already, you have greater vitality here than your teacher ever did. But still, you cannot match me. I have walked in Wyr-mandil more years than you have lived."

That didn't make sense. But then, nothing about *Anant-kal* had ever made sense. "Why have you drawn me here?" asked Kyra, sheathing her blade. "What do you want of me?"

"Two things," said Menadin. "For you are twice in my debt."

Kyra frowned. "How so?"

"The first, when you killed my brother Darril. Do you remember him, Kyra? He was younger than me and not as handsome, but our mother loved him best.

"I tracked you one day to the hillside behind your caves and watched while you did silly exercises in the rain. I imagined how it would be to kill you. I could have snapped your neck with one swipe of my paw. It would have helped me lay Darril's ghost to rest. But I let you live."

Kyra's throat was dry. She remembered the third and final wyr-wolf hunt she had ridden in last year and the wyr-wolf she had killed. How easily her blade had opened its—*his*—chest. She wet her lips. "And the second?"

Menadin bared his teeth. "When we helped you flee your Order after Shirin Mam died. We led Tamsyn a merry dance through the woods, and you escaped to the hills of Gonur."

Kyra closed her eyes. It was too much to take in. The wyr-wolves were *people*. Of a kind. People who had helped her. Who would ever believe her? *Unless* . . .

Her eyes flew open.

But Menadin seemed to know what she was thinking. "We cannot manifest ourselves as human except in Wyr-mandil. You are the first person in centuries with the talent to be here strongly enough to see us. Even Shirin Mam was not able to see or hear us, although she sensed our presence. We, on the other hand, could hear her every thought."

That didn't seem believable. "Why should I do anything to help you?" demanded Kyra. "If there was anything remotely human about you, you would not prey on our young."

"We *don't* prey on your young, Kyra Veer," said Menadin. "It is you humans who prey on ours."

Kyra bit her lip. She remembered the tales she had heard about hunters discovering dens with pups and the slaughter that followed. Tamsyn herself had delighted in stalking pregnant wyr-wolves.

"I always spoke against the killing of any human, young or old," said Menadin. "And I am the leader of the Vulons, the most powerful pack in the Ferghana. My people listen to me. But I cannot control every wyr-wolf that comes down from the mountains, howling for revenge because he has lost his mate and his young ones. Besides, were you to look more deeply into the matter, you may find the truth somewhat different than what you imagined. Wyr-wolves may have injured or killed human adults, but they are not behind the loss of any children. Perhaps you have predators among your own kind. The stories of wyr-wolves carrying off children are just that—stories with which mothers frighten children and killers hide their crimes."

"You expect me to believe that?" said Kyra, summoning up scorn, but her heart was not in it. Menadin's words had the ring of sincerity, unpleasant though they were.

"The truth is always difficult to accept," said Menadin, "and easy to distort. I promise you this: if you grant the first of our two requests, I will do everything within my power to keep my people away from yours. Any wyr-wolf that dares disobey this edict will have his throat torn out."

"And the first of your requests is?"

Menadin spread his hands. "Leave us alone. Stop the killing. Issue an edict of your own that wyr-wolves are not to be hunted, on pain of death."

"I can't do that," Kyra burst out. "Everyone will think I'm mad."

"You are the Mahimata of Kali, aren't you?" said Menadin. "You can do anything you set your mind to."

"It's not that simple," said Kyra. "Even if I do believe you, you're asking me to overturn centuries of fear and hatred with one decree."

"When has doing the right thing ever been simple?" countered Menadin. "Did Shirin Mam teach you nothing?"

Kyra glared at him, knowing that he was right. She said, "You haven't told me what else you want."

"Later," said Menadin. "It's time you were getting back. Your elders are beside themselves with worry." He spat into his hand and held it out. "Come."

Reluctantly, Kyra extended her hand toward his. As they touched, she screamed; his hand felt like a gigantic paw, hairy and clawed.

The world faded.

CHAPTER 8

DOORS AND DREAMS

Kyra jerked upright and winced at the sudden, stabbing pain in her side. She took a moment to orient herself. She was back in her cell—no, wait, this wasn't her cell. It was Shirin Mam's. And her chest hurt worse than ever. Various other parts of her body were also clamoring for attention, complaining loudly.

"Thank the Goddess you're awake." Navroz Lan hovered above her, face drawn with worry.

"We thought we'd lost you," added Felda, her voice tight.

All four elders clustered around Kyra's bed. Their anxiety sent a rush of guilt through her.

"I'm fine, Elders," she assured them. "What . . . what happened?"

"We found you lying unconscious in a clearing in the forest, surrounded by wyr-wolf tracks," said Mumuksu. "We must have scared them off."

That was not what had happened, but Kyra held her tongue. "What about Akassa?" she asked. "Is she all right?"

Chintil snorted. "She'll be all right, once she knows that you are. She's been blaming herself for the incident. As well she might."

"Do you recall anything?" asked Mumuksu.

Kyra took a deep breath. She had discovered a revolutionary truth about the wyr-wolves, but how much should she tell the elders? How much would they believe? Before she died, Shirin Mam had instructed Kyra not to let anyone know about *Anant-kal* or the lessons she had given Kyra on how to enter that realm.

At last she said, "I don't remember everything that happened. I followed Akassa, but I lost her and ended up in the clearing. Rinna threw me, and while I was unconscious, I had the strangest dream. I talked with a wyr-wolf."

"Talked with a wyr-wolf?" repeated Felda, knitting her brows. "How is that possible?"

"Because wyr-wolves are half-human," said Kyra simply. "This wolf—Menadin—he told me I was in his debt. He asked me to issue an injunction against the killing of his people."

Silence greeted her words. The elders regarded her, varying expressions of disbelief and surprise on their faces. Kyra held herself straight. She was so weary, all she wanted to do was sleep for days. But her strength and conviction right now would make all the difference in the days to come.

"An interesting dream," said Navroz finally. "And perhaps it means something. But dreams are not to be taken literally."

"This one is," said Kyra firmly. "There is to be no more hunting or killing of wyr-wolves in our jurisdiction. The wyr-wolves in turn have promised not to harm the humans who live here."

The objections were immediate.

"Kyra, you've been hallucinating," said Mumuksu soothingly. "The wyr-wolves are beasts. Not people to make bargains with."

"Not to mention, the clans will never stand for it," added Felda, shaking her head.

"The clans?" scoffed Chintil. "Try telling Ria Farad this. You'll have a rebellion right here in the caves!"

"Markswomen have been hunting wyr-wolves for as long as the Order itself has existed," said Navroz. "Did not the Goddess herself battle demons that plagued the earth? Should her disciples do any less?"

And on and on. Finally, Kyra held up a hand to stop them. "Please, Eldest," she said in a meek voice, "I'm tired. I'd love some of Elena's pain medicine." Obviously she wouldn't, but it was the best way to deflect them all.

"I'll ask Elena to brew a fresh batch," said Navroz at once, solicitous. "You need to sleep and recover from your ordeal."

Felda was not so easily distracted. "This wyr-wolf you spoke with. Suppose he was lying about his promise?"

"It was a *dream*, Felda," said Mumuksu, exasperated.

"Yes. And dream wyr-wolves can't lie," said Kyra with an innocent smile. Mumuksu hadn't meant that, of course, and she opened her mouth to protest, but Kyra quickly sank back against the pillow. "Please, Elders, I must rest now. We will issue the edict in the morning. I would like you to send runners to all the clans and let me know when they return." She added, with as much sincerity as she could muster, "I would not ask this of you if I did not believe it was the right thing to do."

Navroz pursed her lips and rose. She clearly still had reservations, as did they all. But Kyra had given an order, and she would not disobey her Mahimata.

The realization made Kyra feel hot and cold all over. She needed them to obey her—but now that it was happening, she felt deeply uncomfortable. These were the women who had trained her since she was a child. No matter what mistakes they had made with Tamsyn and Nineth, they were still her teachers and guides. She was asking a great deal of them.

She hoped with all her heart that she was right about Menadin.

The other three followed Navroz's lead, saying nothing more as they moved to the doorway.

Before they could leave, Kyra said, "Not you, please, Elder Felda. I have something to ask you."

A look of surprise crossed Felda's face, but she managed to smooth it away. When Navroz, Chintil, and Mumuksu had departed, Kyra exhaled, trying to breathe out her pain. Felda's brow creased as she sat down next to Kyra's bed.

"You were in no shape to go wyr-wolf hunting and you know it. Why not get rid of Tamsyn's blade and leave such matters to us?"

Kyra looked at the tranquil, square face of the stocky woman sitting beside her. If there was one elder she felt she could trust completely, it was Felda Seshur. Still, she felt reluctant to reveal the bond she had with Tamsyn's blade. She wasn't quite sure why. "I have my reasons, Elder. But that's not why I asked you to stay. I want to know . . ." She hesitated. Shirin Mam had told her to ask Felda about the visions she had seen in the secret Hub, pointing out that no one knew more about Transport than the Order's talented mathematician. But Kyra didn't know where to start, how even to begin to describe what she had experienced.

"You want to know about the codes Shirin Mam gave you," said Felda. "About Transport. Yes?"

Was she always going to be this transparent? Kyra stifled her irritation. "Yes, please."

"Years ago, I deduced that although each door has a unique code, there must exist a special sequence that can override those codes," said Felda. "I worked on re-creating a formula that could be used to open a door—*any* door. Last year I succeeded; at least, I thought I did. I told Shirin Mam, and she instructed me to stay quiet about it. She took the list of numbers my formula had generated and gave it to you." Felda's face relaxed into a smile. "The pyramid is beautiful, is it not? It makes such perfect sense."

"Er . . . yes. But what I saw in the Hub—none of *that* made any sense, Elder."

The words tumbled out. Kyra told Felda what had happened— how the first three doors in the secret Hub had shown her visions of the child Tamsyn, the dead Shirin Mam, and the emptiness beyond the world. And how the fourth door had made her *lose time*, a fact that always brought a wave of nausea whenever she thought about it.

It was a relief to confide in Felda, to be able to share the terror she had experienced. But it also brought back to the surface everything she had suppressed, and Kyra found herself having to stop more than once to ease her breathing and calm herself.

"And, Elder, I could have sworn that . . . after the voice said 'code override,' there was an awful sort of *laugh*." Kyra was unable to keep the plea out of her voice. "Do you think I could have imagined that?"

Felda's expression had become graver and graver as Kyra spoke. "I cannot explain it, but I don't think you imagined anything. You must remember that the Hubs are old, older than anything else in Asiana." She clasped her hands together. "Perhaps something has gone wrong with them, something with their mechanics that we cannot even begin to guess at. Or perhaps they pine for the Ones."

"You talk as if the Hubs are alive," said Kyra, goose bumps erupting on her skin.

"And why should they not be?" countered Felda. "Think of the Hubs as one vast mind. Parts of that mind are falling into disuse or madness. Other parts are perfectly aware of that, and still functioning valiantly."

"But what about the things I saw?" asked Kyra.

"Kalishium is the key that unlocks the doors," Felda mused. "Kalishium, that can look into our minds and know our every thought. Perhaps the visions came to you through the blades you carried. Perhaps they are simply what the doors chose to show you. As for losing time, I think that must have been an error made by the Hub. If you consider that the doors move us using dimensions that we cannot see, a mistake in that calculation would explain the lost time. Still, we must all approach that particular Hub with caution from now on."

"Yes, Elder," said Kyra dutifully.

But inside, she was remembering the dreams that had haunted her since childhood—dreams of a door that opened up to swallow her, casting her into the emptiness beyond. She had learned to her horror that this door actually existed in the secret Hub. And she had seen its image carved on a pillar in the hall where Shirin Mam had given her one last lesson in words of power. *For each of us it is different*, Shirin Mam had said. *For you, a door. For me, it was a blade. This word of power tells us how we will leave the world.*

CHAPTER 9

UP THE HOLY MOUNTAIN

The village of Bankot clung to the foothills of Kunlun Shan, a ragged cluster of huts that looked as if they would be washed away by the next landslide. The wind whistled down the slopes, bringing the scent of pine and the promise of snow.

Rustan sat on a tree stump outside the lone teahouse and gazed at the mountains in awe. He had stopped in the village at noon to rest his horse and eat, and in all that time he had been unable to tear his eyes away from the magnificent peaks that pierced the tattered clouds above.

"You'll die out there," said one of the four oldsters sitting on the rickety bench opposite him. "Just like all the others." His companions grunted in agreement and sipped apricot tea, looking for all the world as if they hadn't stirred from that sunny spot in years.

"Have you been up the mountains yourself?" asked Rustan.

One of them snorted. "Him? He hasn't gone farther than the next field in the last twenty years."

The first man scowled. "I've been to Igiziyar, haven't I?"

"That was half a century ago," cackled a third.

Rustan finished his tea and rose from the stump, shouldering his knapsack. He hadn't been able to glean much information about the way ahead. The locals were either genuinely ignorant or suspicious of strangers, and he was reluctant to use the Inner Speech on them.

"Can I take the road through the valley of the Green Jade River?" he asked.

"It's not much of a road anymore," said the man who had first spoken. "A landslide blocked it many years ago. Take it if you want; you'll have to abandon that pretty horse of yours."

"Not worth risking your neck on those cliffs," added the second man. "Ice Mother, Heart of Stone, and Snow Pyramid do not look kindly on trespassers."

The three main peaks of Kunlun Shan. "Thank you for your advice," said Rustan. "Perhaps I'll go a little way and return." He bowed to them and mounted his horse.

There was no coming back for him until he had found what he was looking for, but they didn't need to know that. Rustan guided his horse toward the dried riverbed on the edge of Bankot, mulling over the little he had learned. The road must have been important once, before the landslide. He could follow it until the way was blocked and then try to find a path up the mountains. The air was clean and crisp, the sky a deep blue, and the voices within him silent. There was something uplifting in the names of the three peaks that towered above the rest: Ice Mother, Heart of Stone, Snow Pyramid. How hard could it be to find a way up Kunlun Shan? He was young and fit; he'd make it.

A couple of hours later, he wasn't so sure. The path was strewn with boulders and his horse stumbled often on the loose stones. The boulders gradually became larger and the ground more uneven, until it was well-nigh impossible for the horse to find its footing.

Rustan dismounted and turned it around, giving it a pat.

"Go on," he said. "Go back to the village. They'll take care of you."

The horse trotted away, and he continued on foot, clambering over the rocks, breathing hard from the exertion, yet feeling lighter than he had in weeks. Something in the mountains had called to him from all the way across the desert. Surely that something would not let him return empty-handed.

He arrived at a place where the boulders formed a solid wall in front of him, just as the old men had warned. He hunted around until he found a rough path—scarcely more than a goat track—that threaded up the sides of the range to his left, and he followed it.

The path wound uphill through a dense forest of oak, pine, and birch. An unseen bird called in alarm at his approach. Small animals darted away into the ground cover. Branches slashed at his face; pine needles and jagged stones caught on his boots. More than once, he had to use his mother's blade to hack his way through the underbrush.

Rustan hoped to make his way above the tree line before nightfall, but dusk found him still in the forest, moving slower now as light stole out of the world and darkness closed like a fist. He paused to rest against a gnarled oak tree trunk and wiped the cooling sweat from his forehead.

He was considering whether to continue in the dark or search for a hollow bush to shelter beneath for the night, when something crashed madly through the undergrowth and the noxious smell of carrion assailed his nostrils.

Without hesitation, Rustan spun, grabbing the rough bark and digging his foot into a crack in order to haul himself up to the nearest branch. His heart pounded; the air around him vibrated with deep growling. There was a moment of stillness, and then the tree shook as a huge weight hurled itself against the trunk.

Rustan bit down his fear. It was an animal of some kind—but what kind of animal could make a massive oak tree tremble? He climbed faster, ignoring the cuts and scratches to his palms, praying that whatever it was couldn't climb trees.

Midway up he stopped and risked a glance down. Nothing but darkness and that growling again, low and angry, setting his teeth on edge. The tree shook once more, and Rustan clutched the crooked branches he had lodged himself between. *No.* He would not let go. Sooner or later the tiger—if that's what it was—would give up and go after other prey.

The night wore on, endless. Rustan grew stiff and cold. It was difficult to keep his eyes open, difficult to remember why he was there. But this was also part of his penance, was it not? To sit like this, though every limb ached, to hold his mother's blade and repeat to himself, *I am a Marksman of the Order of Khur. I am Rustan, a Marksman. I have a blade, though it is not mine. It will keep me safe.*

At times he would hear the animal moving through the

undergrowth, and the carrion smell would fade, and he would begin to hope that it had gone away. But always it came back, and the stench would wrap itself around his throat once more, as if to promise, *I will not let you go.*

In the mist of dawn, he woke from a restless, broken sleep filled with disturbing visions. He undid his knapsack and took a few sips from his waterskin, but they brought no relief to his parched mouth. And still the creature prowled around the base of the tree, waiting for him.

Was this to be the final sentence of his story? To be ripped apart by a wild animal that should not exist? Snap of neck, crunch of bone, and the grinding of meat. The door of death opening to welcome him in.

He closed his eyes, practiced breath control, and summoned his inner strength. And then he slid down the tree onto the fog-wrapped forest floor, though every molecule screamed against it. He fought against his own sense of self-preservation and opened himself up to whatever it was that stalked the forest.

"COME THEN," he subvocalized in the Inner Speech. "KILL ME. I ACCEPT MY FATE. SEE, I WILL NOT RESIST YOU." He let his mother's blade drop from his hand onto the ground and waited, slowing his breath, stilling his fear.

The carrion smell grew overpowering. A massive striped creature approached, bigger than a tiger, bigger than any animal Rustan had heard tell. Thick, fetid breath blasted his face. Talons, long and sharp as knives, caressed his throat. Fangs, stained with the blood of hundreds of men, halted mere inches from his head. All this Rustan sensed and did not see, though he strained his eyes in the half-light.

You will see me better with your mind.

Rustan closed his eyes and sought the calm of a meditative

trance. The form before him contracted and solidifed into the shape of a man, with the face of his mark. "I am innocent," the mark said, tears running down his cheeks. "Please don't kill me."

"I'm sorry," said Rustan desperately. "Please . . ."

But it was too late. A katari buried itself in the man's throat—Rustan's katari.

"No!" cried Rustan, and broke out of his trance, sweating and shaking.

The man was gone.

So was the beast.

The dawn mist dissipated; somewhere a bird called, heralding sunrise.

Rustan sank against the tree trunk, trying to breathe. Trying to understand what had just happened. Was he truly beast-haunted, or had he imagined it all?

After a while, his pulse slowed, and he moved at last, retrieving Shirin Mam's blade from the thick carpet of leaves and twigs on the forest floor. He was still alive, still on his quest.

He climbed without a break that day, despite his fatigue, determined to make it out of the forest before night fell again. Yet the sun had dipped below the horizon when the trees finally thinned and gave way to moss-coated rocks. He paused to catch his breath and saw the distant lake below the forest, twilight blue in the dusk.

There was no path now, only the merest suggestion of one. Still he continued to climb, convinced he was going in the right direction.

Darkness fell in earnest, and it began to rain: freezing rain mixed with snow that soaked his skin and chilled his bones. The going was treacherous; Rustan was reduced to crawling forward on his hands and knees, trying to find toe- and fingerholds in the icy stone. His face and hands became numb; the sweat froze on his forehead.

At last, hours later, he crept into the shelter of a little cave on the rock face. He collapsed on the floor, shivering and exhausted. His hand touched something smooth and hard, and he jerked away, wary.

A long thighbone gleamed in the dark. A rib cage curved above it, grotesque. Rustan pushed himself away as far as possible from the remains. A human body, decades old. Was this one of the seekers who had escaped the creature in the forest only to die of cold? He hoped some vision had come to the seeker before death closed his eyes, some truth or beauty to alleviate the pain of the end.

He slipped in and out of dreams, seeing strange shapes and faces. Once, he sensed the approach of an animal, its long, low form blocking the mouth of the cave. He felt no fear. The beast was within him, not without, and he would have welcomed the rank breath of a bear, the howl of a wolf, or the snarl of a leopard.

The rain stopped, and the wind sang outside. Pale moonlight shone into the cave, and he opened his eyes.

Two figures bent over him, their faces hidden by hoods. He tried to get up, but his legs would not obey him. For a moment he panicked, wondering if the cold had robbed him of the use of his limbs. But the men grasped his shoulders and helped him up and led him out of the cave.

He tried to speak, to ask them who they were, but no words emerged from his lips.

How he made it outside and up the moonlit path was a mystery, for his companions were slight of form and he felt only the lightest touch of their hands on his arms. He must have been walking on those useless legs of his, but he couldn't feel the ground beneath him.

They rounded a steep bend, and the rectangular shape of a building obscured the moon. The edifice perched impossibly on the mountainside, rising out of it with what seemed like sheer will. It appeared to be made of stone; there were two levels topped by a wooden pagoda. A monastery? But the path ended before reaching the doors, and Rustan stopped in confusion. There was nothing but a gaping chasm before him. His two companions urged him on, and he continued, hoping that a path existed even though he could not see it.

They walked—*floated*—on a trail Rustan could not see, until they reached the great wooden doors of the structure. The doors opened, and the warm yellow light of oil lamps welcomed them.

Once inside, Rustan could stay upright no longer. His legs buckled, and the two men eased him down onto soft rugs. They peeled off his wet clothes and rubbed his skin with rough, warm cloths. Pain crackled through his limbs as feeling returned.

Rustan's saviors had removed their hoods, and he saw that they were old—older than Astinsai, the seer and katari mistress of Khur. Their withered faces and bald heads were covered with liver spots, their mouths innocent of teeth. Their scrawny necks gave them the appearance of ancient twin cranes. They were so thin beneath their loose saffron robes, Rustan wondered if they ate at all.

Despite their age, they had strong, fast hands, and they rubbed him down expertly until he began to think he would live after all. When he could sit up, one of them offered him a musty saffron robe and a cup of hot, strong tea, both of which he accepted with gratitude. He tried to thank them, but they waved at him to be quiet.

Rustan sipped the tea and blearily surveyed the room. Oil lamps set in the corners showed rough stone walls, a rug-covered floor, a battered kettle, a glimpse of rickety wooden steps winding up to the second story, and a dark opening at the back of the room—an opening to caves inside the mountain, he guessed. And the two monks, sitting opposite him with folded hands, faces split in wide, toothless grins.

He set down his cup. "Please, who are you?" he croaked. "Where are the others who live here?"

The monks glanced at each other, and then back at him. The answer came in a wave of sadness.

There are no others. We are the last of the Sahirus.

Rustan began to shake. *They are telepathic*, he thought, and then—*I have found the Sahirus.*

One of the monks waved a bony hand at him. *Rest now. Talk later.*

A thick drowsiness overcame Rustan, and he did not resist as they gently pushed him down and covered him with a rug. Perhaps it was the fatigue, or perhaps the Sahirus had something to do with it, but no voices or dreams came to haunt him that night.

CHAPTER 10

AMADERAN

Rustan woke to sunlight streaming through the open doors of the monastery. He could hear birdsong nearby and the sound of bells chiming. Birds and bells. No mad voices splitting his skull in two. No beast, sniffing him with its carrion breath, debating whether to end his guilt-ridden life.

He stretched out on the rug. His body ached, and numerous small wounds competed for his attention. But as he turned his head, he saw the monks were already up and about, sweeping the floor and hanging up robes to dry before the fire. He watched them for a minute before hauling himself up and asking them how he could help.

In response, the monks fixed a rope ladder for him by the doorway of the monastery, so he could get down to the path without their help. He fetched water from a stream and put the kettle on to boil while the monks milked two goats they kept in a shed just behind the building.

They broke their fast with tea, yoghurt, and caraway-seed-sprinkled naan that the monks roasted in a brick oven. The food was simple, yet nothing had ever tasted as good to Rustan as that first meal with the Sahirus. They accepted his presence as natural, and he wondered at that. Why had they brought him, an outsider, into their sacred home? He paused in the act of dipping a piece of bread in the honey-sweetened yoghurt and blurted out, "Why did you save my life?"

We dreamed of you. We have been watching you for weeks now.

"What of the others?" he asked. "The other seekers."

You are the first we have seen in many years. Few undertake the journey; fewer still make it here alive.

Rustan remembered what Nursat had said about bodies being found, sometimes mutilated or missing limbs. "I met something in the forest," he said. "Some kind of animal, perhaps. I thought it would kill me. What was it?"

You met nothing that was not yours.

"I don't understand," he said.

Everyone who seeks us must first confront the worst in themselves. Most do not survive.

A test, then. But . . . he hadn't imagined that carrion smell, those talons caressing his throat. And all those other seekers who had been killed—that was no illusion.

"How . . . ?" he began, but the monks waved at him reprovingly.

Food is best enjoyed in peace and quiet.

This abashed him enough that he ate the rest of the meal in silence. But it was a comfortable silence, with the monks wordlessly pressing more food on him and eating with evident enjoyment themselves, despite their lack of teeth.

Afterward, he washed up while the monks disappeared into

the cave opening, armed with a torch. They soon returned, dragging an old wooden chest behind them. Rustan sprang up to help them bring it to the center of the room, then watched as they fiddled with the rusty lock. It was hard to distinguish between the two of them, they were so much alike. They were even dressed the same, in identical saffron robes wrapped around frayed maroon shirts. However, one of them deferred to the other, and he guessed that one was the older of the two. Ever after, he thought of them as the Elder and Younger Sahirus, although the word *young* had not applied to either of them for several decades.

The lock creaked open, and the trunk lid groaned as the Elder Sahiru pried it open. Rustan leaned forward, and his eyes widened at the contents; inside was a veritable treasure trove of old books, scrolls, and maps, neatly stacked together.

Our legacy.

The Younger Sahiru withdrew a green, cloth-covered book from the trunk and handed it to Rustan. He took it gingerly, afraid that it would come apart in his hands.

But the book felt sturdy enough. He opened it, and his sense of wonder grew. The ivory pages were silken yet tough, and the writing was a clear, uniform print. It wasn't a script he had ever seen before, but what amazed him was the texture of the book and the quality of the printing. He turned another page and came to a map, beautifully colored. It appeared to be a map of Asiana—at least the outline was familiar—but it was all wrong. There was a dense network of towns and fortifications where none existed, rivers and forests in the heart of the Empty Place, and thick lines curving everywhere, like roads.

A historical account of Asiana. Printed before the Great War.

Rustan's jaw dropped. "But—nothing survived the war."

We did.

Rustan laughed. "You are not eight hundred and fifty years old."

The monks merely smiled at him, displaying their toothless gums.

Rustan fingered the pages, marveling at the wealth of knowledge the book contained. "Can you read the script? Will you tell me what it says?"

We will do better than that. We will teach you how to read it.

Rustan stared at them. What they offered was a gift beyond measure, but learning to read this would take ages. How long did they expect him to stay?

The monks ignored his consternation. The Younger Sahiru withdrew a single parchment from the trunk and gave it to the elder one before carefully packing the rest away.

The Elder Sahiru beckoned Rustan to sit next to him. *Come. We will start.*

"What, right away?" asked Rustan, surprised.

Why not? countered the monk, and to that he had no response. So he sat cross-legged next to the Elder Sahiru and tried his best to listen and understand. It had to be important if it was the first thing they wanted to teach him. If what they said was true, the book they had shown him was written at a time when the Ones were perhaps still present in Asiana. Which meant there was much he could learn from it.

The monk had an odd way of teaching. He would point out a fat, swirly word and explain what it meant, then point to a different set of squiggles elsewhere in the text and say why it was almost the same.

It finally dawned on Rustan that the script was not fixed. The shape of the letters varied depending on what the writer had to say, how it was said, and why. A tremendous amount of information could be conveyed by a single word. But there was no way of starting a sentence without also knowing how to end it. You couldn't change your mind halfway through.

He was so absorbed in the intricacies of a language that felt ancient and modern all at once that he had no sense of the passage of time. At last, the Elder Sahiru took the parchment away from him. *Enough. You will dream in this language tonight, and by dreaming you will understand it better.*

Rustan rubbed his eyes in exhaustion and thanked the Elder Sahiru for the lesson.

He stretched his cramped back. It dawned on him that hours had passed, as, judging from the aroma wafting from the iron pot on the fire, the Younger Sahiru had cooked the evening meal. Rustan rose to help him serve it. It was a soup of some sort, thick with vegetables and beans. They ate it with bread, the monks dipping pieces into the soup to soften it for their gums to chew.

After the meal, instead of resting, the Sahirus donned their boots and gestured to him that they wished to go outside. Rustan followed them obediently, hugging himself and rubbing his arms briskly to ward off the cold. The Younger Sahiru held what looked like a wooden staff or stand. The Elder Sahiru cradled a dark metallic tube, which he offered to Rustan.

This is a scope to make distant things appear closer. Would you like to see the stars from the top of Snow Pyramid?

What Rustan wanted was to rest his tired body and sleep as he had the previous night, without demonic voices jostling for space in his head. But he stifled his yawns and accepted the tube, which was surprisingly heavy.

Follow us. A clear night such as this is rare at this time of the year.

Despite their advanced age, the Sahirus hopped ahead of him on the path up the mountain with an alacrity that put his fatigue to shame. Rustan had to run to keep up with them. In thirty minutes he was sweating, despite the cold air and the snow that crackled underfoot. His heart thudded and he gasped for air, and still the monks climbed, sure-footed as mountain goats.

At last, when he thought he would have to stop—or pass out from exhaustion—the path leveled out to a broad plateau. The monks halted and pointed skyward. Rustan dragged himself up the final bit of the slope, thrust the scope at them, and fell to the ground. Let them think what they wanted. He could see just as well lying on his back. One of them chuckled, a gentle humor that he chose to ignore.

Rustan gazed up at the bright, star-speckled sky, his breath slowing. So easy to lose yourself in that wondrous sight. He felt the earth move beneath him in the timeless cycle of the heavens.

The monks mounted the scope on the wooden stand so that it was trained to the sky. When they had set it up, they beckoned to him. He got up and knelt before it.

Close one eye. Look through the end with the other.

At first, he couldn't understand what he was seeing. He blinked and put a hand over one eye and tried again. An orangey red sphere crystallized in his line of sight.

The Red Planet. Fourth from our sun.

He gazed at it, entranced by the dark patterns on the fourth planet's surface. He could have observed it for hours, but the Sahirus took the scope from him and trained it on a different part of the sky. He watched them closely, trying to memorize and understand what they were doing. But it was tricky; he had no words for their thoughts, which came to him as a jumble of emotions and images.

Finally, it seemed they were ready, and they beckoned him to look through the eyehole again.

Rustan leaned forward and beheld a tiny, bright disc surrounded by faint bluish dust.

Amaderan. Home star of the Araini. You know of them as the Ones.

Rustan jerked away from the scope and stared at them, his mind reeling.

No. It was not possible.

Yet—why not? If anyone could know the true name of the Ones and their home star, it was the Sahirus. They sat on their haunches, patient and unmoving, waiting for him. He grabbed the scope and looked through it again.

How long did light from Amaderan take to reach his eye? Into what distant past was he looking now? Would there ever be a chance for humans to cross that void? Rustan studied the bright disc, hope and longing filling his heart. At last, the Sahirus took his arm and folded away the scope.

Time to go.

"But I want . . . I want . . ."

No more. Later.

Rustan let them lead him away, back down the path. All the time, the image of Amaderan glimmered before his eyes, beautiful and unreal and impossibly far.

PART II

A lesson on words of power, taught by Navroz Lan of the Order of Kali

Following the events of the last clan assembly and the disappearance of Tamsyn Turani, the elders and I feel it is time we held a class on words of power, so you may understand what happened. There are wild stories circulating in the valley about Kyra's duel with Tamsyn. I've heard rumors of black magic, alien witchcraft, even the reincarnation of the Ones.

This is all complete nonsense. Kyra used a word of power to defeat Tamsyn. The knowledge was passed on to her by Shirin Mam and— Yes, child?

No, I do not know the word of power Kyra used. She tried to tell me, but I forestalled her. Words of power can be extremely dangerous, and the fewer who know the truly advanced ones, the better. If I have need of it, the Goddess Kali will see fit to pass the knowledge on to me. For it is the Goddess herself who empowered her disciples with these reality-bending words.

The story goes that when Lin Maya, the first Markswoman of Asiana, discovered these caves, the words were written or drawn on the walls of the central cavern, interwoven with the paintings of Kali we see today. Once Lin Maya had learned the words by heart and understood what each could do, they vanished. Or perhaps she found a stone tablet with the words engraved on it. Whatever the exact circumstance of their discovery, words of power are a gift from Kali to her children and— Yes, Sandi?

Yes, I know other Orders use them too. The Order of Kali was generous in sharing this sacred knowledge with the newer Orders of Asiana. But it was so long ago that the others have forgotten, or refuse to acknowledge, that we were the ones who taught them these words in the first place.

It is likely that not all the words Lin Maya found were passed on to her successor. With every generation, some words have been lost, until now barely a few dozen remain. Some are relatively harmless—the ones you all know, for instance. Even an apprentice can light her blade with a whisper. Others are far too risky to even think about— Yes, Tonar?

No, I am not going to teach you any new words today. You must have patience. You will learn new words as you progress through your craft, and not a moment before.

Coming back to the duel, Kyra used a word of power to banish Tamsyn into her past, where she fell from a bridge and drowned, obliterating herself from the present.

While I cannot pretend to understand how this happened, let alone explain it to you, I am sure you will agree with me that the duel proves words of power are not to be used lightly. Not even the most straightforward ones. You must have dire need of them. For instance, do not attempt to light your katari if you can light a candle instead. The simplest solution is always the best in any situation. Words of power are a last recourse, when none other is left. Remember this, and you will be spared the tragic and unnecessary fate suffered by a Valavian Markswoman who tried to get mangoes to fall off a tree and ended up buried alive beneath the roots.

No, Elena, she did not survive. The tree never bore fruit again, but the Valavians preserve it as a reminder to their young ones that the price of foolishness is often death.

CHAPTER 11

THE COUNCIL
OF FERGHANA

The ice outside the caves of Kali had melted by the time Kyra's wound healed enough to remove the bandages. The sutures had dissolved; what was left was an ugly red scar, itchy and tender. At least it didn't hurt so much anymore, and she was able to take up some of the duties of a Mahimata: meeting petitioners, answering letters, reading reports from the other Orders, and most importantly, planning for a concerted attack on the outlaw Taus. The Order of Valavan had written, asking her to select warriors from the Ferghana clans to aid in the coming battle. Barkav had sent his wishes for her speedy recovery and told her the Marksmen were ready to fight when she was.

The Ferghana Valley was too far west of the Thar Desert to be directly impacted by Kai Tau's growing reign of cruelty, but Kyra examined the accounts of refugees, many of whom had been witnesses to the most brutal crimes imaginable. Sickened, she read of mothers separated from children, men whose hands had been hacked off for daring to resist the Taus, and elders who had been slaughtered because they were too old to be "useful."

Her resolve to do everything in her power to end Kai Tau and bring peace to Asiana hardened. She asked Navroz and Chintil to send missives to the clans of the valley to be ready to deploy warriors and weapons in aid.

She sent Ria and Sandi with Mumuksu on a scouting mission to the villages nearby to see if they could find any trace of Nineth. The elders had already covered this territory when Nineth first vanished, but Kyra hoped they might find some clue they had missed earlier, when they were in Tamsyn's thrall. But they returned no wiser than before.

Kyra refused to give up hope. Nineth was still alive, and somehow, she would find her.

With the elders' approval, she started giving a meditation class to the four novices. They regarded her with equal parts awe and fear, mirroring the way she had felt about Shirin Mam when she herself was a novice. Their dependence on her, their complete trust in her ability to protect and teach them, strengthened her like nothing else could. Meditating with them anchored her to the present moment; she could forget for a while the storm clouds that hung over her world, both past and future. It was a brief reprieve, nothing more, and she treasured every moment of it.

Under Chintil's guidance, she also began to learn how to fight in the first-level meditative trance. It was the highest level of Hatha-kala, reserved for the most accomplished Markswomen, and Chintil warned her it was dangerous. It took every ounce of Kyra's energy and skill and left her feeling drained afterward.

But she persisted in her lessons. A Markswoman who could fight in the trance could slow down time and see the true face of her opponent.

Twice she had to deal with the irate clan leaders of the Ferghana Valley, who couldn't believe that the Order of Kali was no longer going to protect them from wyr-wolves—that the Mahimata had actually issued an edict *banning* the killing of the beasts. The first time, it was a small delegation of three, and she managed to mollify them with a blend of logic and thought-shaping, assisted by Navroz Lan.

But the second time, the inter-clan council of Ferghana arrived in full force: twelve elders representing twelve of the biggest clans that dwelled in the valley.

Kyra met them in the central cavern, flanked by the Kali elders, trying to hide her dismay. Six men and six women, their faces hard, their thoughts rebellious. The most powerful clan elders in the valley, and not a trace of respect for her in their minds. *Upstart*, they thought. *Witch*. And, worst of all, *tainted*. She had to delve deeper to understand that, and then wished she hadn't. Apparently, she was tainted by fate itself, by the killing of her own family, and the untimely death of two accomplished Mahimatas. She would destroy the Order of Kali with her ill luck, destroy the clans too if they let her.

Ignorant fools. Kyra fought down her anger and practiced Sheetali, the Cooling Breath. She needed their cooperation. Felda gave her arm a quick squeeze from behind, and Mumuksu sent her a wave of reassurance. *We are with you. Do what you must.*

Kyra took a deep breath and began: "Councillors, welcome to the caves of Kali. To what do we owe this honor?" She used just a slight inflection on the last word, so anyone paying attention would know what she really meant.

Lips tightened; glances were exchanged. A blue-robed woman with ash gray hair stepped forward. "We wish to protest your edict banning the killing of wyr-wolves and your demand for able-bodied combatants from each clan."

No greetings, no introduction from the headwoman of the Chan tribe. Mumuksu gave an almost audible hiss, for the Chan was *her* clan and the headwoman a distant relative, if Kyra was not mistaken.

This was rudeness bordering on dishonor. They would never have behaved this way with either Shirin Mam or Tamsyn Turani. Shirin would have quelled them with a single glance. As for Tamsyn, they wouldn't have dared even meet her eyes.

Well, Kyra was neither Shirin Mam nor the feared Hand of Kali. She was only herself, and they would have to learn to accept her. "Your protest is duly noted," she said. "Rest assured that the safety of the Ferghana remains our top priority, which is why we have asked for your help. For the first time."

"Fighting outlaws is *your* task," said an elderly bearded man on the right of the blue-robed woman—an elder of Tushkan, Kyra remembered. "So is keeping the valley safe from wyr-wolves. The monstrous beasts kill our sheep and steal our children. The Order of Kali has always protected us from them. Why else do we pay tithe?"

Kyra sensed a current of anger run through Navroz, Mumuksu, Felda, and Chintil. *No, please,* she thought to them. *Let me do the talking.*

"You pay tithe so that you may sleep at night while we keep watch," said Kyra, keeping her voice calm. "You pay tithe so that you may live without fear. You pay tithe so that we may carry the burden of justice for you. We are all that stand between you and darkness. War is coming to Asiana; we must have your support to prevail. Have you forgotten your vows of fealty to the Order?"

"We are not the ones who have forgotten," said the elderly man. "The wyr-wolves—"

"Will not bother you any longer," cut in Kyra, hoping she was right. "If they do, let me know, and I will send one of my Markswomen to investigate. Be warned that any lies or traps will be severely dealt with. Now, shall we talk about how many armed men and women you can spare, or has the council of Ferghana nothing better to do than waste our time arguing over a nonnegotiable decree?"

The headwoman of Chan reddened. "You cannot dismiss us like this. We have rights!"

How dare she. Kyra drew herself up. She gathered her anger, let it build, and held it coiled inside her. "You are telling me what I can and cannot do?" Her voice, laced with the Inner Speech, rang through the cavern. "Here, in the caves of Kali?"

Still they did not back down. "Shirin Mam would never have treated us like this," said the Tushkan elder, putting as much scorn as he could into the words.

No. Because you would never have dared defy her. Kyra unsheathed her blade; it flared green and fierce, enveloping her in its glow. Power flowed into her, and she took a single step forward.

The faces of the councillors changed, becoming wary.

"We do not fear you," said the headwoman of Chan, although her voice wobbled a bit. "You are honor-bound to keep us from harm."

That is exactly why I must do this.

Kyra closed her eyes and concentrated. A halo of power danced over her blade. All she had to do was unspool it into twelve threads—there, like that. And then flick a single thread at each councillor to bind him or her. She opened her eyes and surveyed them. They stood frozen in various poses, expressions ranging from terrified to angry.

Good, let them feel helpless before her.

"Kneel before your Mahimata, and swear your allegiance to the Order of Kali," she commanded. Behind her, the Kali elders gasped. Never in living memory had the council been *forced* to do anything.

The councillors fell to the floor, eyes darting around in desperation as the mental bonds of the Inner Speech fell over them and tightened like a noose. They began to speak, a halting, terrified chorus that smote her. These were the people she was supposed to protect. But she steeled herself and did not betray her conflicting emotions. One hard lesson would last them a lifetime. Better this than a series of small transgressions that would fray the hold the Order had over the clans of the valley.

"I swear on my blood, my ancestors, and my land, that I will be forever faithful to the Order of Kali, obey the Kanun of Ture-asa at all times, and be ready to serve as the Order sees fit. Nor will I, through any thought, word, or deed, suffer any harm to come to the Orders of Peace. To the Goddess I commit my soul; to the Order of Kali I commit myself, my goods, and any property I own. Protect us, guide us, and bring the light of the Kanun into every corner of the valley, that our children's children may know the peace we do."

Silence followed. Kyra studied them one by one, holding the threads of power taut, although she was feeling the strain. They had obeyed her because they had no choice. If she weakened now, it would all be for nothing. "You will not move, until you mean every word you have just said," she announced.

She sat down to wait. She could sense the anxiety of the Kali elders, but she had no energy to spare them. She concentrated on maintaining the links she had created.

It took a long time, and it cost her, but she did not let anyone see that. The council members were in pain, in shock, and in fear of their very lives. But their pride was greater than all these things, and it was this she sought to break. She sent them images, one after the other, drawn from the testimonies she had read: the carnage Kai Tau was wreaking in the Thar Desert, the dead bodies of innocent men and women, the hacked limbs of those who tried to resist, the staccato beat of gunfire. She made them feel what a victim would have felt, the feelings she knew only too well; hadn't her own world been destroyed by Kai Tau when she was but five?

She showed them the dark weapons and how one had tried to speak to her, to turn her to evil. *See*, she tried to tell them, *the true threat comes not from the wyr-wolves you have demonized for generations, but from kalashiks and the outlaws who wield them.*

At last, one by one, the council members rose from the floor on shaky legs, trembling and weeping. One by one, the threads of power snapped back, dissolving into Kyra's blade. Navroz glanced at her and she nodded. *Go to them.*

The Kali elders helped the councillors stand or sit up, soothing them and murmuring reassurances. Kyra watched, knowing she had to stay apart. Her head was pounding. She longed to return to the quiet stillness of her cell. But this wasn't over yet.

When all the councillors were upright again, she stood. "On behalf of the Order, I thank all of you for your trust," she said, making her voice strong yet free of the Inner Speech. Aiding the fight against the outlaws was something they needed to do of their own volition. "We will not fail you. We will protect the

Ferghana Valley with every blade, every last drop of our blood. You have seen what I know. Kai Tau isn't going to stop with conquering the Deccan. He is amassing an army and clearly means to overthrow the Orders and replace them with his own rule. You know what such a rule would mean, the darkness it will bring to all of Asiana. So I ask you now, will you aid us? Will you give us warriors to fight by our side against him?"

"We will, Mahimata," said a woman who had not spoken before—Aruna, the headwoman of Kalam, a clan of horse breeders. "We will give you our best fighters and strongest horses."

Kyra recognized her from the time she had gone with Tonar to the Kalam camp and taken down a band of outlaws bent on revenge. She felt a rush of warmth for the headwoman, who had not spoken against her and been the first to volunteer help.

One by one, the affirmations came from them all. The town of Tushkan promised weapons from their smiths, and the Chan vowed to give both men and supplies.

Negotiations and discussions followed. Kyra let the Kali elders do the talking, the listening, the jotting down of numbers and dates. Exhaustion threatened to overwhelm her, but she smiled at whoever looked her way. Not that this happened often. If it did, it seemed to be by accident, and they hastily averted their eyes.

After a ceremonial tea served by the novices, the council members finally left. Kyra allowed herself to slump back, tension draining from her shoulders. The elders looked at her askance, as if they could not recognize who she was anymore. Navroz murmured something about her "very advanced Mental Arts," and Mumuksu added, rather unnecessarily, Kyra thought, that Kyra had been among the worst at it as an apprentice.

But that night as she lay on her rug, she wondered at it herself.

Who was she turning into? Would Shirin Mam have approved? She thought of Tamsyn's blade, lying a few feet away, and a deep unease took hold of her. Was it possible that the blade was influencing her thoughts and actions in ways she had not anticipated?

She slept ill that night and dreamed of a door she could not open, no matter how hard she tried. Behind that door, someone sobbed and shouted for help, but whether it was Nineth or her own lost self, she could not tell.

Chapter 12

THE FUNERARY
CHAMBER

Whether it was the effect of the unsettling dream or her use of the Mental Arts on the council of Ferghana, the next morning Kyra finally gathered her courage to unsheathe Tamsyn's katari. She was unsure what would come of it; she knew only that it was time to uncover the weapon. It had lain dormant in a corner of her cell for months, and always the pain of her wound had flared up in its vicinity. But her wound had healed, and she was no longer afraid of it. Tamsyn's katari belonged to her now, as much as a kalishium blade could belong to anyone.

Kyra withdrew her own blade from its carved wooden scabbard and held it ready. Her gaze went to the black metal case that lay in the farthest corner of the cell. Tamsyn's blade, calling out to her, its voice dark and soft. *Nineth*, it sang, and Kyra's heart leaped. *Yes.* She scrambled to her feet and reached for Tamsyn's katari with trembling fingers. She sensed the longing of the kalishium blade to be free and hesitated.

Nineth, it said again, and she could no more have stopped herself than if Nineth had stood there calling out to her. She unsheathed the blade.

For the first time since Navroz drew it out of her flesh, her enemy's blade was liberated from its cage. Pain lanced Kyra's chest, and she gripped her own blade harder. Tamsyn's katari glowed with a faint reddish light, as if a shadow of its owner still dwelled in it somehow. Its power rippled through her, like a river of all the blood Tamsyn had shed, and Kyra fought the urge to throw it down. It felt—not *evil*, but unclean. Uncontrollable. *Wrong*. Her own katari pulsed green fire, pushing against the red tide that flowed from the alien blade, and Kyra's breathing evened out. She could do this; she could work her will on the katari, now that Tamsyn was gone.

"Tell me," she commanded. "What happened to Nineth?"

Images flashed through her mind, gray with time and distance. Nineth attempting to run away. Being caught and taken before Tamsyn to be punished. Her katari confiscated, her face wet with tears. And then the penance: forced to meditate alone on a hill behind the caves of Kali. Until, one day, she simply vanished.

Tamsyn's blade could not tell her where, because Tamsyn had not known. She had been furious at Nineth's escape and hidden Nineth's blade where no one would think to look for it.

"The funerary chamber?" Kyra was stunned. No wonder the elders hadn't been able to sense where Nineth was. She turned Tamsyn's blade over in her hand, but it had gone cold and silent, as if the effort of communicating with her had been too great.

The funerary chamber of the Order was reputed to be an eerie cavern two levels below the main living area, just underneath the armory. Kyra had never seen it; only elders had access to the chamber, although now that she was the Mahimata, they could scarcely prevent her from going there. She sheathed Tamsyn's blade and made up her mind; she would ask the elders for help in recovering Nineth's katari.

She found Mumuksu and Navroz in Felda's cell; Chintil was outside, teaching Hatha-kala. She explained to them what had happened and what she wanted.

"You will use Tamsyn's katari to trace Nineth's?" Felda's eyes gleamed. "That is a clever idea."

"But dangerous," Navroz pointed out. "Tamsyn's imprint is on that blade; it will harm you if it can."

"I know, Eldest," said Kyra. "But there is no other way that I can see. In truth, if I hadn't been wounded, I would have done this much sooner."

"She's right," Mumuksu told Navroz, surprising Kyra. "If there is the faintest possibility we can trace Nineth, we must take the chance. I will go with her to the funerary chamber and make sure she comes to no harm."

Navroz nodded. "Go at the hour of meditation tonight," she said, her voice heavy. "It is a favorable time to visit the spirits of those who have passed. But be prepared for what you might find."

None of them said it aloud, but Kyra knew what they were thinking: Nineth might be dead, her blade cold as a corpse.

"Careful," said Mumuksu for the fourth or fifth time.

Kyra gritted her teeth and lowered herself down the rope

ladder. She could not see the bottom of the vertical shaft they were descending. It was like being swallowed by darkness.

"Why are there no torches here, Elder?" she asked. The higher levels of the caves were always well-lit. Even the armory had a few metal sconces, their dim light falling on the racks of spears and swords that leaned against the walls.

"We are entering the dark zone of the caves," said Mumuksu from above her. "Natural light does not reach these depths; torches die out soon after being lit. We think it has to do with how the caves breathe."

Despite the green glow of the katari slung around her neck, Kyra felt the cold and clammy fingers of panic pinch her nostrils. She couldn't breathe; her head swam. She was drowning in nothingness, and whose face was that, just beyond her vision, mouth open in a scream, eyes filled with terror?

Her own.

"There is oxygen enough for us," said Mumuksu, a note of reproof in her voice. "Do you not sense the air currents? Calm yourself."

Kyra counted her breaths, focused on putting one foot below the other. Her head cleared, and her pulse slowed. The simplest of meditations were the most effective, Shirin Mam had always said.

The air smelled dank; from somewhere, Kyra heard the faint murmur of water. By the time her feet touched the floor, several minutes had passed. She exhaled, stepped back, and bumped into a rock wall. She bit back a curse and held her blade aloft; as far as she could judge, they were in a rift: a tall, narrow passage, scarcely wide enough to walk through.

Mumuksu climbed down the last few rungs and joined her in the cramped space. "The Goddess Kali walked this path to the funerary chamber," she said, "leaving bloody handprints on the walls as a mark of her passage."

Kyra peered at the walls as she followed the elder. Dark smudges resolved into rough handprints—were they truly inked with blood?—and she shivered. "How come I've never heard this story, Elder?" she asked.

Mumuksu stopped and turned. In the dim glow of the kataris, her face lay more in shadow than in light. "As you rise in the ranks of the Order, so also must you go deeper. You have not been the Mahimata long enough, but one day you will see and understand even more than we do now. Do you believe the Goddess watches over you?"

Thrown off-balance, Kyra stuttered, "Yes—of course. But I try not to think about it."

Mumuksu's teeth flashed in the dark. "Come. It is time you saw her."

Kyra had already seen the Goddess—or at least, a vision of her maternal aspect, Tara. It was nothing she wanted to repeat. But she followed Mumuksu; she had no choice, if she wanted to retrieve Nineth's blade. Every step that took them deeper inside the hill sharpened her unease. Once they came across green patches of phosphorescence, crawling on the walls as though they were alive. Kyra shrank back from them, hugging the opposite wall; they burned as an afterimage on her eyelids long after they were past. Something skittered over her boots, and she stifled a shriek.

"Cave spiders," remarked Mumuksu. "Utterly harmless, unlike the scorpions. Don't worry, Eldest has an antivenom."

Kyra did not answer; she was too busy concentrating on where she put her feet. The passage broadened at last, and a diffuse light filtered through the darkness, revealing the mouth of a chamber, shoulder-high.

"Here it is," said Mumuksu, "the final resting place of Markswomen." And she led the way inside.

Kyra ducked, stepped through the entrance, and gasped in wonder. The chamber was *huge*, much bigger than the central cavern of Kali. Crystalline pillars extended from the damp floor to the distant roof. Calcite made crazy shapes on the walls: swirls of flowers, bunches of coral, banded shawls. Beyond the pillars was a dark, still lake, and on the far side of the lake were rows of recessed shelves that held the urns with the ashes and kataris of long-dead Markswomen. It was from here that the light emanated, dancing and spinning over the crystal formations until they seemed sentient.

"It's beautiful," Kyra said breathily. And it was. But it was also eerie, and she had no wish to linger. Mumuksu strode ahead with the ease of familiarity and vanished behind a dense forest of needle-like crystals.

"Elder?" called Kyra, picking her way carefully across the ribbed and slippery floor. She rounded the mineral forest and almost screamed.

Towering above her, shining with an inner light, the four-armed Goddess meditated in the lotus position. On her forehead glowed a half-moon. In one hand she held a sword, in another a cup of blood. The third and fourth hands were held out in symbolic gestures of fearlessness and boon-conferment. Her eyes burned like coals, and her hair rippled in turbulent waves to her feet. Her face was both beautiful and terrible. Kyra backed away, suppressing the desire to flee. The eyes of the Goddess pierced her, flipped her inside out, exposing every flaw.

Not the Goddess. Just a mineral statue. Get a hold of yourself.

"Bhairavi the Fierce," said Mumuksu from behind her. "The fifth of the ten forms of the Mother Goddess. The story goes that she came here to meditate eons ago and left an image of herself behind."

"It's a statue, Elder," said Kyra, recovering her voice. *A rather lifelike one.*

Mumuksu smiled. "And yet it is only at her altar that a candle will stay lit in this chamber. Will you?" She nodded toward the candles in a black metal holder at the base of the statue.

Kyra knelt over the altar and struck a match with shaking hands. The flame flickered, mirroring her own faith. But it did not die out. She lit one of the candles, straightened, and cleared her throat. "Most interesting, Elder. But we are here to find Nineth's blade."

"Of course," said Mumuksu. "We were only paying our respects. Do you know where to start?"

Kyra's gaze went across the black water to the far side of the chamber. "In the urns," she said with conviction. "Tamsyn hid it in one of them."

"There are hundreds," Mumuksu pointed out.

"Tamsyn's blade will guide us," said Kyra. She could see the elder did not like this. She didn't particularly like it either. But it was either that or disturb the ashes of hundreds of dead Markswomen, and Kyra knew which she preferred.

They crossed the lake in a small boat, using wooden oars to row themselves. Kyra was glad to put some distance between herself and the larger-than-life statue of the Goddess. Not that she was afraid, she told herself. It was a *gift* to have seen the statue, to have lit a candle at her altar. Nevertheless, it was a relief to turn away from that all-knowing gaze. She wondered how long the statue had stood there, guarding the entrance to the chamber, and who had made it. Or whether, as Mumuksu seemed to believe, the Goddess had truly walked these halls and left an image of herself for her devotees to find.

As they neared the other side of the lake, the urns shone with golden light, as if the blades inside knew they were coming and were welcoming them. Kyra stepped out of the boat onto the slick stone floor and withdrew Tamsyn's blade from its scabbard. It glowed crimson; a fierce joy radiated from it, and Kyra had to strive to remain aloof.

"We should leave it in an urn here," said Mumuksu. "This is where it truly belongs."

Kyra did not reply. She knew in her heart the elder was right. But she wasn't going to part with Tamsyn's blade until it had revealed all its secrets to her.

Show me, she thought. *Where is Nineth's blade?*

The crimson light from Tamsyn's katari stabbed at one of the urns on the topmost shelf.

"There! Do you see it, Elder?" Kyra sheathed Tamsyn's blade and corded it to her waist, grinning with triumph.

After that, it was a minute's work to fetch the urn, ask forgiveness of the Markswoman whose ashes they were disturbing, and retrieve Nineth's katari.

It came out a dull, lifeless gray but mercifully free of ash. Kyra turned it over in her hands, trying to feel Nineth, while Mumuksu restored the urn to its rightful resting place.

"Talk to me," Kyra whispered. "You know who I am. You know how much I love her."

Was it her imagination, or did a feeble vein of blue light spark inside Nineth's blade? Kyra quashed her mounting excitement and closed her eyes. *Focus. Remember Nineth: her face, her voice, her smiles, her fears.*

Mumuksu made a small sound; Kyra felt the heat of the blade in her hands, but she did not open her eyes. *Show me. Show me what happened to her*, she willed the blade.

The images started, hesitant at first, then unfolding like a story. Unlike the images from Tamsyn's blade, these were sharp and clear, full of color and emotion, and Kyra felt herself falling into them. She saw Nineth, bereft and angry at Kyra's abrupt departure from the caves of Kali, saddling Rinna with the crazy, half-formed plan of following Kyra to wherever she had gone. She felt Nineth's fear and dismay when she was caught by Baliya and hauled to the Mahimata's cell. Tamsyn leaning forward, smiling that snake smile, saying: *Give me your blade, Nineth.* Nineth's tears as she was forced to obey.

And then the *real* nightmare began. Kyra watched in helpless horror as Tamsyn used the Inner Speech to force Nineth into the lotus postion on an isolated hill—for *four days*. Even four hours would have been deeply painful. This was no penance. It was torture. And it had happened barely half an hour from the caves of Kali. How must Nineth have felt, to be so close to home and yet unable to leave or call for help? Kyra's stomach clenched at the cruelty of it. And when Nineth was driven by hunger to forage for berries and walnuts on the hillside, tears welled in Kyra's eyes.

"Please," she whispered. "Stop." She couldn't bear it; Nineth's suffering was *her* fault.

But, having started, there was no stopping the flood of images from Nineth's blade. When Tamsyn punched Nineth for daring to eat berries, Kyra staggered back from the blow, feeling the sharp pain of it in her own jaw, tasting blood on her own tongue.

Somewhere far distant, Mumuksu cried out her name.

Night fell on Nineth's fourth day of exile, and something shifted in the mood and tone of the images. Someone was bending over Nineth, *picking* her up. Slinging her over his back, like a sack of coals. Moonlight fell on his face and Kyra felt a shock of recognition. Hattur Nisalki, the red-haired young man with too-large teeth who had tried to flirt with them at the festival of Chorzu the night that Shirin Mam had died. What was he doing, heaving Nineth onto his horse? Kyra seethed with anger. How dare he put his hands on her! Just wait till she caught him. She'd rope him to Rinna and drag him across the valley until he begged Nineth's forgiveness and swore never to touch a girl again without her consent. And then she'd do it some more, just to drive the lesson home. And, oh, if he had *harmed* Nineth, she wouldn't let him live at all . . .

The scene switched. Nineth laughed. Sunlight fell on her face and hair, giving her a halo of happiness. She sat on a horse; Hattur Nisalki walked beside her, his face soft and foolish as he gazed up at her. Kyra blinked. *What?*

The scene shifted again. Now Nineth was in a field of some sort, balancing on a rope a couple of feet above the grass. Her arms were outstretched, her face screwed up in concentration. She was going to fall. Of course she was. Dear, clumsy Nineth. Kyra almost could have smiled. Until Nineth fell into Hattur Nisalki's arms, and he—the cheek of him!—dared to kiss her forehead, as though she were a common village girl, not an apprentice of the Order of Kali.

No. This was not to be borne. Kyra's fist clenched around the blade as if she would break it.

But there was more, much more. Kyra's breath stopped as she beheld the cozy, lamp-lit interior of a tent. Hattur was kissing Nineth, running his hands through her hair. And Nineth— Nineth was tugging off his shirt. *Stop, you idiot!* Kyra wanted to scream. Except, of course, this had already happened, and there was nothing she could do about it.

This wasn't fair. This wasn't right.

It should have been me and Rustan.

She whirled around in fury and threw Nineth's blade into the dark, uncaring waters of the lake.

At the altar of the Goddess, the lone candle flickered out.

CHAPTER 13

NINETH

Nineth sat bolt upright, her heart thudding wildly. A nightmare. It had to be a nightmare. It was those awful sheepskin rugs in her tent. The hair got into her nose and made her sneeze. It must have gotten into her sleeping brain too. She pushed away the blankets with a spasm of distaste. Nightmare or vision, one thing was clear. She was not spending another night with Hattur's caravan. No matter what Hattur and his gaggle of aunties said, she had recovered as much as she was going to from the trauma Tamsyn had inflicted upon her. It was time she returned to the caves of Kali and confronted her fate.

She crawled out of the tiny tent that stood at one end of the camp and stretched. A soft wind rustled through the grassy field, bringing the sounds of the night: the song of crickets, the distant bark of a fox, the warble of an unseen night bird. Nineth closed her eyes, trying to will strength into her limbs. Despite the fact that she had done little but eat and rest over the past several weeks, she was spent, completely drained of energy.

Hadn't she felt like this ever since Tamsyn had taken her katari?

Nineth's heart clenched. She had sensed for some time that her katari was no longer with Tamsyn. Now it was no longer . . . anywhere.

She thought back to her nightmare. Kyra, looking quite unlike herself, her face suffused with anger. Nineth's blade, glowing in her hands, as if calling out to its owner for help. And Kyra, throwing the katari in a wide, heartless arc. The small, sad splash as it sank into the dark waters of a lake. The images made no sense.

If Kyra was alive and well and back with the Order of Kali, it meant that Tamsyn was gone. Or maybe it was Tamsyn who had thrown Nineth's katari, and it was Nineth's own wishful thinking that had shown her Kyra's face. Because Kyra would never throw Nineth's katari; Kyra would use it to find her and bring her home.

Wouldn't she?

Nineth sank onto the grass and hugged her knees, wishing she knew the right thing to do. Here in the wilds of the Tajik Plains, news was slow to filter from the heart of Asiana. A million things could have happened, and she wouldn't know it until the caravan decided to head back to the Ferghana Valley. And if the rumors she'd heard were right, that would be a long time coming.

She ducked back into her tent and tugged on a cloak one of Hattur's great-aunts had given her. She tied the food she'd been hoarding for this day in a bit of sackcloth: nuts, dates, dried berries, a loaf of stale bread. Pitiful as it was, it would have to do. At least she would not starve the way Tamsyn had starved her.

When she emerged from the tent, ready to leave, she was not particularly surprised to see Hattur standing outside. The man had the stubbornness of an ox and the perceptiveness of an eagle.

"Move," she said without preamble. "I'm going."

He raised an eyebrow and grinned, teeth flashing white in the darkness. "On foot?"

"I was going to borrow one of the horses," said Nineth, annoyed.

"You will take Neri," he said. "But you don't know the way. You were half-dead when I brought you here."

Nineth bristled. "I will find the way."

"Or you can take me with you," he said.

"No," said Nineth firmly. "You stay right here with your family. You're in enough trouble with them as it is for bringing me to the caravan without asking permission."

He closed one eye and grimaced. "You have two choices, dear lady. You take me, and we leave quietly, and in the morning they all go, 'Oh look, the lovebirds are gone, how sweet, maybe we will have babies come next winter . . .'"

She swatted him, and he ducked, laughing like a hyena. *Idiot.* One or two kisses and he thought she was madly in love with him. Although, she had to admit, it had been fun kissing him. Not at all like kissing a horse, which was what she had compared it to when she first saw him. Not that she had ever kissed a horse.

"Quiet," she hissed. "You'll wake the whole camp."

He sobered up. "Your second choice is to try to go alone. And I will raise the alarm."

"You wouldn't."

He stuck his chin out mulishly. "I don't understand why you want to return. You've only just recovered. That witch could still be looking for you."

"That is exactly why you must stay here," she said. "You'll probably die horribly with a blade sticking out of your chest if you come with me."

He clutched his chest and pretended to swoon. "Oh, my heart has already bid me goodbye, what is this miserable life without you? Take me, take me even to my death, dear lady."

Nineth gave a sigh. "Can you be serious for once? I must return, and you would be in danger if you went with me."

"You might be in danger too," he pointed out. "I'd rather share your fate than waste away with worry here."

Nineth snorted. She couldn't help it. The thought of Hattur "wasting away" was too much. "I doubt you'd skip a meal on my account," she said. "You eat more than Neri does. You'd devour all my provisions if I let you."

"I'll pack extra," he said earnestly. "Just give me five minutes."

"No," she said with finality, and she knew her tone had had the desired effect when his face fell.

She liked Hattur. Perhaps it was the countless number of times he had apologized to her for carrying her off without her permission; never mind that he had saved her from Tamsyn's torture. Or perhaps it was the way he listened to his aunties, who were forever making him do little jobs for them, fixing their tents or hunting for the hard-to-find plants needed for their herbal remedies. Or maybe it was the way he had taken care of Nineth during the journey to his family's camp, spooning awful-tasting gruel into her mouth and not even flinching when she spat it back out into his face.

It had taken many days to trust him. She had been at her weakest, saddest, and angriest. And he had responded with humor, kindness, and, when she accused him of kidnapping her, abject shame.

After a while, Nineth had let go of her anger. He'd believed he was saving her life, and in truth he probably had. But he had also taken her far away from her katari. It was this that hurt most. With time and distance, the pain had dulled, but it was always there, a constant ache in some part of her she could not put a name to.

Hattur didn't know that, though, and she would never tell him. He wouldn't be able to understand. And he had been so full of remorse that she had forgiven him. Gradually, he had become a friend.

But she wasn't going to let him follow her back to the Order. Not only because it was dangerous for him, but because she didn't want him getting ideas about her. Or rather, more ideas than he already had. Whatever he felt for her, there was no future between them, and she had to make him see that.

She looked up to find Hattur's gaze on her, as if he was trying to memorize every detail of her face.

"I'm sorry," she said. "You cannot follow where I am going."

"You don't love me," he said. It wasn't a question.

Nineth shook her head decisively. "Hattur, I like you very much, and I have no wish to see harm come to you—but I don't love you. Stay here with your family, and if all goes well, perhaps we will meet next summer at the festival of Chorzu."

He gave a wan smile. "You will visit my tent full of Marvels and Magick?"

"I will," said Nineth. *If I'm still alive. If my Order hasn't come apart. If I can find my blade again.*

"I'll saddle Neri," said Hattur in a leaden voice. "And pack you some extra food."

"But Neri's *your* horse," said Nineth in surprise. "Won't you get into trouble?"

"You were going to borrow her anyway, weren't you?" he countered, with a shadow of his old grin. "And my father will probably just be happy that you're gone." Hattur's father had been furious with him for running off and capturing one of the Kali "witches," as he called them, and deathly afraid that the wrath of the Order would burn them all to the ground. If not for Hattur, and all his aunts and great-aunts, he would have made Nineth leave the day he'd realized who she was.

"I'll take good care of her," Nineth promised. To her surprise, she had to swallow a lump in her throat. As Hattur melted away into the night, she reflected on the strange nature of friendship.

She thought of Kyra. The nightmare vision came back to her, and she was filled with unease.

Hattur returned with Neri, carrying a small sack on his shoulders, and she put away her disquiet. She gave him a hug and mounted the mare before they could both become maudlin.

"I'll see you again, the Goddess willing," she said.

"Mind you return my horse," he replied, shaking a finger at her. "With interest! I want a baby horse too."

Which was just Hattur being Hattur, but his teasing helped somehow, and the knot within her loosened. "Absolutely," she said. "You can always pass it off as yours."

She laughed as he sputtered and blew him a kiss. "Stay well!" she cried, and then Neri was off, cantering away from the caravan into the unknown night.

CHAPTER 14

IN THE CAVERN

I t had been happening more and more frequently over the
past few days. A sudden pain would pierce Rustan in the
head or chest and he would keel over, blind with agony. And
then it would be gone, leaving him gasping and disoriented.
If the Sahirus knew what was happening, they kept it to
themselves. He didn't want to ask them about it. It was a puzzle
he had to solve, maybe a test they were putting him through.

They had fallen into a routine that began at daybreak with
meditation. After the daily chores and a simple meal, they sat
down to work. The monks showed Rustan how to use different
herbs to make medicines and tried to teach him the ancient
script in which their books were written. At times Rustan felt
close to understanding the heart of the language, but more
often it was all so much gibberish that danced across the page.
More than once he came close to throwing their precious
books down in frustration.

He asked the Sahirus why they had not taken in novices to pass on their knowledge to future generations, but after spending several days with them, he could guess the answer. They could not take just any student. The chosen one would appear to them in their dreams and must come to the monastery on his or her own, surviving the cold, the fatigue, and the beast in the forest. This had happened less and less over the centuries, until only the two of them remained.

He questioned them again about the seekers, and they told him that a very few people had made it to the monastery over the years and been granted an audience. Most never reached them. Who could tell what anyone was really looking for? Some sought answers, but most sought the freedom of death.

"An innkeeper told me that I reminded him of the last seeker, a man called Rubathar," said Rustan, recalling Nursat's words. "Did he ever manage to find you?"

Their faces grew grave. *He did not survive the beast in the forest. There was much in him that was good and noble, but he had not the strength to face what he had done. He was a warrior of some repute, until he decimated an entire tribe in revenge for an attack on his own.*

Rustan remembered the face of the innocent man he had killed and felt a pang of sympathy for the unfortunate Rubathar. "Do I remind you of him too?" he asked.

To us, you are only yourself.

And with that he had to be content.

Thrice Rustan went down to Bankot—the little settlement at the base of the mountain—for ink, parchment, grain, oil, and other supplies. The villagers regarded him with awe, silently giving him whatever he needed and refusing payment of any kind. He realized that they knew about the Sahirus and must have kept the secret for generations. Now they viewed him with the same respect as they did the monks. It made him uncomfortable, but he didn't know what to say to convince them that he did not deserve their reverence. That he was nothing more than a trained killer who still carried a weapon.

He brought this up with the monks one stormy night, speaking over the hail that battered the wooden pagoda of the monastery.

"I am a killer," he said.

We know. We too are killers.

He looked at them, dumbfounded.

They smiled. *Killers of ignorance.*

Rustan sighed. "Not that kind of killer. I mean, I have killed men. Real, living men. I am a Marksman and I carry a weapon, even here in your sanctuary." He brought out his mother's katari and unsheathed its gleaming blade, waiting for their disapprobation.

It never came.

We know this. How else do you think we are able to communicate with you?

Rustan blinked. The monks laughed, thin shoulders shaking beneath their saffron robes. At last he understood. The Sahirus were able to commune with him because of the telepathic metal of his mother's blade.

He persisted. "Why do you teach me when you know what I am?"

We teach you because *we know what you are.*

"I am a Marksman of the Order of Khur," said Rustan. "I will return to Khur when my penance is complete."

This did not seem to disturb the monks. They simply nodded and smiled.

Rustan raked a hand though his hair, trying to think clearly. "I came to you because I killed an innocent man and was burdened by guilt. I needed to atone. I do not want to kill anyone ever again, but I will, if I must. War is coming to Asiana, and I cannot let my Order down. So you see, I am not the one you have been waiting for."

The monks gazed at him with compassion and did not respond.

Rustan found himself floundering for words, trailing off into silence in the face of their peaceful acceptance.

The next morning, he was woken by a pain so sharp that he vomited the remains of his dinner over the side of his bed.

He tried to wave the Sahirus away, but they ignored him and mopped up the mess. When he tried to help, they pushed him back onto his bed.

Rest.

But he could not. Something gnawed at Rustan, something he needed to do. It would wait no longer. The puzzle had to be solved before it finished him off. When he got shakily to his feet, the monks did not try to stop him. They exchanged a quick, wordless glance and led him to the back of the room, where the mouth of the caves opened into blackness. The Younger Sahiru plucked a lantern from the wall and thrust it at him.

Go. Here you will find your answers.

What did they mean? Their withered faces gave no clue as to what they were thinking. A continuation of the test, perhaps. Like the pain. He accepted the lantern and stooped to enter the caves.

The lantern cast a small pool of light around him. It wasn't enough to see the ceiling or the other side of the chamber.

Rustan followed the wall, feeling his way forward with his hand. From the light of his lantern he could make out paintings beneath the hand he trailed along the wall. He stopped to study them, but they were too faded and intricate for him to figure out. Something to explore later.

A bit farther down he stopped. A faint blue-green light shone in the distance. He made his way toward it and discovered a tunnel just tall enough for him to walk through. The light grew brighter as he walked, and he quickened his pace.

The tunnel opened onto a vast, glowing cavern. He blinked, trying to adjust his eyes after the relative darkness. Then he saw what was emitting the light and inhaled sharply.

Kalishium.

The cavern was lined with shelves. Row upon row of kalishium sculptures stood upon them. More kalishium than he had dreamed existed in Asiana. What Barkav would give to know the existence of this treasure trove.

A large, shining white globe stood by itself in the center, balanced on a stone pedestal. Rustan walked along the walls of the cavern, circling the globe, gazing at the statues in wonder. Kings and queens, gods and animals glowed green and blue, some familiar and some alien. Many wore masks, both hideous and beautiful. Each image told a different story, beckoning him closer, until he was falling into them, becoming a part of their history.

Shirin Mam's katari sparked a warning, and the spell broke. He stepped back, wary.

The sculptures belonged to the monks who lived here, who had guarded them for generations. This hoard must be the source of their telepathic powers.

His gaze went to the globe in the center of the cavern, and

his pulse quickened. This was the heart of it, he was sure. This was where his answers waited. What were his questions, though?

The most obvious thing he needed to know was the source of the phantom pain that kept seizing him and how to stop it.

Rustan set down the lantern, walked to the globe, and after hesitating only for a moment—what could happen, after all?—laid his palm upon its shining white surface.

CHAPTER 15

THE SEEING STONE

The pain was so intense, he couldn't breathe. His skull felt as if it were splitting in two. Rustan shouted and tried to wrench his hand away from the globe, but it wouldn't budge. He called for help, but the Sahirus did not appear.

The globe grew until it filled his vision. There was nothing else, no monastery, no cavern filled with silent statues—just the globe growing bigger and darker, and then a single yellow glow off in one corner, like the inside of a hut. Shadows danced and solidified into the shapes of men, bent over a figure crumpled on the floor. One of them kicked the figure and it doubled over. Rustan gasped, feeling the blow in his ribs.

The figure on the floor moaned and turned his way. The face was swollen, smeared with dirt and blood, but Rustan would have known the Khur elder anywhere. Barkav had sent Ishtul to spy on the Taus, but the blademaster had been caught. Rustan's stomach clenched at the sight of his combat teacher lying broken and bloody on the floor. One of the men brought down the hilt of a sword on Ishtul's mouth, smashing it open. "Stop!" cried Rustan, but they did not hear him.

The scene shifted. The sun shone on a barren field. In the middle of the field, on the branches of an old khajri tree, six bodies hung lifeless, broken-necked and fly-covered. Their clothes were in tatters, and their flesh had been eaten away. What had happened here?

A noose tightened around Rustan's neck, and he choked. A strong curved beak hooked into his forearm and ripped out a piece of his flesh. He screamed in agony. "No more, please," he begged.

The scene shifted. A dim, hot room filled with fire and smoke and the clamor of hammers on anvils. Five sweating, bare-chested men worked the bellows and hammered sheets of metal, surrounded by tables and shelves cluttered with tools. A smithy, but what were they forging?

One of the men picked up a long, black metal tube and caressed it as one might a lover.

Kalashiks. They were trying to duplicate the ancient guns. Rustan barely had time to wrap his mind around this horrifying thought before the scene shifted yet again. A dozen people squatted in a village square, hands tied behind their heads. Two guards armed with swords and spears stood on either side of the wretched little group. The captives ranged in age from young boys to elderly grandfathers. Rustan could taste their terror, feel their hopelessness.

A tall man with stringy gray hair hanging over his face stepped out of a white building, and the terror sharpened. *Kai Tau.*

He moved slowly, almost shambling, as if he was drunk.

He was covered in a cloak from the neck down, and there was something wrong with his face, but Rustan couldn't see it clearly.

Then the cloak parted, and the long barrel of a gun emerged. A flood of panic swept over the captives and they got clumsily to their feet, bumping into each other. Thinking, perhaps, to make a run for it.

But they never had a chance. The gun began to fire, cutting the prisoners down like chaff. A gloating delight emanated from the death-stick. *Yes, this is what I am meant for: to shed blood and drink souls. Thank you, Master.*

When the gun finally stopped, the earth was stained red with blood and littered with corpses.

No. Rustan dropped to his knees, shaking. *Enough.* His hand slid from the globe and he returned to the cavern, surrounded by the glowing kalishium sculptures. He rested his head between his knees, trying to anchor himself to the present moment. Shirin Mam's blade smouldered by his side, a comforting presence.

He sensed the Sahirus approach and raised his head. "What was that?" he asked, his voice husky, as if with disuse.

Answers.

Answers. The truth of what was happening in the Thar Desert and, perhaps quite soon, the rest of Asiana. Rustan tasted blood in his mouth and remembered Ishtul's swollen face.

The Sahirus helped him up and led him back to the main room of the monastery. He could barely walk straight. The ghost of all the pain he had witnessed sat on his shoulder, taunting him. He slept, woke, slept again. The next morning, he rose from a thick, dreamless sleep to a monster of a headache ravaging his skull. The Sahirus sat next to him, watching. When he tried to get up, the Younger Sahiru pushed him back.

The Elder Sahiru waved a stick of incense under his nose; the fumes were so strong his stomach churned.

"What is that thing—that white globe in the cavern?" he asked, struggling up onto one elbow.

But they made him wash and eat breakfast before answering. Later, after he had eaten and felt a bit stronger, they told him.

The Seeing Stone is made of kalishium, forged by the Araini themselves. We believe they carved intent into it. Did it answer your question?

Rustan licked his lips, haunted by the blood he had tasted in his vision. In Igiziyar he had dreamed of a human skull. Now, finally, he knew to whom it belonged. Somewhere in the Thar Desert, his teacher was being beaten and tortured by Kai Tau's men. And here he was, whiling away his time trying to learn a dead language and revive the dead hopes of a pair of ancient monks.

He got to his feet. The Sahirus did not try to stop him this time. They gazed at him with concern and something of sadness in their faces. Had they sensed his thoughts? Did they know he was about to leave?

Rustan was overwhelmed with guilt and shame. The Sahirus had saved his life, his sanity. They had shown him the wonders of the sky and taught him about the Ones from the stars. He began to tell them what he had seen and how he had to help the people of the Thar Desert, the words tumbling unsteadily from his lips. But the Sahirus interrupted him:

We know. The Seeing Stone does not lie. Go with our blessing.

"You don't understand," said Rustan. He swallowed. "I may die. Even if I live, I may not be able to return."

Every day brings us closer to death. You still have much to learn, young one.

"Perhaps you will find another novice if you dream of one?" said Rustan, without much hope.

They laughed then, their wheezing chuckles following him as he turned to pack his little bag. His cheeks flamed. Fine, let them believe what they wanted. The visions from the Seeing Stone were a wake-up call. He was still a Marksman; he still had his mother's blade, a weapon of ancient power. It would suffice.

His only problem was time. It would take nearly a week to ride to Yartan, the nearest Hub. Unless the Sahirus knew of a secret door close by? He turned to them, but even before he had asked the question, they shook their heads.

There is a door in the foothills of Kunlun Shan, but it has shifted. It might take you out of time; it is far too dangerous.

Rustan gritted his teeth. "Then by the time I reach the Thar, they will have forged many more weapons. Hundreds more will die. It will be too late."

You cannot know that. The Seeing Stone looks into the past, the present, and the future. Consider this journey the last part of your penance. Do not be afraid.

"I'm not afraid to die," said Rustan.

But you are afraid to live. There is something in you that pushes life away. When you finally embrace life, you will also conquer death.

"I know that if I do nothing, many innocent people will suffer," said Rustan. He slung his bag on his back. "Thank you for everything you have taught me. If there is any way I can repay even a small part of what you have given me, please tell me. I will do whatever is in my power."

Return to bury us. That is all we ask.

Those words stopped Rustan in his tracks. "What?" he asked, dumbfounded. "But . . ."

On the roof of the world, in Ice Mother's arms, you will see and understand everything. Go now.

Rustan paused, torn between wanting to begin his journey and wanting to make sense of what they'd said.

The monks did not give him the option. They thrust a package of food at him and hustled him out, chattering like silent birds with each other, their thoughts too fast for him to catch.

And then he was outside in the bright sunshine, on the path below the monastery, while the two ancient monks stood at the massive wooden door, waving goodbye, their robes flapping in the breeze. They looked so frail, so alone. The last of the Sahirus, and he was abandoning them. A lump came into his throat.

"Suppose I cannot return?" he asked, his eyes stinging. "What will you do?"

What we have always done. Go, Rustan. May you be fearless as the eagle, nimble as the mouse, and slippery as the fish.

The words followed him as he climbed down the mountain, filling him with hope and strength.

CHAPTER 16

MESSAGE FROM KAI TAU

As long as she lived, Kyra would never forget the moment she threw Nineth's blade into the lake in the funerary chamber. It was the moment she realized how deeply Tamsyn's katari was influencing her. It was something Tamsyn would have done in a fit of rage. Not *her*. All Kyra wanted was for Nineth to be back safe and sound. And yet, maddened by what the images from Nineth's blade had shown her, she had reacted just like Tamsyn.

We are more alike than you think, little deer, Tamsyn had said once. Kyra had repudiated those words then and forgotten them until now. Tamsyn's blade was altering her thoughts, feelings, and actions to *make* her more like the former Mistress of Mental Arts.

But Kyra could not let it go. Night after night, she unsheathed Tamsyn's blade and turned it over in her hands, studying it. There was something the blade was still trying to tell her, if only she could understand it. All that came through was a jumble of emotions: sadness, pain, anger, and a deep sense of having been wronged. Whether they were her own emotions or Tamsyn's—or Nineth's, for that matter—Kyra could not fathom.

The elders had been quite cold to Kyra since the day she threw Nineth's blade. She didn't blame them. She had no explanation, no excuse to offer for her behavior that wouldn't result in them demanding, quite reasonably, that she give up Tamsyn's blade.

And wasn't there a part of her that truly *was* angry with Nineth? She knew she was being unfair; Nineth did not know Tamsyn was dead, after all. Still, Kyra couldn't help wondering how Nineth could stay away from the Order for so long. Why did she not at least try to send word that she was alive or find out what was happening in the valley? Surely she'd heard rumors of Kai Tau's army and knew the Orders stood on the brink of war.

But the worst, the very worst, was the flare of jealousy she had felt when she saw Nineth and Hattur kissing. It horrified and shamed her, and yet she could not stop thinking of it. And of Rustan.

Kyra had not acted as the Mahimata should. She had allowed Tamsyn's blade to bring out her worst instincts. She would have to fix what she had broken, although she did not see how, not yet.

She apologized to the elders but refused to talk it over with them. She couldn't tell them what she had seen; she dared not. Quite apart from revealing the influence of Tamsyn's blade on her, it would also reveal to them how she truly felt, and they'd pounce on Kyra if they suspected her of harboring romantic feelings for anyone. Even Rustan. *Especially* Rustan. No matter that Shirin Mam herself had broken the law and borne a son; the elders of Kali had been as aghast at that as anyone else. Besides, Shirin Mam was safely dead when they found out about it; they couldn't very well confront her about her past.

Kyra couldn't even bring herself to confide in Elena, whom she loved and trusted above all others. Elena seemed to spend most of her time with Akassa these days, the apprentices growing close in a way Kyra wouldn't have believed possible a few months ago. She felt envious each time she saw them, heads bent together over a healing recipe or a mathematics challenge posed by Felda. Which was silly, she knew, but she couldn't help it. She thought with longing of the simpler days when Shirin Mam was still alive, when she would go riding or swimming with Nineth and Elena, laugh with them over private jokes, and whisper secrets.

In short, she felt very much alone.

🪷

Some days after the visit to the funerary chamber, Kyra was woken at dawn by a hesitant voice saying, "Eldest requests your presence in the cavern, Mother."

She groaned and rolled over to face the opening of her cell. She rubbed the sleep out of her eyes and focused on the small, white-robed novice hovering in front of her.

"Urgent, is it?" she mumbled, dragging herself up.

"Yes, Mother," murmured Helen, with downcast eyes. "Eldest told me to tell you that it's very important. They are waiting for you in the central cavern." She bowed and backed out of the cell.

Kyra lit a candle and changed into her black robe, racking

her brain to try to remember which important missive she may have failed to answer in the last few days. Nothing which could justify being woken at dawn came to her mind. She left her cell with a sense of foreboding that grew stronger with every step she took.

The four elders stood in a circle around the raised slab in the main cavern. Their mouths were drawn in tight lines, their eyes locked on an oval, linen-wrapped package on the slab. Tension practically vibrated in the air around them. Kyra had never seen them like this, not even when Shirin Mam died.

"What is the matter, Elders?" she asked, approaching the slab.

Then the smell hit her, and she recoiled. "By the Goddess, what is it?" she cried.

"A message from Kai Tau," said Navroz grimly. She reached for the package. "Prepare yourself, Kyra."

Kyra took a step back, fighting a sudden, nauseous fear. "Eldest? Wait—"

But Navroz did not wait. She knew, perhaps, that there was no way to be ready for such a thing as lay hidden in the package, its sickly sweet odor fouling the air of the cavern. She untied the strings that held it together and unwrapped the layers one by one. Felda, Chintil, and Mumuksu held themselves rigid, and Kyra prayed, *Please, Mother Goddess, let it not be him, let it not be him.*

The stained linen fell away to reveal a human head, severed at the neck. Kyra came out of her paralysis, horror and relief warring within her. *Not Rustan. Thank Kali.*

"You know who this is?" asked Navroz. "The package is addressed specifically to you."

Kyra forced the bile down her throat and studied the

discolored lump of flesh that had once been part of a person. Recognition came in a sick, painful twist of her gut.

The eyes had been gouged out and the long, hooked nose broken, but Kyra did know who it was. If she hadn't been in such a terror that it might be Rustan, she would have known right away, even before Navroz unwrapped the layers of cloth. The Khur elder had taught her, after all. Suspicious of her motives at first, he had accepted her as a pupil toward the end and demanded the best of her, just as Chintil always did. Kyra had traveled with him across the Empty Place to the Kashgar Hub; she had survived a sandstorm with him and helped him clean a gash on his cheek afterward. She had touched that face when it lived and breathed, and he had thanked her.

"Ishtul," said Kyra, and it was hard to speak, hard to say that name. "The blademaster of Khur." The Maji-khan had sent him to the Thar Desert to spy on the Taus. The best of their duelists, and Kai Tau had killed him. The suffering he had endured before he died was evident on his ruined visage. Her heart contracted. *I'm sorry, Elder.* It was her fault—all of it. Kyra's first mark had been Maidul Tau, Kai Tau's son; she had killed him and driven Kai Tau to take revenge on the Orders of Asiana. Perhaps he had been planning his war for years before that, but her action was the spark that had set the Thar on fire.

"I don't understand," said Chintil. "Why send this to you and not to the Maji-khan of Khur?"

"It's a challenge," said Kyra, speaking with difficulty. "He's showing me what he's capable of, goading me into taking action before we are fully prepared."

"Then you must not fall into the trap," said Navroz. "No hasty decisions."

"I hear you, Eldest," said Kyra.

She reached forward and touched the matted black hair on the head. She swallowed the hard lump in her throat. "Goodbye, Elder," she whispered. "I will avenge you. I swear it."

Felda cleared her throat. "Should we build a pyre? He deserves the last rites."

"No," said Kyra. "The Order of Khur has its own customs. I believe the dead are buried in a grove behind the camp. We must return the remains to them. Anyway, the Maji-khan needs to know what happened. Eldest, can you devise a way to . . . to make this look and smell more like Ishtul? It would be more respectful, both to his memory and to his Order."

Navroz pressed her lips together. "I will do what I can. I cannot reverse the decay that has already set in, but I will make sure it goes no further."

"Thank you," said Kyra. "As soon as your preparations are complete, please arrange to have it sent to the Kashgar Hub. I'll write a letter to Barkav. The Turguz clan will deliver it to Khur." She stopped, unable to go on.

"And you, Kyra?" asked Mumuksu. "What do you intend to do?"

"I intend to sleep," said Kyra. "I will think on the best course of action after a few hours of rest."

"That is wise," said Navroz. "This has come as a shock, and you need time to recover, so you can make decisions in a calm and rational frame of mind." The others nodded.

Kyra turned so they would not see the expression on her face. Since when had she become adept at lying to the elders of Kali? Perhaps since she had become their Mahimata. Or perhaps only at this moment, when she felt the full weight of her past actions like a yoke around her neck. She couldn't undo what she had done; she couldn't shrug off the burden. She would have to walk with it until the day she died.

She returned to her cell and lay down. She hadn't told a complete lie, of course. More like a half-truth.

"I'm going to kill you, Kai Tau," she whispered. "And I know just who can help me."

She sank into the second-level meditative trance and sought the bridge to *Anant-kal*.

CHAPTER 17

TWO WORLDS

Kyra stood on the now-familiar broad, sunny road lined with purple bougainvillea.

Tall towers and metal domes gleamed against the blue sky, and a cobweb-thin bridge stretched behind her over a yawning chasm. She felt for her scabbard and sighed with relief. This time her katari had traveled with her. Surely that was an improvement.

She set off down the road. Menadin would show up when he wanted to, no doubt. She didn't have to stand around waiting for him. She could go to the hall of pillars again, the place where Shirin Mam had given her a last lesson on words of power. Perhaps she'd find something to help her defeat Kai Tau.

She had to walk up and down a couple of times before she spied the road that Shirin Mam had taken. And—yes—that was the tower she had entered. She waved her hands in front of the metal door at the base of the building; it slid open, just as it had the last time. She stepped through and emerged into a vast marble-floored hall.

Everything was just as she remembered: massive, carved pillars reaching up to a distant ceiling, diamond-shaped windows that glittered in the sunlight. She half-expected to see Shirin Mam again, black-robed and serene, waiting to give her another lesson.

But there was no Shirin Mam, of course. The hall was empty save for the thirty-six pillars with their rather grotesque carvings. Each of those carvings represented a word of power in the ancient tongue—the language of Goddess Kali herself, according to the lore of the Order.

Kyra paused at the first pillar. As she studied it, she frowned. The image was about the same as what she remembered: a three-headed monster that Shirin Mam had said represented the past, the present, and the future. But the image was no longer sharp, no longer distinct. The face of the woman astride the monster was in shadows, as if someone had tried to rub her out. What did this mean?

She went to the next pillar, and her heart sank. The image on this one had blurred too. A fire raged through a field, burning people, animals, and trees: the cleansing fire that destroyed falsehoods and showed the truth. In the original image, the Goddess Kali alone stood untouched by the flames. But now her face was distorted, and the lines of her figure melted into the fire.

Kyra examined every image in the hall before coming to the inevitable conclusion. Something was wrong with *Anant-kal*, or at least with this version of it. And Shirin Mam had made these images for *her*. So whatever was wrong, it had to do with Kyra.

When she came to the last image, she stopped. It was the carving of a door, plain and unadorned. *This word of power tells us how we will leave the world*, Shirin Mam had said. But whereas the door had been closed the last time she'd seen this image, now it was slightly open. As if death was closer, beckoning her in.

Kyra backed away and averted her eyes. She didn't want to see this one, to remember what it meant. It was where she would one day go to die.

The next thing she knew, she was back outside, shaking, with no memory of how she had left the hall. She crossed the street to a walled garden opposite the building and vaulted over the ivy-covered stone. Her feet sank into soft grass. The Shining City was dotted with these pretty gardens, which said something about its builders. If only they were still alive. If only there was someone to talk to.

A fountain sparkled in the sun, making a rainbow. Kyra went over to it, carefully avoiding the red flowers in the grass, and sat down in the lotus position. Perhaps she could summon Menadin by sheer will. She closed her eyes and sought the peace of the first-level meditative trance.

"We meet again, Kyra Veer."

The suddenness of his deep voice almost stopped her heart. Her eyes flew open and she regarded the tall, shaggy-haired man. "Took your time, didn't you?" she said coolly, trying to slow her pulse.

"I run in the other world too; it is as much our home as this one." He crouched opposite her and yawned, revealing his sharp yellow fangs. He was too close; she could smell the wolf on him, and something else. Blood? He had been feeding. She fought the urge to shrink back.

He indicated the building from which she had emerged. "It was important that you see what is happening."

"What *is* happening?" asked Kyra.

"We don't know for certain," said Menadin. "But our elders think Wyr-mandil is dissolving, mirroring the dissolution of your own world."

"How is that possible?" cried Kyra. "Shirin Mam said that this is the world as perceived by our kalishium blades."

"The blades that exist in *your* reality," said Menadin. "Your katari, in particular, now travels with you between worlds. It knows the suffering of your people and senses the unraveling of order and justice. If Asiana burns, so will Wyr-mandil." He bowed his head. "We will cease to exist as people."

"I must stop Kai Tau," said Kyra. She clenched her fists, nails digging into her palms. "I will kill him before he can destroy both our worlds."

"Yes, Kyra Veer," said Menadin. "That is what you must do, what Shirin Mam always knew you would do. And you seek our help with this task, do you not?"

"Yes," said Kyra. She didn't want to ask him for help or guidance. But there was no one else. "I have kept my part of the bargain. I have outlawed the killing of wyr-wolves in our jurisdiction."

"So we have heard. And yet, it may take more than your words to stop the slaughter. You may have to make an example of someone. We will be watching you."

"Watch all you like," she snapped, rising to her feet. "Perhaps you'll learn something of how *real* humans should behave."

To her discomfiture, Menadin burst into laughter.

"What is so funny?" she demanded.

"Just that you think we ought to aspire to be like you. How little you know. I should remember that you're still a cub."

How dare he call her a cub? She, the Mahimata of Kali. Kyra turned her back on him and marched away.

"Not so fast, prideful one," said Menadin, catching up with her in a couple of easy strides. "It is time for our second pact."

"What more do you want from me?" said Kyra, crossing her arms. "Sheep left for you at strategic points? I'll have a full-scale rebellion on my hands if I give any more concessions to your people."

Menadin threw his head back and laughed again. Kyra didn't know which was worse—watching him laugh or watching him snarl.

"We don't need sheep," he said at last. "We need kalishium. And so do you."

"What?" she said, taken aback. "What could you possibly need kalishium for?"

"It will help us remember who we were," said Menadin. "And our elders may be able to use it to stabilize Wyr-mandil."

Kyra shook her head. "Even if I wanted to, I couldn't give you kalishium. We have none left." Shirin Mam had bemoaned that fact often enough. There was no more kalishium, and no one left with the ability to forge a true katari. Apart from Astinsai, the katari mistress of Khur, who hadn't accepted a new commission in years.

"We need only a very little," said Menadin. "But you will need quite a lot."

"Why?" said Kyra, confused. "How will kalishium help me against Kai Tau?"

"What is the one thing in Asiana that is impervious to the dark weapons?"

Realization dawned on her like sunlight breaking through a

storm cloud. How had she not thought of this herself? Given enough kalishium, they could forge shields against the kalashiks' bullets.

"It is a fine suggestion," she admitted. "But as I said, I don't know where I could find any kalishium, let alone that amount."

"You have the blades of those who are gone to the stars," said Menadin.

"What do you mean?" asked Kyra.

"Those who have died," said Menadin. "Kalishium is indestructible, no matter what you do to it. Surely you have hundreds of ancient blades in your caves."

"We cannot take those," said Kyra reluctantly. "They contain the memories of all the Markswomen who bonded with them. If our Order is to have any sort of future, we must hold on to our past; we will need those blades. Is there no other place I can get kalishium?"

"Not as easily," said Menadin. "The last hoard of kalishium in Asiana hides in a monastery cave, high up a mountain. One of our elders found it many years ago. But it is a difficult and dangerous journey to make. The way is treacherous; you must pass through a forest full of traps. And you must go alone."

"Why?" asked Kyra. "What has my being alone got to do with it?"

Menadin shrugged his powerful shoulders. "I do not know. It is the nature of the place, that it reveals itself to only a few, and only to those who are alone. When we tried to find the kalishium again, we failed. The monastery had fallen to ruin and the mouth of the cave had been blocked by a landslide."

"Tell me where it is," said Kyra. "I will leave at once."

And he told her. *Kunlun Shan.*

Within her, something quivered at the sound of that name, as if it needed waking up.

The next day, after a late breakfast, Kyra summoned the elders to her cell and told them what she had discovered.

"Kunlun Shan," said Mumuksu thoughtfully. "The Spirit Mountains. A reclusive sect known as the Sahirus are said to have lived there long ago. Apparently they had deep knowledge of the Ones. But those mountains are the most dangerous in Asiana."

"Who told you of this secret hoard?" asked Felda, somewhat suspiciously. "None of us has heard of such a thing."

"I dreamed of it," said Kyra. She hated to lie to them, although it seemed to get easier by the minute.

"Really, Kyra?" said Navroz. "How gullible do you think we are?"

"I'm sorry, Eldest," said Kyra at once, flushing. "I did dream it, in a way. The wyr-wolf told me."

"Oh, the *wyr-wolf*," said Navroz. "That makes perfect sense. Why didn't you say so earlier?"

"Let us assume your information is correct," said Felda, before Kyra could react. "What do you plan to do about it?"

Kyra gave her a grateful smile. "I plan to go there and retrieve what I can. We can use the kalishium to make shields that will protect us from the dark weapons. I am sure I can persuade the katari mistress of Khur to help us work the kalishium."

"That is a good plan," conceded Navroz. "*If* the hoard

exists. But your wound has barely healed. One of us should go instead."

"I offer myself," said Mumuksu. "I have long wished to meditate in the Spirit Mountains."

"Thank you, Elder," said Kyra hastily. "But this is something I must do myself." She turned to Felda. "Can you please find me the closest door to the place I have described?"

"There is no safe door close to Kunlun Shan," said Felda, frowning.

"There's nothing safe about Transport anyway," said Kyra. "I'll take whatever there is." Goose bumps ran over her arms at the memory of the secret Hub and what it had shown her. She hoped Felda wouldn't tell her to use that one.

Navroz spread her hands out in frustration. "If you must go, at least take one of us with you. We might be able to help."

"Not that you listen to us," added Mumuksu. "Even Shirin Mam used to consult us more than you do."

That wasn't fair. Shirin Mam had always done exactly as she wished. But Kyra knew she had given the elders the *appearance* of consulting them, at least.

"Fine," she said, sitting at her desk. "This is what I know: there is a kalishium hoard hidden in a cave in the Kunlun Shan Range. It might be the key to defeating Kai Tau and his dark weapons. I must find the kalishium, and I must go alone. Time is of the essence. Please advise me, your Mahimata, how best to go about it."

The elders looked at each other, varying expressions of concern on their faces. At last Navroz gave Felda a barely perceptible nod.

Felda grimaced and turned back to Kyra. "There is, perhaps,

a door that you can use," she said. "In the Deccan Hub, there used to be a door to a forest in the foothills of Kunlun Shan."

"Used to be?" said Kyra, not liking the sound of that. "What happened to it?"

"What usually happens," said Felda. "It shifted. It has not been used in more than seventy years. The last Markswoman who went through was never seen again."

There was a moment of silence while they all digested this.

"Then the door is unusable?" asked Kyra, almost hoping that Felda would say yes.

"Not if you use my special formula that overrides the codes." Felda grinned. "It has the effect of anchoring the door in question to its original destination. At least, that's my hypothesis."

"Wonderful," said Mumuksu. "So we are going to risk our Mahimata's life to test your hypothesis?"

They went on debating like that for a while. Kyra disconnected herself from their wrangling. She had used Felda's code before, and the doors had shown her visions and made her lose time. So Felda's hypothesis could be wrong.

Although, now that she thought about it, she had overridden the code of only a single door, and that one had taken her straight to the Empty Place, where Rustan had been waiting.

Rustan. She wished she could talk to him now, more than anyone else. Where was he? Did he think of her at all? If only she could make him feel the way she did, make him miss her with the ache that hollowed her own insides, as if something were missing that could never be replaced. If only she could find a door that would always lead to him, no matter where he was. She reached down and touched the letter that Shirin Mam had addressed to him. She always kept it in her pocket, as if it were a talisman. As if it could conjure them both, mother and son.

"Kyra?" said Navroz. "You are not listening."

Kyra snapped guiltily to attention, hoping the elders hadn't sensed her thoughts about Rustan. She had become better at hiding her feelings from them, but she was no Shirin Mam. Or Tamsyn, for that matter.

"Sorry, Eldest," she said. "I was thinking of Transport, and how the door in the secret Hub made me lose time. I hope that doesn't happen again."

"It is a risk you will have to take if you wish to go to Kunlun Shan," said Felda. "The Deccan Hub is quite stable; the Valavian Markswomen use it all the time. It's not like that disused Hub you found in the hills of Gonur. I will give you a map of the Hub and tell you which door to use. If all goes well, you should be back here within a few days."

The way Felda spoke made it quite clear she didn't even believe that herself. But Kyra pushed aside her misgivings and started preparations for the trip. The Goddess willing, she would find the kalishium and return with it.

CHAPTER 18

THE APPRENTICE SMITH

The sun was low in the sky and a cool wind had sprung up by the time Rustan tethered his camel near an animal enclosure on the outskirts of Jethwa. Tents sprouted everywhere on the barren fields surrounding the village; he was stunned by the sheer number of soldiers and camp followers the Taus had gained. *Many hundreds*, he decided. *Close to two thousand.*

His journey to Jethwa had taken a little less than a week. He had retrieved Basil in Igiziyar, then left him in Yartan in the care of a camel herder, with instructions to bring him to Kashgar with the next caravan. He had not gone to the camp of Khur; it would have added days to his travel time, and every hour he wasted surely brought his teacher closer to death. But in Yartan he had sent a missive to Barkav, using a simple code he had been taught, outlining what he had learned from the Seeing Stone. From Yartan he had Transported to Kashgar, then to the Deccan Hub, and from there to Jhelmil, a small town at the northeastern edge of the Thar Desert, where he had rented a camel.

Now he was there, at the threshold of the Tau camp. One wrong move would get him killed, or worse.

Men and women gathered around small fires, some cooking the evening meal, others bent over swords and bows, repairing or polishing their weapons. There was little talk and less laughter. Faces were surly and closed. No one gave him a second glance as he walked between the cookfires. He wondered how many had joined the Taus of their own free will, and how many had done so at gunpoint.

Something hard jabbed Rustan's back, and he winced. A tall, burly man stood behind him, a wooden staff in his hands. "Who are you?" the man demanded.

So much for his hope that he would be dismissed as just another camp follower. But Rustan had his story ready—a story that might grant him access to the dark weapons forge, as well as allow him to find Ishtul.

"Aruth, at your service," he said, with a small bow. "I've come all the way from the village Munger. I heard Jethwa needs smiths. I apprenticed for a year at the Munger forge, and I was hoping to find work."

The man leaned on his staff and frowned. "Work there is, and plenty of it. But why did you leave your own village?"

Rustan tried to look bashful. "Doesn't pay well and . . . there's this girl, see. I need something put by if I want to ask her father for her hand. I've heard he wants three camels and ten goats as her bride price."

"Do you have references?" asked another guard, a heavyset man with a scar on his face who had strolled up to join the first.

Rustan hung his head. "No. I ran away from old Wahid,

didn't I? He would cut off his fingers before giving me a reference. But I do good work; just give me a chance."

The first man grinned, showing rows of broken yellow teeth. "You'd better be good if you want to survive here."

"What's the pay like?" asked Rustan.

The second guard laughed. "Tell him, Dastug."

"He'll find out soon enough."

Rustan allowed a worried expression to cross his face as he was led by the two guards beyond the chaos of the tents to the mud walls of the village. Inside, he felt elated. He was being taken into the heart of enemy territory by the enemy themselves. He would soon be able to find where Ishtul was being kept. He hadn't been able to sense the elder yet, but that could be because Kai Tau had taken away his blade. Or maybe Ishtul was not in Jethwa at all. Rustan did not allow himself to consider the worst possibility.

The guards took him to a shed where their captain, a lean, sour-faced man called Cemed, questioned him before telling him the rules:

"You get three meals and a place to sleep. You start tomorrow at dawn. The metal we work with is precious; make a mistake, and you will pay for it with your skin."

Rustan opened his mouth to ask about wages, but closed it again at Cemed's expression. This was not a man to be trifled with. He followed one of the guards to the hut he would share with the other workers. No one was around, and he flung himself down in a corner to rest until the others returned. He was bone-tired, not so much from the journey, hard though it had been, but from the strain of deception. And now he would have to pass himself off as an apprentice smith.

He tried to calm himself enough to sleep, but his nerves

thrummed with anxiety and fear—both for himself and for Ishtul. Rustan knew nothing of working with metal. But he hadn't been able to think of a better way to get into Jethwa. How long before his ignorance was discovered? Perhaps he could glean some information from the other apprentices. He didn't dare delve too closely into anyone's mind; Kai Tau would sense the use of invasive Mental Arts.

At dusk his fellow workers returned to the hut, grimy and sullen. There were six of them, two quite massively built, and Rustan wondered how they would all fit into the hut at night.

They were a grim lot and resisted his attempts to draw them into conversation. They hung up their overalls and trooped out in silence, presumably for the evening meal. Rustan followed them to a queue at one of the cookfires outside the village, his stomach rumbling—a reminder that he had eaten nothing since morning. When it was his turn, the dour-faced server slapped a heap of flat green beans and potatoes on a hard round of millet bread and handed it to him.

Rustan stared at the small serving and thought with longing of the simple, wholesome meals the monks had prepared. But the food they had packed for him was long gone.

"Not very lavish with the helping sizes, are they?" he remarked, squatting down beside his fellow workers on the ground. No one answered. They were busy wolfing down their share of the food. Rustan took a bite, and immediately his mouth was on fire. The green beans must be half-full of chilies. He made himself swallow it, though. He'd stick out like a fountain in a desert if he was the only one not eating the meager, unappetizing fare.

After the meal, they drank and washed up at a communal pump. On the way back to the hut, Rustan tried to draw them out again, but to no avail. At last, one man called Tej, older than the rest, snapped, "Shut your mouth. You'll know soon enough what it's like here." At that Rustan subsided into silence.

The next morning, Tej was the one who woke him, prodding him with his foot. Rustan groaned as he staggered out along with the others. From the way everyone obeyed him in silence, he guessed that Tej was the master smith.

They had a drink at the pump, and Tej distributed some dry millet bread that could be swallowed only with the help of water. Thus began a long, grueling day.

The smithy was located at the east end of the village, and Rustan felt a jolt of recognition as they approached it. It was identical to the one he had glimpsed in the Seeing Stone. The dark weapons forge.

They entered a large stone structure with a roof and a chimney for letting out smoke. One side of it must have been open once to reduce the risk of fire, but a wall had been built, blocking it from curious eyes.

The air was hot and tasted of metal, and flames roared behind a black furnace, blazing red against the dim, smoky air. Tej ordered Rustan to work the bellows—a simple enough task, but after three hours his arms ached intensely, and he thought he would pass out from the heat of the furnace and the never-ending clang of hammer on anvil.

He tried to make out what the others were doing, but nothing gave the place the appearance of anything but an ordinary smithy.

They broke at noon for a meal. Rustan stumbled out with the others, sweating and panting. The sun shone fierce and bright, but it was positively cool after the infernal interior of the workshop. He began to understand why the rest of them didn't talk much.

The food was as sharp and spicy as the previous evening. He tried to swallow it quickly without tasting, but it was hopeless. His mouth still burned.

They went back to work after their meal. All the while, Rustan strained himself to the utmost, trying to sense if Ishtul was nearby without revealing himself. He caught odd thoughts now and then and saw disturbing visions that made no sense. In one of them, Kai Tau sat on a throne of skulls, wrapped in a bloodred cloak, his face in shadows, men and women prostrating themselves before him. But the skulls were alive; they moaned and twisted beneath Kai Tau, gazed at Rustan out of their hollow sockets, and whispered: *Help us, Marksman. Set us free.*

People had been killed in Jethwa. The entire village council had been hung on the branches of an old khajri tree for the vultures to feast on. This too the Seeing Stone had shown him. Rustan could barely control his fury. He would have to make his move soon; there was no way he could stay here for much longer without betraying his presence.

In the afternoon, a powerfully built man with iron gray hair and a chin beard entered the workshop, accompanied by guards armed with kalashiks. Everyone except Tej continued to work. Tej wiped his hands on his apron, stepped forward and bowed. "Oleg-dan," he said, placing his hand on his heart.

One of Kai Tau's captains. Rustan dropped his gaze and continued to work the bellows. His heart thudded. In the moment that he had looked at Oleg, he had caught a vision: Ishtul's swollen face, smeared with blood. *But his eyes were gone.* What did this mean? Where was his teacher?

Oleg spoke to Tej, and from the corner of his eye Rustan saw him give the smith a sheaf of parchments. There followed a low-voiced consultation that he couldn't hear above the noise of the workshop. Oleg left as abruptly as he had come, and Tej spent the good part of an hour studying the parchments that the outlaw captain had left with him.

Rustan's eyes burned from the smoke and the heat. His stomach roiled with anxiety. Finding Ishtul was his primary concern. But the parchments had to be important too.

That night, when the hut was still and silent except for heavy breathing and the occasional snore, Rustan rose and padded toward the rug where Tej lay. The smith had shoved the parchments beneath him. But he was asleep now and would not know if Rustan took them.

Gently, ever so gently, Rustan slid his hand beneath the rug. Just as his fingers brushed the papers, an arm shot up and gripped him by the elbow. Tej's eyes glared at him in the moonlight. His mouth opened to give a warning shout.

Rustan brought down his other hand sideways in Chopping the Tree, and Tej's head lolled back, the whites of his eyes showing. Hopefully, he would be out for a while.

Everyone else was still asleep, oblivious to the drama playing out in their midst. Rustan withdrew the bundle of parchments from below the rug and straightened them out. It was too dark to see what was written on them.

Keeping his head down, he crept to the window, where the moonlight filtered in, and studied the parchments. There were six of them, covered in dense, spidery writing and diagrams. Some of them looked like the insides of a kalashik. Others were of things he could not recognize: strange shapes, bits and pieces of metal, globes filled with odd parts. They had just one thing in common. They were all machines designed to kill.

Sweat beaded his forehead. This was beyond him. He needed

to get this to Barkav and Astinsai right away. But first, he would do some damage.

Rustan tucked the sheets into his belt and stole out the door. He flattened himself against the wall and scanned his surroundings. Nothing stirred except the wind.

He ran to the smithy, staying in the shadows, blending into the night. He did not have Barkav's ability with camouflage, but he could make himself unobtrusive. No one challenged him; not one of the sleepy guards lounging outside the council hut or in the village square gave him a second look.

It took him three minutes to start the fire. It blazed in the hearth with a vengeful light. He took a smouldering log and tossed it on the wood heap in one corner of the smithy. It caught, and the fire came into its own, taking on life. Rustan laughed as he tossed burning pieces of wood everywhere, even as his eyes watered from the smoke. This was what he had wanted to do from the first moment he saw this hellish place.

He ducked out of the doorway just as it came splintering down with a satisfying crash. Guards were running up to the burning smithy now, shouting. Rustan edged past them, concealing himself behind huts, trees, the council house. At the village wall he paused and looked behind him.

Flames engulfed the smithy. Smoke roiled skyward. People were shouting for water to put out the fire.

Water. In the *desert*. That was a joke. There would be no putting out this fire. It would burn the building to ashes before it died. Happily for the people of Jethwa, there were no huts near enough the smithy to share its fate.

Time to find Ishtul. In the chaos of the fire, no one would notice him. He walked in the shadows cast by the crumbling mud wall, delving lightly into the minds of the men and women who ran past him. But he found no sign of the elder—no one who was tasked with the care of a special prisoner, no memory of a Marksman's blade.

Halfway around the village was a wooden gate, and there Rustan stopped and doubled over, gasping as a sudden pain pierced him.

They dragged him out from this gate. But not all of him.

The pain grew until it was unbearable. Rustan ran and ran but he could not escape it, and finally he stopped and forced himself to see what had happened to his teacher. And he wept because he was too late.

CHAPTER 19

THE DOOR TO KUNLUN SHAN

There was no direct door from the Ferghana to the Deccan Hub, and Kyra had to connect via a small Hub in the southern tip of the subcontinent. This was annoying, but perhaps just as well. It wouldn't do to have too easy access to another Order's jurisdiction.

As Kyra entered the second Transport Chamber, she repeated the steps of her mission in her mind like a mantra: find the door to Kunlun Shan, override the code, get the kalishium, get back home. Simple. Nothing to worry about. Apart from the door that had shifted, of course. She couldn't help thinking about the poor Markswoman who had last used it and never been seen again. Was she stuck somewhere between doors, still trying to get home?

Kyra pushed down her unease and reminded herself that she possessed something the lost Markswoman hadn't: Felda's override code. It *had* to work. She clutched her katari; warmth and reassurance emanated from it, but they were muted somehow, dimmed by the presence of Tamsyn's blade around her neck.

The elders hadn't wanted her to carry it, of course. They had argued, cajoled, threatened, pleaded. But in the end, she had overruled them. "I need it," she had said, and retreated to her cell to pack a small bag. Tamsyn's blade was not anywhere near as old or as potent as Shirin Mam's, but it had a hunger and sharpness of its own. In a fight, it might serve Kyra well. At least, that was what she told herself. And surely, now that she knew it was trying to influence her, she could resist its manipulation.

When the spinning Transport Chamber slowed to a stop, Kyra rose, recalling the map Felda had drawn for her. She would emerge from the sixth door in the Transport corridor of the Deccan Hub; she had to walk four doors down to the tenth.

She pushed open the door of the chamber and stepped out into the corridor: a narrow passage lined with the glowing slots of doors on one side, a smooth wall on the other. At one end was the main door of the Hub. Should she go through that, she would emerge below the Temple of Valavan. Everything was just as it should be, and yet Kyra could not slow her racing pulse.

Do it, then. Get it over with. What's the worst that can happen?

Actually, quite a lot. It didn't bear thinking about.

She walked down the corridor, counting. Seven, eight, nine, and finally the tenth door. She braced herself and laid her palm upon the cold metal. Nothing happened—no strange visions, no faces from beyond the door of death, no horrific emptiness waiting to swallow her. She exhaled with relief and inserted the tip of her blade into the glowing slot on the door. A screen slid out, and she tapped in the tenth code from Felda's pyramid of palindromic primes. The screen withdrew, and the door swung open as if it had been waiting for her. She entered the circular Transport Chamber, heart pounding. She had been expecting it this time, and yet, when the silken voice spoke in her ear, she almost screamed.

"Code override. Code override."

Kyra steeled herself. "Yes, I overrode the code," she said defiantly. "I need to go to Kunlun Shan."

Nothing answered; had she really expected it to? She sat down on one of the seats melded to the floor. It moved beneath her, adjusting to her weight, and she recoiled in distaste. She remembered what Felda had said about the Hubs being one vast mind, as if they were alive. As if the walls of the chamber were the skin of a womb, the Transport corridor the inside of a throat.

Okay, stop. She was being fanciful. The chamber began to spin, and she closed her eyes to meditate.

It was then that the whispering started. Tiny, incomprehensible voices in her ears, her hair, her skin. Kyra jerked to her feet in alarm, almost losing her balance, and flailed at the air with her hands.

"Stop," she stuttered, but the voices did not stop. They rose in pitch, acquiring an edge of insistence, as if to say, *Know us. Understand us.* Like ghosts they gathered about her, thick with want. She dropped to her knees and pressed her palms against her ears. But the voices were inside her skull and there was no getting away from them, their anger and their pain.

Abandoned. That's how they felt. And— *We will show you,* they whispered.

The spinning slowed and stopped. For a while, Kyra could

not make herself get up. However terrifying the Transport Chamber, it was a familiar place, unchanging in appearance. What lay beyond the door was unknown. And after what had just happened, she had not the slightest hope she would emerge in the time and place she was seeking.

At last she stood and went to the door. It was that, or give in to despair and rail against herself, against Felda, and most of all against the makers of the Transport system, who had built something that would outlast them all in years, but not in sanity.

Kyra left the chamber, stepping into a short, dark passage. There were no doors save the one she had emerged from, and a door at the end of the passage, which she presumed led outside. A Hub with a single Transport door—perhaps a door that shifted every time it was used. She offered up a brief and fervent prayer to the Goddess and pushed it open before she lost her courage.

The heat struck her face like a blow, and she flinched. She stepped out onto a bleak, bare hillside, taking care not to let the door close behind her. Nothing grew, nothing lived for as far as the eye could see. The sun shone in a blue-white sky, but something was wrong with it; the sun appeared bigger, fiercer than it should. The air was dry and difficult to breathe. Even the Empty Place at the height of the noonday sun was pleasant compared to this.

Dark spots danced in front of her eyes. Her throat and skin burned, and she retreated into the blessed coolness of the Transport corridor, shaking.

She fumbled for the waterskin in her bag. After a few reviving sips, she returned to the Transport Chamber, feeling light-headed, the sun still burning the backs of her eyelids.

She had spent less than a minute outside. A few minutes more would have killed her. What was this place? It was nowhere she recognized; not even the Barrens at the western edge of Asiana were this lifeless.

It is the future. The voices were a cold caress in her ear. The horror of it sank into her.

"How many years?" she asked, her heart in her mouth. But no answer was forthcoming. She hoped this future was far enough away that the people of Asiana had found another planet to call home by then. Or perhaps they had learned to live in underground cities.

The chamber began to spin again. Avoiding the seats, Kyra sat on the floor. She steeled herself for the invasive voices, but they did not return. Perhaps they were done with her, and the door would open to the present-day Kunlun Shan this time.

But it did not. When Kyra emerged for a second time from the tiny Hub, green grass covered the hillside. The sun looked quite ordinary, and a cool wind rustled her hair. But she was not alone. Climbing up the hill were a dozen men and women clad in bright saffron robes. Now and then they stopped to talk and laugh or pick a flower. Some carried baskets; others carried pitchers. A picnic of some sort? Their destination appeared to be a red and gold pagoda on top of the hill.

Who were they? When was this? Kyra longed to run up the hill after them and ask. But part of her doubted they would be able to see and hear her, and another part was terrified that if she let the door close behind her, it wouldn't open again for her blade. And that would be the end of Kyra Veer, the youngest Markswoman of Asiana. Perhaps she'd live out her days with the saffron-robed men and women. At least they seemed like a cheerful bunch.

She was debating whether to call out to them when the sky darkened. At first Kyra thought it was a thundercloud. But the men and women froze, their faces like stone as they gazed upward. She raised her eyes to see what had troubled them and almost screamed.

A vast rectangular structure blotted out half the sky; it was charcoal gray, covered with runes of some sort, the underside studded with cylindrical pods. That was all she had time to see before one of the pods dropped out of the sky and tore off half the hillside. The men and women who had just seconds ago been laughing and talking with each other disappeared in the fireball.

The explosion threw Kyra back inside the Hub. The door slammed shut before the fire could reach her. She lay stunned for several minutes, her ears ringing, her head feeling as if it would burst. The violence had happened so quickly she could not process it. One moment those poor people had been walking up the hill for a picnic; the next moment they were obliterated by a machine worse than twenty death-sticks. How sick must a mind be to design a weapon like that?

Kyra tried to stand and could not. She felt dizzy and disoriented. After a while she managed to sit up. She made herself drink some water and wiped her face, which was sticky with soot and tears. She crawled away from the door on her hands and knees.

You have seen the past, whispered the voices as she entered the Transport Chamber, but they didn't have to. She already knew. She had caught a glimpse of the Great War that had consumed Asiana all those centuries ago. Despite their technological marvels, her ancestors had lacked the most basic feelings of decency and compassion. They had treated their fellow human beings like a diseased herd to be culled.

Why show her this? And what horror would the Hub inflict on her next?

But when she stumbled out of the Transport door the third time, she found herself back in the long, smooth corridor of the Deccan Hub. Back where she had started. Fury built in her until she thought she would burst. After all that it had put her through, the chamber had spat her out at her starting point.

"You useless piece of junk!" she cried. "Take that." She kicked the Transport door again and again, until her foot felt as though it would break. Stupid, childish behavior, but it gave her some satisfaction, as if she were punishing the Hub instead of her own foot.

"Kyra?" came a disbelieving voice. "Is that you?"

She whirled, her stomach clenching.

Rustan. Standing before her, disheveled and wide-eyed, his face ghostly in the bluish light of the corridor. A hallucination spun by the Hub to punish her for her insolence, her temerity? *Not this, please. This I cannot bear.*

"Kyra," he said again, and held his arms out. She ran into them, half laughing, half weeping. Whatever the Hub had done to her, she forgave it in that one, perfect moment when she stepped into the circle of his arms and he wrapped them around her, as if he would hold her forever.

CHAPTER 20

TIME OUTSIDE TIME

How long did they stand in the dim, cool Transport corridor, holding each other? Later, Kyra would think of it as a time outside time, immeasurable and precious. She rubbed her cheek against his, rough with stubble, and inhaled the jagged scent of him, a confusing blend of desert and mountain, anger and serenity, sweat and grief. When Rustan bent his lips to hers, the kiss was already there, like a word waiting to be said. Sweeter, wilder than all her fantasies of him. She tightened her arms around him, afraid that he would break the contact and step away from her.

But he didn't. He pulled her head back and traced his lips on her throat, turning her insides to liquid, obliterating all her fear, all her reason. She gasped and twisted against him, forgetting everything except her need, the loneliness she had kept in check these long, dark months. He stroked her blade, and she felt it through the scabbard, more intimate than a caress on her skin.

"I've missed you so much," he whispered into her hair.

"I've missed you too," she said, her voice muffled against his chest. "Don't you dare leave me again."

He made a small sound of protest. "You're the one who left. You're the one who nearly died." She heard the ache in his voice, the ghost of the pain he had suffered when she was stabbed by Tamsyn's blade.

He traced his thumb against the nape of her neck, giving her goose bumps. "Are you well now?" he asked. "Does your wound still hurt?"

"No," she lied, but the exhaustion and trauma of what she had been through caught up with her then, and her knees buckled, as if in the presence of Rustan, her body could finally relax and let go. He caught hold of her, concern tightening his face.

"I'm all right," she muttered, leaning against the wall, pushing him away. Her legs felt like Tarshana's noodles. "Just need to rest a bit. Been a long day."

"You do that," he said. "I'll keep watch."

She lay down on the corridor, using her bag as a pillow. Rustan sat beside her, looking as though he needed to lie down more than she did. She gripped his hand, as if he might try to run away, and he gave it a reassuring squeeze. *I'm here*, he thought at her, and raised her hand to his lips. *Rest easy, my love.*

She smiled and, watching him, drifted off to sleep. A while later, she woke in a panic that he was gone. But he was still there, his long body stretched out next to hers, one arm thrown across his head, breathing the deep, even breath of sleep. She exhaled in relief. *Still here. Still with me.*

She slipped an arm around him, feeling the rise and fall of his chest, the hard muscles beneath his Marksman's robe. He stirred but continued sleeping, and she smiled, feeling such a rush of tenderness that it was difficult to breathe. Rustan— her friend, her teacher, her lover, her other half. Did not the Goddess herself have a male twin?

But thinking of the Goddess reminded Kyra of her Order and the mission she was on.

She closed her eyes, wanting to prolong the moment of stillness before action, the moment of togetherness that no one would be able to take away from her, no matter what came after.

Slowly, bit by bit, she separated herself from him. It was a painful awakening. She remembered who she was and why she was there. The strangeness of it came to her then, the glowing slots on the Transport doors, how Rustan had been there at the precise moment when she emerged from the chamber. How all Transport corridors looked much the same, and this was not the Deccan Hub at all, but somewhere else. Or some*when*.

She jerked upright, heart thudding.

Next to her, Rustan stirred. "You all right?" he asked, his voice still heavy with sleep. He caressed her back with his fingertips, and she suppressed a tiny sound of pleasure. What she wanted most was to lie back beside him and touch him the way he was touching her, to make him feel the way he made *her* feel.

But not here. Not now. Glad of the darkness that concealed the flush on her face, she said, keeping her voice light, "Just wondering where we are, and what you are doing here." She would not show him her discomfiture.

But he saw it anyway. He sat up and stretched. "I was on my way to Kashgar, back to my Order," he said. "The Deccan Hub was the closest. What's the matter?"

Kyra waved a hand. "The Deccan Hub is the most heavily trafficked in the subcontinent. We've been here for hours and not seen another living soul." She paused. How much to tell him? Hubs with minds of their own—he would think she was crazy.

But Rustan did not seem to think anything was amiss. "Hours?" he said. He reached for his blade—*Shirin Mam's* blade—and slung it around his neck. "I have to get to Barkav as soon as possible. Take a look at this."

He withdrew a sheaf of parchments from his knapsack. Kyra unsheathed her blade and whispered the word of power to set it alight. She studied the parchments in the glow of her katari, her alarm growing as Rustan described how he had infiltrated the Tau camp and set their forge on fire.

"You did this on your own?" Kyra was stunned. "You could have been killed."

He bowed his head. "Somebody did die," he said. "I was too late to save him."

And it dawned on Kyra whom he was talking about, and why he smelled of grief and anger. "Ishtul," she said.

His head jerked up, and he raked her face with his eyes. "What do you know of it?" he demanded.

It was hard, telling him what Kai Tau had done. But she saw from his bleak, flat expression that he already knew, that the only surprise for him was the fact that Kai Tau had sent the severed head of the blademaster to *her* and not to the Order of Khur.

"He means to force my hand," she concluded. "But I'll not go up against him until I am ready."

Rustan frowned. "There is no way to be ready for kalashiks. Those bullets can pierce anything."

"Except kalishium," she said, and was gratified to see a look of astonishment on his face. She plunged ahead and told him of her plan to use a secret kalishium hoard to build armor and shields. She left out the bit about Menadin, making it sound as if it was her own idea. She didn't want to withhold the truth from him, but somehow it didn't feel right, telling him about the wyr-wolf. It was not her secret to share.

Rustan folded his arms. "There is no more kalishium in Asiana," he said. "Where is this hoard that you are so convinced exists?"

"It does exist," said Kyra, nettled. "I just have to find it. It hides in a monastery cave in the Kunlun Shan Range."

"And how do you know that?" Rustan's voice had gone soft and dangerous.

Kyra was bewildered. She had thought Rustan would applaud her idea. In truth, she had hoped he would offer to join her, to help her look for the kalishium—forgetting, for the moment, that this was something she needed to do on her own. But Rustan was acting as if she had done something wrong.

"I just know," she said. "I dreamed of it," she added.

His eyes narrowed. "Don't lie to me," he said. "It is disrespectful, both to yourself and to me."

"Fine. Somebody told me, okay?" She tried to keep the defensiveness from her voice. "I can't tell you who—it's not for me to tell. I just know that I have to—*prove* myself, in some way. And that a door to Kunlun Shan exists, right here in this Hub."

"You will never find the monastery," said Rustan, sounding as if he was trying to convince himself.

"Then help me," she said, a plea in her voice. "Come with me to Kunlun Shan. Once I find the kalishium, we can return to Khur together and ask Astinsai to forge it." She slipped her arms around his neck, but he was stiff, unyielding. "What is wrong?" she whispered.

He relaxed and touched his forehead to hers. "Nothing's wrong," he said. "Not yet. And I will go with you. Of course I will."

Kyra should have felt reassured by his words. Yet she could not shake the feeling that he did not mean to help at all.

CHAPTER 21

THE BEAST
IN THE FOREST

The third time Kyra tried the door to Kunlun Shan, it worked like an ordinary door in an ordinary Hub. Perhaps the fact that Rustan was with her made a difference. Or perhaps, having shown her the past and the future, it was content to lead her into the present.

They stepped out of a door embedded in the trunk of an enormous tree into a dense, wild forest of oak and pine. Kyra inhaled the sharp, fresh scent with gratitude. It was good to be outdoors again. Birds chittered, and the undergrowth rustled. A shaft of late-afternoon sunlight caught Rustan's face, his expression trapped between astonishment and some other emotion she could not identify. Anger? Regret?

No, that was not possible. Why would he be angry? And what was there to regret? Not the moments of tenderness they had shared in the Hub, surely. She was imagining things. Although now that they were out of the Hub, everything that had occurred inside it seemed distant and dreamlike, as if it had happened to someone else. Rustan stood so close to her, yet she could not have reached out and touched him. This thought cut her to the quick, but she hardened herself. He had distanced himself from her for some reason; she wouldn't make herself vulnerable again.

"The forest at the base of Kunlun Shan." Rustan traced the edge of the door with the palm of one hand. Now that it had closed, the door was hard to distinguish from the bark of the tree. All that was left was a faint rectangular outline and a tiny slot.

"Told you," said Kyra, trying to sound confident, as if this was exactly what she had expected. She had explained to him Felda's pyramid of codes and shown him the one to override this particular door. What she hadn't mentioned was her growing suspicion that the codes were not a one-way device to unlock the doors of recalcitrant Hubs, but more like a conversation—a conversation with an entity that was no longer quite sane. And how was it even possible to stay sane if you could look into both the past and the future? If you were doomed to survive until the last days of the Earth before it was swallowed up by the sun?

"Yes, you did tell me," said Rustan. "You were right about the door. You are right about the stash of kalishium too. But I pray you do not find it." He stepped toward her and grasped her arm. "Trust me. Turn back now before it is too late."

"What?" Kyra was flabbergasted. "Why would I turn back? Why should I not find the kalishium?"

"You think this is an ordinary forest?" His pressure on her arm increased, and his eyes trapped her, blue and intense. Shirin Mam's eyes. Shirin Mam's son, who had taught her, and held her, and kissed her, and whom she still did not understand.

"It doesn't matter what kind of forest it is," said Kyra, keeping her voice calm. "I have been called here, and I will stay until I find what I seek."

"It is your own death you seek," said Rustan. "The forest is guarded by a beast you cannot kill, for it is born of your deepest fears. I am the first to have escaped it unscathed in many decades."

"Unscathed?" Kyra shook his hand off, anger growing inside her. "Are you sure of that? Perhaps the beast has damaged you in ways you cannot see."

"Would you rather it had ripped my arms off? Because that too can happen." A note of frustration entered his voice. "Believe me, Kyra. This is not something you can fight."

"And yet I must, if I am to pass through the forest and climb the mountain," said Kyra.

He stepped back, and his face shuttered. "And if you were to vanquish the beast, and climb the mountain, and find the place where the kalishium is hidden—if you were to do all that, you would then have me to reckon with."

"What?" Kyra stared at him in dismay. "Why?"

"The kalishium is not ours to do with as we wish," said Rustan. "It is a legacy of the Ones, and it might contain their memories. This particular stash you are seeking is made in the images of the kings and queens of Asiana and their gods. They are too powerful and dangerous. Touch them, and you could lose yourself."

Kyra's skin prickled; she wrapped her robe more closely around herself. "How do you know all this? And is it my safety you fear for, or the kalishium you wish to protect?"

"Both," he said. "Each image tells a story; destroy it, and the story is gone from us forever. I know this because I have been there and seen it with my own eyes."

Kyra shivered. She was cold, within and without.

Rustan was not going to help her. He was going to try to *stop* her. And his reasoning was not without merit. After all, she hadn't wanted to use the kataris of the long-dead Markswomen of Kali precisely because their memories were too important for the Order to lose.

But she didn't have the luxury of worrying about the ancient history of Asiana, not with war threatening the stability of her world and the safety of her people right now.

"Kai Tau is killing innocent people in the Thar," she said. "We will have to move against him soon. I must do whatever I can to gain the slightest advantage."

"There has to be another way to defeat him," said Rustan. "Come back with me to Khur; let us show Barkav these weapon designs and ask Astinsai's counsel. We will fight him together."

"Nothing can stand against the bullets of the dark weapons except kalishium," argued Kyra. "And I don't plan to take *all* of it—just one or two of the images you're so concerned about."

"You will not take even one," said Rustan, his voice like granite. "Not while I'm around to prevent it." He folded his arms and regarded her, challenge in every line of his taut body.

Kyra's heart sank. He had made up his mind to stop her; she could see it. Nothing she said would make any difference.

She had three choices now. She could give in. She could fight him. Or she could run.

She ran. If she had stopped to think more about it, she could not have done it, could not have left Rustan, his face slack with disbelief, her own heartbreak reflected in his eyes. *Don't leave me. Don't go.*

Branches slashed her face. Kyra hacked her way through the undergrowth, breathing hard, her eyes stinging. Behind her,

Rustan gave chase. "Kyra!" he shouted. But his voice faded, and the forest closed around her, thick and watchful. As if it had been waiting for a chance to separate the two of them all along.

She pushed aside her growing sense of dread and fought through the forest. It was what Rustan had done; he had battled with the beast and earned his way through. She would do no less. Had he not taught her, after all? And was she not the Mahimata of Kali, with the fate of Asiana resting on her shoulders?

But the forest did not yield to her. She had to fight every step of the way. When darkness fell, she came to a halt, scratched and filthy, bleeding from a hundred tiny wounds.

Now the beast will come.

But it didn't, not right away. Kyra spent the night leaning against the roots of a massive tree, trying not to succumb to sleep. The canopy closed above her, blotting out the night sky. No light but the light of her blade, no voice but her own. It had been stupid to run away from Rustan. Stupid to throw away the chance to be with him, fight with him. And for what? To walk circles in the labyrinth of this endless forest? Perhaps it would all be for nothing, and she would die, just as Rustan had warned.

Something sparked a warning, and Kyra started. Not her own blade. Her katari lay unsheathed on her palm, giving her its light and comfort, small in the immensity of darkness that surrounded her.

It was Tamsyn's katari. Kyra withdrew it from the scabbard around her neck, and it blazed, red and triumphant, sending a thin current of courage and power into her veins. Kyra drew a deep breath and stilled herself. Her erstwhile enemy's weapon was now her ally. Tamsyn would have appreciated the irony of this, perhaps even applauded it.

A great roar split the night, and Kyra leaped to her feet, her pulse racing. Something huge crashed through the undergrowth, and a smell of carrion assaulted her senses, making her gag.

Goddess protect me. Kyra fell into the stance of Twin Blades at Dawn, her arms crossed in front of her face, a blade in each hand. A deep growling shook the ground, setting her teeth on edge.

"Come on, then," she shouted. "I am here. I am ready for you."

Something moved to her right, but when she twisted her neck, she saw nothing. And then it was behind her. No, to her left. Kyra spun, holding her stance, keeping it in front of her. It prowled always at the periphery of her vision, but she sensed enough to know that it was huge, clawed, and fanged.

Then it stood directly before her, and her eyes skittered over it, because it was impossible—such things did not exist. *Should not* exist. Like an unholy cross between a wyr-wolf and a tiger, only much, much bigger. The head alone was wider than the span of her arms. The eyes glowed crimson, and the fangs curved like tusks. And she thought she could kill it?

"Attack, why don't you?" she screamed, and it sprang.

Kyra closed her eyes and opened herself to the first-level meditative trance. To fight in the trance was terribly risky—Chintil had warned against it—but she had no choice. She needed to slow down time if she didn't want her bones crushed in those massive jaws.

Time elongated, and the beast flew at her in slow motion. Kyra's own body moved much faster, her right hand already reaching back to throw the katari in a killing strike. But as the beast sprang, it metamorphosed. It dissolved, lengthened, shifted, until it resembled nothing so much as a man. And not just any man.

Rustan. Kyra had no time to stop the flow of her own body in response to the threat. Perhaps, if it were just her own katari that she had been wielding, she could have controlled it. But as the figure solidified, Tamsyn's blade flew from her hand into his heart, and shattered into a million pieces.

Kyra fell out of the trance, screaming Rustan's name. Her hand—the one that had held Tamsyn's katari—burned as if it had been set on fire. Her own blade had gone cold and quiet in her other hand.

After a while, she made herself stop screaming. The forest was still, silent but for her own heavy breathing. No beast, no Rustan corpse stained the ground before her. A dream, but for the fact that Tamsyn's katari was gone. She felt its absence like a pit in her stomach. It had been with her so long, she had taken its power for granted. Without it, she felt smaller, diminished.

No, not diminished. Just plain Kyra with her own katari, the way it was meant to be.

She kissed her blade and coaxed a tiny, answering spark from it. *Goodbye, Tamsyn*, she thought, and swallowed a lump in her throat. Odd that she should feel grief. Tamsyn had been a killer and had met a much-deserved end. While she'd held Tamsyn's blade, though, it was as if a part of Tamsyn was still with her. Not the murderous, apprentice-torturing part, but the part that hungered, that felt pain, that knew the darkness she had fallen into. Kyra thought back to what she had seen of Tamsyn's past—the harsh life on the streets, the murder of her brother—and felt regret. What might Tamsyn have been under different circumstances?

But there was no changing the past. And holding on to it

only embittered you and made you undeserving of the present. Kyra had fantasized enough about her own dead family to know that.

She took a few swallows from her waterskin. Dawn's light filtered through the trees, and the forest awoke around her. Birdsong filled the air.

It was time to move on.

⁂

Kyra continued to climb all that day, and as she walked, she replayed the encounter in her mind. Why had the beast taken on Rustan's face and form when she went into the first-level meditative trance? Had she actually hurt him in some way? She prayed not; she hoped he had given up on her, gone back through the door to the Deccan Hub, and returned to Kashgar.

Her mind chased itself in circles, and her body ached as the climb grew steeper. Exhaustion began to wrap itself around her, until it was sheer force of will that made her carry on.

Her thoughts went to Nineth. Her friend was tired too. Kyra didn't know how she knew this, or where Nineth was— just that the ache in her limbs mirrored Nineth's. *Stay safe*, she thought, as if Nineth could hear her. *Come back home.*

Finally, just when she was ready to drop, the trees thinned, and she emerged above the tree line. The peaks of Kunlun Shan towered above her, majestic in the setting sun.

The wind sharpened, and the path grew icy. She slipped and stumbled on the sharp stones, but she never once thought of stopping. Time was her enemy now; it circled like a hungry wolf. Every hour that she spent resting was an hour that Kai Tau gained power.

When she saw the stone edifice clinging to the rock face, her heart sang, even though she was numb with cold and it was a near-vertical climb. This was the monastery she sought; she was sure of it. The place Rustan had tried to prevent her from reaching.

As night fell, she continued on her hands and knees, the going cruelly slow and hard. Her black robe was ripped; her palms bled. But the moon rose in the sky and shone on the path leading up to the monastery, lighting the way for her. She crawled forward, shivering, determined not to give in to the cold, the pain, and the fatigue.

Just a little more. You can do it. Her teacher's voice—or her own?

And then she was at the massive doors, and they swung open, and a figure stepped out. *Rustan. Another illusion.*

But he bent down and picked her up and rubbed his face against her cold cheek, melting away the horror of what she had been through. "I thought I'd lost you again," he said, and his face was wet with tears.

CHAPTER 22

A DUEL AND A THEFT

Rustan carried her inside the monastery and laid her down, wrapping her in moth-eaten blankets that smelled musty but were warm. She tried to tell him what she had seen, how the beast had taken his form and how she had killed it, but she sounded incoherent even to her own ears. At last, he stroked her cheek and shushed her.

"We can talk tomorrow," he said. "You will do no good to anyone if you fall sick." He turned his head this way and that, as if listening for someone. "I wish they were here," he muttered, before pushing a bowl toward her lips. "Drink—hot butter tea will do you good."

Kyra took a sip and almost spat the tea out. By the Goddess, it was as bad as one of Navroz Lan's brews. Rustan cajoled her to keep sipping it, though, and she felt better when it was inside her, warmth and life returning to her limbs.

"Rest now," he said. "Honestly, you must be the most stubborn creature to walk this planet. You should have listened to me and returned to the Hub. I don't know what the monks will make of you."

What monks? They were alone in a large, lamp-lit room. It didn't look as if anyone had lived here for a long time; the fireplace was cold and dark, and the air smelled of dust—the kind of thick dust that takes years to accumulate. The only bit of heat came from the stove; Rustan must have lit it to make that awful, salty tea.

Drowsiness took hold of her. She was warm, she was safe, she was reunited with Rustan, and the kalishium was close. She could afford to sleep for a few hours.

⁂

Kyra woke to sunlight and birdsong. She felt rested and clear-eyed. Rustan had thrown open the doors of the monastery, and the fresh morning breeze had chased away the musty odor of the previous night. A pot bubbled on the stove, giving off a rather dubious aroma.

"Breakfast," said Rustan cheerfully. "Not as good as they make it, but I found a few things that haven't gone bad. Not *all* the way bad."

"Who are 'they'?" she asked, sitting up.

"The last of the Sahiru sect," said Rustan, ladling gruel into a bowl and passing it to her. "They saved my life. They taught me so much. I was with them for a while before I went to the Thar Desert to look for Ishtul."

"But no one has lived here for years," Kyra pointed out. "You can see that for yourself."

He had no answer, but she could see that he didn't understand their absence and it made him unhappy.

They ate in silence. Kyra was loath to break it, but at last, when the frugal meal was over, she could put off her question no longer. "Where is the kalishium?" she asked. "We should take it and be on our way. If we leave soon, we could be at the Hub by nightfall. I don't fancy another night in the forest." As if it was just a matter of logistics and Rustan would fall in with whatever she suggested.

"I cannot let you take the kalishium," said Rustan, gentle yet implacable.

Kyra threw up her hands. "Why?" she cried. "How can it matter more than the lives we might save?"

"The images here are also alive, in a way different from our blades," said Rustan. "You would be killing something precious."

Kyra gritted her teeth. "I will deal with the guilt. It will be my burden, not yours."

"You misunderstand," said Rustan. "In the absence of the Sahirus, the guardianship of this monastery and all it contains falls to me. I can no more let you desecrate it than I can commit such an act myself." He stood, relaxed and ready, and gave her a tender smile. "I love you, Kyra Veer," he said, and it was true, but she realized to her horror that it didn't change anything. He would not yield on this, because he thought he was right. She wanted to cry.

Instead she rose, drawing in her strength.

Anticipate me, or all the moves of all the schools in Asiana will not keep you on your feet.

She blinked, startled. But it was only a memory, an echo of a time when Rustan had stood beside her, teaching her how to fight, preparing her for the duel with Tamsyn Turani.

She would not draw her blade, no matter what he did. And with that thought, Kyra flowed into the dance of Empty Hands. She fell into Hidden Snake stance, and he responded with Striking Mongoose. She answered with Flying Arrow, and he blocked with Rhino's Tusk.

Kick, parry, retreat, punch, withdraw, sidestep, block, and thrust, switching forms every time. And all of it nothing but a show, a match with no end. Kyra made her moves, anticipating every one of Rustan's, and he did the same. The blood pounded in her ears and her breath came short and sharp. *He* didn't even look winded.

I know you, Rustan, and you know me too well. With that thought, Kyra let her arms fall and allowed Rustan to kick her so that she flew across the room and landed with a painful thud against the stone wall. For a moment she could not breathe. Then the pain sank in and she moaned. Her head hurt where she had hit it against the wall. Her chest felt as though it were on fire. She hoped she hadn't broken a rib. So soon after her old wound had healed too. Navroz would disown her.

Rustan ran across the room and crouched by her side. "I've hurt you," he said, his face taut with worry. "Why did you not block that? You *saw* it coming . . ."

Yes, I did. Kyra swallowed her pain and summoned the Inner Speech before he could come to his senses:

"You will lie down on the floor. You will not move or speak."

Rustan froze as the mental bonds settled on him. Then he dropped like a stone to the floor.

Good. She would never have been able to do this if she hadn't caught him unawares. Perhaps a bit of Tamsyn's power still clung to her, despite the loss of her katari. Kyra dragged herself to her feet, massaging her chest. She put all her remaining strength into her voice, hoping it would be enough:

"You will stay here until I release you."

His slate-blue eyes followed her, full of shock at her betrayal.

"Don't look at me like that," she snapped. "I'm doing what I must." But her heart clenched within her as she stumbled away from him, leaning against the wall for support.

She'd tricked him; she'd broken the rules. *Never use Inner Speech against another Marksman or Markswoman.*

She was no better than Shurik, no better than Tamsyn. Shirin Mam would have exiled her from the Order and confiscated her blade.

But Shirin Mam was gone; the rules were made for times of peace, not war. She needed the kalishium to defeat Kai Tau. Even at the cost of hurting the one person whom she loved above all others.

Menadin had said that the kalishium was secreted in a cave in the monastery. Kyra explored the room, running her hands over the rough walls. It did not take her long to find the dark opening that led inside the mountain; it had been blocked by a heap of rotting firewood, as if that could hide it. She kicked it aside and bent to enter.

"Don't." It was just a whisper, and it must have cost him. Rustan's forehead gleamed with sweat and his face worked with the effort of speaking against her order.

Kyra hardened herself and the bonds she had laid on him. "Do not move or speak."

He closed his eyes, exhausted. *I'm sorry. I'm so sorry*, she thought. Tears blurred her vision, but she turned away from him. She had a task to complete. She could blame and punish herself later.

Although what punishment could be worse than this? The feeling, as she entered the cave, that she was leaving all light and love behind. The memory of the hurt in his eyes, sharp as a blade. And the knowledge, bitter-tasting, that even if Rustan forgave her, she would never forgive herself.

She held out her katari to illuminate the way. "Show me where the kalishium is," she commanded, but she could feel the reluctance of her blade grow as she went deeper into the cave. Its radiance wavered, unsteady, and a needle of doubt pricked her. She ignored it and continued, following the wall, bending the katari to her will. It was *hers*. It would do what she wanted.

A faint blue-green light shone in the distance, and Kyra quickened her pace down a narrow tunnel, at the end of which the light grew stronger, brighter, making her blink after the pitch-dark.

Kyra stepped into a huge, luminous cavern. A magnificent white globe glowed in the center. She shielded her eyes and circled the cavern, her heart beating like a drum within her chest. Faces gazed back at her, both grotesque and beautiful.

Kalishium, in the form of hundreds of sculptures, lined the walls. Her gaze skittered over them; she was afraid to look too long, knowing the spell she could fall under. No wonder Rustan had warned her not to seek this place.

But he had underestimated her. An ordinary person might well be sucked into the void and lose their mind. She had her blade, and it would protect her from the worst.

A dark trio of eyes flicked in her direction, and she almost screamed.

But it was only an image of the Mother Goddess. Kyra fell against a pillar and tried to control her breathing. A sculpture of the Goddess in her aspect of Bhuvaneshvari, the World Mother, red-skinned and four-armed, with a garland of lotuses around her neck. A crown with a crescent moon rested on her braided hair.

Was this the right image to take back with her?

No. Kyra didn't even have to think about it. She could barely bring herself to look at the sculpture. The eyes seemed alive, all-knowing. They followed her as she circled the cavern, as if judging her actions.

Why had the alien Ones carved an image in the likeness of the Goddess? Had they too worshipped her? Or had they made it for their human counterparts? No way to know.

On her second slow circle around the cavern, Kyra's gaze snagged on another image: a four-legged wolflike creature with a not-quite-human face snarling at her. Her katari sparked a warning, but she ignored it and approached. The image reminded her of Menadin. It was both familiar and unpleasant, but it did not frighten her the way the image of the Goddess had. Before she could think too much about it, Kyra screwed her eyes shut and reached down to grasp the two-foot-high sculpture. Her fingers touched cool metal and a jolt of memory shook her.

I run; I run like the wind with my brothers. I taste the terror of the buck before it falls, crashing to the forest floor. And then we are upon it, tearing open its throat, feasting on its delicious flesh. I eat my fill, growling when a young one tries to push between my legs. But there is enough, enough for all. I sit back on my haunches when I am done, licking my chops. It is difficult at times like this to remember that I am also a man, that I become a man whenever the Araini call.

I wear robes and sip tea and study the stars and am greatly envied by the ordinary ones for my duality. And when I ask the Araini why they have made me like this, they only smile and answer that one day I will know.

Come back, Kyra. Rustan reached out to her with his mind, trapped as he was in the bonds of the Inner Speech.

Kyra surfaced from the memory, gasping and shivering. She snatched her hands back from the wolflike image; it gleamed before her, opaque once more.

She had not erred. This was the image she would carry back with her, saving a piece for Menadin. Perhaps it would tell Menadin more than what it had told her, or perhaps it told everyone a different story. But the memory was sharp and clear within her still. The Ones had made the wyr-wolves; to what end, only they could tell.

She went back to the monastery and returned with a tattered rug. She would not touch the statue with her bare hands again. She wrapped it in the rug and heaved it onto her shoulders, lurching under its weight. Goddess, it was heavy. It would be hard to carry it all the way down to the door at the base of Kunlun Shan. She would have to make a sled of some sort out of the pile of firewood.

"I have found the image I need," she announced as she staggered into the room where she had left Rustan. "I am taking only one."

Rustan's eyes were closed; if he heard her, he gave no sign. She set down her load and ran to him, her fingers flying to his wrist. His pulse was faint but even. *Thank the Goddess.*

"You can move after two hours, but you will not follow me," she said in the Inner Speech. "You will not use the Kunlun door until three full days have passed."

His face twitched and he sighed, as if waking from a dream.

Kyra paused and swallowed. "I love you, Rustan," she whispered. "If you love me, fight by my side."

She bent and kissed his damp, cool forehead. "Goodbye," she said, and rose to leave before she could change her mind, release him from her bonds, and beg his forgiveness.

Before she left, she removed Shirin Mam's letter for him from her pocket and laid it by his side, where he would see it when he awoke.

CHAPTER 23

THE SECRET OF
THE SAHIRUS

When Rustan woke, he remembered the kiss and Kyra's parting words, but it took a while to recall everything else.

He sat up, his head spinning, his heart heavy.

She had used Compulsion on him. *Compulsion*. And she had stolen a kalishium image from the cavern. He had failed to protect the kalishium, and he had failed to protect her.

He had told her he loved her, and she had betrayed him.

Two hours, she had said; he could move after two hours. He still had time to catch up with her if he ran.

But Rustan found he was unable to go much farther than the doors of the monastery with the intention of following Kyra. Every limb ached, and his head began to pound when he tried to descend the path curving down from the monastery to meet the broader track as it disappeared around the side of the mountain. The path the Sahirus had helped him traverse, when he had not the eyes to see it. The path that Kyra had climbed to the monastery without any aid or any knowledge of it. Perhaps the monks had expected her, had *wanted* her to come. How else could she have seen where to place her feet?

But where were the Sahirus? He had left them less than two weeks ago. Surely they would have sensed his return. Had they hidden themselves from him as yet another test?

Rustan drank fresh, cold water from a stream outside. He sat down to practice the forms of internal strength while waiting for the monks to make their presence known. After a while, he succumbed to fatigue and fell asleep again. When he woke, sandy-mouthed and gritty-eyed, the Sahirus had still not returned.

That was when he noticed the bulky letter, lying a few feet away from him. *Rustan*, it said on the cover, the *t* hidden by the jute string that held the sheaf together. He frowned and picked it up, turning it over in his hands. It was smooth and familiar to the touch, as if he had held it before, or as if he knew quite well the person who had written his name in such clear, beautiful script. The letter had Kyra's scent on it, but it was not her writing.

It was his mother's.

Rustan began to shake but forced himself to stop. He held Shirin Mam's last words in his hands. His mother, who had once told him she would acknowledge him to the world and then fulfilled her promise in the most unexpected way. Here, perhaps, was the secret of his birth, the reason for his existence. Maybe he was part of a bigger plan, and Shirin Mam had foreseen the role he would play and chosen to defy the ancient Kanun to bring him into the world.

Or maybe his birth was an accident, the embarrassing result of a youthful indiscretion, best forgotten.

He wanted to tear the letter open and devour its contents. Instead, he touched it to his lips and tucked it into his robe. While it remained unread, his past and thus his future were limitless. Once he read it, all those possibilities would collapse into one reality, perhaps a banal one.

He scanned the familiar old room, truly observing it for the first time since his return. The kettle was rusty, the fireplace dark. The sunlight that shone through the half-open doors revealed a thick layer of dust on the walls. Only his and Kyra's footprints had disturbed it on the floor. The food stores were mostly gone, sacks of grain eaten away by rats and tea leaves crumbled to dust. And now that Kyra had left, he sensed that he was alone. Not even ghosts kept him company here.

He climbed the creaky wooden staircase to the second level and checked the three rooms upstairs without much hope. Nothing but dust and age, battered trunks on the floor and frayed hangings on the walls. One hanging in particular caught his eye, because it was illuminated with the ancient script the Sahirus had been trying to teach him. He read it, coldness settling in the pit of his stomach as he translated the words in his mind:

To the faithful Sahirus this grace is given:
All debts forgotten, all sins forgiven.
Keepers of Kunlun, hold on to the ways
Until you join us at the end of days.

Return to bury us. That is all we ask. They had not said when. They had given him no hint how near the end was—or that the end had already happened and they were reading him a story from an earlier time, a different age. He had thought them near-immortal, but maybe the truth was stranger than that. Maybe they had been phantoms.

Or perhaps he was the phantom, unsure and unaware of the part he had to play.

Rustan went back downstairs to the great wooden doors of the monastery. The rope ladder no longer hung below the entrance, but it did not matter anymore. Rustan studied the path and saw the way the monks had taken—how long ago?—up the mountain.

On the roof of the world, in Ice Mother's arms, you will see and understand everything.

Ice Mother, the name of the highest peak of Kunlun Shan.

Rustan walked down the narrow path of the monastery to where it met the broader one and began to climb. Not the route they had taken up the mountain when they showed him the home star of the Araini, but a different path, to a different peak.

Snow and ice and loose stones slid underfoot, and the sunlight blinded him. Rustan sweated and shivered as he made his way slowly up the steep, treacherous path. He thought of Kyra, and then wondered why he thought of her in this moment, when a strong gust of wind might knock him over and send him tumbling down the cliffs. *Perhaps I am close to death, and that is why I think of her.*

It took Rustan hours to reach the summit of Ice Mother. By then the sun had dipped into the west, and the sky flamed red and orange above him. The air was thin and sharp, imbued with the many colors of dusk. And it was in this transitory light that Rustan saw what the Sahirus had meant for him to find.

A massive oblong structure, unlike anything he had ever

seen, rose from the snowfield before him. Its smooth, silver walls glinted in the dying light. It did not look like a temple, a monastery, or a dwelling place. It looked like the inverted hull of a strange ship, or perhaps a Hub. A few feet in front of it, a boot stuck out of the snow.

Rustan rested, breathing the cold, clean air, letting the exhaustion leach away from his bones. Putting off the inevitable, painful discovery. Trying, and failing, to find his inner calm.

At last he walked toward them, his dead teachers, the two ancient Sahirus buried beneath the snow, frozen in time. He dug them out, his eyes stinging, his hands numb with cold.

How long had they lain here, waiting for him? Months? Years?

He laid out the two tiny corpses, brushing the snow away from their faces. They had asked him to bury them. They had been trying to get inside the oblong building—of that, he was certain.

Rustan rose and circled the building, trying to find a door. There wasn't one. He touched the cold metallic surface with his palms and nothing happened. He unsheathed his mother's blade. As a last resort, he would try to cut an opening into the metal walls.

But there was no need to. As soon as the kalishium blade touched the building, the outline of a door shone silver-bright in the dusk. Stunned, Rustan stepped back. The outline faded.

The building had to be an artifact of the Ones. It had survived the war and the burning and eight and a half centuries of snow and wind. Once again, Rustan touched the walls with his mother's blade, and once more the outline of a door appeared. He pushed it with trembling hands.

The door swung open at his touch. He picked up the bodies of the Sahirus, one by one, and brought them inside. When the door swung closed behind him, blue lights came on, illuminating the vast space. Just like a Hub—but this was no Hub.

Rustan stood at the entrance of a great white hall lined with glass-covered caskets. A hall that was surely bigger on the inside than it appeared on the outside. He walked in, his heart hammering, and peered into the first casket. It held the body of an old woman, perfectly preserved. Her hands were folded on her chest and she appeared to be asleep. A Sahiru?

He walked along the line of caskets, counting as he went. Twenty-two, twenty-three—and there he stopped, for the few caskets that remained were empty. Nearly as many men as women, and all in the same perfect state of preservation.

What art was this? And what would be their ultimate fate?

Rustan laid his teachers in two of the empty caskets, folding their hands and smoothing their foreheads. When he stood back, glass covers slid over the caskets with a smooth hiss. There was nothing now to distinguish his teachers from their fellow Sahirus.

He stood there awhile, remembering what they had taught him, thanking them for all they had done for him, and apologizing for his failures. Only then did he allow himself to check if there were any empty caskets left.

There was one.

Rustan sighed and moved toward it, touched the smooth metal, and closed his eyes. This one was for him. If only he could have lain down on it right away.

But of course, he could not. His time had not yet come.

If you love me, fight by my side.

It was hard, but Rustan made himself turn away, walk out of the building, and into the freezing night. It had begun to snow; the driving wind pelted bits of ice into his mouth and eyes. He tied his headcloth over his face and went down to the monastery, the secret of the Sahirus a burning coal in his heart.

PART III

Shirin Mam's letter to Rustan

My son. The words feel strange in my mouth, yet you have never been far from my thoughts. If there is one regret I have, it is that I will not set eyes on you until you pass through the door of death and join me on the other side. Many times over the years I have imagined how you must look, first as a boy and then as a grown man. Many times I have longed to make the trip to Kashgar and summon you to my side.

But I lost that right when you were born, and I gave you up into the care of others. And I lost it for the second time when I took you away from your adoptive clan and delivered you to the Maji-khan of Khur.

It is better so. And yet how it hurt. I did not know it would hurt like this, to give you up. Before you were born it was like a game, hiding my condition from my eagle-eyed council. Poor Navroz, she will never forgive me.

Will you?

Let me tell you a story, a story of when I was young. Not yet the Mahimata of Kali, but I was the Mistress of Mental Arts and very proud of myself too. Not bad for a daughter of shepherds from the Uzbek Plains, yes?

One day, Ananya Senn, my Mahimata, told me to judge a riddling game at the festival of Chorzu. The prize would be whatever was asked, if it was in our power to give: forgiveness for a crime, a combat lesson, a tour of the caves of Kali—not that anyone ever asked for that.

This might surprise you, but in those days we mingled more with the ordinary folk. We were active participants at the festival, sometimes offering a confessional for those whose hearts were weighed by past misdeeds, sometimes enacting a mock duel. I put a stop to all that, for reasons that will become clear.

The riddling stage was a patch of grass beneath an ancient banyan tree at the edge of Chorzu. Twenty riddlers showed up on the day of the festival, all keen to test their wits against each other. Of the twenty were nineteen I could read and one—a man called Rubathar—whom I could not. He was impervious to the Mental Arts. This is not an unknown skill, but it is quite rare, and it disturbed me. He was disturbing to look upon too, with his piercing eyes, ragged clothes, and wild hair, and the long, curving sword that hung on his belt. A sword that was drenched in the blood of hundreds, if I was not mistaken.

But I did not betray my unease. I paired the contestants and sat back to watch. I reasoned that he'd be gone soon enough, eliminated by the more experienced riddlers of the valley.

The rules were simple. The contestants posed riddles to each other, carrying on until one or the other failed to guess the correct answer. As was customary, the entire village had turned out to cheer the contestants and judge the quality of the riddles posed.

The afternoon wore on and dusk fell. Lanterns were lit, and spice tea was brought to slake the thirst of onlookers and riddlers alike. By midnight, only two riddlers were left: Rubathar and Piyaret, a medicine woman from a neighboring village. I had underestimated the stranger's abilities, and this annoyed me deeply.

At last, Rubathar stood and stretched. "This is my final riddle of the night, for I grow weary and have a long way to go," he said. "Listen:

"Known to all, I speak but to one.
More precious than gold, yet never sold,
My work is never done.
Who am I?"

Piyaret hesitated for the first time that evening. Of course, I had guessed the answer even before Rubathar finished speaking, and I couldn't help myself. "That is not a fair riddle," I announced.

"It is the simplest riddle I know," said Rubathar. "But I will give you another clue:

"Drenched in blood and bits of bone,
Smoother than silk, harder than stone."

This was too much to be borne. I stood. "Do you make fun of us, stranger?" I demanded.

Rubathar turned to me. "Make fun of the Markswomen?" he said, his voice mild. "Think you I harbor a death wish?"

And right then, I knew. This man wanted to die. Had perhaps wanted to die for a very long time, for the sins he had committed. "I declare this competition null and void," I said.

Protests and murmurs rippled through the crowd gathered around. No one dared voice their objections more strongly than that, but it was clear that everyone thought I was being unfair to the stranger.

Rubathar smiled at me. "But you know the answer to my riddle. And the rules say that as long as someone can guess the answer correctly, the riddle is valid."

"I make the rules," I said. "You would do well to leave. Now."

Everyone quailed before the use of the Inner Speech, but it had no effect on Rubathar. Instead of leaving, he turned to the confused Piyaret and said, "I give you a third clue. Listen again:

"Untouched by fire, wind, or cold,
Shaped by secret ways and old,
Sometimes light, and sometimes dark,
I know what lies in your inmost heart."

Comprehension dawned on Piyaret's face and she shouted: "Katari! The answer is a katari."

"No matter," I said. "I have declared the competition null and void." By then I was quite angry with this man who dared defy me in front of the entire village.

"Why, mistress," said Rubathar. "Will you not riddle me for the prize? Or does an elder of Kali fear the poor wit of an ignorant forest dweller?"

I confess to you freely that it took all my self-control not to take out my katari and throw it at your father. Which, of course, is what he wanted. Instead, I said in my coldest voice, "You are evidently a stranger to our ways. Perhaps you have dwelled alone in the forest too long and forgotten the courtesy due to the Orders."

Rubathar bowed and, perhaps repentant of the public breach in etiquette, dropped his mental defenses and allowed me a glimpse into his mind.

It is a moment that is seared into my heart. Sometimes we go through our entire lives not even knowing that we are searching for something. And sometimes we realize it—and we find it—but too late. Too late to change ourselves, and far too late to change the world.

I suppose your father could have been a Marksman. He had the ability, and more. But he had not the temperament. He loathed killing. And he was unable to come to terms with what he had done, the numberless men and women he had killed in revenge for an unprovoked attack on his tribe. But that I found out later, and it does not belong in this story, which, after all, is your story.

"You asked for a riddle," I said. "You shall have it. Listen well:

"Time without end,
Neither foe nor friend,
A starry host,
Neither man nor ghost."

"The Araini," said Rubathar. "I believe I have won this contest."

It is the first and only time I have heard the true name of the Ones spoken aloud. I was so stunned that I was rendered speechless. Around me the onlookers burst into cheers. I found my voice and announced Rubathar as the winner of the riddling contest.

"And what is to be your reward?" I asked, when the cheers had died down. Although I suspected I knew what he would say, what he would ask for. I was not wrong.

"A foretelling," he said. "Show me where my path lies, where I will meet my death."

There was utter silence. I do not like foretelling. It hides far more than it shows. I have always concealed this gift, this curse. But this man knew I had the talent—something even my own Order only guessed.

"Ask me for something else," I said at last. "There has been no true far-seer in the Order of Kali for three generations."

Except you, mistress. He did not say it aloud, but I heard it all the same. What he said was: "Give me death, then. I have been looking for it for a long time. I've thrown myself off a cliff, walked into a tiger's den, waded into the shark-infested Yellow Sea. I've tried everything, yet it evades me."

"It will evade you awhile longer," I told him. And then I

dismissed them all: the gawking villagers, the defeated riddlers, the children staying up late the one night in the year they were allowed to do so.

It was the middle of the night and a full moon hung low in the sky. We stood in silence and took each other's measure. "How did you know?" I asked.

He shrugged. His own powers did not interest him anymore.

And so I succumbed; I did a foretelling for him. I shut down my senses and sought the wisdom of the third eye. I saw his world line, entwined with mine for a brief, glorious moment. I saw you as you would be, tiny and perfect, blessed with our powers and free from our limitations. And I saw a shard of my gift splinter and pass on to him.

His eyes widened when I told him that. But he did not flinch. "If that is the price I pay, then so be it," he said. "Tell me where my path lies."

And I told him. Having foreseen it, I had no choice but to reveal it. It is a place that will call you too, sooner or later: a monastery deep in the heart of Kunlun Shan, where you will find the answers to some of the questions that haunt you. Perhaps you will meet the spirit of your father. I like to think so. I like to think that you will find us both again, in one way or another.

That night I spent with your father under the bright midsummer moon of the Ferghana sky. This I did against the Kanun, and I have paid for it many times over. In the morning he was gone, and I never saw him again, for he died, as I had foretold, on the slopes of Kunlun Shan.

Do not grieve for him. He made his peace with himself before he died. As I will too.

One final word. Beware of Kyra Veer. I love her like a daughter but—like me—one day she will betray you. Try to forgive us if you can.

CHAPTER 24

THE TEMPLE
OF VALAVAN

When Kyra emerged from the Transport Chamber into the Deccan Hub, it had altered beyond recognition. Where before the corridor had been silent and empty, it was now a hive of activity—which hardened her suspicion that when she and Rustan found each other, they hadn't been in the Deccan Hub at all. They had been . . . . elsewhere. But she could not regret it; no matter what the Hub had put her through, it had reunited her with Rustan. That time alone with him had been a gift. He had told her he loved her, and he hadn't lied.

Then she had to go and destroy it all. He wouldn't ever trust her again, and rightly so.

Kyra found herself close to tears and resolutely pushed all thoughts of Rustan away. She needed to focus on her surroundings. She had planned to go straight back to the caves of Kali, and then to the Order of Khur, but something was amiss.

Valavian Markswomen hurried down the passage with their blades drawn, herding people in front of them, shouting instructions in a language she did not understand. Men and women milled about, some holding weapons, others clutching children. Kyra sensed fear, bordering on panic. Somewhere, a baby started to cry.

Kyra put down her load and plastered herself against the wall to avoid the crowd. What was happening? She could not see anyone's face clearly, despite the glow of the blades and the occasional lamp.

A Markswoman stopped in front of her and raised a lamp to her face. "Kyra Veer?" she cried. She turned to the others. "It is the Mahimata of Kali," she announced in a shocked tone.

A petite figure hurried toward her and bowed. "Derla Siyal of the Order of Valavan," she said by way of introduction. "The Goddess herself must have sent you. I was on my way to the caves of Kali to ask for help."

Help? Since when had the Valavians deigned to ask anyone else for assistance? They numbered seventy-five strong—the largest of any Order—and were known far and wide for their fierceness and fighting skills. "What's going on?" asked Kyra.

"You'd best come and see for yourself, Mahimata," said Derla. "Here, let me help you carry that." And she reached for the rug-wrapped kalishium image that Kyra had stolen from the monastery of Kunlun Shan.

"No thank you," said Kyra, blocking her. "It is my burden, and no one else may touch it."

"As you wish," said Derla, straightening, eyes agleam with curiosity as Kyra heaved the bundle onto her back, trying not to groan. Those eyes said what Kyra already knew; Derla would take the first opportunity to peek at the bundle. Once discovered, the kalishium would be whisked away from her for "safekeeping" or some such excuse. The Valavians would not relinquish such a treasure.

"I'm going to leave it in the Transport Chamber so I don't have to carry it," said Kyra. "I can retrieve it later."

"*That* one? That's the door you used?" Derla's voice was heavy with doubt. Kyra ignored Derla's sharp intake of breath as she keyed in the code to the Kunlun door and it swung open.

"That door shifted many years ago," said Derla slowly. "The last Markswoman to use it never returned. And we should know, because she was a Valavian elder."

Kyra placed the kalishium image on the chamber floor and let the door close again. It would be safe—at least for the next couple of days, until Rustan could follow her. "I just happen to know a special code," she said, dusting off her hands and making her voice bright. "Now, isn't there a matter of great importance we must attend to at once?"

Derla's face clouded. "Of course. Please follow me."

"Where are you taking all these people?" asked Kyra, as they inched along the wall, against the tide of humanity rushing past them.

"Somewhere safe," said Derla over her shoulder. "These are farmers and villagers who live near the Temple of Valavan. They were the first casualties when the outlaws rode in. All who survived ran to the temple for safety."

A finger of ice brushed Kyra's spine. "Kai Tau is here?"

They had arrived at the main door of the Hub, propped open by a young girl with frightened eyes. An apprentice, most likely, seeing her first real battle.

"We don't know if Kai Tau himself is here, but at least two of his death-sticks are," said Derla. "One to the north, and one to the south, they hold us captive—at least for now."

They crossed the threshold and hurried down a narrow, underground passage. The stream of people fleeing the fighting had slowed to a trickle, and it was possible to walk faster. They went up a short flight of stone steps, and at the top, Derla turned and gave Kyra a short bow. "Welcome to the Temple of Valavan," she said. "I would that you could have seen it in circumstances different from these."

Kyra followed her down a corridor, at the end of which Derla took off her shoes, explaining that they must be barefoot within the temple precincts. Kyra followed suit, glad to escape the confines of her boots. They emerged into a vast, domed space so bright it hurt the eyes. Kyra blinked until her vision had adjusted to the light, then gazed around in awe.

She stood on a white marble floor laced with a black cobra-hood pattern. The ceiling that soared overhead was studded with intricate carvings and rectangular panes of painted glass. All around, the walls were gilded with a mosaic of mirrors. Kyra could see endless images of herself, reflections of reflections, stretching into an infinity of glass. Except, that wasn't what she really looked like, was it? That arrogant smile, that crimson blade—those belonged to Tamsyn. And the gray hair, the black robe—those were Shirin Mam's. As for the striped skin, the overlong canines—those were utterly inhuman and did not, could not, belong to anyone she knew.

"Welcome to the Hall of Reflection." A deep, musical voice broke her vision, shattering it to pieces and leaving Kyra disoriented. She looked down at her empty hands, then up at the tall, dark-skinned woman bearing down on her. Faran

Lashail, the head of the Order of Valavan, every bit as imposing in person as Shirin Mam had been at the height of her powers.

Kyra inclined her head in thanks, resisting the urge to bow. She must meet Faran Lashail as an equal, despite the differences in their age and experience. The Order of Kali was the oldest in Asiana, and she must never let anyone forget it.

"What did I just see?" she asked, indicating the mirrors.

"You saw yourself, as you are or as you could be," said Faran. "We bring murderers here before we execute them. The truth is often harder to bear than death."

"If only there was a way to bring Kai Tau here," said Kyra.

Faran gave a humorless smile. "There are those who know what they are and don't care, and on them the mirrors will not work. You see an image only if you also have one to maintain. I have witnessed men throw themselves on the glass and scratch it until their fingernails bled. But I doubt Kai Tau would fall in that category."

"What do *you* see?" blurted out Kyra, then wished she hadn't, as Derla stiffened and threw her a warning look.

But Faran did not seem put out. "I see what I should," she said. "And now you have too. What you do with it, if anything, is up to you."

A young Markswoman entered the hall and bowed. "Elder Ishandi is back, Mother," she announced.

Faran frowned. "What about Ikana?" she demanded. "She left before Ishandi did."

But the Markswoman did not know, and Faran asked Kyra to accompany them to the council room where the elder waited.

"Ishandi and Ikana are the best among us at camouflage," said Faran, as she strode down the hall, Kyra and Derla having to almost run to keep up with her. "I sent them north and south to spy on the outlaws. Ikana should have been back by now."

They walked down a corridor lined with bas-reliefs of horses, elephants, and tigers, up a steep flight of marble steps, into another hall lined with paintings, and down a different corridor, turning left and right and left again until Kyra had lost all sense of direction. The temple was a vast maze of rooms and passages that could easily have housed thousands of Markswomen instead of just seventy-five. Kyra wondered if the Order of Valavan too had diminished with time.

As if she had read her mind, Faran glanced at her and said, "At its peak, our Order numbered over two thousand Markswomen."

There was a trace of bitterness in her voice, and also resignation, as if the gradual decline of the Orders was inevitable and there was nothing to be done about it.

Kyra took a deep breath. "Some months ago, I met Astinsai, the last living katari mistress. She said that the ability to bond with kalishium was becoming rarer because—because Markswomen do not have children and cannot pass on their talents to future generations."

Faran stopped and wheeled to face her, astonishment and disapproval writ large on her face. "Markswomen have *never* taken mates. It is not a trait that is *inherited*, like eye or skin color. I don't know what Shirin Mam taught you—"

"Shirin Mam never did anything without good reason," interrupted Kyra. Her cheeks burned with embarrassment but she pushed ahead, knowing she would not get the chance to say it again. "Her son is one of the best in combat in the Order of Khur."

Faran snorted. "The Order of Khur, safely tucked into the

middle of the Empty Place, five days from the nearest usable door. They are the ones who spawned the outlaw filth that has invaded the Deccan and now stands at our threshold."

"They will help us fight Kai Tau," said Kyra. "I have the Maji-khan's word. I was on my way to the camp of Khur to confer with them."

"You will waste ten days," said Faran. "That time would be better served in preparing for the battle of the soul of Asiana. Because that is what this is."

"Why are Kai Tau's men even here?" asked Kyra, hoping to deflect her. "What do they have to gain from splitting their forces and attacking the Temple of Valavan?" The temple was known far and wide as an impenetrable stronghold. Bullets might damage its stone walls, but they would not bring it down.

Faran hesitated, and Kyra knew at once that her question had hit home.

"We will speak of this in the council room," said Faran at last. "It is on the third level."

Derla explained to Kyra as they walked that the temple was a step pyramid with nine platforms, each symbolizing a level of enlightenment. "The base levels represent the world of desire, where most people dwell," she said. "The middle levels represent the world of form, and those belong to us: Markswomen who have gone beyond material desire. The highest three levels represent true reality, beyond self and form. It is this state of liberation that we must aspire to."

"And you would have us slip to the bottom," said Faran without turning around. "You would have us take mates and bear children like commoners."

"Shirin Mam was not a commoner," said Kyra, keeping her voice even. "Perhaps she saw and understood something that we do not in our blind arrogance. Perhaps the ability to bond with a blade *is* inheritable. If a Markswoman wished to have a child—"

"Enough!" said Faran, her eyes flashing. "No Markswoman of mine would wish it."

"But I would do it, if you asked it of me," murmured Derla. "Just to test the hypothesis."

"I do not ask it," snapped Faran. "I expressly forbid it. Why are we even discussing this?"

"Because there is a possibility that the last living katari mistress and seer might be right," said Kyra, exasperated, "and Shirin Mam went against her vows and her own nature to set an example for us."

Faran rolled her eyes. "Yes, let us all reproduce like rabbits until we repopulate the Orders with our amazing and talented offspring. Your thinking is diseased. It is not your fault, of course. The Order of Kali has suffered greatly in recent months, and you are far too young to shoulder the terrible responsibility that has been thrust upon you. Perhaps, when this is over, you can spend some time meditating in the upper levels of our temple. You would be most welcome, and it would benefit you."

"Thank you for the invitation," said Kyra, torn between amusement and anger. "I will be sure to communicate it to my elders. Is this not the council room?"

They stood at an archway through which Kyra could see a rectangular hall with a long table and map-covered walls. Several women with tense faces stood around the table—the elders of Valavan, Kyra guessed.

She was right; Faran led the way in and introduced her to the council before sitting down at the table and demanding a report from Ishandi, a small, slight woman with a faded air who looked like she might vanish any moment.

"There are more than two hundred fighters, armed and horsed," whispered Ishandi, her voice so soft that Kyra had to lean forward and strain her ears to hear it. "Two kalashiks, as far as I can judge, and the rest have bows and arrows, spears and clubs. They have set up camp a mile north of us, just beyond the sacred grove." She paused, and a somber expression crossed her face. "They are cutting the banyan for fuel."

Faran made a whistling noise between her teeth. "They will pay for this sacrilege with their lives," she declared. "Each and every one of them."

"They have posted lookouts, Mother," said Ishandi in the same barely audible voice. "They will see us approaching in the daylight, but perhaps we can take them down at night, one by one."

"No," said Faran. "Not if they have kalashiks. The evil weapons will tell them when we're close enough to kill. The guns form a bond with their handlers, a sick and twisted version of the bond we ourselves have with our blades."

Kyra started. How did Faran know so much about the death-sticks? Realization dawned, slow and cold. Rustan had destroyed the Taus' weapons forge. The only reason Kai Tau would risk dividing his forces at this juncture was if he had the chance to procure more death-sticks. She remembered, now, that Tamsyn had spoken of the dark weapons kept by the Order of Valavan during the Sikandra Fort assembly, just before the duel. How could she have forgotten?

"You have a cache of guns here, don't you?" she said. "That's why Kai Tau sent his men to attack the temple."

"It is not a secret," said Faran with a cool smile. "We

guard the weapons so they do not fall into the wrong hands. Your elders know this, even though they don't seem to have mentioned it to you."

The Markswomen turned to stare at her. The weight of their judging looks was crushing, but Kyra refused to bow under it. She sat up straighter and said, "There is much the elders and I have not had time to discuss. I was fighting for my life for several weeks after the duel. There was rather a lot on our minds. But I survived, and I have a plan. A plan that will decimate the outlaws with little danger to you, although the greater danger comes from the guns you hide here."

"And what is this plan of yours?" asked Faran, ignoring Kyra's last comment. "Do you propose to decimate the outlaws yourself through some magical strength only you possess?"

Kyra summoned her confidence. "Not by myself," she said. "But with the help of wyr-wolves."

There was a small, shocked silence. *Help me convince them, Goddess.*

"That is the strangest thing I have ever heard," said a white-haired Markswoman at last. She leaned toward Faran. "I was against going to the Order of Kali from the beginning. They have enough ill luck to poison the whole continent."

"Such superstition," said Kyra, keeping her voice calm and cold. "I am surprised at you, Elder. When the time comes to fight, we must use what weapons we have. And I consider the wyr-wolves to be weapons. The kalashiks will ignore their presence. They will sneak up on the guards and overpower them, and that's when it will be safe for us to move in."

"And wyr-wolves will do this—why, exactly?" asked Faran, with the air of one who is humoring a child.

"Because I request them to," said Kyra. "And because you

will issue a ban on the hunting and killing of wyr-wolves in your jurisdiction."

At that, pandemonium broke out across the table. The Valavians leaped to their feet and began to shout at Kyra. One told her she was mad. Another said that she was a demon, in league with evil beasts. Through it all, Faran watched her with thoughtful eyes, not joining the din but not trying to stop it either, as if she was testing Kyra, deciding which side of sanity she was on.

What ended the clamor was not an order by the head of Valavan, but a sudden flurry of activity by the archway of the hall. Kyra recognized the young apprentice who had held open the main door of the Deccan Hub as they exited it.

"Ikana is dead," the apprentice announced, and burst into tears.

Chapter 25

A BURIAL AND
A PROMISE

The Valavians had not lost a Markswoman in decades. Ikana was precious to them—a gifted elder who had taught the art of camouflage to Ishandi. When the apprentice made her terrible announcement, Faran brought her fist down on the wooden table so hard it cracked. The elders gasped and reeled back as if they had been struck. Ishandi rushed to question the girl, gripping her shoulders with impatience and comforting her at the same time.

Kyra was forgotten. She watched the outpouring of grief and anger, feeling small and insignificant and helpless. This was how it had been when Shirin Mam died. When Ishtul died. There were so few of them left with the gift, every death was a blow that weakened the foundations of the Orders of Asiana. And without the Orders, who would uphold the law? Who would keep the peace? Above all, who would remember the past?

From Ishandi's questions and the girl's broken answers, Kyra gathered what had happened. Ikana had been shot; she had managed to make her way back to the base of the temple, and there she had breathed her last, bleeding out her life-force onto the stone steps.

Kyra stood. A part of her railed against what she was about to do. *Let them grieve*, it said. *Have you no shame?* But another part knew this was exactly the right time to speak.

"Elders of Valavan," she said, using the barest hint of the Inner Speech to get their attention. It didn't work. "ELDERS OF VALAVAN," she repeated, stronger now, and they turned to her, faces blank with shock.

"Elder Ikana will be avenged," she continued in a normal voice, holding their gazes with her own. "Every one of the outlaws will die, as Faran Lashail has decreed. This I swear as the Mahimata of Kali and a disciple of the Goddess. But why should we risk the lives of more Markswomen? Let the wyr-wolves help us. They are not evil beasts to be hunted. They are intelligent, self-aware beings. Indeed, they are half-human. I know this because I have spoken with them. Two moons ago I issued an edict to ban the killing of wyr-wolves in the Ferghana Valley. In return, they have sworn to help me fight my enemies."

Faran Lashail found her voice. "How did you manage to speak with them? And what do you mean, they are half-human?"

Kyra hesitated. She could not tell them about *Anant-kal*. They would not understand her, and what they could not understand, they would not believe.

"Trust me," she said at last. "I speak to them in dreams, and they answer. In my dreams, they appear as men. If you will but give me one night, I will ask them to help us defeat the killers of Elder Ikana."

"Have we come this low, that we should seek the help of animals?" said one of the elders. "I am not afraid of the outlaws or their guns."

"It is not a question of fear, Elder, but logic," said Kyra, with as much sincerity as she could muster. "It is time to change if we wish to survive. The wyr-wolves will not do much harm in the Deccan, beyond making off with a goat or two, if you enter into an agreement with them. But those who carry kalashiks are beyond reason, beyond redemption. How many innocent villagers have they killed already? Dozens? Hundreds?"

There was an uneasy pause. Kyra held her breath, hoping against hope they would come around.

"Do it," said Faran at last. "Speak to your wyr-wolves tonight. Tomorrow night, we will move against the outlaws."

Kyra bowed, filled with jubilation. "Thank you for the trust you have shown me. I will not let you down."

Faran nodded. "Derla will take you to a chamber where you can rest and meditate. This evening, you will join us in bidding farewell to Ikana."

They filed out in somber silence. Derla led Kyra up a flight of stairs and down several turns of a corridor, stopping at last in front of a carved wooden door.

"We hope you find this room comfortable," she said. "We do not often have guests." She pushed open the door to reveal a small, neat room with a large window that let in the afternoon sunlight. A narrow bed with a plain white sheet stood beneath the window. Off to one side was a washbasin, and on the other was a table with a pitcher of water and a plate of what looked like rice, lentils, and potatoes. Kyra's mouth watered. She had forgotten how hungry she was. The frugal breakfast she'd had with Rustan seemed long ago and far away.

"Please eat and rest," said Derla. "I will send someone to escort you when it is time for the last rites."

Kyra thanked her, relieved. There was no way she could navigate the labyrinthine temple on her own. It must take novices several months to learn how to get around unaided. Maybe that was the first test of a Valavian novice—although, come to think of it, Kyra hadn't seen any novices so far. Perhaps they dwelled in a different part of the vast temple complex.

When Derla had departed, Kyra took off her cloak and washed herself at the basin as best she could. It would have been nice to be able to change into a clean robe that wasn't torn, but that was a luxury she didn't have.

She should contact Menadin as soon as possible, but she didn't feel up to it, not right now, and definitely not on an empty stomach. She dragged the table to the bed and fell to, eating the food with relish even though it was a tad spicier than Tarshana's cooking.

After eating and drinking her fill, she lay down to rest. But instead of sleep, her thoughts went immediately to Rustan. Her stomach knotted as she remembered how she had left him unmoving on the stone floor. She hoped he had risen by now and recovered from the ordeal she had put him through.

Would he ever recover, though? She had betrayed his trust in the most personal of ways. Adrenaline had carried her through the past few hours so that she hadn't dwelled too much on it, but now the full horror of her actions sank in. She knew what it felt like to be under Compulsion. Shurik had misused his powers in the Mental Arts to try to force her to run away with him, to leave her blade and her goal of dueling Tamsyn behind.

Rustan had also been without the protection of his katari in the monastery. He must have felt as helpless, angry, and stunned as she had been when Shurik broke the law, broke the faith with her.

She had known precisely what it felt like, and yet she had done the same to Rustan, Rustan who had loved her.

The tears came in earnest then. *I'm sorry*, she thought, as if he could hear her. *If there's any way to make it up to you, I will.*

But there wasn't, not for something like this, no matter how many penances she gave herself. All she could do was plow ahead and hope the kalishium was worth the crime she had committed. Rustan might never heal from the hurt she had inflicted on him, and that would be her burden to bear.

But on the matter of wyr-wolves, he would approve of what she was trying to do. Of that she was certain. The Order of Khur already believed them to be half-human. It was but one step further to believe that they had once been people and the Ones had made them as they were.

Perhaps he would be a little less angry if she explained she needed to give the wyr-wolves a piece of kalishium to make them remember their history. And perhaps one day, when this was all over, she'd find a way to atone and regain a piece of his trust. Such a beautiful, precious thing, trust, and how easily she had shattered it. The look in his eyes as she had walked away, leaving him bound—but here Kyra found she could not continue, could not bear to remember any more. She closed her eyes and counted her breaths, emptying her mind until her skin cooled and her thoughts drifted away.

The next thing she knew, it was evening, and someone was knocking at the door. She leaped up, guilty at having fallen asleep. Outside, the sun was about to set; the last dying rays of light slanted through the window, turning the room a dusky gold. Kyra pulled on her robe and smoothed her hair, then opened the door to find no fewer than five Valavian Markswomen. Under this stately escort, Kyra climbed up to the higher levels of the temple.

"Where are the last rites held?" she asked.

"On the ninth level, at the very top," replied one of the Markswomen.

Kyra couldn't help thinking this was rather inconvenient; they would have had to carry Ikana's body up several hundred steep steps to get to the top. And what did they do with the body up there? Burning was out of the question; the risk of fire spreading to the temple rooms was too great. Perhaps they had a special tomb on the top level. She couldn't remember learning about the last rites of the Valavians in Navroz Lan's class—but then, she had often not paid much attention in History.

She soon found out what the Valavians did—and wished she hadn't. When they pushed through the trapdoor to the circular rooftop—Kyra huffing and puffing and the Valavians not even out of breath—she saw that Ikana's body had been placed on top of a flat slab of stone. But the body was no longer whole. It had been hacked to pieces. Kyra's stomach lurched; she averted her eyes from the horrifying sight, but it was not a thing that could be unseen. She swallowed and took her place in the circle around Ikana.

Faran, dressed in mourning white, held a stick of incense in her hand. It gave off a sweet odor that wafted in the breeze. She began to chant in a language Kyra could not understand. It was not the speech she had heard in the Deccan Hub but something older and more melodic. The incense stick was passed from hand to hand as, one by one, the Valavians prayed over Ikana's remains.

And that was it. At a nod from Faran, the Markswomen lined

up to descend through the trapdoor. Kyra contrived to place herself beside Derla and whispered, "What will happen now?"

Derla was unable to conceal her surprise at Kyra's ignorance. "The vultures will eat the flesh," she whispered back. "That is why the body has been disassembled. When only the bones are left, we will ground them with flour and offer them to the crows that patiently wait for the vultures to leave."

Kyra suppressed a shudder. But truly, what did it matter what you did with a body? The spirit had gone, leaving an empty house behind. Bury it or burn it or feed it to the birds—it was all one to the departed soul.

Mulling over this, she found her way back to her chamber with Derla's assistance. She refused the invitation to join them for the evening meal. She had eaten enough; any more and she may not be able to detach from her physical self and enter *Anant-kal*. As it was, she found it difficult to sink into the second-level meditative trance. It was even harder to find the bridge to *Anant-kal*. She wandered in the fog of the trance, willing her blade to light the way.

But her blade seemed uncertain and subdued. She bent her mind to it and imagined the door that would take her to the Shining City. At long last, it complied. She rushed through the rectangular opening of light before it could fade and found herself in the familiar landscape of *Anant-kal*: the grassy cliff, the cobweb bridge curving over the gloomy chasm to the other side, the tall towers, the white domes.

But something was wrong with the once-beautiful city. As Kyra crossed the bridge, taking care not to look down, it seemed to her as if the buildings faded in and out of view, too quickly for her mind to process. From the corner of her eye, they appeared to shimmer, winking in and out of existence.

When she looked straight at something, it just hurt, as if she was trying to look at the sun.

It made her head spin, and after a while she gave up trying to observe the shifting landscape. She made her way down the road to one of the walled gardens. Even the flowers and fountains appeared fuzzy at the edges. She sat against a wall that seemed solid enough and hoped Menadin would be along soon. He would be able to tell her what was wrong with *Anant-kal* . . . although she suspected she knew the answer.

When Menadin finally appeared, she felt a rush of relief. He wasn't faded at the edges like everything else. But he'd gone thinner, and there was a red scar on his neck that hadn't been there before.

"What happened?" she blurted out.

"What do you mean? Oh, this little scratch." He gave a feral grin. "Why, Kyra Veer, one would almost think you were concerned about my well-being."

Kyra crossed her arms. "Of course I am concerned. You are my ally in the fight against the outlaws of Asiana."

"Oh, is that all?" he said, mocking her. "And here I was thinking you had finally succumbed to my many charms." He held up a massive, hairy hand, forestalling her. "It's nothing to worry about," he said. "Just putting a cub in his place. As the leader of the Vulon pack, I do get challenged from time to time. Especially now that I have forbidden my pack from going near humans and their herds. My people are hungry, and game is scarce."

"I don't think we would begrudge you a sheep or two," said Kyra, choosing her words with care. "Just don't hurt any humans."

"Humans often protect their herds with their lives. They try to fight us with their puny weapons, even though they know how pointless it is." He shook his shaggy head. "We will try to stay out of sight."

"I will instruct the clans to offer compensation to those who lose their livestock to wyr-wolves," said Kyra. "That should reduce the potential for conflict." She waved a hand around them. "But what is happening here? The city looks like it's fading."

"It is," said Menadin. "Remember what I told you about our two worlds being connected? Asiana stands on the brink of chaos. If the Orders fall, Wyr-mandil will cease to exist."

"Help me, then." Kyra leaned forward. "The first battle will be fought tomorrow night near the Temple of Valavan." She recounted what had happened in the Deccan, how Kai Tau had split his forces and surrounded the temple. "There are at least three, perhaps four kalashiks with them," she said. "We have a chance of taking on all four or five hundred of the soldiers— but not if their kalashiks warn them of our presence. The dark weapons would ignore you."

Menadin stroked his chin. "The kalashiks would ignore us at first. But the instant we attack, we are as good as dead. My people hate and fear the death-sticks. Far more than your kataris."

"Of course," said Kyra. "There is no comparison. The kalashiks are deformed, evil of intent. Do I not know this? They have no place in Asiana."

"Then get rid of them," said Menadin.

"How?" asked Kyra. "They cannot be cut, burned, buried, or drowned."

"You are the Mahimata of Kali," said Menadin, frowning. "If you truly wish it, you will find a way. A door, perhaps, that waits for you to open it. Swear to me in the name of your clan that you will at least try."

The breath left Kyra's body. *A door that waits for you to open it.* She knew such a door. It had haunted her dreams since childhood. Its image was carved on the last pillar in the hall where Shirin Mam had taught her about words of power. The last time Kyra had seen it, the door was slightly open. She knew, without a doubt, that if she returned to the hall and that pillar, the door would appear to have opened wider still. The time to use it was drawing near.

"What's the matter?" growled Menadin, not understanding the emotions rippling through her. "Do you or do you not swear?"

"I swear it," she whispered. "I will do all in my power to rid Asiana of the dark weapons, even if it brings my own death closer."

Menadin rubbed his hands. "Good. Then we shall help you, even though you have not yet brought us the promised kalishium."

"I *have* procured the kalishium," she said. "But I must take it to the katari mistress of Khur to forge into shields. I will ask her to leave a small piece for me, and I will bring it back to you."

"Then you have done well indeed," said Menadin. "My people will be pleased. It will be something for me to barter with, when I ask the Deccan pack to risk their lives for you."

"What?" She was dismayed. "Then you won't be there?"

"I run in the Ferghana Valley," he reminded her. "Many days' travel from the Temple of Valavan, even at our speed."

"I could use the Hub to bring you here," she said, without pausing to think.

They both stared at each other, for what Kyra had suggested was so radical, even Menadin was rendered speechless.

CHAPTER 26

THE LAND OF
THE LIVING

A strong, musky odor, like that of a wolf, stole across the room, jerking Rustan out of the first-level meditative trance.

Two days had passed—perhaps three—since Kyra had left, and her bonds no longer held him. Yet he had not pursued her. He had roamed the caves behind the monastery, feeling his way in the dark, not caring if he got lost and could not find his way back. All of his life thus far had felt like that: a blind movement in the dark toward death and oblivion.

But always his feet took him back to the cavern with the kalishium images; always the light of the Seeing Stone banished the worst of his bitter thoughts, leaving him lighter, stronger, until at last he turned his back on the caves and sat on the dusty floor of the main room to meditate.

The bright rays of the morning sun angled across the room, trapping dust motes in a ghostly dance. Rustan could not remember having opened the door of the monastery. And there was that smell, alien yet familiar. He stood, wary, reaching for his mother's blade.

A huge, gray-furred beast with a long snout and pointed, black-tipped ears materialized at the doorway. *A wyr-wolf.* Twice as large as an ordinary wolf and far more dangerous. Rustan swallowed and gripped his blade. The wyr-wolf prowled into the monastery, swishing its bushy tail, regarding him with light yellow eyes with what could have been curiosity. Or hunger. *Do they eat people?* Rustan couldn't recall having heard anything to the contrary. Not that he'd heard much; the Order of Khur, despite its ancient reverence for wyr-wolves, hadn't had any actual encounters with them, living as it did in the Empty Place.

As if it had read his mind, the wyr-wolf dropped to its haunches. Sitting, it was no less powerful, but it *was* less threatening—maybe it wasn't planning on eating him after all. It raised a massive paw and began to lick it with a long, forked tongue.

Rustan sheathed his mother's blade and knelt, forcing his breathing to slow. The wyr-wolf wasn't here to attack him. Its purpose was different, and if he was patient and did not succumb to fear, he might discover it.

A small brown wren flew down from the open door of the monastery to the floor, distracting Rustan. It scratched the floor, searching, perhaps, for insects. *Fly away, little one, before you are gobbled up.* But the bird, with a complete disregard for its safety, hopped closer to the wyr-wolf, and then right *through* it.

Rustan blinked and memory returned, sharp with clarity. He had seen this apparition before in the death hut of the Ersanis, a clan of cultivators and carpet weavers. The villagers had told him it was Varka, their ancestral spirit, and they had claimed to be descended from wyr-wolves. Seeing the spirit had saved both Rustan and Samant, the Master of Meditation, from the wrath of the villagers. They had told him it was exceedingly lucky to be able to glimpse the spirit. He hadn't thought much about it at the time, grateful just to be able to make his escape with the elder without having to resort to killing anyone.

Now here was the ghostly wyr-wolf once again, quite far from its ancestral grounds.

"Varka?" whispered Rustan. The wyr-wolf stopped licking its paw and yawned, revealing two rows of hideous fangs. Fangs that could tear Rustan's limbs off.

But the wyr-wolf didn't appear to be very interested in him, for all that it had manifested in front of his eyes. It rose, shook its massive head, and turned to leave.

"Wait," called Rustan, scrambling to his feet.

Varka stopped at the door. He turned his head and regarded Rustan with that same expression of curiosity.

"Aren't you going to . . . ?" Rustan's voice caught. "Aren't you going to tell me anything before you leave?"

You are not your father or your mother.

Rustan took a deep breath. "What do you mean?" he asked.

Return to the land of the living.

And then he vanished.

Rustan exhaled, staring at the spot where Varka had disappeared, as if he could will him back. He went to the door and studied the ground, although he knew it was pointless. No paw prints embellished the muddy path that led down from the monastery. No tuft of fur, no rattle of stones, no echo of that voice.

The wind blew soft against Rustan's face, birds called in the trees, and he closed his eyes. He felt hollow inside, as if he teetered at the edge of an abyss or a revelation, he didn't know which. There was nothing to anchor himself to. The Sahirus were gone. He had failed to rescue Ishtul. The Order of Khur felt far away. And Kyra . . .

Kyra had tricked and betrayed him.

It was this, somehow, that hurt the most. He had found her and lost her, found her again, only to lose her yet again in the most devastating way. He understood why she had done it, but understanding did not make it any easier to bear. It did not lessen the hurt. And it did not excuse what she had done.

If you love me, fight by my side.

Ironic, that she should talk of love after having used Compulsion to bind him.

No, Kyra, if you love me, then free my bonds and return the image.

That's what he would have said, if he had been capable of speaking.

He would fight the menace that loomed over Asiana because it was his duty to do so—personal feelings did not enter into it, although he did still love Kyra, even after what she had done to him. Love was not something that could be granted or withheld based on reason. But his love now had a painful edge to it, like a hook in his chest that made it hard to breathe.

It was time to leave the monastery. His penance was over, and he had done what he could for the Sahirus. What had Varka said?

Return to the land of the living.

Rustan went back inside and packed his knapsack. He gathered his things, forced himself to eat the remaining gruel, and filled his waterskin from the stream outside. All the while, his heart ached, as if he were going into exile rather than returning from it.

CHAPTER 27

RETURN TO FERGHANA

It was much harder than Kyra had anticipated to use the Ferghana and Deccan Hubs to Transport Menadin and eleven of his pack members to the Temple of Valavan. The first hurdle was Faran Lashail's council of elders. They claimed the temple was a sacred place and the presence of wyr-wolves would pollute it eternally.

"You use wyr-wolf blood in your ceremonies," Kyra pointed out. "You have wyr-wolf pelts in your halls. Why is a dead wyr-wolf more acceptable than a living one?"

"That is different," one of the elders argued. "We offer them as *sacrifice*."

"As you have agreed to ban the killing of wyr-wolves, that practice will have to cease," Kyra returned. "And I do think it would be better for you to remove all pelts from the Hall of Reflection, because that is where the wyr-wolves will pass. I will escort them out of the temple at once. I'm quite sure they will not wish to linger here. They are creatures of the forest and the mountains."

"Then that is where they should remain," muttered another Markswoman.

"They come to help us," said Kyra for the hundredth time. "They will be risking their lives."

In the end, Faran Lashail agreed, on the condition that Kyra accompany the wyr-wolves at all times and act as translator. She seemed to think Kyra could communicate with them freely, and Kyra did not disabuse her of that belief. Things were difficult enough without making them more so.

"And you should talk to your elders," Faran added. "Alert them to the danger we are in and your plan to seek the wyr-wolves' help. They may have advice for you."

Faran was right. Kyra had to let her elders know what had transpired in Kunlun Shan and the threat the Temple of Valavan was facing. Besides, the kalishium image would be safer in the caves of Kali. Rustan would follow her as soon as he could, and if he found it in the Transport Chamber, he would almost certainly return it to the monastery.

Derla accompanied Kyra down to the Deccan Hub and bade her farewell. Kyra retrieved the kalishium image from the Kunlun Transport Chamber, relieved to see that it was still there, still intact. The lack of a direct door between the Deccan and the Ferghana Hubs meant not only that she would have to take two doors to get home, but that her job of herding the wyr-wolves to the temple would be twice as hard.

Herding. As if they were sheep. She remembered Menadin's fangs and pressed her lips together. She had best not make the mistake of thinking them tame or altruistic. The wyr-wolves had goals of their own, and in this case, their goals aligned with hers—to rid Asiana of its dark weapons and stabilize Wyr-mandil. Even then, Menadin had put a price on their aid.

Kyra took the door to the connecting Hub, and then the second one to the Ferghana. As she sat down to wait in the Transport Chamber, she realized with a start that Transport no longer terrified her. The mind that was behind the Hubs had thrown her into a warring past and a dead future. It had shown her visions and made her lose time. But it hadn't hurt her, not yet. And one day, a door would open into darkness that would take her away from everything she knew and loved.

But that day was not here, not now. When the room stopped spinning, Kyra rose and exited the door with a sense of inner calm that she knew would have made Shirin Mam proud. She emerged from the Hub and breathed the familiar air of the sun-drenched Ferghana Valley, gladness stealing into her heart. The snow had melted, and spring would soon fill the green valley with wildflowers. If not for the burden on her back, it would have been a perfect homecoming.

Elena was the first to sense her return. Her friend came bounding up the hill to meet her with very un-Elena-like excitement, her plaits flying behind her, as she trailed a scent of sacred basil and mint. She must have been working with her beloved herbs.

They embraced, Elena half laughing, half crying, and Kyra felt the familiar tug of guilt in her heart. She had left those who loved her behind, and she would have to leave them again soon.

To her surprise, Akassa came running to meet her as well and gave her a fierce hug that warmed her heart. She held the girl out at arm's length and smiled. "Did you know I was back too?" she asked.

"Elena knew you were back," said Akassa, "and I always

know what Elena is thinking." A shared look of affection passed between the two girls—a look that excluded Kyra. But the twinge Kyra felt was not of jealousy, but of wonderment. And relief too, that Elena had someone to rely on and comfort her. That they had each other.

As they walked down the hill, Kyra gave the two girls a condensed version of what had transpired, leaving Rustan out. Their eyes widened as Kyra described the secret hoard of kalishium she had discovered and the image she had borrowed—*stolen*—from the cave. But when she came to the part about using wyr-wolves to help the Order of Valavan, Elena shook her head.

"The elders won't like it," she said flatly. "They'll have visions of you being torn limb from limb. Kyra, can you actually *control* the wyr-wolves?"

No, of course not. The very idea was absurd. Before Kyra could speak, though, they had arrived at the entrance to the caves of Kali, where the elders stood waiting for her, a mix of emotions emanating from them: joy and relief tempered with wariness, as if they sensed that she intended to implement a dangerous and unorthodox plan.

Kyra set down the rug-wrapped image and straightened her shoulders. "I have succeeded in obtaining the kalishium, Elders," she announced.

"And in not dying," said Navroz, a touch acerbically, but the corners of her mouth twitched.

"My codes worked," said Felda, unable to conceal her triumph. "You didn't have any trouble with the door, did you?"

"Not exactly," Kyra hedged. She was loath to tell them what the Kunlun door had shown her, but she had to let them know how dangerous doors that had shifted could still be, Felda's codes notwithstanding.

A look of alarm crossed the mathematician's face. "What happened?" she demanded. "Tell me quickly!"

"What Kyra should do *first* is take a bath," interjected Mumuksu. "What she should do *second* is eat a meal in the communal kitchen, so everyone can greet her. Then we will talk."

Felda grumbled a bit, and Kyra shot Mumuksu a grateful look. Elena called the novices, and together they lugged the kalishium into the central cavern of Kali, with strict injunctions not to unwrap the image.

It was lovely to take a proper bath in the small rock-filled pool not far from the caves. The cherry trees that surrounded it would soon be in full bloom, and Kyra was reminded of all the times she had played here with Elena and Nineth when they were younger, splashing water on each other and diving down to the sandy, weed-covered bottom.

She felt a wave of shame when she remembered how she had thrown Nineth's blade into the funerary chamber lake. It was not something she could ever forget, but in the chaos of all that had happened since she took the door to Kunlun Shan, she had pushed the memory to one side. If she came out of the battle of Valavan intact, she would find a way to retrieve the katari and contact her friend. She would beg her forgiveness. With Tamsyn's blade gone, she could see even more clearly how it had held her in its thrall. Her actions in the funerary chamber felt both foolish and inexplicable.

For a few precious moments, she allowed herself to relax to the sound of water tumbling down the rock face behind her and the warmth of the sun on her face, contrasting with the coolness of the water. Then, reluctantly, she rose and dried herself and headed back into the caves.

Tarshana had prepared a delicious meal of vegetable pilaf and creamy yoghurt. Kyra sat cross-legged on the kilim-covered kitchen floor and ate with relish. Akassa insisted on serving her; she grinned and winked at Kyra as she bent to put the plate in front of her. Kyra nodded and smiled when anyone else in the kitchen caught her eye. Which, admittedly, was not very often.

"What's wrong with them all?" she muttered to Elena, who was seated next to her. "Why aren't they looking at me?"

"Because you're the Mahimata, you ninny," Elena whispered back, and Kyra burst into laughter. It was almost like old times. Not quite, of course. Nineth was missing.

At least she still had Elena. And Akassa, and Tonar, and Sandi, and Noor, and all the rest. How few they were, how tight they would have to hold on to each other, their way of life. This was her world, worth living for and worth dying for.

After the meal, Kyra went to Shirin Mam's cell—she still couldn't think of it as *hers*—where the elders awaited her. They sat on the rug, rapt, as she told them what had happened—once again, she omitted mention of Rustan. Surely it was not relevant, she told herself. She had met Rustan through happenstance, nothing more. But she remembered how the Hub had brought them together and felt a stab of unease. She couldn't keep him out of the story indefinitely, for she would also have to confess her crime of using Compulsion on him sooner or later.

Felda was dismayed at what Kyra had to say about the door to Kunlun Shan. "It took you *where*?" she said, stunned. "It showed you *what*?"

Kyra began to repeat herself, but Felda held up a hand. "Don't tell me," she said grimly. "I need to go back and check my formulae."

Navroz and Mumuksu shared a quick, worried glance, and

Kyra suppressed her mirth. It was quite obvious what they thought Felda should do with her precious formulae. But they wouldn't dare say it aloud. The Order of Kali had always revered its mathematicians, and Felda was one of the most gifted they had ever had.

Chintil cleared her throat. "You were telling us about the troubles facing the Order of Valavan," she said.

Kyra returned to her narrative, filling them in on the siege of Valavan, the attack on their people, and the death of a Markswoman. "Which is how," she concluded, "they agreed to let me ask the wyr-wolves for help."

"Ask the wyr-wolves for help?" repeated Mumuksu in disbelief. "Kyra, it is one thing to ban the killing of wyr-wolves in our jurisdiction. It is quite another to seek them out. Suppose they turn on you?"

"They will not," said Kyra, with more confidence than she felt. "And the Valavians have agreed already."

"Why can you not let the Valavians deal with the outlaws?" said Navroz. "Seventy-five of them and yet you think they need *you*?"

"You have a greater mission," said Felda. "You need kalishium shields so we can confront Kai Tau himself. Now that you have procured the kalishium, you should go to Astinsai without further delay."

"Suppose you are injured?" demanded Chintil. "You cannot trust the wyr-wolves. How do you communicate with them, anyway?"

Kyra heard them out with patience. She reminded herself that she had not told them everything she knew about wyr-wolves; it was natural for them to react like this. At last she held a hand up. "I hear your concerns. But I must mention one of my own. You did not tell me the Valavians have hidden death-sticks in their temple," she said.

All the elders fell silent. At last Navroz spoke. "The Valavians have guarded them for years, ever since the slaughter of your clan. They rounded up all the death-sticks they could find and buried them with whatever little kalishium they could spare. The kalishium deadens the evil voices of the guns, at least to some extent. That is all I know."

"It is too dangerous," said Kyra softly. "You know this, Eldest. The arrival of Kai Tau's force there is no coincidence."

"What is the alternative?" asked Navroz. "They are as safe as they can possibly be in Asiana."

"Then maybe we need to take them *out* of Asiana," said Kyra, then wished she hadn't when she saw their expressions. "But stopping Kai Tau must be our priority," she continued. "I need to contact the wyr-wolves. I will be escorting them to the temple tonight."

Mumuksu frowned. "If it is not too much to ask, you should give the entire Order a class on wyr-wolves. It appears you know much more than any of us, and it is only right that you communicate that knowledge before going into battle."

Although Kyra chaffed at the delay, she knew the truth of Mumuksu's words and acquiesced.

The entire Order came together for her class, seated beneath the mulberry tree, gazing at her with rapt expressions. The slanting rays of the afternoon sun fell on the familiar faces, young and old. The elders stayed at the very back, their faces serene, as if the Order did not stand at the very edge of extinction. The four novices sat right in front, all agog, as if a combined class taught by their Mahimata was the very pinnacle of excitement. Nearby were the two apprentices, Elena and Akassa, who both loved her—and each other—in their different ways, although she did not deserve it. Everyone looking to her for guidance, for knowledge.

How could she bear to leave them?

Kyra pushed the thought away. *One day at a time. One lesson at a time.*

How to tell them about the wyr-wolves? Shirin Mam had warned her to keep *Anant-kal* secret. But now that some time had passed, Kyra wondered if Shirin Mam's insistence may have been so that Tamsyn did not get wind of it. The wily Mistress of Mental Arts would have done her utmost to access *Anant-kal* and twist it to her own ends, consequences be damned.

But Tamsyn was dead now, and no matter what Shirin Mam had intended, Kyra owed her Order an explanation. No more than one or two in every generation showed the ability to enter *Anant-kal*. Suppose such a one ever came to the Order of Kali as a novice? It would be far better for the elders to know in advance what such a gift could do.

So she began, aware that she was repeating Shirin Mam's words from long ago. "When we bond with our blades at the end of the coming-of-age trial, we come into contact with the second part of our soul. The bond with our blades is like a bridge. Cross the bridge and you enter another world. *Anant-kal*: the world beyond time. The world as perceived by our kalishium blades."

She talked on, and they listened, spellbound. No one interrupted her. When she grew hoarse, after an hour or two, a novice ran to fetch her tea. She told them how Shirin Mam had taught her to enter *Anant-kal* before her death. How she had taught Kyra words of power by carving memory images into pillars in a vast marble hall. And then how Kyra had used a word of power to defeat Tamsyn in the Hall of Sikandra. When she came to the part about how wyr-wolves walked as humans in the world beyond time, there were cries of amazement. Even the elders looked stunned. Ria Farad was the most distressed, as well she might be, given that she was their most lethal hunter.

At last, when the sun was about to set, Kyra stopped. "I know you will have questions," she concluded. "I will do my best to answer—but not today." Her throat felt raw and so did her heart. Talking about Shirin Mam had brought back the grief of her loss, sharp as ever.

It was a subdued group that made its way to the communal kitchen for the evening meal. And so the day ended, unusual in its near-normalcy for Kyra, and all the more precious because of it.

After they had eaten, she bid farewell to the Order before setting off for the Ferghana Hub, where she had asked Menadin to meet her. She managed to dissuade the elders from coming with her—even Chintil, who was quite determined to join the fight. "Please, Elder," she said, "the wyr-wolves may not accompany me if there is anyone else about."

She did not know the truth of this, but it sounded plausible, and Chintil backed off. Kyra could not afford to risk any of her Markswomen—especially on the chance that this mission failed. They would be needed in the fight against Kai Tau.

So she went alone up the hill to the Hub, the wind cold in her hair, the stars bright in the sky, and her blade glowing at her side.

CHAPTER 28

AN UNEXPECTED ALLY

The moon slipped into the sky and the Ferghana Hub shone silver against the shadows of the night. Kyra's skin prickled as long, dark shapes flowed up the hill toward her. Until this moment, she had not given a thought to how it would feel to be surrounded by the beasts in their fearsome wolf shape. She had grown so used to talking with Menadin in *Anant-kal*, she had quite forgotten what he was like in the real world. In *her* world.

A gigantic wyr-wolf emerged from the shadows and ambled toward her. Kyra fought down her fear. It was only Menadin; she recognized him, with his thick gray mane and the white streak on his ridged forehead. But it was hard to remember, hard to suppress her own ingrained terror of the deadly form he inhabited.

Menadin stopped in front of her and flicked his ears. *What are you waiting for?* he seemed to be saying. *Hurry up and open the door.*

Kyra swallowed and bowed. "Thank you all for coming," she said. "We must take two doors to reach the Temple of Valavan. We will exit the temple through a hall lined with mirrors. Please follow me out without looking at the mirrors; they can be dangerous. I will lead you to within five hundred feet of the outlaws and then stop. You must choose two or three of your strongest to attack the men with kalashiks. Give me a signal of some sort—a howl, maybe—and we will launch our own attack. We will encircle the outlaws, so they cannot escape."

She paused. More of the wyr-wolves had slunk up while she was talking. They surrounded her and Menadin in a tight circle, eyes glowing yellow fire. Eyes you could fall into, if you were not careful. Kyra tore her gaze away from them and reached for the Hub door with shaking hands. Time to go. She had gambled everything on this. *Goddess, I hope I'm doing the right thing.* She inserted the tip of her katari into the slot and it swung open. Just like always.

But there was no precedence for the company that followed her in. The dozen wyr-wolves crowded into the Transport corridor, their rank smell overpowering in the confined space. When the last wyr-wolf had squeezed in, the door swung shut. She was alone with them in the dark, huge furry bodies pushing against her, radiating heat, their luminous eyes the only visible part of them.

I will not scream. I will not faint. Kyra took a deep breath and almost gagged at the animal reek.

"Stand . . . stand back, please," she said, hating the tremor in her voice. "I need space around the Transport door."

The eyes drew back a smidgeon—not enough for her to feel anywhere near comfortable, but enough for her to take another breath and fumble for the slot on the Transport door.

She tapped in the code and the door opened onto the familiar blue-lit space of a Transport Chamber. Kyra sat on one of the seats, wondering how the wyr-wolves would take to Transport. Surely not even their ancestors had traveled in such a style. Would they be nervous?

But the wyr-wolves spread out on the seats and the floor as if they'd been Transporting all their lives. Even when the chamber began to spin, they did no more than flick an ear or twitch a bushy tail. A couple of them even yawned, displaying their hideous fangs and forked tongues.

Menadin rose from the center of the chamber and padded toward her. To her astonishment, he sprawled on her feet. She flinched slightly at his weight, his nearness. He turned his head and regarded her, tongue lolling out lazily, as if enjoying her discomfiture.

Well, two can play the game. Before she could think about what she was doing, Kyra reached out a hand and touched Menadin's ridged forehead. Menadin froze, the expression of surprise on his lupine face almost comical. Kyra grinned and pushed her hand deep into the thick gray fur of Menadin's back. She wasn't afraid of him now. She'd *never* be afraid of him again.

Menadin jerked his head back and snapped his jaws, lightning fast. He trapped her arm in the cage of his teeth. *One bite and I can take your arm off.*

"Not afraid of you," said Kyra through gritted teeth, and although every part of her screamed out to struggle, to fight, what she did instead was to use her other hand to stroke the side of his massive head. She could sense the others watching, wariness stealing over the pack. Would Menadin lunge at her and try to subdue her the way he would an insolent pup?

The chamber stopped spinning and the door swung open.

Menadin released her and stood; he was as tall as she was while seated. Kyra made to rise, but he blocked her with a low growl that vibrated through the chamber.

"Oh, all right," she said, irritated, wiping her arm against her robe. "I will not touch you again without your permission."

Menadin gave a small whuff and allowed her to get up. She led the wyr-wolves out into the corridor and on to the next door. The second half of their journey was quiet and uneventful. Kyra took care to keep her hands and feet to herself, and Menadin left her alone. She couldn't help but wonder, though, what had made him sprawl across her feet like that. There had been nothing doglike about the gesture, although that was how it may have appeared to a stranger. It had been more as if he was claiming her as his in front of the other wyr-wolves.

Well, next time he attempted something like that, she'd pet him and call him a good boy. That would probably be enough for the beta male of the pack to challenge him.

When they arrived at the Hub of Valavan, Kyra thought it best to give the wyr-wolves some warning of what they might expect. She stood and cleared her throat. They listened to her with grave regard.

"The Valavians have agreed to stop hunting wyr-wolves," she told them. "But they have always regarded you as enemies—as I did, before I met your leader in Wyr-mandil and spoke with him. It will take time to change how they feel and think. You will sense their fear and hatred. I ask you to forgive them."

They were, at least, expected. Two Valavians stood in the corridor outside, on either side of the door. The wyr-wolves flowed out, ignoring their presence. Kyra noticed how the Markswomen's hands tightened over their blades, how the muscles in their faces went rigid. But they were too well-trained to show any other outward sign of the panic they must surely be feeling.

Derla Siyal waited at the main door of the Hub, her face a mask. "Welcome to the Temple of Valavan," she said, and Kyra was glad of the strength and firmness of her voice. It could not have been easy, saying what she did without a tremor as a dozen deadly beasts trotted up to her.

"Thank you," said Kyra. "We will leave the temple through the Hall of Reflection. Is Faran Lashail there? I want to speak to her."

Derla frowned. "Yes, Faran awaits you in the hall. And so does someone else."

She turned before Kyra could ask who it was, leading them down the underground passage and up the stone steps to the hall. Kyra slung her boots around her neck; she couldn't wear them in the temple, but she would need them outside.

The wyr-wolves followed Kyra up the steps, so close they were practically breathing down her neck. "Back off a little," she hissed. "And remember what I said: do not look at the mirrors."

They emerged into the vast, domed space of the Hall of Reflection. The wyr-wolves trotted past her, their claws clicking on the marble floor. The mirrors on the walls reflected their monstrous forms, and it seemed as if the Temple of Valavan had been overrun by the beasts and would crumble beneath their weight.

But what snared Kyra's gaze was the man who stood in the middle of the hall next to Faran Lashail, his body held in relaxed readiness, as if he belonged there as much as Faran herself did.

"Rustan," she croaked when she had found her voice. "What are you doing here?"

"Precisely what I asked," said Faran. "We do not need the help of yet another Order. But he will not leave, and I am reluctant to employ more forceful means to evict him. Perhaps he will listen to you?"

"We were in the middle of a duel, Kyra Veer," said Rustan. His voice was like a knife. "Will you not finish it?"

"The duel was . . . a draw," said Kyra, choosing her words with care. "I am deeply sorry for what I did to you. But we have more important things to focus on right now."

"Nothing is more important than trust," said Rustan. His gaze held no accusation—and no affection. "Not when there is a war to be fought. I am here. I will fight the outlaws. But first, Kyra, you will duel me with honor." And to her horror, he withdrew Shirin Mam's blade. It shone, iridescent in the bright light of the hall.

Not this. Please, not this, she thought numbly. She heard Derla's intake of breath and Faran's voice, commanding: "I want no bloodshed in my temple."

"There will be none," said Rustan. "Not by my mother's blade."

Faran and Derla looked at her. The wyr-wolves gathered around them in a loose circle, watchful.

"Not by mine either," said Kyra, striving to stay calm. She unslung her boots and put them aside. Then she dropped into a defensive stance.

"Draw your blade," said Rustan, uncompromising.

"I will not," she said.

He raised his eyebrows. "Why? Are you afraid to show me how well—or how ill—I have taught you?"

At that she did draw her blade, knowing he would be satisifed with no less.

And so it began.

It was nothing like any of their mock duels. It was nothing like the dance of Empty Hands. It would have been easier to give in, to yield before either one of them got hurt. But that would do him dishonor, and she had wronged him enough already.

They circled each other, each looking for an opening. Kyra's blade burned in her hand. She remembered how Rustan had taken her through the thirty-six known styles of katari duel and wondered which one he would start with.

Then he was upon her, and it took every scrap of her skill and training to deflect him. He slashed, and she danced away, feeling the wind of his katari on her face. She threw a backhanded punch to the side of his head, which he evaded with ease, sliding underneath her arm and pushing Shirin Mam's blade up to her throat. She gasped and flung up her own katari, blocking it, feeling the clang reverberate up her arm.

He spun, feinted, and grabbed her wrist, trying to twist her katari loose. She fought to regain control, aiming a side kick at his groin. He blocked her with his knee, and she staggered back. In that moment of imbalance, he flung Shirin Mam's katari at her, his blue eyes ablaze with deadly concentration.

The blade stopped an inch from her forehead. Right above the mark it had left there years ago, when it had branded her as an apprentice of Kali. The breath left Kyra's body. She tried to stay absolutely still. The katari was balanced on air, on his will. There was utter silence in the hall. Sweat trickled down her face. She pushed aside her fear. Rustan would not harm her. Neither would Shirin Mam's blade.

Rustan walked toward her, still that look of abstraction on his face.

"I yield," she managed to say.

He looked at her then, and something flickered in his eyes. Concern? Regret? He reached forward and grasped the hilt of the blade, and she swayed in relief.

"Well, that was impressive," said Faran drily, although there was no hiding the relief in her voice too. "I'd love for you to teach my Markswomen how you did that. Are you two quite done with each other?"

"We are," said Rustan, sheathing Shirin Mam's blade, calm as ever. "Thank you for allowing us to complete our duel."

"Are you all right?" Derla asked Kyra.

Kyra took a deep breath and stood straighter. "I'm fine," she said. "Not a scratch." And that was true. But her head spun. And her heart hurt.

Menadin gave a small whuff, as if he knew what she was feeling and was trying to buck her up.

Kyra rallied. She had brought the wyr-wolves here, and she would stay strong and focused for their sake, as well as her own. "If your honor is satisfied," she told Rustan, "we have a battle to fight tonight. Will you join us?"

"That is why I am here," said Rustan. He gave the ghost of a smile. "I follow your trail, and it takes me to the front line."

Kyra wet her lips. "But I thought—did you not need to return to your Order?"

"I do. As do you," said Rustan. "I will accompany you to Khur once this is done." He eyed the wyr-wolves, who had now gathered in a tight pack around Menadin, in front of one of the mirrors—*oh no, they were looking at the mirrors*—and added, "You have powerful friends, Kyra Veer. This will be interesting."

"Menadin," said Kyra, urgent. "Tell your people to get away from the mirrors."

"Why?" said Rustan, sounding mystified. "What's wrong with them?"

"You do not know?" asked Kyra, astonished. "Did you not look?"

He turned and craned his neck. "Yes, I did. They seem ordinary enough to me."

"He sees only himself," said Faran, a complex emotion in her voice that Kyra could not identify.

"Which is the real reason she let him stay," murmured Derla.

Another puzzle, but one that could wait. For now, she had to get the wyr-wolves away from the mirrors and out of the temple. Kyra crossed the hall to them, taking care to avoid looking Rustan's way, but feeling his gaze on her back as if it were something physical.

"Menadin," said Kyra. "You have to get away from here." She pushed her way through the pack and crouched next to him, where he sat on his haunches, gazing at the hundreds of wolf images with every appearance of raptness. "Look at me."

Menadin raised one gigantic paw and placed it on the mirror. The glass splintered, cracks spreading across the surface. Behind her, Kyra heard cries of alarm and distress, but she had no time to spare for the Valavians; in the moment of splintering, the images before her changed. It was no longer Menadin the wyr-wolf she saw, but a man. And not the wild, rough man she had met in Wyr-mandil, but a well-groomed and well-dressed one, as if he was a noble at a king's court. Golden-eyed and brown-skinned, he wore a pristine white robe and an amused smile. His long gray hair was neatly tied back in a half-bun. Kyra stumbled back in shock, and at last Menadin turned to face her. In his unfathomable eyes she saw the truth.

Menadin and his pack saw themselves as human in the

mirrors. It was their past, or their future, or some version of themselves that was as true as anything else.

"Time to go," she said, her mouth dry. "Please."

"Yes," said Faran, her voice tight with anger. "Please leave, before the cracks spread across the entire hall and I go down in history as the one who allowed the destruction of our most sacred artifact."

Menadin swung around, almost knocking Kyra over, and padded across the hall. The rest of the wolves followed him, silent. Kyra hurried to catch up with them, Rustan close behind her.

"What was that about?" he whispered, but she shook her head, unable to speak of what she had seen. He seemed to understand, for he did not press her.

A young, tense-looking Markswoman ushered them out of the hall, down a corridor, into another hall, and then at last to the great double doors that led outside. The doors opened with a tremendous groan onto a massive plinth, and the wyr-wolves spilled out into the moonlight, blending with the night. They were back in their domain. Far in the distance stretched the sacred groves that surrounded the temple. Beyond the groves, Kai Tau's men waited with their weapons.

Kyra pulled on her boots and inhaled deeply as they descended the steps from the plinth to the ground. Her heart thudded—leftover adrenaline from the duel, she decided. Not because Rustan was right next to her, so close she could have touched him. She glanced sideways at him, but his face gave nothing away. She remembered how they had kissed in the Transport corridor, and a lump came into her throat.

"The kalishium image—" she began hesitantly, but he interrupted her.

"I did not ask you about it," he said, a warning note in his voice.

"I'm sorry," she said softly. "But I—*we*—need it."

Rustan swung around and gripped her shoulders. His eyes blazed in the moonlight, but she stood before him unflinching.

"You broke the law," he said. "Or do you now think you are above it?"

"No," she said, meeting his fierce gaze. "But I will do what needs to be done. Whatever it takes to defeat Kai Tau. And you know it."

His arms dropped; his shoulders sagged. "I know," he said. "Why didn't you *talk* to me, Kyra?"

"I tried," she pointed out, "but you would not listen. I could have talked till I was blue in the face and it wouldn't have changed your mind."

He raked a hand through his hair and sighed. "Perhaps not," he admitted. "But it does not absolve you."

"You are right," she said, her heart contracting. "I will ask the elders to give me a penance, when this is over. If they refuse, I will give one to myself."

He reached forward and brushed the mark on her forehead with his fingertips. "Were you afraid?" he asked, his voice suddenly, unexpectedly tender. *When I threw that blade?*

Not once.

He bent down and touched her forehead with his lips. "You were never in danger," he murmured.

"I know," she said, her voice husky. She wanted, in that moment, to melt into his arms. Only her awareness of the wyrwolves made her draw back.

Rustan's gaze went to them. "Will you introduce me to your friends?"

"They're not exactly my *friends*," she said. The wyr-wolves sprawled at the base of the steps, waiting for them. Even at this distance, and in the dark, they could not be mistaken for anything other than what they were— dangerous, hulking beasts, neither wolf nor man, but something more terrible than either. And yet, had she not pushed her hand into the gray fur of Menadin's back? Had he not held her arm in his mouth, so carefully that he did not even break the skin?

"They are not your friends, and yet they are willing to risk their lives for you?" said Rustan. "For the Orders?"

"We pledged to stop hunting them," said Kyra. "And," she added in a smaller voice, "I agreed to give them a piece of the kalishium I took from the monastery."

"It is not yours to give," Rustan reminded her.

Kyra sighed. "Kalishium does not belong to *anyone*. Well, except the pieces that form our blades, the ones that we bond with. And that too is only temporary, until we die."

"Did you never wonder why the Ones left it behind?" asked Rustan. "That it may serve a higher purpose than what we can see and understand?"

"It's going to serve a higher purpose, all right," said Kyra. "That kalishium is going to save the lives of my Markswomen when we attack Kai Tau. Now, did you not wish to be introduced to my 'friends'?"

Rustan's mouth quirked and he followed her down the steps. She was beyond grateful he was there. Though he had bested her in front of the Valavians. Though he was still angry about how she had stolen the kalishium. There was no better warrior than Rustan; having him on her side made her feel more confident. But it also made her feel more anxious; she wouldn't be able to bear it if something happened to him tonight.

At the bottom of the steps was a stretch of tended grass and here Menadin lolled in the center of an adoring circle. One of the wyr-wolves playfully nipped his ears, and he nudged her with his muzzle. *His mate?* Kyra hoped not. She wanted to think Menadin's family was safely back home in the Ferghana Valley.

She cleared her throat. "Menadin, I present to you my friend, the Marksman Rustan of the Order of Khur."

But she had no need to speak. The wyr-wolves rose and pushed past her. She turned to find Rustan kneeling, surrounded by the massive beasts, and for a moment she was overcome with fear and horror. Suppose they hurt him?

But they only sniffed at him, uttering low whuffs. Rustan murmured to them in a respectful voice, words Kyra could not hear. One of the wyr-wolves butted his shoulder and he gave a joyful laugh, and Kyra felt a sudden stab of jealousy, which was stupid. She *needed* them to like each other, but somehow, the fact that what had been so hard for her appeared to come easily for Rustan was deeply annoying.

"Faran said we would start at midnight," she said, unable to keep the asperity from her voice. "Which is in a few minutes. Have you talked with her?"

"Of course." Rustan leaned forward and traced a rectangle on the grass. "Here is the temple, surrounded by groves of trees. Here are the two main contingents of men, to the north and south. Faran and I agreed that there are probably spies to the east and west as well. She has sent forty Markswomen, ten for each direction, to neutralize them. They used a door, emerging not too far from here. They'll double back and cut off any retreat from the rear. Twenty more Markswomen, including Faran herself, will come with us. The rest will remain at the temple."

"We will have to split up," said Kyra, although she hated the thought of it. She didn't want to be separated from Rustan, not for this. "Half of us go north, and half south."

Rustan nodded. "I will go north, and you lead the party south. Faran said there are two kalashiks with each contingent, if not more." He said this in such a matter-of-fact way, as if he didn't care at all—as if their fates were not intertwined and it was all right if one died while the other lived.

The double doors of the temple swung open, and Faran stepped out. Markswomen streamed out behind her, kataris gripped in their hands, the light of battle in their eyes.

"Markswomen!" roared Faran, stabbing her silver-lit blade toward the sky. "Kai Tau's men have killed Ikana, they have cut our sacred trees, and they dare stand at our threshold, armed with kalashiks. Will we let them defile our land?"

"Never!" came the resounding response.

"Will we let them hurt our people?"

"We will not!"

"Will we let them *live*?"

"No! Death to the intruders," bellowed the Valavians.

"Then march with me," shouted Faran. "March for the glory of Valavan!"

The blood thundered in Kyra's ears and the katari sprang into her hand.

It had begun.

CHAPTER 29

THE BATTLE
OF THE WOLVES

The sacred groves were as silent as graves. Kyra, trying to keep track of Ishandi as she darted through the trees ahead of her, could imagine they walked through a mausoleum. Perhaps it was the presence of those supreme hunters, the wyrwolves, prowling beside her. Or perhaps it was the bloodlust of the Markswomen themselves that kept the nocturnals away, but not an owl hooted, not a bulbul called.

A light wind rippled through unseen leaves and touched her cheek, bringing the scent of moonflower. Kyra practiced Sheetali, the Cooling Breath. It helped her rein in her feelings about Rustan and fix her attention on the present. She had to keep Ishandi in sight so she could lead the others. The distant canopy was too thick to let in moonlight; instead, Kyra had to rely on the glow of their blades.

Menadin had chosen to stay with her, sending six of his pack mates with Faran and Rustan in the opposite direction. Behind

Kyra were the ten Valavian Markswomen Faran had assigned to her. There were elders among them, Markswomen more skilled in combat than she was. But for this attack, Faran had ordered them to accept Kyra's lead. She was thc one who could "talk" to wyr-wolves, after all. And she *was* the Mahimata of Kali, even though it was clear some of them thought she was an upstart who had reached her current position more by accident than merit.

Well, that wasn't far from the truth—but it didn't matter. Now was the time to show the Valavians what she was capable of. Kyra's grip on her blade tightened; if it had been made of anything but kalishium, it would have drawn blood.

Ishandi turned and signaled a halt.

"No farther," she whispered. "The kalashiks will sense us."

Menadin gave a low growl, a deep vibration that lifted the hair on the back of Kyra's neck. He trotted forward and pawed the ground, as if he couldn't wait to attack the outlaws.

"Go, then," said Kyra. "We will await your signal."

Menadin leaped forward, and the pack sprang after him in a rush of powerful bodies.

"Take care and good luck," called Kyra in a low voice, but they were already gone, vanished into the night.

The seconds ticked by. Kyra waited, taut as a drawn bow-string. The Valavians looked as tense as she felt. Every minute that passed seemed longer than the last, and she was unable to stop herself imagining the worst—bullets cutting down the wyr-wolves mid-spring, blood seeping from their broken bodies . . .

Screams split the night, followed by a long, piercing howl. *The signal.*

"Go!" shouted Kyra. They ran, uncaring now of the noise

they made, feet thudding across the forest floor, snapping twigs and crackling leaves. Ahead of them came the roar of gunfire and more shrieks.

Kyra raced to keep up with Ishandi, who flew ahead of them seemingly unhindered by the branches that tore and snagged at everyone else. Kyra put in an extra burst of speed; she wanted to arrive first at the camp, so she could assess the level of danger and signal a retreat if it was unacceptably high. The pain from her old stab wound reared its ugly head, but she pushed it down.

Then they were out of the grove and in the open ground, in a version of hell straight from one of the old stories of the Great War.

Before them stretched a clearing dotted with tents and cookfires. Horses tied to posts were bucking and neighing in terror. Men shouted and passed weapons to each other, trying to organize themselves in the wake of the unexpected attack. One group huddled behind a cart-like contraption on wheels mounted with a nasty, elongated tube that put Kyra in mind of a death-stick. A catapult of some sort?

Bodies lay crumpled on the ground, with necks torn and faces gouged out; among them was the body of a wyr-wolf. Off to one side, another wyr-wolf snarled as it was surrounded by more than a dozen men with spears and swords. The remaining wyr-wolves Kyra could not see, but judging by the screams, they were spreading mayhem throughout the camp.

All this she grasped in a fraction of a second. But the kalashiks—where were the kalashiks? They had fallen silent moments before.

"The Goddess go with you," Kyra told the Markswomen, and the Valavians uttered their war cry—a bone-chilling shriek that froze the tableau before them—and fell upon the outlaws.

Kai Tau's men screamed and died as kataris found their hearts and the Inner Speech took their minds. Kyra took advantage of the chaos to check the wyr-wolf sprawled on the ground amid the humans. *Please don't let it be Menadin*, she prayed.

It wasn't. Kyra grasped its head in both hands and turned its face up. Dead eyes stared sightlessly back at her, and blood trickled through a hole in its forehead. Kyra cursed and laid down the head.

That was when she noticed the gleaming black gun beneath it.

Heart thudding, she used the blade of her katari to pry it out from beneath the wyr-wolf's corpse, taking care not to touch it with her hands. She sensed a tiny movement behind her and threw herself aside just in time to avoid the bolt that plunged into the dead wyr-wolf instead, spilling out its guts. *Goddess, that was too close.* Her blade slipped from her sweaty palm.

The man who had attacked her stood several yards away—too far for the Inner Speech, but Kyra had to try. She slowed her pulse and focused. The man fitted another bolt in his crossbow and aimed.

"You will not move," said Kyra. The man hesitated a split second, and that was all she needed. She grabbed her blade and threw it. The katari flew straight and true into the man's chest. Blood spurted out and the crossbow dropped from his hands. He fell to his knees, clutching his chest as if he could somehow stem the flow. Her fourth mark, but she could not think of that then, for there was the kalashik, shining in the moonlight, begging to be picked up, to be *used*, to punish these men like they deserved.

Take me, mistress. Its oily voice coiled around her, gripping her by the throat. *I have waited so long for you. Do you remember how your family died?*

Kyra stood, breathing deep and slow, though every sense screamed at her to run, run hard, away from that dreadful voice. She called back her katari and, thank the Goddess, it listened. She gripped it in both hands, letting its soothing warmth wash over her. Then she unslung the bag from her shoulder, untied the string, and kicked the gun into it. Faran had given her the bag before they parted, warning her not to touch any kalashik with her bare skin. As if she needed to be warned.

Coward. Weakling. Kyra froze in the act of retying the bag. *Just like all the others. Tell me, who is brave and strong enough to wield me, if not you? Who can tame me, if not you? Who deserves me, if not you?*

It came to Kyra, clear as glass, what she *should* be doing. She should be taking the gun in her hands and slaughtering the outlaws who had dared threaten the Temple of Valavan. Not a single one would she leave alive. Let them taste the bullets, let the pain of shattered limbs and leaking guts be theirs. They had killed her mother, her father, her sisters. They had massacred every single member of her clan. They had destroyed her world. And now she would destroy theirs.

Time stopped. Kyra no longer heard the cries of the battle that surrounded her. There was only herself, and the dark weapon that called to her with a need that matched her own. She reached inside the bag with shaking hands.

"Look out, Kyra!"

The Inner Speech shattered the spell the death-stick had woven. Kyra dropped the bag and gripped her blade. Time flowed back, and with it the heat and noise of battle: the snarls of wyr-wolves, the shouts of men, the fierce cries of the Valavians, fire crackling through the tents, burning canvas like parchment, smoke rising through the air, stinging her eyes.

And right in front of her, the thing the Valavians had been trying to warn her about. The cart-like contraption she had noticed earlier was pointed directly at her. Men turned a lever behind the tube, their faces grim with concentration. They were too far for the Inner Speech or her katari, and the Valavians were caught in clashes of their own, keeping at bay the hundreds of fighters who poured out of the tents.

Someone thrust a brand into the mouth of the tube and a deafening roar split the night.

Kyra stood rooted to the spot, watching in fascinated horror as a giant fireball arced through the air toward her.

A huge body knocked her aside, sending her sprawling to the ground. *Menadin.* His eyes locked with hers, his mouth open in a red snarl. Firelight framed his face and then they were burning, and Kyra gasped for air but there was none; all the oxygen had been sucked out of the world and this was how they would die, locked together, eye-to-eye, none of the promises fulfilled.

Reality returned with a distant boom. Menadin slumped over her, crushing her beneath his weight. Kyra's eardrums popped; she took a deep breath of smoky air and coughed. She pushed aside the wyr-wolf's massive body with an effort and stood. Her chest burned with every breath. Deadly flowers of fire sprouted around her. Menadin did not move. Her eyes stung from smoke, and from something more painful, but she *must* not think about him right now. She ran instead, dodging the projectiles that whistled about her, leaping over fires, ignoring the heat searing her face and limbs.

Through the smoke, the weapon came into view, the hellish black snout pointed toward her, men pumping frantically to deliver another charge. But she was close now, close enough to count six men, three women. She threw the bonds of Inner Speech at the nearest two, freezing their limbs. Her katari got a third, toppling him to the ground. And then she was upon them and it was the dance of Empty Hands, and was that not the most beautiful, purest dance of all? She whirled in the middle of the frenzied, diminished group. One of them landed a blow to her shoulders, and she almost doubled over with pain. She recovered and threw a kick to the side of his skull, feeling the sick crunch of bone beneath the bridge of her foot.

How long did it last? Kyra had no memory later of the last minute or two of the fight. But she must have killed or maimed them all, for when the Valavian battle cry sounded to the rear of the camp, she stood alone in the midst of a heap of unmoving bodies. The catapult, or whatever it was, stood unattended. She brought her blade down on the elongated tube mounted on the cart, and the awful clang of metal on metal jarred her whole body.

But nothing could resist kalishium. Kyra brought her blade down again and again, until her jaw ached and every bone screamed in protest. Finally, the tube was reduced to a mess of distorted parts that were fit only for melting.

Valavians poured through the camp, cutting down the outlaws who were still fighting or attempting to flee. Kyra retrieved her bag with the kalashik and went hunting for the remaining one, ignoring the chaos around her. The Valavians would deal with the surviving outlaws. The most important thing was to find the second death-stick.

Something butted her from behind, and she almost fell. It was a wyr-wolf, the one that had playfully nipped Menadin's ears, the one Kyra had thought might be his mate. From some-where, a name came to her, like a gift: *Sudali*.

"Where is the other kalashik?" she asked, urgent.

The wyr-wolf loped ahead of her, leaping over fallen bodies and the fires that sprouted all over the battlefield. Kyra followed as best she could. Sudali led her deeper into the camp. Had the kalashik been passed from hand to hand, retreating ever farther as defeat became imminent?

At last Sudali stopped in front of a heap of burned and broken corpses. Her ears flattened, and she growled.

The air stank of metal and smoke and burning flesh. Kyra swallowed hard. There was something here that belonged to her, and she would take it.

Goddess make me strong, so I can do what needs to be done. She reached down and began to move aside limbs and torsos, trying not to be sick. Most of the men and women had died from bullet wounds; a few had been hacked apart by swords. They had turned on each other—why?

The answer lay cradled in an arm at the bottom of that distressing heap—an arm without a body attached to it. The gun gleamed dark and bright, unsullied by the human blood and brains that stained the ground and Kyra's own hands.

At last you are here, and we shall both be free.

Kyra clutched her blade, but it was no good; this time the voice was stronger—amplified, perhaps, by the blood it had shed.

Take me, Markswoman. I will lead you to the man who killed your family. You need me, you want me, you know you do.

The voice so seductive; the words so cold and true. As in a dream, Kyra saw herself reach for the dark weapon.

Razor-sharp teeth caught hold of her hand, and she yelped in pain. *The wyr-wolf.* The seductive tones of the death-stick vanished, replaced by fury.

Kill it. Kill the dog that dares stand between us.

Kyra trembled at the onslaught of that voice. She looked at the katari in her free hand, and the wyr-wolf, still hanging on grimly to the other. Blood trickled out of Sudali's mouth. *Her* blood. At least she hadn't snapped off Kyra's hand. She was probably being as gentle as she knew how.

"You can let go now," said Kyra. "Please, Sudali," she added.

The wyr-wolf released her hand and backed away, wary.

"Thank you," Kyra muttered, wiping her hand on her robe and trying not to wince. She opened her bag and kicked the gun in. Its voice rose in a protesting screech, but somehow it had no more power over her.

"I'm going to get rid of you all," she said, tying the bag closed. "Forever. Prepare for oblivion, you evil thing, because that's where you're going."

Then, and only then, did she retrace her footsteps to Menadin. Sudali followed her, and the other wyr-wolves fell in step behind them, until they arrived at the place where their leader had fallen.

CHAPTER 30

THE GUN IN HIS HAND

Rustan walked behind Faran Lashail, relying on the glow of his mother's blade to light his way. The wyr-wolves ran ahead of them, occasionally stopping to glance back, impatient for the humans to catch up. Odd, how calm he was before the battle. But Shirin Mam's katari was warm in his hand, her letter tucked safely in his robe, and both were talismans that would hold the worst at bay.

He had read Shirin Mam's letter several times, even though the words were burned in his mind, indelible. Every time he read it, a fresh question rose, demanding to be answered.

But there would be no more answers from his mother, no secret missives waiting to be found. Her life and her death remained a mystery to him—almost as much of a mystery as the man called Rubathar. Rustan could not think of him as his father, not yet.

To what end had she lived, and to what end had she brought

him into being? Shirin Mam, the most powerful woman of Asiana, had done a foretelling, and what she had seen had made her go against the Kanun of Ture-asa.

Beware of Kyra Veer, she had warned, but the words came too late to make any difference. Whether the betrayal she spoke of was Kyra's breaking the law and stealing the kalishium, or whether it was some other betrayal that waited in his future, Rustan did not know. What he knew was that his fate was entwined with hers, as long as he lived, and he could no more have separated himself from her than he could have severed his own limbs.

When Rustan climbed down the mountain and took the door to Kunlun Shan, Kyra's trail burned bright for him. Even three days on, he could see the afterglow of her blade as he moved down the Transport corridor. When he caught up with her at the Temple of Valavan, the feeling of rightness returned to his world. Even through the duel, even through his own pain and hers. This was where he needed to be: fighting the outlaws by her side. Barkav would have approved.

And Shirin Mam? Surely she would have approved as well. She had loved Kyra. While love could be blind to imperfections, a Mahimata's love was not given lightly.

He believed Kyra would defeat the outlaws and return peace to Asiana. And he, Rustan, would help her in this mission, paying back in some small measure the blood debt his Order had incurred when Kai Tau turned renegade and killed Kyra's family. Kai Tau, after all, had once been a Marksman of Khur.

The Sahirus too would have understood. He owed them his life and his sanity, but they had known from the beginning that different loyalties tugged at him. And did it make him any less of a Sahiru, that he was a Marksman too? Did it make him any less of a Marksman, that he was a man too?

Twigs crackled underfoot, and Faran shot him a warning glance. No one spoke, but Rustan could sense the thoughts and emotions of the Markswomen around him. Anger, fear, outrage—and overriding them all, an unwavering determination to punish the men and women who had attacked the villages surrounding the temple and desecrated their sacred groves. There would be killing tonight, plenty of it, and Rustan was unsurprised to find distaste growing within him in anticipation of what he would witness—of what he would be forced to do.

The kalashiks, he reminded himself. Once those were secured, the outlaws wouldn't be able to harm them, and could, perhaps, be reasoned with. But would the Markswomen be willing to negotiate a surrender? Somehow, he doubted it. The outlaws had killed one of the Valavians, and the light of vengeance was in all their eyes, Faran's words in their hearts. *Will we let them live?* she had asked. *Death to the intruders*, they had answered.

Faran halted and made a sign for everyone to stop. The wyr-wolves sprang ahead, and the rest waited, tense. Rustan felt the cold brush of inevitability, and his skin prickled. *Death will come, but not by my hand, not if I can help it.*

Howls pierced the silence of the night and Faran shouted, "Come on!"

They ran through the forest, and as the trees thinned, fires danced into view, burning fitfully before the tents that rose from the ground like tumorous growths. Gunshots rang through the air; a bullet whistled past Rustan and struck a tree, dislodging a branch.

"Watch out," shouted Faran. "They are still armed!"

On cue, the Markswomen spread out far and wide, keeping to the shelter of the trees, careful not to break cover. As another bullet ricocheted off a massive tree trunk and nearly grazed his cheek, anger welled up inside Rustan. Whatever ancient knowledge had created these weapons, it was dead and gone; only its offspring remained to work their evil upon Asiana.

Faran had reached the edge of the clearing, where the forest gave way to stumps—the trees had been hacked by the men for firewood. To Rustan's astonishment, two men walked up to her, weaving between the tree stumps, helpless terror on their faces. And then he realized she had used every ounce of the Mental Arts in her power to draw them to her over the distance. But to what end?

He soon found out.

The men broke into a run, away across the open ground, moving together diagonally in perfect synchrony, shielding Faran Lashail behind them.

She was using them as human shields. Bullets tore into the men and they fell to the ground, spurting blood, but by then Faran had already reached the camp. The man who held the kalashik stood on a cart-like machine, protected from the wyr-wolves by a thick knot of men and women armed with spears and swords. Many lay dead, their throats gouged out by the snarling wyr-wolves, but as many, Rustan guessed, took their place from the ranks of the fighters spilling out of the tents.

And then the man with the kalashik turned and began to fire on his own people. Rustan watched, sickened, as dozens died in mere seconds, bodies disintegrating into bits of flesh and bone before his eyes.

He sprinted out of tree cover to join Faran, who crouched

a few yards away from the man with the kalashik. The other Markswomen fanned out, careful to stay out of the path of the bullets.

"Stop," said Rustan. "It is over. They are running away."

Faran's face was beaded with sweat, her fierce eyes turned inward with concentration. The man with the kalashik continued to shoot at his fleeing, wailing companions.

Rustan summoned the Inner Speech. "STOP NOW," he said, and Faran collapsed against him, shaking.

Rustan laid her down and ran to where the man now stood alone, surrounded by a heap of dead bodies, staring at the kalashik as if he did not know what to do with it.

Then he turned, saw Rustan, and raised his gun, awareness returning to his eyes.

Rustan flung Shirin Mam's blade, and it lodged itself deep in the man's forehead. Incredibly, the hand holding the gun did not falter. Rustan watched in horror as it pulled the trigger and a single shot rang out, deafening at this proximity, before the man toppled over.

Rustan blinked. He raised his hand and touched the side of his stinging face. His fingers came away covered with blood.

"Damn fool thing to do," said Faran next to him, making him jump.

Rustan took a deep breath, trying to calm his pounding heart. "A small flesh wound, nothing more." He was lucky the bullet had only grazed him. "And you, are you all right?"

"Of course," said Faran. "Time to mop up." She jerked her chin and her Markswomen moved forward, slow and deliberate.

Rustan went to the dead gun-bearer and pulled out Shirin Mam's blade from his forehead. It came out with ease, leaving a sticky mess of bone and tissue behind. Rustan's guts churned and he turned away. Someone's brother, someone's son. What could this man have become, if not for Kai Tau?

The death-stick had fallen from the dead man's hand onto the ground. It gleamed, not with light but with an intense blackness that drew the eyes and demanded attention. Rustan picked it up, studying its shape, puzzling over its contours. The bullets, he had heard, were self-replicating, the gun taking power from its handlers and the surroundings to replenish itself.

"Put down the dark weapon. Are you mad?" Faran cried out.

Rustan looked up, bewildered. "I am just observing it. What is the matter?"

"What is the matter, he says." Faran summoned the Inner Speech. "PUT IT DOWN. Now."

Rustan frowned. He could have tried to resist the command, but the other Markswomen had gathered behind Faran and were looking at him with equal parts horror and fear. Moreover, he could discern, just at the edge of his hearing, a faint, high-pitched voice emanating from the weapon. It was disquieting, to say the least. He laid the death-stick down on the ground and opened his palms.

"There you go. Satisfied?" To his relief, the voice faded away.

Eyeing him as she would a venomous snake, Faran edged over and used her booted foot to kick the gun into a bag. Only when it was securely tied did her shoulders slump with relief. "Never let a dark weapon touch your skin," she told him. "It can take over your mind. We are protected by our kataris, but not even they can help us if we fall under a kalashik's spell. Did you not know this?"

Yes, he did know it, but he had ignored that knowledge. Why?

Rustan examined himself and realized, with stomach-clenching clarity, that the gun had made him forget how dangerous it was.

But there its influence had ended. "It couldn't reach me," he said. "It was able to make me pick it up, but it was unable to make me listen to its voice."

"Praise all the gods and goddesses," remarked Faran. "Or we would all be dead, and so would half of Asiana. I wonder," she added, "what protected you?"

He shrugged, uncomfortable. "Shirin Mam's blade?"

"Powerful as it may be, it is still only a katari," said Faran.

"And I am only a Marksman," said Rustan.

"Are you?" she said, and flashed her teeth. "When this is all over, if we are both still alive, I would welcome an . . . *exchange*. One of my Markswomen can visit your Order to learn what she can from your people. And you can stay with us and learn what *you* can."

An invitation to live and learn with the Order of Valavan? Barkav would be delighted. This would do much to lessen the isolation of the Order of Khur. "I thank you on behalf of my Maji-khan," said Rustan, and he bowed.

Perhaps it was the act of bowing, or perhaps it was a delayed reaction to the loss of blood, but as he bent forward, darkness fogged his mind and he toppled over.

CHAPTER 31

THE NAME OF THE BLADE

Menadin was dying. Kyra knew it as soon as she crouched beside him and heard his labored breathing. His eyes were closed, his entire back burned raw. But it was a deeper hurt inside that was killing him.

"Hang on," she whispered. "I'll take you to Navroz Lan; she's the best healer in all of Asiana. You'll soon be up and running again." Knowing, even as she said it, how empty of meaning her words were.

Menadin's eyes opened, and his tongue flicked out. Wyr-wolf venom, he had once told her, could transpose someone to Wyr-mandil.

"Later," she said, desperate, slipping her arms around his shaggy neck. "First, we have to treat those burns, get you some medicine . . ."

Menadin snarled at her with a return of his old fire and

thrust his snout into her face. She gasped at the cold, prickly sensation of his tongue, and squeezed her eyes shut. *If this is what you truly want in the last minutes of your life, so be it.*

When she opened her eyes again, she was in *Anant-kal*. She sat in a garden, her back against a stone wall, the sun caressing her cheeks. Around the garden, the tall towers and familiar domes of the Shining City pierced the blue sky. Lounging in front of her was Menadin, an easy grin on his feral face, his back straight, unharmed, *alive*.

"Menadin!" she cried, and leaped to her feet. She wanted to run and hug him, but she checked herself. "You're okay? You're going to be all right?"

"Look around," said Menadin, instead of answering her question. "Observe. Tell me what you see."

Kyra frowned. She took in her surroundings: the lush garden, the fountain in the distance, the towers of the city, the disc-shaped structure hanging unsupported in the sky.

And then it hit her. "It's not fading in and out anymore," she said, and relief rushed through her. "It's just as it used to be."

"Not exactly," said Menadin. "But things are improving. You've struck a blow against Kai Tau today, and Asiana has taken a small step back from the brink of chaos. Wyr-mandil will hold on a little longer. But don't get complacent. You have won a battle, not the war. For that, you will have to kill Kai Tau himself and rid Asiana of the dark weapons. Then, and only then, will Wyr-mandil truly be safe."

"Stay with me, and I can take on any outlaw and his army," said Kyra. How had she ever thought him ugly or unclean? True, he had the look and smell of a wolf, but he was handsome in his own shaggy-haired way. And he had saved her life—a debt she could never repay.

Menadin was quiet for a moment. At last he said, "Kyra Veer, my running days are over."

Her heart gave a little swoop of fear. "What do you mean? You look the picture of health."

"I can control how I appear to you in Wyr-mandil." He raised a sardonic eyebrow. "Would you rather be talking with a dying, gasping, burned-out husk of poor old Menadin? Perhaps that would feel more authentic to you?"

Kyra swallowed. It was what she had feared, but it was easy to forget; what the eyes saw in *Anant-kal* was not the way things truly were, not in the real world. "I'm sorry," she said in a small voice.

"I'm not," said Menadin. "It was a fine thing to fight by your side. I die with honor. My flesh will feed the forest, and my soul will walk Wyr-mandil till the sun sets over the horizon and the Ones come down from the sky."

"That means I can see you here again?" asked Kyra, hope flowering inside her.

Menadin sighed. "No. That was me being poetic. Look, give the kalishium to Sudali. She'll come to the caves of Kali when you're ready for her. She'll take care of things when I'm gone, keep the Vulon pack in line."

Pain lanced her. "Sudali, your mate?"

"My mate," he said, and added proudly, "We have four cubs."

Kyra hugged herself against the coldness within her. "You're dying because of me. Your children will not have a father because of me."

He stepped forward and grasped her shoulders. His amber yellow eyes bore into hers. "So make it worthwhile," he growled. "Make Asiana and Wyr-mandil safe for my children, and their children after them."

"I will," she promised. "With all the strength of me and mine." Her eyes stung.

"He's a good man," said Menadin, almost grudgingly. "He'll help you. You could have done worse."

"Who? What?" asked Kyra, bewildered.

He blew out an exasperated breath. "Your mate. The Marksman."

Rustan. Kyra's face grew warm. "He's not my mate," she said. "He's just . . ."

"Yes?" prompted Menadin.

"A friend," she said.

Menadin closed one eye and gave a wicked grin. "Only mates carry the scent of each other. I know what I know."

Kyra pressed her lips in a thin line. *How dare he?* She could not trust herself to speak.

"I approve," he added mildly. "He is a good match for you. We two would never have worked out, you know. Both too fiery, too much alike."

What?

But Menadin was laughing, his shoulders shaking with mirth. "Your face," he hooted. "I wish you could see your face."

"This conversation is over," said Kyra through gritted teeth.

He stopped laughing and nodded his head. "Yes. It is time. Goodbye and good luck, young one."

It struck her then, what he had been trying to do, and she was furious both with him and with herself, but overriding that fury was the sense of impending loss. She reached out and hugged him. "Don't go," she said, her voice muffled against his chest. It was like holding the world's largest, furriest dog. "Don't leave me."

He ruffled her hair. "Death is but another door I walk through. Isn't that what Shirin Mam told you?"

She did not reply, but held him tighter, as if that could put off the inevitable. It was quiet and peaceful in the garden. They stood there awhile, and it could have been anywhere, anywhen.

At last Menadin stirred. "I have one more gift for you before I go," he said. "A gift of truth. I have been debating with myself whether to give it to you."

She released him, puzzled. He looked infinitely sad. "What do you mean?" she asked. "What truth?"

Menadin held both her hands in his—it was like being grasped by two gigantic hairy paws, but whereas before, the sensation would have made Kyra cringe in fear and revulsion, it now comforted her. As if no one could hurt her while she was being held like that.

"A truth you have known for a long time," said Menadin, "but have denied to yourself."

"If you're talking about Rustan . . ." she began.

"I am talking about Shirin Mam," said Menadin, and again that expression appeared on his face, as if he pitied her. "Do you still believe Tamsyn killed her?"

Kyra's stomach clenched. She tried to pull away from him, but his hands held her in a steel trap.

"Answer me," he said, implacable.

"Yes, I believe Tamsyn killed her," said Kyra, striving to stay calm. "Shirin Mam told me so herself when I met her in *Anant-kal*. Why are we talking about this *now*?"

"Because I'm dying," he said. "And if I don't remind you of the importance of critical thinking, who will? Remove the barriers you have erected in your mind, and you will know whose hand held the blade that killed your teacher. Remember Shirin Mam's exact words to you and tell me if I am wrong."

Kyra succeeded in freeing herself from Menadin—or perhaps

he let her go—and strode away, deeper into the garden. She tried
to still the hammering inside her chest.

The garden was larger than she remembered from earlier,
and wilder. The grass had grown to her knees and the trees
clustered thickly where before they had stood in decorous rows.

"Kyra," called Menadin from behind her. "What did Shirin
Mam say?"

Tell me, who killed you? Kyra had asked. *The Mahimata of Kali,*
Shirin Mam had replied.

The realization hit her with such force, she stopped breathing.
She slid down the trunk of a tree and leaned back against its
roots. If only the earth would swallow her up right then. If only
she could stop feeling. If only she could un-know what she knew.

Of course. Shirin Mam would not lie.

The Mahimata of Kali had killed herself.

She dug her nails into her palms. "Why?" she whispered.

Menadin crouched before her and cocked his head, regarding
her with compassion. "Would you have challenged Tamsyn
Turani to a duel if you did not think she had murdered your
teacher?"

"Then I have been nothing but a pawn," said Kyra slowly.

"Untrue. In every heart there is a blade, and the name of the
blade is love. The more we love, the sharper the blade. Shirin
Mam loved you. She had a foretelling, a vision of the multiple
branches the tree of life could grow. On every single one of
them Tamsyn subverted you, and the death-sticks multiplied—
except on this one."

Kyra closed her eyes in pain. She remembered how upset
she had been after Shirin Mam refused to let her go back to
the Tau camp for a second mark. How Tamsyn had intercepted
her afterward and spun her a vision of a future where *she* was

in charge. *If it were up to me*, Tamsyn had whispered, *I would command you to kill the Taus. I would not rest until I had seen you avenge your family. I would walk with you into their camp, blade to blade, and butcher them in their sleep.*

How difficult it had been to free herself from that vision, and how terrible she had felt afterward, as if she were betraying her Mahimata. Shirin Mam had known, had seen the weakness in her that Tamsyn would exploit, and had sacrificed herself rather than risk Kyra following Tamsyn's corpse-littered path.

"Tamsyn swore a blood oath to Shirin when she was initiated as the Mahimata of Kali," said Menadin. "Such an oath cannot be broken, not without consequences. But *you* swore no such oath to the Mahimata."

It took a moment for what he was implying to sink in. "I would never have betrayed my teacher," said Kyra, clenching her hands.

Menadin smiled without humor. "Which one, though?"

Bitterness rose within her. "Shirin Mam didn't think much of me, did she?"

"On the contrary, she died for you, and for Asiana," said Menadin. "She took the one branch where you might have some hope of bringing peace to our world."

"What about you?" said Kyra. "Was there a branch on which you might have lived?" Her vision blurred. Tears in *Anant-kal*—real or not?

Menadin pretended not to notice. "You indulge yourself," he said, standing. "Go back to those who need you. The mate who will fight by your side. The members of your Order and the clans of your valley. The wyr-wolves to whom you owe your protection and your kalishium. Go, and do not return to Wyr-

mandil until Kai Tau is dead. I, Menadin Vulon, challenge you."
He spat into his hand and extended it to her. "Do you accept?"

Kyra wanted to stay, to question him awhile longer, the last
person who could claim an understanding of Shirin Mam greater
than her own. Above all, she couldn't bear the thought of never
seeing him again, this half wolf, half man whom she had once
feared and despised, and who had become her friend and ally.

But it was time to go, and he had thrown her a challenge. She
would not disappoint him. She wiped her face with her sleeve,
stood, and laid her hand on his. "I accept."

Menadin smiled a smile that twisted her heart. "Stay strong,
Kyra Veer," he said, and raised his other hand in farewell.

The world warped into a ribbon of colors. Kyra's head swam,
but she stood her ground, anchored by Menadin. Then the
warmth of his hand slipped away from hers, and she fell back
into the battlefield with a sickening lurch of awareness. The
darkness of night, the glow of fires, the wyr-wolves beside her,
the Valavians walking up to them, blades drawn, faces grim.

And Menadin, his head cradled in her arms, his eyes looking
beyond her to a place she could not see.

CHAPTER 32

AFTER THE BLOOD

I n the end, Menadin did not go through the door of death alone. Four of his pack mates went with him, as well as three Valavian Markswomen. Many of the others were injured, but all would survive. How much worse it would have gone for them if not for the valor of the wyr-wolves.

Kyra's thoughts chased themselves in circles: grief over their deaths, grief over what Menadin had revealed—what he had forced her to acknowledge.

Everything Kyra had done, from the moment of her teacher's death, had been based on the belief that Tamsyn had killed Shirin Mam. A belief that had no foundation in reality. A belief that had been fed by her own prejudice and dislike of the Mistress of Mental Arts.

Yes, Tamsyn was cruel. She had starved and beaten Nineth. But she had not killed her.

And she had not killed Shirin Mam.

This was what Tamsyn's blade had been trying to tell her. This was why she had been unable to let go of it for so long.

What else was untrue? Had she been right to trust Shirin Mam?

There was no way now to be sure of anything. Kyra looked at herself and saw a headstrong girl who had jumped from one conclusion to another without pausing to think. It was a painful realization, and if not for the fact that they were on a bloody, grimy battlefield, she would have broken down. Only the presence of the Valavians and the exhausted, grieving wyr-wolves stopped her.

The wyr-wolves had fought with ferocity and courage. If there had been any doubt in the Valavians' minds about the dual nature of the beasts, it was banished forever.

Faran Lashail issued the edict in the battlefield, after rejoining them with her contingent. Rustan was nowhere to be seen; Kyra learned that he had suffered a minor wound and been sent back to the temple for first aid. Worry for him mixed with her grief at Menadin's death and a dark jumble of emotions for Shirin Mam and Tamsyn. Kyra could not tell where one feeling began and the other ended, but her heart ached. She longed to see Rustan. But she couldn't pester Faran for details, not now.

The head of the Order of Valavan stood over Menadin's still body and thanked the wyr-wolves for their sacrifice. "We could not have achieved victory today with such few casualties without your help," she told them, her voice full of suppressed emotion. "You have my gratitude and my vow. As long as I live, wyr-wolves will be regarded as our equals."

Her words could not lighten the pain of Menadin's death, but they did him honor. Kyra, bowing her head and standing beside Sudali, imagined Menadin flicking his ears in amusement at the irony of it. It took the death of a wyr-wolf to earn respect for him and his kind. *Pity I'm not around to enjoy it*, he seemed to be saying. *What a eulogy!*

Sudali was rigid with sorrow. Kyra could not bring herself to touch the wyr-wolf; it would have been presumptuous on her part. But Sudali turned and breathed on her hand—the one she had injured in her attempt to free Kyra from the death-stick. The pain in Kyra's hand flared anew, then receded. Kyra lifted her arm and examined it in rising astonishment. The blood had dried, and the wound had sealed.

Wyr-wolf saliva was rumored to contain enough venom to paralyze a horse. But perhaps the truth was much stranger than that. Before she could ask Sudali for clarification, the wyr-wolf trotted away to her remaining pack mates.

Half the Markswomen stayed in the battlefield, to ensure that no outlaw remained within their territory. Those who were still alive would be subjected to the Inner Speech, their weapons and memories taken so they no longer posed a threat to the Deccan.

Two elders were dispatched to fetch the strongest and bravest villagers to help dispose of the dead bodies safely. The corpses would be burned, the ashes mixed with the earth.

"Perhaps," said Faran, "a time will come when the souls we have freed return to Asiana as peaceful, law-abiding, productive citizens. Meanwhile, their remains will nourish the soil."

The three Valavians who had perished would be given a sky burial at dawn. The dead wyr-wolves, including Menadin, would be left in the forest, as was their custom. Kyra would escort the rest back to Ferghana, as soon as the healers were done tending to their wounds. She said a final farewell to Menadin, and stepped away from him, her eyes stinging.

"What about the death-sticks?" she asked the head of Valavan. "What do you plan to do with them?"

"Put them with the others in the underground vault that only I have access to," said Faran. "Why, do you have a better idea?"

"One day," said Kyra slowly, "I will find a way to remove the dark weapons from the face of Asiana. On that day, you will deliver them to me. *All* of them."

Faran studied her and nodded, her face expressionless. She did not betray any curiosity about how Kyra would do such a thing, although Kyra could sense her trying to work it out. At least Kyra had earned her trust during this battle, and Faran would not dismiss her claims outright. But she knew she would have to provide the head of Valavan with a more complete explanation before she would agree to deliver the death-sticks to the Order of Kali.

They returned to the temple, carrying the wounded on make-shift stretchers of bamboo poles and canvas torn from the outlaws' tents.

In the Hall of Reflection, Kyra slowed, watching herself shape-shift in the mirrors. If she screwed her eyes up and looked sideways, she could glimpse Menadin in the mélange of images. He was part of her now, she thought. She did not care if it was wishful thinking.

A vast room off the hall had been converted into a temporary sick bay. Kyra carefully laid down her end of the stretcher and backed away. Healers shouted orders and apprentices ran up with balms, bandages, and hot water. The smell of blood and antiseptic hit her nostrils, and a wave of blackness passed before her eyes.

A hand gripped her arm, steadying her.

"Rest," said Derla, looking as exhausted as she felt. "Tomorrow is another day."

Kyra tried to smile. "I don't think I can manage all those stairs tonight."

"Sleep anywhere," said Derla, waving a hand. "Or go to the kitchens and ask for food. You look terrible."

"Do you know where Rustan is?" asked Kyra. "Faran said he had been wounded."

"A mere graze," said Derla. "Although apparently he blacked out. I tried to get him to lie down, but he gave me the slip when my back was turned. Perhaps you will find him upstairs with Faran. I know she wanted to talk with him."

She hurried away before Kyra could respond, which was just as well. Kyra grabbed a blanket from a pile by the door and headed back to the Hall of Reflection, meaning to give it to Rustan when she found him. Why did Faran want to talk with him right now? He needed to rest. For that matter, where had Faran disappeared to?

The Hall of Reflection had a grand staircase that spiraled up to a narrow, wraparound passage on the second floor—a whispering gallery, one of the Valavians had told her, that amplified the slightest sound so it could be heard at the other end of the hall. Kyra headed for the passage, certain that Rustan had taken it just moments ago. She could sense his presence—or perhaps it was the trail of Shirin Mam's blade she followed.

Your mate, Menadin had said. But Menadin had been teasing. It was impossible to think of Rustan as such. And yet, it was impossible to imagine a world without him by her side.

Kyra heard low voices, faint in the distance. Rustan and Faran? The acoustics of the whispering gallery were tricky. She circled the passage before taking a narrow opening into another corridor, cursing the mazelike interior of the temple. She climbed up a steep flight of stairs lit by torchlight, and the voices became clearer, louder.

Somebody laughed—a low, rich sound—and Kyra halted, dark seeds of suspicion clouding her thoughts. Carefully, she edged up the last stair and peered down a long, dim corridor. She was just in time to see Faran open a door and usher Rustan inside a room. She was too far away to be sure, but Kyra thought he was smiling.

She sat down, trying to slow her breathing. So he was wounded, was he? He had refused to stay in the sick bay. He had sought out the head of the Order of Valavan as soon as she returned, instead of trying to find Kyra. And now he was closeted in a room with Faran—to do what?

Maybe Faran had taken her words seriously, about how Markswomen could not pass on their talents to future generations because they did not have children. Maybe Faran had decided to put this to the ultimate test. And who better to test this on than Rustan, whom Kyra herself had foolishly revealed as one of the best in the Order of Khur?

No, she was being ridiculous.

Still, no harm in checking out what exactly they were up to. Kyra gripped her blade and started down the corridor.

She stole up to the door, laid her hand on it, and held her breath. She heard a murmur of voices, indistinct, and again that low laugh, almost seductive in its tone.

Kyra threw open the door and leaped in, ready to pounce.

Eight bewildered faces gazed at her from around a table

covered with maps. Faran rose. "Ah, Kyra. Just the person we needed," she said. "I was about to send for you." She paused, frowning. "Why is your katari in your hand?"

"Oh, this?" Kyra sheathed the katari, her face hot. "I don't know. I'm still all jumpy from the battle." *And my brain is not working properly.*

"And the blanket?" said Rustan, his mouth quirking into a grin.

"I'm cold," said Kyra. She sat on one of the chairs, wrapping the blanket around herself, not looking at him. She emptied her mind so they would not see how flustered she was. Although she could tell that Rustan knew.

"Well, thank you for joining us," said Faran. She smoothed the edges of a detailed, hand-drawn map on the table, and pointed. "The Tau clan has set up camp in a village called Jethwa, fifty miles from the door in Jhelmil. It is likely that the door is being watched now. If we want to use it to Transport people and weapons, we will first have to take down the spies. Or else find another door. Time is of the essence." She turned to Rustan. "You have been there. Tell us what you found."

As Rustan began to speak of his journey to Jethwa and how he had burned Kai Tau's weapons forge, Kyra allowed herself to relax. All eyes were on him, so hers could be too, with no one the wiser. There was a bandage on the side of his face, and his eyes betrayed exhaustion, but otherwise he appeared to be fine.

She wished, suddenly, that they were alone, and she could get a detailed account from him of what had happened. She longed to tell him about Menadin, their unlikely friendship and his ultimate sacrifice.

She would never be able to tell him about Shirin Mam,

though. It would hurt him too much. Just like it hurt her. Pain and anger squeezed her heart. Shirin Mam had loved her enough to die by her own hand. But she had not trusted Kyra with the truth, had instead let Kyra believe a lie.

But Menadin was right. If Kyra had not been so blinded by her own prejudice, she would have known the truth without anyone's help. Shirin Mam had once taught Tamsyn. Tamsyn had sworn an unbreakable oath to Shirin Mam when Shirin became the Mahimata of Kali—just as all the Markswomen were now sworn to Kyra. The Mistress of Mental Arts could not have killed her own teacher. Not without paying a grave price.

But Kyra had run away from the Order of Kali before Tamsyn was inducted as the new Mahimata. Kyra had never sworn to Tamsyn, and so she was able to challenge her to a duel in the Hall of Sikandra without breaking a blood oath.

It made sense, but it felt wrong. Tamsyn did not deserve to be in a position of power, perhaps, but she had not deserved to die. Kyra remembered *how* she had died—carried away by the swirling waters where once her own father had tried to drown her—and felt a deep sadness. She was glad she no longer carried the burden of either teacher's blade.

"Kyra?" Faran's voice was loud, as if this was the third or fourth time she was trying to get her attention.

Kyra snapped guiltily back to the present. "Sorry, I . . . I was thinking over what everyone said."

"And your conclusion?" said Faran, tapping the map. "Which door should we use, and when?"

"I must discuss this with my elders," said Kyra, hoping she sounded lucid. "But we have another door to the Thar Desert, to the west of Jethwa. Although it is farther than the Jhelmil door to the Tau camp, the advantage is that it is well hidden and will not be watched. I propose that we use both doors and coordinate our assault to surround the camp. The Order of Kali can lead the first attack from the west, throwing the Taus into disarray. The Order of Valavan can follow by attacking from the east."

"So even if they have spies, it will do little good," said Faran thoughtfully. "They will already be under attack, and you will draw off their forces to the west. Before they can counter us, we will encircle them."

"We don't know how many fighters they have gained in the past few days," said one of the elders—the Mistress of Combat, Kyra guessed. "Nor if they have succeeded in building the weapons the young Marksman mentioned." She nodded at Rustan. "But we had best move fast. I will summon the clan elders of the Deccan to contribute soldiers and weapons. And you, Mahimata, what do you propose? Will you return to the caves of Kali to prepare your Order?"

"Yes," said Kyra, "but first, I need something from Astinsai, the katari mistress of Khur."

There were raised eyebrows at this; apparently Rustan had not told them about the kalishium or her plan for using it to make shields. Good.

"What do you need from her?" said Faran. "The Order of Khur is five days' journey from any usable door. Anything can happen in that much time."

"It's vital," said Kyra. "Something that might help save lives. Please," she added when the elders sitting around the table frowned. "You've trusted me this far—believe me when I say it's crucial. We need ten days anyway to mobilize our fighters. And we need the Order of Khur by our side."

Rustan stirred. "I will accompany you," he said. "I must report to Barkav, and the Desert of No Return isn't the safest of places to travel alone."

Kyra was about to argue that she didn't need his protection when Faran said, "You should stay here and recover from your wound, Marksman. Kyra can fill in the Order of Khur on your behalf. A Markswoman is perfectly capable of taking care of herself."

Although this was exactly what Kyra had been about to say, what she said instead was "Of course I am capable of looking after myself, but I carry something more precious than any of you can imagine. It would be wise to have more than one person on this journey, one to keep watch while the other sleeps." No way she was leaving Rustan with the Order of Valavan, not with Faran Lashail regarding him with such open interest.

And so it was decided, without any more words being said. At dusk the next day, when Kyra escorted the wyr-wolves back to the Ferghana Valley, Rustan went with her.

PART IV

Fragment of parchment found in Kunlun Shan

Our time is coming to an end. All things end, and this should not grieve us, but it does. We grieve not for ourselves but for Asiana. Once the last Sahiru is gone from this world, the last living link with the Araini will break. The world will forget us. But it should not forget the Araini. It should not stop hoping for their return.

We remember the Araini, even though they left before we were born. For we have the memories of the first Sahiru, just as we have the memories of the last one.

The first Sahiru was Vamika the Wise. She was part of the trade delegation sent to negotiate with the Araini when they landed in their vast, elegant ships on the Uzbek Plains. Like small planets they were, those leviathans. And now only one is left. It sits like an iceberg on top of a mountain, revealing a fraction of what it hides. There we will go when our work is done, as our elders have gone before us.

Vamika the Wise stayed with the Araini in one of their ships to learn their language. It is said that her goal was not wisdom, but the securing of a better deal for her own people. But the longer she stayed, and the more she learned, the less inclined she was to leave. The day came at last when she mastered the language and became other-human, for she saw then our thousand-year history unfurl before her like a scroll. She saw humanity teeter on the brink of greatness and misery, death and resurrection. She went into silence, knowing the terrible power of words. But the Araini sent her from their ship, bidding her work to the best of her abilities. Knowing the arc of history does not release us from the pain of living it.

The Araini made three kinds of other-humans: Those who could bond with kalishium, so they could communicate their thoughts, even if they could not grasp the language of the Ones. Those who could, like the Araini themselves, change shape and heal wounds. The latter abilities were greatly coveted, and if not for the fact that most humans could not bear the pain of transformation, there would have been a stampede to their ships. Still, several hundred were successfully transformed by the Araini over the years, and they formed an important link between the Ones and the natural world of Asiana.

But of us, the Sahirus, there will only ever be twenty-six. Very few can learn the language of the Araini. Fewer still can learn it and stay sane. And of our precious number, twelve died during the Great War alone, in an unprovoked and cowardly strike on our people.

Few though we are in number, we have played our part. Did we not build the world where all other-humans may meet as equals? The world that will come to be called many names in many tongues, but which we will always call Anant-kal, the world beyond time. At the height of our powers, we used to meet our compatriots every new moon, gathering in a large hall in a beautiful city of gleaming towers and white domes—a mirror of the city that flourished on an island state in the Dead Sea.

The real city was ravaged by war, the island sunk under the ocean. But the one in Anant-kal will outlast us all.

Our end draws close.

The last Sahiru is yet to be born. But we have seen him cross the desert and climb the mountain in search of our monastery. He will ride through a firestorm and crawl over icy stones to reach us. Bleeding from wounds unseen, stumbling in the dark of his mind—that is how we will find him.

We must go forward to await him. We must teach him what we can, even though he will have little time with us. It will have to be enough. He is the key that will release us from our earthbound prison.

This is the Araini's gift to us—to know and to remember past and future, within the living memory of our sect. A thousand years of history, and it will die with us. None will find these scrolls. They will crumble to dust, and our monastery will fall to ruin. It will be the end of an age, and we cannot see what comes after.

Yet we leave these seeds of knowledge in the hope that we are wrong. In the hope that some day, they will fall into the right hands and spread the light of truth.

CHAPTER 33

A FRIEND'S FURY

It was a perfect evening, the residual warmth of the setting
sun dispelling the last cold dreams of winter. Green shoots
covered the Ferghana Valley with new life. Night birds sang,
and squirrels chittered—sounds that were abruptly cut off when
the wyr-wolves slouched out of the Ferghana Hub, close behind
Kyra and Rustan.

Kyra knelt in front of Sudali, the alpha female. "Thank you,"
she said, her throat constricted. "I will not forget your bravery
and sacrifice. And I will not forget my promise to Menadin."

Sudali locked eyes with Kyra. *Till we meet again, Kyra Veer.*
She lowered her great head and rested it on Kyra's shoulder before turning away. The wyr-wolves vanished behind the tamarisk
bushes that covered the hill.

Kyra rose and noticed Rustan breathing deeply, gazing at
the twilit valley with awe.

"Welcome to my home," she said, smiling at his expression.

How many times she had dreamed of this moment—to bring Rustan to the place that she loved above all others and introduce him to her "family."

"It's beautiful," said Rustan. "You live in paradise. I can see why you risked your life to return to it."

Kyra cleared her throat. "Er, yes. Please follow me." She turned so he could not see the flush on her cheeks. The memory of her duel with Tamsyn was forever tainted with the knowledge that Tamsyn, whatever else she was guilty of, had been innocent of the crime of killing the Mahimata of Kali. It hadn't been a fair fight. Kyra wouldn't have *won* a fair fight. She had gained the position of Mahimata because of Shirin Mam; she did not deserve or desire it. But there was no way out of it now. It made her feel helpless and angry and impotent all at once, because Shirin Mam was *dead*, beyond her reach. And so was Tamsyn.

"If I see you again, Mother, I'll throttle you," she muttered.

"Did you say something?" asked Rustan from behind her.

"Nothing," said Kyra. "Watch your feet, make sure you don't sink into a burrow."

From the horse enclosure came a whinny, and Kyra couldn't help grinning. Rinna knew she was back.

Elena and Akassa should have known too, as well as the elders, but no one came to greet them. It was what Kyra had expected—she had, after all, brought a Marksman with her—but it still annoyed her.

They reached the grassy meadow at the base of the hill, and Kyra pointed to the gnarled old mulberry tree that stood before the caves. "We often have classes here in good weather," she told Rustan. "The novices pick the mulberries when they're ripe and Tarshana—she's our cook—makes the most delicious pies."

Rustan drank it all in, a wistful look on his face. Kyra longed to slip her hand into his, to smooth his furrowed brow. But they were within sight of the caves now, and she would have to be more careful. Instead, she tried to send him a wave of reassurance and comfort.

I know what it is to lose a mother, twice over, she thought.

The corners of his mouth twisted. "And yet I envy you, for you spent years with Shirin Mam that I did not. Isn't that foolish of me?"

Not foolish, no. It was natural. But Kyra did not trust herself to speak without betraying her own mixed feelings for her old teacher. "Let me show you the entrance to the caves," she said. "You have to crawl the first few meters, but then it broadens to a fairly big passage."

She showed him the crawlway. He was examining it with interest when Ria Farad materialized before them with her usual suddenness. Kyra should have been used to it by now, but it never failed to startle her.

"Welcome back, Mahimata. And you too, Marksman," said Ria, with a glint in her eyes. "You may enter our abode, once you have relinquished your weapon."

"What? The Marksmen never asked *me* to do that!" said Kyra indignantly.

"I don't have my katari," said Rustan. "It is back in Khur with the Maji-khan—a matter of penance. I do carry Shirin Mam's blade, though. Would you like to keep it for me?"

He withdrew the katari and proffered it to Ria. The blade sparkled, throwing a ghostly light on his face.

Ria stepped back, uncertain. "You survived a separation from your katari?" She shook her head. "You may keep Shirin Mam's blade. Let the elders try to take that from you, if they will."

Kyra resolved not to allow anything of the sort. Rustan had told her how his mother's blade had helped stave off the madness that threatened to consume him when he was parted from his own katari. She'd order the elders to stand down with every bit of authority she possessed as the Mahimata of Kali.

But in the end, she did not need to. The elders were waiting in the torch-lit central cavern, relief emanating from them at her safe return. Felda grinned at her, and Chintil even nodded at Rustan. Mumuksu betrayed nothing in her expression. Navroz looked disapproving, but that was only to be expected from Eldest.

The rest of the Markswomen were not in the cavern, but Kyra could sense them in their individual cells; the elders must have told them to make themselves scarce, given the unexpected arrival. She could imagine the curiosity, especially among the younger ones. And she could literally *feel* Elena and Akassa bursting with questions. With a pang, she remembered her own arrival at Khur and how Shurik had befriended her.

"Elders," said Kyra before any of them could speak, "I present to you Rustan of the Order of Khur, the son of Shirin Mam. He helped me practice in preparation for my duel with Tamsyn Turani, and I owe him a great debt. He also helped the Valavians fight the outlaws. We will give you a full account of what transpired, after we've had a chance to wash and eat."

"Welcome," said Navroz Lan in as cold a voice as Kyra had ever heard from her.

"You look so much like your mother," said Felda Seshur, beaming.

Rustan bowed. "Thank you, Elders," he said. "I am honored to be here."

"The first time a Marksman has entered the caves of Kali

in centuries," remarked Mumuksu. "Let us hope the Goddess does not take offense."

"And if the Goddess does not take offense, neither should her disciples," said Kyra, with a touch of asperity.

Rustan's gaze went to the ocher and charcoal paintings that danced on the walls, lit by a hundred sconces. "May I see the places where my mother meditated and taught class?" he asked. "It would mean a great deal to me to be able to understand how she lived and what she believed. It is my greatest regret that I did not know her while she was still alive."

"Certainly," said Navroz, thawing just a bit.

Kyra hid a grin as the elders led Rustan across the cavern, talking over each other, pointing out the paintings and the passageway to the Mahimata's cell, and explaining the function of the raised slab. If they could only cease to see him as a man, they would get beyond their prejudice, much as the Valavians had.

It wasn't that simple, of course. As Navroz summoned the older Markswomen to meet Rustan, the Mistress of Meditation hung back to whisper in Kyra's ear.

"Why is he here?" hissed Mumuksu. "Why have you brought him?"

He belongs by my side, Kyra could have said, and then watched Mumuksu's face redden with a suppressed explosion.

Instead she said, her voice grave, "It is a pilgrimage, Elder. He wants to pay his respects to Shirin Mam."

Mumuksu's expression cleared and she nodded.

It wasn't even untrue. Kyra knew, as Rustan knelt by the central slab, that his expression of reverence was not fake— not that he was capable of faking such an emotion anyway. It really did mean a great deal to him to touch the place where his mother had been laid after her death. Where Kyra herself had helped lay his mother down after her death. So light the corpse, so frail the body that had commanded the highest power in Asiana.

Death is but another door I have walked through. You see my husk, the part I have left behind, and mistake it for the whole. I am elsewhere, a place you cannot reach—not yet.

Kyra shivered as the words came back to her, like the echo of a ghost.

As Rustan rose, he swayed and gripped the slab for support.

"What's the matter?" Kyra covered the distance in two quick steps, unable to hide her alarm. Rustan's face had gone gray. Kyra turned to Navroz, urgent. "Eldest, will you examine Rustan's wound? He was shot yesterday, and he handled a dark weapon."

"What?" Navroz looked horrified. "Why didn't you tell me right away? I thought that was an ordinary scratch. Come along with me, Marksman. Let's have a look at you."

She led him away, ignoring his weak protests. Kyra watched him go, her heart clenching. Felda and Chintil excused themselves to go back to their cells.

But Mumuksu stayed.

"A pilgrimage, is it?" murmured the Mistress of Meditation when they were alone, raising her eyebrows.

"In a manner of speaking, Elder," said Kyra evenly, wondering how much Mumuksu had guessed. "He will also accompany me to the Order of Khur where I can meet Astinsai. Where is the kalishium?"

"Safe in the funerary chamber," said Mumuksu. "When do you leave?"

"In the morning, if he is well enough," said Kyra. She stopped, swallowed, and continued. "Elder, there is something I need to do in the chamber anyway. Will you come with me?"

Mumuksu's brow furrowed. "Oh no. Not the lake. What do you plan to do, dive in?"

"I owe it to Nineth," said Kyra. "I did something wrong, and I need to fix it."

"You cannot fix this," said Mumuksu with certainty. "Not by yourself. It would take greater power than you have. And I don't know if I can help you."

Kyra took a deep breath. "But I know someone who can."

⚜

Elena smelled of an odd mixture of joy, wariness, worry, and the medicinal herbs she worked with every day.

Kyra hugged her. "How are you?" she asked.

Elena tugged a plait in an uncharacteristic display of restlessness. "Busy. But I miss Nineth." *And I miss you*, she did not say, but Kyra heard it anyway.

And there was nothing she could do about it. Her path was set, and it was not one that Elena could follow.

"And Akassa," said Kyra gently. "How goes it with her?"

Elena gave her a startled look. "She's not the girl we knew as Tamsyn's pet," she said slowly. "As if, in dying, Tamsyn released her to be herself. She's still stubborn as an ox, but I can usually get her to listen to me. She longs for a chance to prove herself, you know."

"We all get a chance to do that, sooner or later," said Kyra. "I wonder what Nineth will make of the change in Akassa. I hope they get along."

Elena's face lit up. "You know where Nineth is? She's *alive?*"

Hot guilt coursed through Kyra. She had known all this time and withheld that knowledge from Elena. "Come with me," she said. "And I will show you."

She led Elena down one level to the ghostly, dimly lit cavern that functioned as the armory. Mumuksu was waiting for them, her face expressionless. Elena bowed to the Mistress of Meditation and murmured, "Elder."

"I cannot remember when last a mere apprentice has been allowed into the funerary chamber," said Mumuksu drily. "But Kyra is right; if anyone can help her, it is you. Watch your step now."

She turned before Elena could ask any questions and guided them down a narrow passage illuminated by a single torch, at the end of which was the shaft that led down to the dark zone of the caves. They descended the rope ladder, Mumuksu leading the way, Kyra in the middle, and Elena at the top, jittery with nerves. Kyra sent a wave of reassurance to calm her friend. *It's all right. I've been here before. Breathe.*

The funerary chamber was exactly as Kyra remembered: dank, imposing, and dominated by the glowing statue of the Goddess meditating in the lotus position. On the other side of the lake, urns on recessed shelves glowed with the light of the blades within them. Crystalline pillars reared up from the calcite-filmed floor to the soaring ceiling.

Behind Kyra, Elena's breath came loud and uneven. Mumuksu bent to light a candle at the altar of the Goddess, and Elena clutched Kyra's arm.

"This is creepy," she whispered. "I don't think we'll find Nineth here. *Last* place she'd try to hide."

Kyra suppressed a smile. "Nineth isn't here. But her blade is. And we're going to call it to us. I couldn't do it alone, but maybe together we can."

"Do you want me to add my voice to yours?" asked Mumuksu.

"Thank you, Elder, but we were—we *are*—her best friends. Perhaps she'll listen to us," said Kyra, praying that this was still true.

She went to the water's edge and settled down in the lotus position. Elena followed suit.

"Hold my hand, and with the other hold your blade," said Kyra. "Bend your mind to Nineth. I'm going to use a word of power I learned at Khur."

Rustan had used that word once to divest her of her weapon while they were mock-dueling. But it would be no simple task, calling Nineth's katari out of the cold, dead water of the lake when its mistress was so far removed in time and space. That was why she needed Elena's concentration to match her own.

Elena slipped a hand into Kyra's and closed her eyes. Her body relaxed into a meditative trance. Her blade glowed silver-blue.

Kyra thought of Nineth: her unruly hair and perpetual smile, her loyalty to her friends and to Shirin Mam. She remembered Nineth's coming-of-age ritual when she had bonded with her katari. *You cannot ever forget that, can you? No matter how much time passes. The bond might weaken, but it can never break.*

From somewhere beneath the waters of the lake, there came a spark. Kyra's throat tightened. *I'm sorry for what I did. Please forgive me and come home. I love you, now and forever.*

Light spread in concentric circles from the middle of the lake, and Mumuksu drew in a sharp breath.

Kyra ignored her. She bent her mind to Rustan, to the word of power he had used to call her blade to him—how it had flown from her grasp into his, and how indignant she had been.

The word arrived, cool-edged and purple-hued, into her conscious mind. "*Ahiya tinmu*," she whispered, and the lights on the lake became a maelstrom. The water began to spin like a whirlpool. Nineth's blade rose from the middle of the whirlpool and plunged toward Kyra like a gannet. Elena pushed her aside with a wordless cry, and the blade clattered across the stone floor of the chamber, sparking and steaming.

Kyra hauled herself up, her heart thudding. She sheathed her blade and wiped her sweaty palms on her robe, hoping the other two wouldn't notice how flustered she was. Mumuksu had a sardonic smile on her face. No doubt she was recalling how Kyra had thrown Nineth's katari into the lake and thinking it served Kyra right that it had tried to stab her on its way out.

"You did it." Elena squeezed her shoulder, her eyes shining.

"*We* did it," said Kyra. She knelt by Nineth's blade and laid her palm upon it. It tingled with expectation and resentment. She met Elena's gaze and nodded. Elena laid her own palm over Kyra's.

And there was Nineth, looking right at them, her mouth open in shock.

"She can see us," whispered Elena, and Kyra shushed her.

Nineth sat on a white horse, moonlight falling on her surprised face. She'd gone thin, and she looked bone-tired. But she was alive and unhurt and that, of course, was the most important thing.

We miss you, Nineth, thought Kyra. Beside her, she could feel Elena's outpouring of joy and excitement. It could not fail to move Nineth.

A disbelieving smile lit Nineth's face. Then she looked directly at Kyra and scowled. Kyra swallowed. *I'm sorry*, she thought, but Nineth's expression did not change. *You hurt me*, it said.

The connection broke. Elena gave a little cry of frustration.

"It's all right," said Kyra, although the words felt like nails being dragged out of her throat. "She saw us. She knows we're okay, and Tamsyn is gone, and her katari is safe. She's on her way back." Knowing, as she spoke, that it wasn't quite as simple as that.

"How did her katari end up in the lake?" asked Elena. "Did Tamsyn throw it in?"

Kyra glanced at Mumuksu. *Please, Elder*, she thought, but the Mistress of Meditation stayed silent, a stern expression on her face. Kyra wasn't going to get any help from her.

"Tamsyn hid Nineth's katari in the funerary chamber, yes," said Kyra at last. "But I'm the one who threw it in the lake."

"What?" Elena looked stunned. "*Why?*"

Because I'm a terrible person and I don't deserve you or Nineth. "Because of something the blade showed me," said Kyra, unable to keep a tremor out of her voice. "I'm so sorry."

Elena crossed her arms. "All this time," she hissed in fury, "I've been worried sick about her. Thinking she was *dead*. But do you care? Do you care for either one of us?"

"Of course I care," said Kyra, stumbling over the words. "I want her to come home just as much as you do."

Elena shook her head. "So much that you threw her katari into the lake? You better hope she forgives you, Kyra, because I certainly won't."

She rose and marched away from them without another word.

Kyra's eyes stung. It was nothing more than she deserved,

but it still hurt deeply. She had never seen Elena so angry before.

Mumuksu laid a calming hand on her shoulder. "The first step in gaining forgiveness is to tell the truth," she said. "You have taken that step. Elena will come around."

Kyra dashed a sleeve across her face. She managed a smile. "I hope you're right, Elder," she said.

But inwardly she wondered. She could try to explain about Tamsyn's katari, but she had no way of knowing what might have happened if she hadn't kept it for so long, or if it was only the will of the blade that had made her act as she did. And what would she do now, if her actions had cost her the friendships she treasured above all else?

CHAPTER 34

TOGETHER, ALONE

Rustan was better the next morning—at least, he pronounced himself well enough to travel, and nothing Navroz Lan could say would dissuade him.

He had been given Kyra's old cell to sleep in, and all that night Kyra had tossed and turned, thinking of him lying on her woolen rug—the rug she had slept on for years—wishing she could go to him. Did he light a candle, as she sometimes did, to ward off bad dreams, or did he sleep in the dark? Would he wake if she tiptoed into the cell and touched his forehead? Just to see if he was all right, Kyra told herself. Just to see if his breath came even, his pulse beat regular. And maybe, just maybe, to brush her lips on his. A brief taste of him, to remember and to hold.

In the end, of course, she did nothing of the sort. No point scandalizing the elders; she needed their cooperation and goodwill. But she ached for his touch, ached to have him beside her.

Finally, at dawn, she left her cell and made for the horse enclosure. Rinna whinnied in delight at being reunited with her, and even some of the other horses trotted up to her and nudged her with their noses. She laughed and patted them, feeling the tension ebb from her shoulders. Then she saddled Rinna and cantered out of the enclosure to enjoy one last ride before she had to leave the Ferghana yet again. Only the absence of Nineth, and Elena's anger, poisoned the sweetness of that hour galloping across the valley as the sun rose in the sky.

By the time she returned, Rustan was up too and in the communal kitchen with the others, sipping tea and munching fruit. Kyra tried to catch his eye, but he was listening to Eldest describe a skirmish she had been in fifty years ago with such raptness that she was unable to get his attention. When he did look her way, he bowed formally, as if they were no more than fellow Keepers of the Peace. Very correct and proper behavior in front of the elders of Kali, but it maddened Kyra, especially as he seemed to relax in front of the novices, showing them the different ways Marksmen gripped and threw a katari, much to their delight. Even Chintil thawed enough to ask probing questions about the Khur style of fighting.

After the meal, the older Markswomen led the younger ones out for a Hatha-kala class. Kyra bid them goodbye, for she would be gone for several days. She hugged the younger ones and bowed to the others. But Elena walked away without a glance at her, crushing her slim hope that sleeping might have abated some of her friend's fury. She wanted to run after Elena, to apologize again, to beg forgiveness, but she held back, knowing she had to maintain her dignity in front of the others.

At last Kyra and Rustan met with the elders in the central

cavern. They were packed and ready to leave, the kalishium image wrapped in oilcloth and slung onto Kyra's back.

"You should stay awhile longer," said Navroz to Rustan. "One of us can accompany Kyra to Kashgar and across the Empty Place."

"I must return to my Order," said Rustan, in a tone that brooked no argument. "I have a duty to report to the Maji-khan of Khur."

Kyra laid a hand on Navroz's arm. "Eldest, we will be back in less than two weeks. Meanwhile, you will gather the forces promised by the clans. We can lose no more time."

"Speaking of losing time, suppose the door to the Thar Desert has shifted," said Chintil. "No one has used it since you did."

Kyra grimaced. She had filled them in on the Valavian battle, and the plan to attack the Taus from both east and west once the kalishium shields were ready. "Any door can shift, at any moment," she said. "We must take our chances. But I will go first to make sure all is well, before I let anyone else follow. Mobilize the clans, Eldest. We will need every able-bodied fighter we can get. Kai Tau's army could have swollen to several thousands by now."

"Blood will flow," said Chintil, her eyes agleam. "We will give the desert a feast it has never seen before."

"Hopefully, it will not be *our* blood the desert feasts on," said Felda drily.

"Yes, Elder," said Kyra. "That is why we need kalishium shields. That is why I must go to Astinsai."

"The Goddess go with you," said Navroz. "Do not tarry in Khur; come back as soon as you have what you need."

Kyra bowed, and Rustan did the same. As they set off up the

hill to the Ferghana Hub, a slow realization sank into Kyra. She and Rustan would be alone together for several days, for the first time ever. That time in Kunlun Shan did not count; then, they had been adversaries of a sort, and it had all felt like a dream anyway. Now he was her ally. *Your mate*, Menadin had said, and she grew warm thinking it. *Knowing* it, even if Rustan did not. When this was over, she would . . . do something. *Say* something. *I belong to you and you belong to me, even as we belong to our Orders.* And perhaps, just perhaps, he would agree.

⟡

Rustan did not speak to Kyra until they arrived at the Kashgar Hub, but it was a companionable silence. He asked her once if she needed his help carrying the image, but she refused; he was already laden with provisions for the journey, and the kalishium was her responsibility.

They emerged from the Kashgar Hub into a bright, clamorous morning. It was market day, and as Kyra weaved her way between the sellers crying out their wares, she remembered the first time she had seen this beautiful, bewildering town. Rustan had found her at the central market square, standing on tiptoe, trying to look at everything. He had shown her around. And he had bought her a bolt of beautiful green silk.

Kyra still had it, safe in a drawer of the Mahimata's old desk. *One day*, she thought, *I will wear it for you.*

Rustan turned to her with a questioning frown, and she shook her head, grinning. It was fun to confuse him; he could still sense her feelings, but she had grown better at concealing herself from him. Perhaps that came from being the Mahimata. Or perhaps that simply came from growing as a Markswoman.

People backed away and bowed as they passed. Kyra couldn't help enjoying how their eyes widened as they took in her black robe embroidered with the symbol of Kali. She had no need to hide who she was this time, and it was a pleasant contrast to her last visit there.

They had no trouble renting a camel for the journey to Khur. Rustan already had his own, Basil, which had been brought over from Yartan to Kashgar in a caravan.

The camel herder refused to take money from them, overcome at the identity of his customers. Rustan forced him to accept ten silver sitaris anyway. They loaded the camels with their provisions and several goatskins of water.

After a quick meal of vegetable soup and noodles at a guesthouse—where, again, they had to force the proprietor to accept their coin—Kyra and Rustan set off for Khur, Kyra wincing as she lowered herself onto the hard saddle. This was the part she was *not* looking forward to.

Midmorning turned to noon as they crested the first large dune. Kyra turned back for a last look, admiring the way Kashgar shimmered below them in the sun like a fable. Then the camel descended the slope of the dune and the city vanished, as if it had never been there at all. The wind rose, whistling down the dune.

"We were caught in a sandstorm last time," said Kyra, tying a scarf around her face to protect it from the sun and the wind. It was not an experience she wished to repeat.

"It's still too early in the year for a really bad storm," said Rustan. "It will be all right." But he sounded ill at ease as he said it, as if he needed to convince himself.

"What is it?" asked Kyra, glancing at him sideways.

He stiffened his shoulders. "Nothing," he said.

Fine. Be like that, she thought.

A few minutes later, he broke the silence. "It's my katari," he said. "I have been parted from it for months. But it knows I am returning. I can feel it"—he frowned—"*pulling* me."

"That's a good thing, isn't it?" she asked. "It means your bond is still strong, even after the separation."

He shook his head. "It almost drove me mad to leave it behind. I thought it would tear me apart. I heard voices, I saw things. And"—he swallowed—"I can hear them again now, very faint."

The look on Rustan's face made her heart clench. It was the first time she had ever seen him look lost or uncertain. Kyra nudged her camel closer to his. When they were alongside, she reached out and encircled his wrist with her hand. "It will be all right." She echoed his words. "And I am with you."

He gave a startled smile. Then he raised her hand to his lips and kissed it. So soft his lips, so rough the stubble of his cheeks. She wanted to trace her hands over him, to know him as intimately as she knew herself. Heat flooded her face and she withdrew her hand abruptly.

"How will we time our breaks?" she said, her voice uneven.

"We have started late in the day, so we should continue until nightfall," he answered. "Tomorrow, if we start at dawn, we will let the camels rest in the afternoon." His eyes lingered on her face, searching, and she pulled her camel away from him.

They continued in silence after that, letting their bodies move in rhythm to the swaying camels. The heat of midday gave way to the slant of the late-afternoon sun. The dune field stretched to the horizon, an austere landscape that brooked no indulgence, no carelessness. And yet, with Rustan by her side, the bleakest setting turned to gold. Kyra let her mind empty and her thoughts drift. It was a bit of peace, all the more precious because of the days that would follow.

But the peace ended all too soon. As darkness fell and stars winked in the sky, and Kyra began to think it was about time they halted and stretched their limbs, Rustan slumped forward in the saddle of his camel. At first, she didn't register it; her mind had slowed, in tune with the landscape that surrounded them. Then she realized with a jolt that she could no longer sense Rustan's warm, comforting presence ahead of her; he had slipped away from her, as if through a door.

She urged her camel forward and saw, with a sickening plunge of her heart, that Rustan lay unmoving on his camel. Only the horn of the saddle had protected him from falling. She commanded the camels to sit and dismounted, her own discomfort forgotten as she raced to Rustan's side. His pulse, thank the Goddess, was regular, though faint. She put an arm around him to try to get him out of the saddle and onto the ground, but he was too heavy for her and she was afraid that he would fall.

"Wake up, Rustan, please, open your eyes," she said, repeating the words over and over, rubbing his cold hands between her palms. At last he stirred and turned his head toward her, bewildered, as if he did not know who she was or where they were. She helped him off the camel and onto the sandy earth. He collapsed, sweat beading his brow. She undid a waterskin with shaking hands and held it to his lips. After a few sips, he revived somewhat. Kyra knelt beside him, feeling her own breathing return to normal.

"What happened?" she asked at last.

"I don't know," he muttered. "Voices. Dark ones. I pushed them away, but it was hard."

"The dark weapons." Coldness crept up her limbs. "They are calling to you. You need Astinsai's help."

"What I need is my own katari," said Rustan. "My mother's blade helps, but I am not bonded to it."

"Then we must return to Khur as fast as possible," said Kyra. It took five days, if you rested at night and in the afternoons. But they could go faster than that; the camels did not need to rest as much as humans did. "Sleep," she told Rustan. "I will keep watch and wake you in three hours so we can continue."

He shook his head vehemently. "No. The voices get stronger at night; if I sleep, they will take over my dreams."

"You must rest," said Kyra. When he began to argue, she forestalled him. "Do you not trust me?" she said, and he fell quiet.

She made him drink more water and eat some dates, then tucked a rug around him and bade him sleep. He tried to resist for a while, but finally his eyes fluttered closed and his breathing lengthened.

Kyra tried to stay awake, leaning against her camel, but she was tired, and the night was cold. At last, unable to help herself, she edged under the rug next to Rustan.

He stirred and moaned, restless. "No, no," he muttered. "Get away." He thrashed his head from side to side.

"Hush," said Kyra, leaning on her elbow and laying a hand on his chest, trying to calm him. "It's okay. It's just a dream."

He threw the rug off and sat bolt upright. "Stay away from me!" he shouted.

Kyra sat up in alarm. In the starlight, Rustan's eyes were unfocused, his face torn with anguish.

"Rustan," she commanded, with a hint of the Inner Speech, "wake up." She knelt in front of him and grabbed his face with both hands, forcing him to look at her.

Slowly, he returned to himself, and his eyes focused on her. His face twisted with pain. "Hold me," he whispered. "The voices are too strong."

Kyra drew her arms around him, cradling his head on her chest. "I'm here," she said, her breath uneven. She kissed the top of his hair, inhaling the heady, confusing scent of him she loved so much: desert and sky, hope and despair, darkness and desire.

He rubbed his cheek against her, his breath warm on her skin. His hands moved up her hips, over her scabbard, and her breath caught as tiny shocks of pleasure sparked in her body.

His arms tightened around her and he pulled her down next to him, slipping his hand under her belt, anchoring her to himself. For a moment it was as if Kyra had stepped outside her own body, and almost she could not recognize herself, this woman who gasped and arched her back as Rustan trailed hot kisses down her neck.

"Rustan," she said in a ragged voice. "Rustan."

"I am here," he breathed in her ear. He gazed at her, the want in his deep blue eyes mirroring her own. Slowly, deliberately, he bent his lips to hers, the kiss soft at first, and then harder, more insistent. A small sound escaped her throat. Her heart beat like a drum, both terrified and exhilarated. He entwined one hand in hers; she could feel every tendon, every callus of his palm. With his other hand he unclasped her belt, and she dissolved, melting into his embrace.

The world vanished; it was as if only the two of them lived and, for however brief a time, it was enough to love and be loved by the one person who could keep the darkness of the whole universe at bay.

CHAPTER 35

TO FORGE KALISHIUM

Rustan and Kyra arrived in the camp of Khur three days later, grimy and exhausted. They had ridden hard, stopping only for a few hours each night to rest the camels. Kyra was trembling with fatigue and Rustan looked in even worse shape. She was sure the voices continued to haunt him; though he did not speak of it again, his eyes betrayed his inner anguish. She hoped and prayed that being reunited with his blade would drive away the vile touch of the kalashiks from his mind. Her spirits soared as they came in sight of the vast dune that shimmered over the camp of Khur.

In Khur, they were expected; the Maji-khan himself stood at the edge of the camp, his visage grave, the elders arrayed behind him in a semicircle. It reminded Kyra of the first time she had arrived in Khur, with one poignant exception: Ishtul the blademaster was missing, and he would never return.

They dismounted, and a couple of apprentices ran up to lead

the camels away. Kyra heaved the sack containing the kalishium image onto her shoulders. Rustan almost stumbled at Barkav's feet. The Maji-khan grasped his arm and helped him up.

"Father, Ishtul . . ." Rustan's voice broke.

"I know," said Barkav tightly. He nodded to Kyra. "Welcome, Kyra Veer. It is good to see you looking well."

Looking *well*? Did she look that different from how she felt? Tired, aching, and hungry from traveling across the Empty Place on camelback with meager rations. Apprehensive about the image she carried, seeing Astinsai, and persuading her to help them. Anxious about Rustan and the upcoming battle with Kai Tau and his death-sticks.

Then she remembered that the last time the Maji-khan had seen her, she had been almost dead from the wound delivered by Tamsyn's blade. Anything would be an improvement.

She bowed to Barkav and the elders. "Thank you," she said. "It is good to be back. If only we had better tidings."

"The Order of Kali sent us Ishtul's remains, for which we are grateful," said Barkav. "We buried him at the edge of the grove, in sight of the dune that protects us. He will be sorely missed."

"We have not had such an accomplished blademaster in decades," put in Saninda, one of the elders. "You are needed here, Rustan."

"He has returned to us," said Barkav. "Have you not, Marksman?"

Rustan took a deep breath. "There is a war to be fought, and I would fight by your side, if you will have me."

Barkav smiled, his expression relaxing into something almost like tenderness. "Then I have something that belongs to you." He withdrew a wooden scabbard from his belt and proffered it to Rustan. "It has been waiting for you these many months."

Rustan grasped the hilt of his katari and slid it from the scabbard. He touched it to his forehead, and Kyra gasped and took an involuntary step back. Soft blue light sprang from the blade and enveloped Rustan in radiance so that he looked, for a moment, like a bygone king.

He sheathed the blade, and the light dissipated. The Maji-khan spoke, his voice ringing in the silence that followed, "Even though we stand on the brink of battle, and our hearts are filled with sorrow at the fate of Ishtul, let us put aside our grief for one day and celebrate the return of a son of Khur."

The Marksmen cheered and bore Rustan away. He twisted his head back and locked eyes with Kyra. She gave him a reassuring smile. Although he looked ready to drop dead from fatigue, his face softened, and he smiled back at her. She watched him until he disappeared in the knot of Marksmen that surrounded him. She could understand how he felt; he was back where he belonged, reunited with his katari. What more could anyone ask for?

The Maji-khan had not moved from his place. He stood, solid as a mountain, and regarded her with his calm gray eyes. "You mentioned in your letter that you have been anointed as the Mahimata of Kali. Please accept my congratulations. You must be the youngest Mahimata in the entire history of your Order."

"The youngest and most foolish, according to my elders, I'm sure," said Kyra drily.

Barkav threw his head back and laughed. "Youth has advantages that old age sometimes refuses to see," he said. "You will always have the support of the Order of Khur, if that is any consolation. Now, we have much to discuss, but you carry a burden that not many shoulders could bear. Will you not lay it down?"

Kyra hesitated. But the Maji-khan had sensed the contents of her sack, even if no one else had. She dropped it onto the ground and sighed, rubbing her shoulders. "It weighs on me," she confessed. "It is not mine; I took it from a monastery. Rustan tried to stop me, but I wouldn't listen to him. We need it, Maji-khan."

She outlined her plan to Barkav, how she hoped Astinsai would forge the stolen kalishium into shields to protect the vanguard of Markswomen who would attack the Tau camp.

Barkav stroked his beard and frowned. "It is not rightfully yours," he said at last. "You will pay the price for this theft, one way or another."

Kyra shivered. This was what Rustan had warned too. "If I must, then I must," she said stoutly. "There is no other way that I can see, not without risking all our lives."

Barkav nodded. "I will speak to Astinsai. You may rest and eat first; I will have an apprentice inform you when Astinsai is ready to see you." He turned, beckoning her to follow him. "You remember the tent where you stayed when you first arrived?"

"Yes, Maji-khan." She hefted her burden once again and followed him.

She had spent more than a month living in the camp of Khur. As Barkav led her to the little tent set aside for guests, Kyra was struck by a pang of sadness. Little had she realized then that, despite Shirin Mam's death and the duel with Tamsyn looming over her, it was one of the most carefree times she would ever know. She had learned new ways to fight; she had made new friends; she had even cooked a meal for them. And a large part of what had made this a happy time for her had been the company of Shurik, the cheerful young Marksman who, in the end, betrayed their friendship in a way she had deemed unforgivable.

But had she not done the same to Rustan? And had he not forgiven her, out of the love and generosity of his heart? Could she do any less?

"You know where everything is," said Barkav, waving a hand to encompass the camp. "Feel free to go to the communal tent and ask for something to eat. Jeev has already placed fresh water in your tent."

When she had first arrived, it had been Shurik who had fetched water for her and shown her around the camp. But she had seen no sign of him since their arrival. What had happened to her former friend? "Please, Maji-khan, where is Shurik?" she asked.

Barkav frowned, the sudden change in his countenance almost frightening. "You need not worry about him," he said. "The boy will not bother you again."

"I'm not worried," Kyra assured him. "Isn't he here, though?" She wasn't afraid of seeing him again; she found that she *wanted* to see him and speak to him. To put the past behind them.

"I sent him to the Thar Desert after his penance," said Barkav. "He meditated in solitude for three months without his blade, and at the end of it, requested an assignment away from Khur to prove himself worthy to rejoin the Order. We knew it would be dangerous, but I thought I was sending him to Ishtul. That was before I realized that Ishtul had been killed."

Kyra's chest tighened. "So you have no idea where Shurik is, or if he's safe."

Barkav shook his head, looking troubled. "I believe he lives, but more than that I cannot say. We will find him again, God willing."

He left, and Kyra ducked into the tent, glad for a chance to escape his piercing gaze. She prayed Shurik was all right and would rejoin his Order soon.

There was clean water in a pitcher, and she drank her fill before using some to wet a piece of cloth and wipe herself down, knowing that was all the bath she'd get before returning to the Ferghana. As she lay down to rest, she wondered how Rustan was doing. If being reunited with his blade had banished the voices plaguing his mind. If being reunited with his friends and fellow Marksmen had healed the old wounds he had tried to run away from. She felt a surge of jealousy as she remembered how they had surrounded him and swept him away. There was genuine love and affection there—both how they felt about him, and how he felt about them. It was clear that he was happy to be back, that he would not leave their side willingly.

And then she was surprised and angry at herself for feeling jealous. She did not *own* Rustan, just as he did not own her. They had loyalties, responsibilities, and friends. What they felt for each other was a small part of the whole, and she had better remember it. Perhaps, when the menace of Kai Tau had been dealt with, they could travel together occasionally. She wouldn't try to separate him from his Order, but she could ask him to accompany her on the most dangerous and difficult missions. Surely the Maji-khan would not object to that. And surely it was possible that on those missions, they would know again the intimacy they had shared so briefly in the desert.

Dreaming of this, of the touch of his skin on hers, his breath in her hair, his hands on her blade, she drifted off to sleep, smiling.

She came to a rude awakening when someone shouted her name from outside the tent.

"Kyra?" It sounded like the apprentice Jeev. "Astinsai says she is ready to meet you, and to bring your gift."

Gift? Kyra sat up, rubbing the sleep out of her gummed-up eyes. "I will be there soon," she called. She peeked her head out of the tent, noticing that the light had dimmed to late evening. Jeev stood on one leg, grinning at her, his face thinner and older than she remembered.

"Nice to see you again," he said shyly. He cast a nervous look around, then produced a ragged bit of parchment from his pocket. "From Shurik," he said, and thrust it at her.

"What?" said Kyra, startled, taking the parchment. The parchment was folded and the edges sealed with wax; she noticed Jeev was still standing there hopefully, as if she was going to open it right away and read it aloud to him.

"Thank you," she said. "I will read it later. Goodnight," she added pointedly, and he finally left.

Kyra tore open the letter. It contained a single word: "Sorry." Below that was the drawing of a stick figure with a sad face— presumably Shurik. His drawing skills left much to be desired, but the sentiment was clear, and her lips twitched. She really hoped he was okay.

She tucked the letter into a pocket and tried to make herself presentable, washing her face with cold water and running a comb through her unruly hair. She stepped out and donned her traveling cloak, glad of its warmth in the chilly wind.

What did the Old One mean, she should bring her gift? Did she mean the kalishium? Kyra hefted the sack onto her shoulders and walked to the Old One's tent. It was slow going. She passed several Marksmen on the way, all of whom stopped to shout a greeting or ask how she was. Quite a change from the last time she visited Khur, and it gladdened her.

Astinsai sat cross-legged on the floor of her tent, looking exactly the same as ever: tiny and ancient, with blackbird-sharp eyes peeking out of a wizened face.

"Welcome, Mahimata of Kali," she said, inclining her head. "The first such distinguished personage to visit my humble abode. I am indeed blessed."

Kyra suppressed her irritation at the palpable falseness of the words. She bowed and knelt opposite Astinsai, laying the sack at her feet. "Greetings, mistress," she said. "Thank you for the welcome. I have come to seek your counsel and your help."

"Show it to me," said Astinsai, her eyes gleaming. "Show me what's inside." She was trembling, as if she couldn't contain her eagerness.

Kyra undid the strings that tied the sack, feeling an odd reluctance as she did so. Her hands felt heavy and slow, as if they did not wish Astinsai to lay her greedy eyes on the wealth it contained.

But that was foolish. Only the katari mistress could help her with what she needed. At last, the wrapping fell away and revealed the precious image inside. The wolf reared its head, snarling, looking as if it were alive, gleaming with an alien light of its own.

Astinsai shrank back, nostrils flaring, looking in that reflected light like an alien herself. She muttered an invocation under her breath and snapped, "Cover it up."

Kyra obeyed, bewildered and shaken. The light dissipated.

Astinsai took a deep breath. "Of all the images you saw, you had to steal *that* one?"

"What is wrong with this one?" asked Kyra, trying to ignore the word *steal*.

"Nothing wrong with it," said Astinsai. "But it is a wyr-wolf image and rightfully belongs to them. You should have, at the very least, taken the image of a human. The repercussions would have been milder."

Kyra remembered the sensations she'd had when she first touched the image, the memories she had been sucked into, and how she had almost lost herself. "I intend to save a piece of this for the wyr-wolves," she said. At Astinsai's disbelieving expression, she outlined, in the barest possible detail and without reference to *Anant-kal*, her connection with wyr-wolves, her ability to communicate with them, and the role they had played in the battle of Valavan.

"Hmmm." Astinsai studied Kyra with her penetrating eyes, as if she knew that what Kyra hid was greater than what she revealed. "That does change things somewhat. Almost as if you have their permission to use this image, which is why you were drawn to it in the first place. Nevertheless, I cannot help you."

"What?" Kyra was too stunned to be angry. "Why not?"

"It is now many years since I have forged a katari," said Astinsai. "You do not know, do you, what it entails? The kind of sacrifice it demands?"

"No," said Kyra, choosing her words with care, knowing they would hurt the katari mistress. "But we all have to make sacrifices in times of war. And in this war, do not forget your own culpability."

Astinsai's face stiffened, but beyond that she did not betray any emotion. "You don't understand," she said. "Kalishium is not an ordinary metal. To prepare it for bonding, we must give it a bit of our soul. I do not remember how many blades I have forged, but a piece of me resides in them all. I am incomplete, and I always will be, until the moment of my death. What I am trying to tell you is, there is not enough of me left to make anything for you."

Kyra's heart sank. Her whole mission had depended upon Astinsai's cooperation.

"Unless . . ." said Astinsai, her expression suddenly sly.

Kyra leaned forward, hope blossoming inside her. "Yes?"

"Unless you help me," said the Old One, with a gap-toothed grin. "You have an affinity for kalishium, and I noticed the beginnings of it when I first saw you. I have never had an apprentice—never dared to. It is such a risk; most people would not survive the witnessing of a true forging. But I am reasonably sure the Mahimata of Kali can not only survive the process but aid it. Would you like to learn how to forge kalishium?"

Kyra sat back, shocked. This was so unexpected that she was rendered speechless.

"Of course," added Astinsai, "you do have to make an offering."

"An offering," echoed Kyra, still unable to wrap her head around what Astinsai had said.

"It is traditional," said the katari mistress. "If you wish to learn my craft, you must offer me a gift, something that I would value."

"And if I refuse to help?" said Kyra.

Astinsai shrugged. "Then you must return, taking that image with you. I cannot do this on my own. It is not death I fear. I am old enough now that death would be a release. But I have no wish to spend eternity trapped in a piece of metal, and that is what would happen."

Kyra was stuck. If she wanted Astinsai to forge shields from the kalishium image, she would have to agree to help her. She had never dreamed she had the kind of affinity for kalishium that Astinsai was talking about. Maybe she didn't; maybe the Old One saw something in her that wasn't there, born from her own wishful thinking.

But it was a risk Kyra would have to take. She bit her lip as she considered her meager options. "All right," she said at last. "I will help you, if that's what it takes."

Astinsai grinned widely and rubbed her bony hands together. "Excellent. Finally, in my advanced age, I find a pupil, even if she is an unwilling one. Come now, where is my offering? I am eager to begin."

"I'm sorry," said Kyra with regret. "I don't have anything of value."

"Ah, but you are mistaken." Astinsai leaned forward and lowered her voice. "You have the code to the Akal-shin door, and perhaps many other doors that have been thought unusable for decades. Give me those codes."

Kyra thought of Felda's pyramid of primes, and her eyes narrowed. "Why do you want them?" she asked.

"Because there are doors that lead out of Asiana," answered Astinsai. "To other lands we have lost all knowledge of. Maybe even the moon. I would like to take such a door. It would be a fine way to die."

A chill went down Kyra's spine. That was *her* destiny. Not Astinsai's. "I am sorry," she said. "But those doors you are talking about are unstable. They are too dangerous. I would be doing you—and everyone else—a great disservice by sharing that kind of knowledge." She held up a hand as Astinsai opened her mouth to argue. "Please. Do not ask this of me. I will not be moved."

"Then there is only one more thing you have that might possibly interest me." The Old One reached for a pipe attached to a clay bowl and inhaled, blowing a smoke ring into the already close air of the tent. Kyra, tense, waited for her to resume speaking. Astinsai removed the pipe from her mouth and said, "A vision."

Kyra looked at her blankly.

"I told you once, you are a girl with many questions," said Astinsai. "Some of the answers you receive may be of value to me. You will drink Rasaynam and tell me what you see."

Oh no. Kyra remembered what Rasaynam was, what it had done to Rustan. Astinsai had offered the potion to her once, and she had refused. Wisely, if what Shurik had told her was anything to go by. Rasaynam showed you the truth, but never a happy version of it, and never the whole of it either. Whatever she saw was bound to make her bitter, angry, or worse, drive her crazy.

But was she not a stronger person than she had been just months earlier? Armed with the foreknowledge of what Rasaynam could do, would she not be able to battle its worst effects?

And above all, what might it tell her that no one else could?

"I'll do it," said Kyra, before she could change her mind. "And then we will forge the shields together."

The Old One sighed with barely concealed pleasure. "Let me brew it then. Return at the hour of midnight, and your apprenticeship will begin."

Kyra bowed and left, trying to convince herself that she was doing the right thing. But as she walked to the communal tent in the cooling dusk, the coldness of fear crept into her limbs.

CHAPTER 36

COUNCIL OF WAR

Rustan sat cross-legged near the entrance of the council tent, surrounded by the elders, the Maji-khan in the middle. He had just finished describing in detail his infiltration of the Tau camp at Jethwa and the burning of the weapons forge. His katari glowed at his side, spreading warmth into his limbs, mitigating the exhaustion he still felt, chasing away the remnants of the evil voices that had pursued him across the Empty Place. His mother's blade was sheathed in a black scabbard. It had kept him sane, but it was Kyra who had reminded him that life and sanity were worth fighting for. Her, and the memory of the two phantom monks who had guided him from the land of despair to the land of hope and self-knowledge.

Barkav and Saninda pored over the diagram-filled parchments Rustan had wrested from the smith Tej the night he burned down the forge.

Ghasil, the Master of Mental Arts, leaned toward Rustan. "You did not see or sense Kai Tau?" he asked. "Or Shurik?" He could not keep the anxiety from his voice.

Rustan shook his head. "I did not sense any kataris in the camp, Elder."

"Shurik will be all right," said Ghasil, as if he was trying to convince himself. "He is the strongest pupil I've ever had."

Ghasil had never praised Shurik before. He must be really worried about him. Rustan filed away the compliment to report to his friend later. If there was a later.

Barkav looked up from the parchments, his face grave. "Rustan, you did well to bring these to me. These designs— they are the product of a sick mind, but a highly intelligent one. Some of them might actually work. Spheres that burst into many pieces, embedding themselves in flesh and bone. Guns that look like crude kalashiks. Machines to rain fire and death from the sky. I see the hand of Kai Tau in this, and I fear this is but one of multiple copies he has made."

"All the more reason for us to attack sooner rather than later," said Ghasil.

Barkav nodded. "We will return with Kyra to the Ferghana when her work with Astinsai is done. Ghasil, you and Saninda will summon the horsemen of the Kushan and Turguz clans. They are good fighters, and they owe us a blood debt. Gather as many as you can and follow us to the caves of Kali."

"The caves of Kali?" asked Saninda in disbelief. "Do you think they will welcome us, Maji-khan?"

"They will, Elder," said Rustan, with as much conviction as he could muster, pushing aside the wariness he had sensed from Navroz and Mumuksu when he arrived at the Order of Kali. "They know they need us if they are to defeat Kai Tau.

And Kyra is now the Mahimata of Kali. They are oath-bound to follow her."

Ghasil exhaled heavily. "I never thought I'd see this day. We are actually contemplating walking into the heart of Kali territory. Let us pray they do not think we are attacking them."

Barkav's mouth twitched. "Kyra will be with us, to prevent any 'accidents.' Let us not waste time and energy worrying about our allies but concentrate on our enemies."

"I want to hear from Kyra about the events at Valavan, and her link with the wyr-wolves," said Afraim.

"After the evening meal," said Barkav. "Why don't you all go to the communal tent, and Rustan and I will join you afterward?"

It was a clear signal for the elders to leave Rustan alone with the Maji-khan. They rose and filed out of the tent, talking in low voices. Barkav waited until they were gone and then met Rustan's gaze. "Come, my boy," he said softly. "Tell me what happened in Kunlun Shan. Because something did happen. I can see it in your eyes."

Rustan's shoulders sagged. He hadn't told them about the Sahirus, what he had learned from them, or the beast he had confronted on the way up to the monastery. It had seemed much more important to tell the Khur elders about Jethwa and the battle of Valavan.

But Barkav knew, even if the others did not, that he had left out the most crucial part of the story—the part that made the least sense. Rustan rubbed his eyes and willed himself to relax. "I don't know what happened," he said at last. "I don't understand it, except in some moments I do, and then I feel I am living a life that is not mine, that I am meant to be elsewhere."

Barkav waited patiently for him to continue.

And so, haltingly at first, Rustan told the Maji-khan everything, from his journey across the desert and up the mountains, to his rescue by the two ancient monks, and his discovery some weeks later of their frozen bodies.

"They had been dead for many months, perhaps years," concluded Rustan. "So who did I meet? And what did they want?"

"They told you what they wanted," said Barkav, his face full of compassion. "They wanted an apprentice who would learn from them and then bury them. I cannot pretend to understand how they reached out to you from beyond the door of death. Perhaps they can manipulate time? There are many strange stories told of the Sahirus, and I have never given them much credence before. But you are indeed fortunate to have lived with them—or whatever version of themselves they chose to show you."

"I think," said Rustan slowly, "that I must return to the monastery one day. That I have tasks left unfinished." *One last coffin to fill*, he thought, a hollow feeling in his chest.

A look of sadness passed the Maji-khan's face. "Go then. After the battle with the Taus is decided one way or another, go back to Kunlun Shan, with my blessing."

Rustan's heart constricted. He had only just been reunited with his Order and his katari. Would he be able to give them up again? And—more importantly—would he be able to give up Kyra?

Lying with her under the bright stars of the desert sky, her head on his chest, the warmth of her body curled next to his in the sweet exhaustion that followed their lovemaking, he had wanted the night to last forever. Despite his doubts, his pain, and the voices that dimmed in her presence but never quite died away, he had felt an odd sort of peace, and wished it could continue—a journey that never came to an end.

Wishful thinking, a child's thinking. Rustan had always tried to do what was right. But when the end came, he wondered, would he still know what the right thing was? And would he have the strength to do it?

CHAPTER 37

A VISION FROM
THE PAST

After the evening meal, Kyra was summoned to the council tent to meet the Maji-khan and the elders. Rustan was already there, looking much healthier than he had during their journey. He kept touching the wooden scabbard at his belt, as if to reassure himself that his katari was back where it belonged—an unconscious gesture of vulnerability that she found endearing. He met her gaze and gave her a warm smile. *I'm all right*, that smile said, and she felt herself relax a little, although she was dreading telling him what Astinsai had asked of her, what she had agreed to.

Astinsai was conspicuous in her absence. *Busy preparing the potion to drive me mad*, thought Kyra wryly.

"Rustan has described to us the battle of Valavan," said the Maji-khan. "But we would hear it in your words, Kyra Veer. Did a wyr-wolf truly save your life?"

"He did," said Kyra, pain returning at the memory of

Menadin's sacrifice. "He died so I might live and fulfill the promise I made to him and his people: rid the world of its dark weapons and return stability to Asiana. You were right about them, Father."

As succinctly as possible, she told them about her link with the wyr-wolves, her ability to communicate with them, and her discovery that they were part human. Something which the Order of Khur had always believed. The elders listened to her, rapt. Ghasil tugged his mustache and muttered, "I knew it!" and Saninda wiped a sleeve across his eye. Even Barkav could not hide how moved he was.

"There will be no more hunting or killing of wyr-wolves in Asiana," finished Kyra. "The Order of Kali and the Order of Valavan have issued edicts to that effect. And none of the other Orders allow it anyway."

The Zoryans had always believed, like the Marksmen, that wyr-wolves were part human. The Order of Mat-su did not believe in killing animals at all, no matter how dangerous.

"Now all that is left is for you to fulfill your vow," said the Maji-khan. "And to do that, we must first defeat Kai Tau. Have you spoken with Astinsai? Will she forge the kalishium for you?"

Kyra hesitated. "Yes," she said carefully. "But she cannot do this alone. The katari mistress says she needs my help. She thinks I have an affinity for kalishium."

A dead silence met her words. The elders stared at her with a mixture of hope and disbelief, and Rustan was the first to speak. "What. The. Sands." His face was furious. "You can't risk yourself, Kyra. You have a battle to fight."

"A battle we will not win unless we can protect ourselves from the dark weapons," she reminded him.

"We will not win without you either—" Rustan began, but Barkav held up a hand, and Rustan fell silent. His eyes, however, raked her face, pleading: *Don't.*

I'm sorry, but I think I must.

"If Astinsai has seen an affinity in you for kalishium, then it is your duty to investigate it," said the Maji-khan. "Astinsai has never taken an apprentice—never even let anyone witness her forging a katari. If you truly have the gift—even the merest hint of it—think of what it means for the future of the Orders of Asiana. The katari masters and mistresses of yore are a dying breed. If you can learn from Astinsai, it would be a boon, not only to your Order, but to everyone else as well."

Kyra swallowed. "I will try my best, Maji-khan." *If I survive the night*, she did not need to add. It was in all their faces.

"Let me stay with you then," said Rustan. "Perhaps I can help."

"No," said Barkav, his voice like flint. "In this, none of us can help her. It is between her and Astinsai."

"Don't worry," said Kyra, in her most reassuring voice. "I am sure Astinsai will not let any harm come to me."

At that, even Barkav looked at her with such misgiving that she changed the subject to the matter of mobilizing and arming the nomad warriors of the Empty Place.

When the meeting was over, Kyra hurried out into the cold night, anxious to avoid Rustan. But she sensed him behind her, striding to catch up, and she halted.

"I'll be fine," she said firmly, before he could speak. "I must do this. Don't try to stop me."

He gave a sardonic grin. "I wouldn't dare," he said. His voice lowered. "But be careful, all right? If something does not ring true to you, then it isn't. Listen to the wisdom of your inner voice before doing anything she asks. You are not honor-bound in this."

Kyra sighed. "I don't trust her," she admitted. "But she isn't lying when she says she needs help. I just hope I have what it takes to be her assistant."

"Of course you do," he said, grasping her shoulders, his touch warm. "You are the Mahimata of Kali. You have the blessings of the Goddess herself. And do I not know that you are the best pupil any teacher could hope to have? The kind of pupil who will outmatch her teacher one day."

Kyra opened her mouth to protest, but he bent down and kissed her forehead, leaving the words trapped in her throat.

"Tell the Old One," he whispered against her cheek, making her heart palpitate, "that if she lets harm come to you, I will kill her with the blade she forged for me. And there will be no more katari mistress of Khur."

He held her tightly for a moment, then released her and stepped back, breathing hard. His eyes burned into hers. Then he turned and was gone, swallowed by the darkness.

Kyra walked to her tent, trying to slow her pulse. It was almost midnight. But she wasn't about to go to Astinsai like this. She ducked inside and splashed cold water on her face and breathed in the lotus position until she had herself under control. Only then did she make her way to the Old One.

Astinsai was waiting for her, a feral grin of anticipation on her face. "I wondered if you would come," she remarked when Kyra was seated opposite her. "Or if you would listen to the young man who is so head over heels in love that he has forgotten where his duties lie."

Kyra gritted her teeth. "He has not forgotten," she assured the katari mistress. "But he has other loyalties now."

"To you?" sneered Astinsai. "How long do you think that will last?"

Kyra flushed with anger. "I was thinking of the Sahirus," she said. "Rustan owes his life to the monks he met in Kunlun Shan. He owes nothing to me. Although," she added, "he did ask me to tell you that if you let harm come to me, he will kill you."

At that Astinsai laughed outright. "Love, lust, *deewangee*," she said softly. "It is what drives us all in the end." She bent her head for a moment, lost in her own thoughts, her own memories. When she raised her head, the sparkle was back in her eyes. "Are you ready?" she asked.

Kyra squared her shoulders. "As ready as I'll ever be," she said, although the words sounded hollow. *Of course* she was not ready.

The Old One lifted an iron pot and poured a measure of steaming liquid into a clay cup.

"Rasaynam," she said, and proffered the cup to Kyra. "You declined it the first time I gave it to you. Remember what I told you then? Come back to me when you're ready. Come back when you think you have no more tears to shed."

Kyra accepted the cup, willing her hands not to shake. "What will it show me?" she asked. "Do I have to think of something specific?"

"No," said Astinsai. "Rasaynam knows the deepest, most urgent question of your heart." She waved a hand. "Drink, drink it all. The potion will do the rest."

Kyra put the cup to her lips. Astinsai watched, her ancient face agog. Kyra squeezed her eyes shut and prayed, *Kali keep me sane for what comes next.*

Then she tilted her head back and drank, without stopping,

until the cup was empty. When she opened her eyes, she was
no longer in Astinsai's tent.

❧

Fidan Veer had escaped her mother's eagle eye and gone to the
central market of Yartan with her cousins. If only it were not
so cold. The girls were clad in sheepskin coats and thick boots,
woolen scarves wrapped around their throats, and they were
still shivering. Ice floated on the surface of the Yartan River,
which coiled around the main market square. The square was
mostly empty; a few enterprising souls had set up stalls to sell
woolens, frozen butter, cheese, knives, and other odds and
ends. It was good to be out, with the brisk air on her face, one
giggling cousin on each arm, the faded blue and pink facade of
the old prayerhouse radiant in the winter sun.

Fidan's cousins paused to inspect a cart full of old-fashioned
bracelets and brooches. Bored, she drifted ahead of them to a
more interesting stall displaying tools and weapons.

It was then that she noticed him. He was watching her from
across the square, holding the reins of a black horse. He was the
most arresting young man she had ever seen, tall and well built,
with piercing green eyes and smooth dark hair tied back in a
braid. He was travel-worn and hollow-cheeked, as if he hadn't
eaten or slept in a while. She wanted, suddenly, to go to him.

She blushed and turned away. What was wrong with her?
Her heart was beating fast and she could feel his eyes on her
back. She should go back to her cousins. They were but a few
steps away, haggling over the price of a bracelet.

Come to me, a voice whispered in her mind, and she obeyed.
Her feet took her across the square, to the man who leaned

against his horse, waiting for her. Panic congealed in her stomach as she approached him. She wanted to run but couldn't. *Don't be afraid*, he said to her, but she was, more afraid than she had ever been in her entire life. Then he did or said something, and her panic dissipated. Her mind fogged and she could no longer remember what she was doing there. He held his hand out to her and she took it, unable to help herself. His touch was warm, possessive, and she trembled. "Please," she said once, "let me go."

He smiled. It was not a smile of cruelty, but of hunger: a deep, deep want that she had never felt before. But she could feel it now, *his* want that was somehow also her want.

The small part of her mind that remained hers recoiled in horror, screamed in warning.

But it was too late. He lifted her into the saddle of his horse and leaped up behind her. He wrapped one arm around her waist and brushed her neck with his lips. "Mine now," he murmured. As they cantered away from the square, darkness came before Fidan's eyes . . .

⁂

"Kyra? Wake up! Fool girl. I should have known it would be too much for you."

Cold water drenched her face, and Kyra sat up, spluttering. "What . . . what happened?" she asked feebly.

Astinsai sat back, her relief palpable. "You passed out after drinking the Rasaynam. What did you see?"

Kyra wiped her face with her sleeve. She felt cold and numb and shaky. Yes, she *had* seen something. The Marksman Kai Tau had misused the Mental Arts to subjugate her poor mother.

She had felt her mother's fear, bewilderment, and confusion. Fidan had been two years younger than Kyra when she was assaulted; how had she recovered from such terrible trauma? Kyra remembered her mother as a sweet-faced, laughing woman with a musical voice and loving hands, yet who could be quite stern when her eldest daughter did something particularly reprehensible, like pushing her cousin into the pond or hiding her grandmother's knitting.

"Tell me," commanded Astinsai, and the yearning in her voice was repulsive, almost like the yearning Fidan Veer had sensed from Kai Tau.

"Are you sure you want to know?" asked Kyra. Something in her face or voice must have given Astinsai pause, for the katari mistress hesitated.

"Why would I not wish to know?" asked Astinsai at last. "Does it hurt you too much to speak of it?" Again that avidness in her tone, as if it was the hurt she wished to see, as much as the vision.

"No more than it would hurt you to listen to it," said Kyra. "Did you not tell me once that perhaps not all things are meant to be known? Otherwise, how would we take sides?"

Astinsai glared at her as if she were a repulsive insect. "You dare throw my words back at me?" she snapped.

"I'm sorry," said Kyra, not feeling particularly sorry. "If you wish, I will tell you."

A long moment passed, Astinsai still glaring at her. "Tell me," she repeated at last, but she sounded almost resigned, and her eyes had lost their avaricious gleam.

So Kyra told her. She described in detail the vision she had seen, the fear she had felt in her mother, the hunger in Kai Tau. She told Astinsai how the Marksman had compelled Fidan Veer to follow him, how he had fogged her mind so she could no longer remember who or where she was. Kai Tau's last thought, before they cantered away: *Mine now.*

When she had finished speaking, there was silence for so long that Kyra thought the old woman had fallen asleep. But when she sneaked a quick glance at Astinsai's face, she saw it was wet with tears. And then Kyra did feel bad, for Kai had been the Old One's favorite Marksman. She had believed the lie Kai Tau had told her, that Fidan had fallen in love and gone with him of her own accord.

Astinsai met her gaze. "It was my fault," she said with difficulty. "What happened to your clan. My fault they died."

Something hard and painful squeezed Kyra's heart. "No. It was not your fault," she said. "It was Kai Tau who killed them, mistress."

"I freed the bonds that had been laid on him," whispered Astinsai. "Love blinded me to his true nature, and by the time my eyes opened, it was too late."

"You loved him?" The words stuck in Kyra's throat. "As a . . . pupil?"

"I loved him like a son," said Astinsai, her voice breaking. "The son I never had. Unlike the others, he was never afraid of me. He used to seek me out, ask my counsel, bring me little gifts from his travels. He used to make me *laugh*. I thought we had a special bond. I never thought he'd lie to me. That he would grow to be a murderer."

Kyra swallowed. "I'm sorry," she said, meaning it this time.

Astinsai rallied and waved a bony hand in dismissal. "No matter. You have given me knowledge, and knowledge is precious, even when it is painful. And I am glad you did not die in my tent. That would have been most inconvenient."

"Especially for me," said Kyra drily. She was beginning to recover from the ordeal, although there was still a bitter taste in her mouth, and her limbs felt heavy as lead. At least her mind was clear. "Are we ready to begin forging kalishium shields?"

"We are ready to begin, yes," said Astinsai. "But as to what we will get as an end result, I cannot say."

"What do you mean?" demanded Kyra.

"I have only ever tried to forge blades," said Astinsai. "*One* blade at a time, losing something of myself with each one. And too, it matters who you are making it for. Do not be surprised if we arrive at something else entirely. Especially considering whose image we are destroying in the process."

Kyra suppressed her unease. She had gone to great lengths to bring Astinsai the kalishium. "Let us at least make the attempt," she said. *And hope for the best.*

Astinsai smiled without humor. "Very well." She opened the door of her stove, reached for some discolored lumps, and threw them in. The flames leaped up inside the stove, and a noxious smell stole into the tent. Kyra wrinkled her nose. *Probably dried camel dung*, she thought. She was thankful for the smoke hole in the top of the tent that funneled most of the fumes away.

Astinsai reverently undid the sack and uncovered the kalishium image. "Accept our gratitude," she muttered, "and our deepest apologies for what we are about to do. Understand our need and help us."

The image glowed, throwing its golden light onto the ragged walls of the tent. Kyra looked into the wolf's eyes and felt herself falling into them.

At last, said Menadin, and he grinned at her, his fangs gleaming.

But that wasn't possible. Menadin was *dead*.

"Pay attention," snapped Astinsai. "I asked you to lift the image and put it on the stove."

Kyra obeyed. The image felt heavier somehow, and resistant

to her touch. But she managed to lay it on the heated top of the flat stove, almost burning her hands in the process.

"What will this accomplish?" she asked. "Kalishium does not burn."

Astinsai grimaced. "No. But it can reshape itself when we use a word of power."

A word of power in the ancient tongue of the Goddess. Kyra should have known that's what it took to forge kalishium.

"Only those with an affinity for kalishium can use the word safely," added Astinsai. "It will kill anyone else who tries, or worse, drive them insane."

"You're going to have me say it, aren't you?" asked Kyra flatly.

"Of course," said Astinsai. "The image is your burden; the forging will be yours too. Now, repeat after me." She leaned forward and whispered, *"Aakaarmaya."*

The stove dimmed. The candles flickered out. A cold wind blew through the tent, and the image lying on the stove turned silver. Kyra stared at it; its eyes followed her, as if it were alive.

Astinsai's bony hand closed around Kyra's wrist so hard, she winced. "Say it," she hissed. "This is the moment."

Kyra swallowed. *Goddess protect me. "Aakaarmaya,"* she said, and squeezed her eyes shut.

Nothing happened. Kyra let out the breath she had been holding and opened her eyes. And screamed.

Astinsai and her tent were gone.

She stood on a vast, smoking black plain. The ground was almost too hot to stand on. Fires licked the sky in the distance. It was like a scene from hell. But it was what loomed directly in front of her that almost stopped her heart.

A huge, silver wyr-wolf, at least thrice her height, rested on its haunches, regarding her with golden eyes.

An interesting word, said the wyr-wolf, its voice a deep, thrumming growl in her mind. *Shape is an illusion, like everything else. What illusion do you seek to create?*

Kyra licked her dry lips. "Shields to protect my Markswomen from the dark weapons," she managed to croak.

You ask too much and give too little, said the wyr-wolf.

"What must I give?" asked Kyra.

Yourself, said the wyr-wolf.

"I don't understand," said Kyra, desperate. She was beginning to feel light-headed. It was too hot and smoky.

You will lose someone you hold dear, said the wyr-wolf. *But you will find them again. A bargain, is it not?* It crouched down and opened its maw. A huge, forked tongue slithered out from the cage of its teeth. A cage large enough for Kyra to walk into. Inside was only darkness. Kyra stumbled back, her heart racing.

But in the darkness, a pale, familiar form glimmered into being: Menadin in his human aspect, with his wild hair and feral grin. He beckoned her, as if to say, *Come on. Don't be afraid.*

But she was deathly afraid. An illusion—wasn't that what the huge wyr-wolf had told her? Menadin was not real. She was only imagining him. But then, she must be imagining everything else as well. She gulped and clenched her fists, mustering her courage. Before she could lose it, she strode into the maw of the beast. Menadin reached for her and touched her hair, a tender expression on his face. She opened her arms to hug him, but her hands closed on emptiness. The darkness *twisted*.

Kyra returned to the tent, gasping and sweating. Astinsai sat before her, her face avid. She glanced at the stove, and an expression of triumph crossed her face. "Look," she said.

Kyra's gaze went to the flat stove top. The image was melting, dissolving before her eyes. Even though this was what she had wanted, the knowledge that she had destroyed something so beautiful and unique smote her.

Not destroyed, came the wyr-wolf's voice. *Changed.*

"Shape it with your thoughts and hands," said Astinsai urgently. "While it is still malleable."

What? Kyra stared at the heaving silver mass on the stove, deeply reluctant to touch it.

"Go on," said Astinsai. "It will not hurt you—no more than it already has."

Kyra plunged her hands into the remains of the image and gasped. The metal was like a cool breeze on her skin. Like touching a cloud. She moved her hands and the fluid metal moved with them, as if it were a dance. *Shields, armor, protection*, she thought disjointedly, wishing she could have practiced at something less important before doing this. It was like going for a first mark without knowing how to use a katari.

But kalishium was too precious, too rare. There was no question of wasting it on anything as dumb as "practice." You had to get it right the first time, and every time thereafter.

Before her disbelieving eyes, the metal began to coalesce into a single elongated shape. *Her* shape. Full arms, high neck, knee-length skirt.

"Kalishium armor," said Astinsai, awe in her voice. "You are indeed fortunate."

"But," Kyra stammered in dismay, "I wanted shields. Many of them."

Astinsai gave her a pitying look. "You are the one who forged it, and you are the one it will protect. No one else."

Kyra touched the armor, her heart sinking. She could not take on Kai Tau's army single-handed. And she could not risk her Markswomen against the bullets of Kai's kalashiks.

The armor was stiff, as she had expected, but flexible, light and thin. Not at all like the image she had carried there, as if the transformation she had wrought had changed the basic nature of the metal itself.

Or perhaps she only felt this way because it was hers now, because she had given herself to it.

"No helmet," observed Astinsai. "Try not to get your head blown off."

Kyra thought of the mask of Kali from the funerary chamber and said, "I have something else that will work as well as a helmet."

"Good," said Astinsai. "You have what you came for. And I have an apprentice."

Kyra shifted, uncomfortable. "About that . . ."

"Yes, I know," said Astinsai, with surprising patience. "You have a battle to fight, and an Order to lead. Nevertheless, if you survive, one day you may find your way back to my tent, and learn more of my art. You have but dipped your toe in the water—and withdrawn it with much haste."

"Thank you for everything," said Kyra, pushing down her irritation at Astinsai's words. "I will leave in the morning."

"Alone?" asked Astinsai slyly. "Or with Rustan?"

"With half the Order of Khur," said Kyra shortly, but her face burned as she bowed to the old woman. She picked up her armor carefully, marveling at its lightness, and spied a small piece of metal beneath it. Her heart quickened as she examined it. It was a perfect likeness of the wyr-wolf image she had brought with her.

"What will you do with that?" asked Astinsai, watching her.

Kyra's fist closed around the tiny image, hiding it from the

Old One's acquisitive eyes. "It is for the wyr-wolves," she said firmly, and bid the katari mistress goodnight.

Outside it was quiet and cold. A chilly wind blew through her hair, making her shiver. There was no moon tonight; the stars shone like bright spears in the dark bowl of the desert sky.

To her surprise, as she passed the Maji-khan's tent, both Barkav and Rustan came out to meet her. The relief on Rustan's face was obvious. Even Barkav looked happy to see her intact.

"A success?" asked the Maji-khan as she walked up to them, and Kyra nodded. She described to them what had transpired, leaving out the word of power and her meeting with the wyr-wolf.

"Excellent." Barkav rubbed his hands together. "This will help us get close to our enemies and disable their minds before they can shoot us."

"Astinsai said it would only protect me," said Kyra unhappily.

"Then you must lead our attack," said Barkav. Rustan's lips pressed together, but Barkav's plan made absolute sense. If Kyra was the only one shielded from the bullets, then it fell to her to pave a safe path for the others.

The Maji-khan asked her into his tent, and although Kyra was bone-tired, she went. Inside, the elders sat in a circle around a large map, arguing in low tones about tactics, supplies, and fighters. She joined the circle, Rustan next to her, his warm presence comforting. She tried to pay attention to what was being said, but at last fatigue overpowered her, and she fell asleep, leaning against the tent wall. She barely stirred when Rustan laid her down and covered her with a rug. The elders talked on, deep into the night.

CHAPTER 38

REUNIONS

The mulberry tree outside the caves of Kali was in full fruit, its branches laden with purple berries. Lush green grass dotted with pink and white wildflowers carpeted the hollow in front of the caves. Morning assembly had just finished, and everyone had dispersed to prepare for the first class of the day. Navroz Lan stood alone underneath the tree, inhaling the heady scent of late spring, remembering how, as a young apprentice, she had plucked berries with her friends: a springtime ritual that had endured over the years.

Most of those friends—and many younger—had now passed through the door of death. Soon it would be her turn to see what lay beyond that door. Only the mulberry tree would remain, a witness to their passing.

But not yet. The Order still depended on her. There was a war to be fought, a tyrant to be defeated, dark weapons to be dealt with. Once Asiana was a safer place, she would finally let go. She could imagine it now, lying in the central cavern with her blade placed over her chest, surrounded by satisfactorily grief-stricken Markswomen. The eulogies that would follow, the fire that would release her to the stars.

"Eldest?" Elena came and stood beside her.

Navroz came to with a start of annoyance, then chided herself. Dreaming of one's own funeral was the height of self-indulgence. "Yes, child?" she said.

Elena looked better than she had in months. She had grown taller, more serious than ever before, but at least the dark circles under her eyes had vanished, and she was sleeping soundly again. Akassa hovered behind Elena, a few steps away, her face scrubbed and her hair tied back in a bun. She bowed to Navroz, and Navroz nodded to the apprentice, her face relaxing into a smile. Akassa followed Elena like a shadow, had even tried to learn the basics of healing from her. She certainly didn't have the gift for it, but it warmed Navroz's heart that Akassa cared enough about Elena to start paying attention in a class that she had once disdained.

Normally, Navroz would have thought such attachment unhealthy and un-Markswoman-like. But given what had happened—how close Akassa had come to despair before Kyra hauled her out of it—she was willing to overlook it.

Kyra's return had done them all some good, although her becoming the Mahimata had been completely unexpected. Still, it made sense, in a way. It was time the Order was led by someone young and fresh—although that knowledge didn't change the fact that there were times Navroz wished Kyra was several decades older and wiser.

Elena held out Nineth's blade. A faint blue glow enveloped it. "It's been like this since morning. Eldest, do you think she's close by?"

Navroz made to take the katari from her, then drew her hand back. Heat emanated from the blade—not hostile, but as a mild warning. Elena could hold it without fear, because she was one of Nineth's closest friends. That meant . . .

"She's coming back today," said Navroz, relief and delight welling up inside her. "Oh, just wait until I get my hands on that girl!"

Elena's eyes sparkled with unshed tears, and she did something that caught Navroz completely by surprise: she slipped her arms around the elder and hugged her. Navroz patted her back. "It's been hard for you, hasn't it?" she said sympathetically. "Both Kyra and Nineth gone their separate ways while you stay here. But the Order is built on people like us, who stay and strengthen its foundations. They depend on us—do you see that?"

"Yes, Eldest," said Elena in a muffled voice. Then she stepped back, wiped her eyes, and gave a watery smile. "I'm going to clean Nineth's cell and air out her rugs. May I?"

"You'll be missing Mathematics," said Navroz. "You can request Felda's permission to do so. I think, when you show her Nineth's blade, she'll have a hard time saying no."

"Thank you, Eldest."

As she watched Elena and Akassa run back to the caves, Navroz smiled. Today was the day they were all coming back; she could feel it in her bones. Her bones might be ancient, but they were never wrong.

❦

They arrived within an hour of each other, almost as if they had planned it.

Just before the midday meal, a shout went up outside the caves. Navroz and Elena, who had been preparing healing salves in preparation for the fighting to come, rushed outside.

A line of men streamed down the hill that housed the Ferghana Hub, a familiar figure at their head.

"Kyra!" screamed Elena. She made to run as Akassa and Tonar did, then checked herself, which surprised Navroz. She sensed a complex mix of emotions in her favorite pupil and wondered at it.

"Kyra and half the Order of Khur," muttered Navroz. Not that anyone heard her. They were all too busy staring at the Marksmen. Bad enough when Rustan had come; the novices had gawked like village girls. But this . . . even *Felda* was staring. It was hard not to; the last time the Ferghana Valley had seen so many Marksmen had been—never.

"Stand with me, Elders," murmured Navroz. "Let's have some dignity here."

Felda, Mumuksu, and Chintil obediently arrayed themselves behind her. "The Maji-khan looks even larger than he did at the Sikandra Fort assembly," whispered Felda. "I wonder what he eats."

"Felda," warned Navroz. "They approach."

Kyra hugged Akassa and Tonar, patted the heads of the novices who surrounded her and smiled at everyone, though Navroz could see the lines of tension on her face and how difficult it was for her to stand upright, let alone bear the strange burden she had slung across her shoulders. Overextending herself as always. Navroz felt a surge of protectiveness, and she struggled to keep it in check.

At last Kyra extricated herself and made her way to where the elders stood. The Maji-khan of Khur walked beside her, a huge mountain of a man who nevertheless moved with catlike grace. Rustan stood behind them, along with two elders whom Navroz recognized from past clan assemblies.

"Elders, I have the honor of presenting to you the Maji-khan of Khur and fifteen of his Marksmen," Kyra announced.

"Welcome," said Navroz, returning the Maji-khan's bow. "I wish that Shirin Mam were alive, so she could see this day." *And deal with you*, she did not say aloud. But he heard it anyway, from the way his mouth twitched.

"The rest have gone to mobilize warriors from the clans of the Empty Place," continued Kyra. "We will launch a coordinated attack with the Order of Valavan. If we leave at dawn in three days, we should arrive near the Tau camp at dusk, around the same time as them. They will approach from the east, and we will attack from the west, as we've discussed."

Three days? Navroz nodded sharply. "The Ferghana clans have dispatched archers, weapons, and horses," she said. "We expect them tomorrow, or day after, at the very latest."

"They had better be here by then," said Barkav in his deep voice. "We can delay no longer. We must join forces with the Order of Valavan if we are to succeed in crushing the outlaws. Jhelmil is but fifty miles from Jethwa. I have asked the Valavians to wait for us, but if the Jhelmil door is being watched, they will have no choice but to engage."

Besides which, the Valavians would not deign to wait for anyone. The Thar was *their* territory. It must rankle that they needed the help of the other Orders to deal with the Tau menace. Kyra had made the right decision to stay and fight with them during the attack on Valavan. It had gained her their trust and respect.

"If they are spotted, it will draw Kai Tau's forces to Jhelmil. It will be advantageous to us, but the Valavians may take heavy losses," said Navroz, frowning.

"They know the risks," said Barkav. "They have the Hub to fall back into, if they are attacked."

"Won't work if they are ambushed miles from the Hub," said Chintil.

"They have planned for that," said Kyra. "They will send scouts ahead, far enough away to get a warning, and close enough to use the Mental Arts. And they won't be alone. The rest of the Marksmen will be with them, as well as the warriors they have summoned." She paused. "Elder, a lot of things can go wrong. We won't be able to anticipate each and every one. Some of us will be injured. Some might even die."

"But are we afraid of death?" thundered Barkav. He turned to the Marksmen clustered behind him. "Are we afraid?"

"No!" came the resounding response.

"We will avenge Ishtul!"

The expressions on the faces of the Marksmen grew grim, and Navroz winced inwardly as she remembered the fate of the blademaster of Khur. A terrible way to die, and a terrible way to remember someone who had taught you, whom you had once looked up to. No wonder the Marksmen were so eager to go into battle.

Barkav turned back to her, his eyes stormy. "My blade is thirsty," he said.

"And mine," said Kyra.

"And mine," said Chintil, and she gave a fierce grin.

"So be it," said Navroz. "In three days, we will take the door to the desert. The Goddess protect us all." And with that, she bade the Marksmen enter the caves of Kali and partake of the midday meal with them.

They followed Navroz through the wide wooden doors into the kitchen, crowding into that roomy space, standing back respectfully to allow both Khur and Kali elders to sit first on the kilim-covered floor. At Navroz's signal, the novices passed around bowls of water for them all to wash their hands, and Tarshana the cook went into a quiet frenzy of activity to prepare for the guests.

Navroz noticed how Kyra sat next to Rustan, the way she kept glancing at him as if she could not help herself, and sadness tugged at her. She could no longer be angry with Kyra for her very obvious and inappropriate feelings for Shirin Mam's son. But she also knew there was no way for them to stay together, if they wanted to belong to their Orders.

Classes were cancelled, of course. Introductions were made, and the ice was broken among the older ones at mealtime by the effusive praise the men showered on the food. Tarshana surpassed herself, producing leek soup, potato samsas, and mulberry pies for them all. Navroz, sitting in a far corner and watching her Markswomen thaw toward their visitors, knew it was the dawn of a new era. No matter what happened in the Thar Desert, the isolation of Khur had ended, for good. Shirin Mam would have approved.

Despite the coming battle, Navroz felt a tiny portion of the burden she bore slip from her shoulders. Nineth would return soon, Elena would one day be the healer of the Order, and Kyra would do what Shirin Mam had foretold, all those years ago, when she first brought the little waif home: she would rid Asiana of the dark weapons once and for all.

She was jolted from her thoughts by a crash that startled them all; Kyra had dropped her cup and jumped to her feet. Everyone quieted and stared at her.

"What is it?" cried Mumuksu.

But Navroz knew, and Elena knew too; joy bloomed on her face and she rose as well, followed by Akassa.

"Nineth," Kyra blurted, and ran out of the kitchen as if she were a novice, Elena and Akassa at her heels.

"Nineth?" echoed Felda, and she too ran after them, looking most undignified. Mumuksu leaned forward to give a few words of explanation to the Maji-khan, who had a bemused expression on his face.

"If you will excuse us," said Navroz, rising, "we must see about an errant apprentice who has finally decided to return home. The rest of you stay here," she added sharply, as some of the others began to get up, disbelieving grins on their faces.

Kyra waited outside, Elena and Akassa a little behind her, shading their eyes against the bright sun. Felda stood with her arms on her hips, her lips moving as if in calculation.

"Listen," said Kyra. "Do you hear her?"

Horse hooves cantered across the valley, growing ever nearer.

Time seemed to stop. Navroz held her breath, her heart quickening in anticipation. And then the horse and its rider came into view, and Elena gave a joyful shriek.

The horse stopped in the glade; the rider dismounted. Nineth stood before them, her robe rather worse for wear, her face grimy and careworn, her hair as untidy as ever. But alive and well, just as her glowing blade had signified.

Elena ran forward, took Nineth in her arms, and hugged her fiercely. Akassa stood back, a little awkward. Of course, she and Nineth had never gotten along. But they would now. Elena would make sure of that. Stranger to Navroz was the fact that Kyra was also hanging back, relief and shame emanating from her in equal parts. Of course, she *had* thrown Nineth's blade into the underground lake—*why*, she had never divulged to the elders.

At last Nineth released Elena. "Well?" she addressed Kyra, her smile changing into a scowl. "Do I get a hug, or are you going to stand there with a hangdog expression for the rest of the day?"

Kyra gave a half sob and stumbled into Nineth's arms. "I'm sorry," she cried. "Please forgive me."

Elena hesitated a moment, watching them, then moved to embrace them both.

Navroz smiled, surprised to find her eyes damp. She was getting sentimental in her dotage. For a while it was impossible to speak. Nineth's return was a sign, a favorable one. Surely everything would turn out for the best.

CHAPTER 39

AN HOUR OF PEACE

Nineth and Elena met in Kyra's cell that night before the hour of meditation. It would have been almost like old times, if not for the fact that this was the Mahimata's cell. And the fact that Kyra could sense Rustan, not thirty feet away from her—they were separated by several walls of rock, but still. The Marksmen had been offered cells to sleep in, but had politely declined, preferring to sleep outdoors, for which, Kyra knew, the Kali elders were thankful.

It had been an eventful day, to say the least. Nineth was not the only one to have returned to the Order. In the afternoon, Helen, who had gone to Chorzu to help Tarshana procure fresh supplies, had run up to Kyra and blurted out, "Mother, Baliya and Selene are back!"

Kyra had not expected this; their return just before the Order went into battle was truly a gift, as they were both accomplished in combat.

When they arrived, Baliya had seemed hesitant, Selene

relieved, but both had been sincere in begging the elders' forgiveness, and both swore their oaths of loyalty to Kyra at once. The elders had supported giving them a penance, but Kyra had ruled that penance could wait until the fighting was done. And then she had embraced them—even Baliya, who had delivered Nineth to Tamsyn. Nineth had been a bit indignant about that, but she knew they needed all the Markswomen they could muster for this fight.

"Besides," she'd said, "Baliya is no longer the Mahimata's favorite. *I* am." And Kyra had to chuckle at that. It felt so good to have Nineth back.

She leaned now against the wall of Kyra's cell, her feet tucked under a blanket. Her blade hung in a scabbard around her neck; she kept stroking it, as if she couldn't believe it was there. Kyra had just finished telling her—for the third time—about her duel with Tamsyn Turani.

"Tell me again," she said, nibbling a leftover samsa she had stolen from the kitchen. "Tell me how you threw her into the river. I wish I could have seen it."

Elena looked from one to the other. "This is fantastic," she kept saying. "You're back—both of you."

Kyra reached over and touched Elena's hand. She was so grateful to have been more or less forgiven, her heart felt it would burst. "I wish I didn't have to leave again."

Elena's face clouded. "You'd better come back alive," she said. "I won't be able to bear it if anything else happens to either of you."

"I'll look after her," said Nineth. "Make sure she doesn't do anything foolish."

"What? Certainly not," said Kyra firmly. "No novices and

no apprentices allowed. Only a full Markswoman may go into battle. That is the rule."

"Only the novices should stay behind in the caves," Elena protested. "The three of us should go with you."

"Three?" said Nineth. "Oh, you mean dear Akassa." She grinned as a flush spread across Elena's face. "You know, forget everything else. Tamsyn dead, Kyra the new Mahimata—I mean, the elders are crazy to do that, but who understands elders anyway? The biggest shock to *me* is the new-and-improved Akassa who follows our Elena like a shade."

"She's trying hard," said Elena. "Don't tease her, all right? It was such a shock when she failed her first mark."

"Good thing she did," Nineth decided. "Took her down several notches. I can almost tolerate being in the same room as her now."

"Do you feel any difference in your katari after being separated from it for so long?" asked Kyra, trying to change the subject, which she knew was making Elena uncomfortable.

"Not a difference as such, no," said Nineth. "It is as if I forgot a part of myself and have remembered who I am again." She paused. "Tell me why you threw my katari into the lake." There was no judgment in her voice—only curiosity.

Kyra squirmed. "I saw you kissing Hattur Nisalki," she answered.

"And you were angry?" asked Nineth.

Kyra thought about it. "I *was* angry," she admitted at last. "It was a stupid thing to do, and I wish I hadn't done it. I wasn't thinking clearly. Part of it was the fact that I was carrying Tamsyn's blade. It affected me more than I realized. By the time I *did* realize it, it was too late."

"So if you hadn't been carrying Tamsyn's blade, you wouldn't have done it?" asked Nineth.

Kyra shook her head. "I don't think so. But I can't just blame Tamsyn's blade for how I felt. I saw you kissing and I was"—she swallowed and made herself say it—"*jealous.* I thought about Rustan and how much I wanted to be with him. How I was stuck here, and it didn't matter what I wanted. And how worried we were about you—and there you were, enjoying yourself, without a care in the world. You didn't even like Hattur that much, and yet you were the one who escaped from here and ended up with him."

"Was kidnapped, more like," said Nineth. She looked thoughtful. "Hattur's not a bad sort. He thought he was saving my life. I like him, but I wouldn't have stayed with him, even if I wasn't an apprentice of Kali. But all of this seems to be more about you than about me. What's going on between you and Rustan?"

Kyra's cheeks warmed as she remembered the feel of Rustan's lips on hers, his hands enfolding her, drawing her to him. The beat of his heart against her own. The hitch in his breath as she ran her hands along his hard, muscled body.

She couldn't tell her friends about that. It was his secret as well as her own. And it meant too much; she would diminish it by talking about it. "He wasn't too well after the battle of Valavan," she hedged. "He's fine now that he's reunited with his blade, but . . ." She waved a hand.

"He's surrounded by his Order," finished Elena. "It won't ever be otherwise for you two. You know that. And what about you, Nineth. Will you see Hattur again?"

Nineth shrugged, popping the last of the samsa into her mouth. "Maybe, at the next festival in Chorzu. I have to return his horse. But I could be a Markswoman by then. Or I *will* be one if Kyra lets me go into battle."

"No," said Kyra at once. "Please, don't ask this of me. I couldn't bear it if you got hurt. It would be my fault." She hesitated. How to tell them what Astinsai had hinted to her, what she herself now believed? "But . . . about Rustan . . . I think we can be Markswomen and still love other people," she said at last. "I know Shirin Mam taught us the importance of detachment, but remember, what she actually did was something else entirely. She bore a son. She must have loved someone enough to have a child with them."

"Or maybe she did it for entirely different reasons," said Nineth.

"Possibly," agreed Kyra. "Astinsai, the seer and katari mistress of Khur, told me that the ability to bond with a kalishium blade is inherited. The reason the number of Markswomen and Marksmen have declined over time is because the trait is dying out. We aren't passing our gifts on to future generations."

There was a stunned silence. Both girls stared at her as if she was mad.

"Have you told the elders this?" asked Nineth. "They'll throw you out, never mind that they've made the grievous mistake of anointing you the Mahimata while I wasn't around to prevent it."

Kyra grimaced. "Not yet, no. But I did tell the Valavians. And I'm telling you. Not that we all have to go out and start procreating—that would be ridiculous and stupid, and I'm sure most of us have no desire to do so. But maybe it's not a bad thing if one or two of us likes a man well enough to have a child with him."

"Well, count me out," said Elena firmly. "I don't feel that

way about boys. Not the way you two do. And even if I did, I'd much rather die than get pregnant. Yuck!"

"I don't want to get pregnant either," said Nineth fervently. "Or what is the difference between me and my poor mother who had five babies because the first three were all boys and we needed a girl to carry on the family name and the fourth was a girl, but it was me, and Mother thought quite rightly that she needed a spare, just in case, and look what happened—"

"Yes, yes," Kyra interrupted, "but there may be others who feel differently. Markswomen who would *like* to have a child. A child who may or may not be born with the gift but would be loved nevertheless." She threw her hands up. "Don't look at me like that. I'm just saying we should all have *choice* in the matter. Choice in who we love and whether we have children. Our bodies, our decision!"

"Not going to happen," said Nineth flatly. "Not if the elders have anything to say about it. And most of the older Markswomen won't like what you're saying either. Just because Tamsyn is gone doesn't mean you can overturn centuries-old rules."

Kyra sighed. "I know. Maybe things will change with time. Otherwise, the Orders may well be doomed to die out." She noticed their expressions and hastened to add, "I mean, much later. Not in our lifetimes."

"Do we have to talk about this kind of dark, terrible stuff?" grumbled Nineth. "I've had quite enough of it."

Kyra gave her an affectionate glance. "Of course. How many samsas did you manage to scarf today?"

"Eleven, I think," said Nineth, with a satisfied smile. "Tarshana's cooking is the one thing I'll miss in the Thar."

"You stay here and recover," said Kyra. "Regain some of your strength. You've gone quite thin."

Nineth shook her head, decisive. "I'm strong enough to fight. Not even Tarshana's samsas will tempt me to stay. I'm going with you to the Thar Desert. You owe me, all right?"

Kyra's head began to ache. She had forgotten just how stubborn her friend could be.

"I'm coming too," said Elena casually.

"You need to stay here and look after the novices," protested Kyra.

Elena gave her a withering look. "I already asked, and Navroz said yes. She needs me. There'll be plenty of wounded, and my skill may save somebody's life."

"That's decided then," said Nineth. "We're all going. Akassa can guard us while we save lives." And she grinned as if they were talking about going on a picnic.

Kyra held her head in her hands and groaned. "I could forbid you from coming."

Elena laid a hand on her arm. "But you won't. Weren't you talking about choice just now? We choose the risks we take. We choose to be with you. Respect our choice."

The gong rang for solitary meditation, saving Kyra from having to reply. And truly, there was no reply, for Elena was right.

CHAPTER 40

SOMEONE TO FEAR

Two days had passed. Rustan slept under the mulberry tree outside the caves of Kali and dreamed of Kyra. He had fallen asleep thinking of her, so this was not surprising, but the content of the dream was. In the dream, Kyra walked up to a door that stood by itself in the middle of nowhere. He stood on the other side of the door, but she could not see him, nor could he call out to her. He tried to open the door, but it refused to budge. He felt himself being sucked away by a terrible wind, and all the while Kyra stood on the other side, unwilling or unable to open the door and come to his aid.

He woke sweating, despite the cool predawn breeze. On either side of him, Marksmen slept, wrapped in rugs that the Order of Kali had thoughtfully provided. Farther out still were the camps of the eighty-odd warriors sent by various clans of the valley who had arrived yesterday. Kyra's face had turned grim as she sized them up. *Not enough*, he could hear her thinking, and he had agreed. He hoped that Ghasil and Saninda had managed to persuade the Kushan and Turguz clans to part with more fighters than this.

Rustan lay back and tried to get another hour of sleep, but it was impossible. Tomorrow they would defeat Kai Tau or die in the attempt. If he managed to survive, he would have to make a decision: stay with the Order of Khur or return to the monastery. Either way, his path would diverge from Kyra's.

He had made a vow to the Sahirus. But his Order needed him too, especially after the loss of Ishtul.

And Kyra, did she need him? Surely not; he had never seen her so relaxed and happy as when she was with her friends Nineth and Elena. But she had kept glancing at him too, and her glance had reflected the yearning of his own heart.

Whether or not she needed him, he knew that he needed her. If only they could find a way to be together and yet fulfill their obligations.

"Can't sleep?" murmured a voice beside him, and Rustan jerked out of his thoughts. It was Samant, the Master of Meditation—the only one to whom he had confessed his love for Kyra.

"No, Elder," said Rustan. "In an hour we must wake anyway and continue our preparations."

"We have been preparing a long while," said the elder quietly. "Ever since Ishtul was taken from us. We will make them pay."

"Yes, Elder, but how many of us will fall so that Asiana might be free of Kai Tau?" asked Rustan. "And how long before some other outlaw with delusions of power tries to steal the kalashiks? How safe are they even in the Temple of Valavan?"

"The guns must leave this world," said Samant. "Or we will never have peace."

Peace. What a fragile thing it was. Asiana had never known peace, not truly since the Great War more than eight hundred fifty years ago. The men and women who had lived in that time were gone, but they had made sure their weapons remained to create havoc among their descendants.

"Who in his right mind would make such a weapon?" asked Rustan. "What kind of evil did men fall into?"

Samant shook his head and sighed. "There are no answers to such questions. There is only the matter of what we are willing to do to protect our people."

They were both quiet after that. The sky lightened and, somewhere far distant, a rooster crowed. The men and women sent by the clans began to stir. Time to sharpen weapons and check horses. The Markswomen had forbidden cookfires so close to their caves, so the men made do with bread, cheese, and berries, supplemented by Tarshana's porridge, which was carried out in steaming vats by the novices.

The Marksmen, of course, were welcome to eat with the Order of Kali. They wrapped up their bedding, packed their knapsacks, and stored them in the cavern before heading to the kitchen. Kyra was already up, sipping a cup of tea, her eyes fever-bright. Rustan dropped down next to her, his heart quickening as it always did in her presence.

"Today is the day you will prove to be a better fighter than any of your teachers," he said, and she smiled, but he could tell how tense she was in the way she held herself.

"I will be with you all the time," he said, putting as much reassurance as he could into his voice. "I promise you that."

She frowned. "I must go forward alone. I am the only one with armor. The Maji-khan and Chintil will lead the main attack force, and you can be with them."

Nineth, who was sitting on her other side, snorted. "Yes,

just listen to her. She is planning on taking on the entire army single-handed, because she's the only one with measly armor."

"Kalishium armor," hissed Kyra. "Impervious to bullets. As I have told you several times."

"You cannot be the sole vanguard," said Rustan. "That doesn't make sense. Even if you are impervious to bullets, enough of Kai Tau's men could surround you to physically overpower you and rip off the armor. The degree of Mental Arts required to control all potential attackers would be enormous. You would be dead long before you reached Kai Tau."

"Yes, that is what Eldest also said," agreed Nineth. "The vanguard must be a team of at least thirteen Markswomen."

"And Marksmen," said Rustan. He noticed Kyra's expression and added, "You cannot protect everyone. The best you can do is stay alive to confront Kai Tau himself. Even Astinsai says you are the one who must do that. The rest of us—we will have our hands full. We will play the roles we are given. And certainly, Marksmen will be part of the vanguard."

"The Maji-khan and Chintil are working it out," said Nineth, pointing to where the two sat together, heads bent, arguing over a sketch.

"You can rest assured you will be nowhere near the fighting," Kyra told her. "You will be at the rear with Elena, to help tend the wounded."

Chintil looked up at that moment. "Kyra, the Maji-khan and I have concluded that a direct attack will not work. This is what the Valavians have warned too. The Taus are expecting us and have had months to prepare. A direct attack will lead to a huge loss of life, both at our end as well as their lowliest fighters, who may well be viewed by their top leaders as mere fodder."

"What do you suggest?" asked Rustan. "The Thar is mostly flat; there's nowhere to hide. They will see us coming for miles."

"Not if we arrive after dusk, as we have planned," said Barkav. "It is a new-moon night; this will be to our advantage."

"Also disadvantage, if our archers cannot see their targets," Kyra pointed out.

"I agree, but the gains outweigh the potential risks," said Chintil. She spread out the parchment in front of her. "We need the element of surprise to turn the odds in our favor. Look."

They gathered around her. She had drawn several concentric circles on the parchment. "Kai Tau is adept in battle strategy. Based on what we know of their numbers and weapons, they will have at least three lines of defense around Kai Tau and his kinsmen. There are only eight kalashiks left, and I'm guessing most of them will be in the innermost line or the heart of the Tau camp. Moreover, given how uncontrollable the dark weapons are, they will not be used right at the start of fighting."

"If they have succeeded in duplicating the weapons, some primitive versions will be in the outermost ring," said Rustan.

Chintil nodded. "I have studied the parchments you took from their camp. In addition to trying to duplicate kalashiks, they have been trying to build explosive balls that they can launch from within their circles. Additionally, they will have a quick-moving line of attack planned—possibly horsemen with spears and primitive guns—ready to split from the main lines and tear through any attacking force." She traced her fingers around the circles. "We will approach from the west and split into three. One force will flow north, the second will flow south, both meeting the Valavian forces pouring in from the east. Thus, we will encircle and trap the Taus. Meanwhile, the third force—our smallest and strongest—will break through the defensive circles and go straight for Kai Tau at the center." She locked eyes with Kyra. "You will lead the third force, Mahimata, in a flying wedge."

Kyra exhaled. "Yes, Elder." The flying wedge was an ancient strategy to break through enemy lines. It was highly effective, if done right, but also perilous.

"Choose twelve Marksmen and Markswomen to go with you, six on each side," said Chintil. "This will be the most dangerous part, and all success depends upon you. A dozen horsemen will protect your flanks, but we need everyone else to surround the enemy. We will press forward, squeezing them in a tightening horseshoe. If our timing is right, the Valavians will close the pincer from the other side."

"I am in favor of leaving an avenue for escape," said Rustan. "They will fight with more ferocity if they are completely surrounded with no hope of escape. We must allow them the opportunity to run away."

Chintil frowned. "We cannot plan this in advance. It will depend on how the battle progresses. There will be an appearance of escape to the east—until the Valavians close it off. We may take heavy losses, in which case I fear that the loss of life on their side must be a secondary concern."

"I agree," said the Maji-khan. He laid a hand on Rustan's shoulder. "The most important thing is to capture the kalashiks and Kai Tau. The sooner we can do that, the faster we can end the battle. I will be part of the third force behind Kyra. I want you there as well."

"To fight by the side of my Maji-khan," said Rustan, and he glanced at Kyra, "led by the Mahimata of Kali. What more can I ask for?"

"To not have to fight," said Kyra. "Let us hope, when this is over, that we have many years of peace."

"Who else will you take with you, Kyra?" asked Navroz.

Kyra calculated. "Elder Chintil, you and Elder Mumuksu must lead one of the forces. Elder Felda, you and one of the Khur elders can lead the second force."

"Ghasil," said Barkav. "We need someone strong in the Mental Arts."

Kyra nodded. "I will take Tonar Kalam, Ria Farad, Sandi Meersil, Noor Sialbi, Ninsing Kishtol, and Selene Deo. The rest will be Marksmen of your choice, Maji-khan."

As she said the names, Rustan noticed the individual Markswomen straighten and glance at each other with tight smiles. They were proud that she had singled them out for the most dangerous mission of all.

"Eldest, you must stay at the rear to treat the wounded," continued Kyra.

Navroz scowled. "I am not so old that I cannot fight better than just about anybody in this room."

"Yes, Eldest," said Kyra patiently. "But we need you for something more important than fighting. All of us can fight. No one has your skill for healing."

"She's right," said Chintil. "Eldest, you and the apprentices must stay well behind the lines—preferably sheltered by a dune. That doesn't mean you won't be in danger. The kinds of weapons Kai Tau has been trying to build, no one will be safe for miles around."

Navroz pressed her lips together but did not argue further.

A shout went up outside, and Barkav stood in a hurry, almost knocking over a wooden cupboard of pots and pans. "Ghasil and Saninda are here," he said in triumph. "We are ready to move."

Kyra put down her cup of tea. She looked as if she was going to be sick. Rustan grasped her hand and she threw him a smile. "Just one more thing I need," she said, and her gaze went to the Mistress of Meditation. "From the funerary chamber. Elder Mumuksu, please get it."

Various expressions flitted across Mumuksu's face: astonishment, horror, resignation, understanding. Rustan had no time to wonder what it was Kyra needed, for the Maji-khan beckoned him, but he would remember Mumuksu's reaction later during the battle, when Kyra transformed herself into someone he could not recognize, someone to fear.

CHAPTER 41

THE RIDE TO JETHWA

They left at dawn, using the Ferghana Hub to Transport to the Thar Desert. Kyra quashed her misgivings about the door and went ahead with just Rustan to test it. Meanwhile, one of the Markswomen was sent to the Temple of Valavan to confirm and coordinate the attack plan.

Somehow, Rustan's presence made the experience seem more ordinary and safe than it actually was. As they sat down next to each other, Kyra took a deep breath. This was her last chance to say anything meaningful to him before the fight. "I'm glad you're with me," she said at last, with a catch in her voice. "There's no one else I'd rather die with than you."

Rustan grazed her cheek with his fingertips. "There's no one else I'd rather live with than you."

"You mean, after this . . ." She stopped, unable to go on, unable to put words to her want.

He bent toward her and kissed her forehead. "We'll find a

way to be together, at least some of the time. If that's what you wish."

It is, oh, it is. Kyra slipped her arms around him and held him hard.

But right then, the spinning room slowed and stopped. Never had the experience of Transport seemed so fleeting to Kyra. She rose with a sigh, Rustan close behind her.

"Let's pray the door hasn't shifted," he remarked cheerfully, as she pushed it open and entered the Transport corridor.

To Kyra's relief, it hadn't. At least, it didn't appear to have; the Hub opened onto a desert, and the scene looked much the same as it had all that time ago when Shirin Mam had sent her to take down her first mark: Kai Tau's eldest son. The only difference was that it had been dark then, and she had been alone.

Now it was early morning; the sun had just risen, and the Thar Desert looked beautiful, rolling sand dunes dotted with thorny plants and the occasional stunted tree. A veritable forest compared to the Empty Place. Kyra moved with care, mindful of the fact that the door could have been discovered and watchers posted to spy on them. However, a mountain of sand had accumulated outside the door. It was clear that it hadn't been touched in a while. There was also no adequate place for anyone to hide for miles around, save for some nearby dunes, and Kyra could not sense any human presence around them.

Time blurred after that. Rustan returned to fetch the others. No more than twenty to thirty people could fit in the Transport Chamber at any time, and it would take far longer to move the horses. Only the novices would stay behind in the caves of Kali. The rest of the Order of Kali, most of the Order of Khur, as well as more than three hundred warriors from various clans and tribes needed to be Transported. Those who had been assigned to fight with the Order of Valavan had already taken the door to the Deccan Hub.

Kyra used the time to don her armor and strap two spears to her back. The armor looked a bit like chain mail, except it was much lighter and stronger, and it moved with her easily. It covered her from her neck down to her knees. It would have to be enough. The mask of Kali—the item she had asked Mumuksu to fetch for her from the funerary chamber—she would wear later, just before the attack. She didn't know why she had decided to wear it, save that it was the mask of the Goddess in her warrior aspect, and this was war. Today Kyra would become the face of Kali, and perhaps the Goddess would be pleased with her disciple and bestow her blessings for victory.

The first batch of Markswomen arrived with their horses, including Rinna. It would take all day to travel to Jethwa, and they would have to be careful to rest and water their mounts. They would need them in fine mettle at the start of the fight. Nineth was there, astride Akhtar, Shirin Mam's old stallion, for which Kyra was glad. Akhtar was the strongest, fastest horse they had. Nineth winked at her and Kyra smiled. *Stay safe*, she sent to her.

When they had all assembled outside the Hub, they formed an impressive sight. The rising sun glinted off the armor of the clan warriors and the weapons they carried: spears, longbows, lances, swords, and machetes.

Rustan had a massive crossbow slung over his back. The Maji-khan was covered in weapons, his gigantic form bristling with swords, axes, and spears. His stallion was huge; Kyra hoped it was strong enough to carry the weight on its back.

Chintil had two swords slung in scabbards on her belt. Felda carried a wicked-looking axe in one hand, and a compass and a map in the other.

"Jethwa lies in that direction, many hours' ride away," Felda said, pointing with her axe. "We had best get started." She gave Kyra a sideways glance. "Any last words for us, Mahimata?"

"Last words?" Kyra shook her head. "Consider these my first—the first that have ever meant anything since I took my oath to you. Today we are going to fight evil. Sometimes evil may wear the face of a man, but make no mistake—the humanity has gone from those who wield the dark weapons." She paused and raised her voice, addressing them all. "Hold fast to your blades; be true. The Goddess Kali guide our weapons and our hearts."

Everyone gave a rousing cheer, and the blood rushed through Kyra's veins. Some of her excitement must have communicated itself to Rinna; the mare stamped and wheeled, impatient to be off.

But Felda bowed to Barkav and said, "Does the Maji-khan have any words for us?" They all quieted down, and Kyra turned her mare around to face him.

Barkav gave a fierce grin. "I can only say how proud and glad I am to fight by the sides of such warriors," he said, his deep voice echoing in the silence. "Never in the history of Asiana has the Order of Khur joined the Order of Kali in battle. No matter what happens today, it will be written and sung about for an age to come. Let them not say there were cowards among us." He raised his hand in benediction. "May you live long and die well."

A more subdued cheer followed his words, and then Felda

gave a war cry, and they were off. Rinna sprang forward, eager to be at the front, and Kyra let her have her head. Rustan came up next to her and they rode together across the desert.

The sun slipped higher into the pale blue sky, and suffocating heat rose from the earth. Under the scarf she had tied around her face, sweat trickled down to Kyra's neck. But she barely felt the heat. The ride was dreamlike, in a way. They rode to their deaths, some of them—and also to Kai Tau's. Of this, Kyra was certain.

Although she had fantasized about killing Kai Tau for years, this fight was no longer about her, or even the slaughter of Veer. It was about making Asiana a safer place. It was to remove the kalashiks, once and for all, from the face of the earth. Anything less, and it would be mere self-indulgence. She saw that now, and almost wished she had not killed Kai Tau's son. The only true purpose his death had served was to bring them closer to this day of retribution. Perhaps that had been Shirin Mam's intention all along.

They stopped in the shade of a massive dune toward midday, drinking and eating a little, resting the horses and making sure they were watered. Although not as bleak as the Empty Place, the Thar had a desolate beauty all its own, punctuated by the occasional thorn tree or line of shrubs. At one point they cantered past a boy herding goats. The goats scattered in terror and the boy stared at them wide-eyed before running in the direction of a clump of thatched huts.

The heat intensified in the afternoon and they slowed down, both to protect their horses as well as to pace themselves. It would not do to arrive before dusk.

In the end, though, they were forced to engage well before the sun had set. As they trotted through a rock-filled valley between two cliffs, Kyra felt a prickling at the base of her neck. They were being watched. Rustan sensed it too. He frowned and drew alongside the Maji-khan.

That was all the warning they had before a hail of arrows plunged into the midst of the company. Some pierced the unprotected flanks of the horses, and they stumbled and almost dropped their riders. One of them caught a Kushan man on his neck; he fell forward, unconscious and bleeding.

"Up there!" shouted Chintil, and she spurred her horse off to the side of the cliff. A small cave punctured the cliff halfway up, and a flash of movement betrayed the presence of their attackers. Above the cave, a pigeon winged across the sky. It was an aberration here in the desert, and Kyra noticed it with a lurch of her heart, but there was no time to target it through the rain of arrows falling around them.

She urged Rinna after Chintil, her pulse racing. From the corner of her eye she saw Rustan, Ghasil, and Felda do the same, while Navroz called out for the rest to fall back and put their shields up. More arrows fell, but this time they glanced harmlessly off their shields or landed on the ground.

The Maji-khan made to dismount, but Ghasil stopped him. "Allow me," said the Master of Mental Arts grimly. He leaped from his horse and strode to the edge of a rough path that snaked up toward the cave.

"Drop your weapons and climb down."

The force of his Inner Speech was so great, Kyra knew she would have crumpled had it been directed at her. In her memory, only Tamsyn, and perhaps Shurik, had shown such power.

The rest of the company felt it too. The clansmen and -women fell back farther, uneasy.

Ghasil repeated his command, putting even greater force into it, and the arrows stopped. A group of seven men emerged, their hands empty, their eyes terrified. They darted glances at each other, and some tried to resist Ghasil's command, falling to their knees and pressing their hands against their ears, but in the end none of them were able to stop themselves from climbing down the cliff.

At last the group halted before Ghasil. "You will not hurt us," said Ghasil. "You will tell us everything we need to know."

The men shook and gasped. One of them fell to the ground, eyes rolling up inside his head.

"How many more of you are there?" asked the Maji-khan, putting some pressure into his voice and addressing the one who appeared to be their leader.

"None here," he said in a shaky voice. "But a dozen men guard the way to Jethwa, ten miles up ahead, and just two miles short of the village."

"What weapons do they have?" demanded Ghasil.

"Bows and arrows, and two guns," answered the man.

Barkav frowned. "Kalashiks?"

"No," said the man. "Although they have long barrels like the kalashiks, they are but imitations, and will only fire once before they have to be reloaded." He hesitated. "I heard that the main weapons forge was burned down, and this delayed the production of better weapons."

"What are the bullets made of?" asked Rustan.

But the man shook his head. Evidently, he didn't know more.

"Was that your pigeon I saw in the sky?" asked Kyra.

Barkav and Ghasil looked at her, startled, but the man quailed.

"Answer," said Ghasil harshly. "Did you use a messenger pigeon?"

The man gulped. "Yes, we have notified Jethwa command."

Kyra's heart sank into her boots. So much for the element of surprise.

"Tell me about the organization of Jethwa's defenses," commanded Ghasil.

But here again, the man could not, or would not, help them. He pressed his hands to his head and shook it, repeating weakly, "No, I don't know."

Ghasil kept increasing the pressure until the man collapsed. "Useless," he said in disgust. "All right, which one of you is next?"

"Please, we don't know," said one. "The Taus do not reveal their plans to any but the topmost commanders."

"How many fighters do they have?" demanded the Maji-khan.

This the man was able to answer. "There are more than five thousand fighters, organized into groups of one hundred, each led by a Tau lieutenant."

Five thousand. Kyra's heart sank further still. There were fewer than four hundred of them, not counting the Valavians and any troops they could muster.

"Weapons?" prodded Ghasil, putting his face so close to the man that he shrank back.

"Longbows, crossbows, swords, knives, guns," said the man, his words tripping over themselves in their hurry to get out. "I don't know how many."

Navroz cantered up to them. "We need to get going," she said. "They have delayed us enough."

"Are there injuries?" asked Barkav.

"A few," replied Eldest. "Only one serious. We have tied him to his horse and he must stay back with the healers. But the rest of them can fight. There are five horses that should be replaced as soon as possible. They will heal in time, and I have put salve on their wounds, but they are in no condition to run."

"We will take theirs," said Ghasil.

The men had tied their horses on the opposite side, in the shade of an overhang. A couple of clansmen went to fetch them. Ghasil and Navroz together emptied the men's thoughts until their minds were blank and they could not remember who they were. They left them there, blinking in confusion, and rode ahead.

Kyra cast a last look back, wondering what would happen to the men. It would almost have been kinder to kill them. It would have been easier too. The use of such invasive Mental Arts was exhausting, and she could see from the strain on Ghasil's face that he would need time to recover.

As if reading her thoughts, Rustan leaned toward her and said, "This way, they have a chance for a new life."

"And if they meet someone they were once close to, like a family member?" asked Kyra. "What happens then?"

"Fragments of the past come back to them, but no more," said Ghasil. "Like dreaming someone else's life."

Kyra shook her head. It was a high price to pay for the lives they'd chosen—and surely some of them had *not* chosen it. It had been forced on them by Kai Tau. She felt a surge of pity for them, and her resolve to punish Kai Tau hardened.

Chintil drew alongside them. "Look," she said, and pointed. A large dune obscured their view of the way east. "There's no other shelter for miles around. This is probably where Kai's soldiers are hiding. They will have a clear view of us. Even primitive guns will do too much damage before we can get close enough to use the Inner Speech."

"We must split up," said Kyra. "The main force continues east, as if we do not know we walk into a trap. A smaller one—I propose myself and you, Elder, and perhaps two more—goes south, the long way around the dune to the windward side. It is possible that they will be too caught up tracking the main force to notice us. Plus, they likely hide on the lee side of the dune."

"A good plan," said the Maji-khan. "I will come with you. I have some ability with camouflage."

"Please, Maji-khan," said Kyra. "We need you with the main force in case things go wrong." *In case they see us coming and shoot us dead.*

"Then you will take Ghasil and Rustan," said the Maji-khan.

Rustan flashed her a grin. *Don't think you're going anywhere without me*, he thought at her.

"I will go too," said Ria, riding up to them. "Honestly, I should be the only one, seeing as I have the true gift of camouflage, which none of you do."

Kyra threw her a grateful look. "You may have the gift of camouflage, but your horse does not," she pointed out. "And you cannot just walk there; it would take hours. You can go ahead of us once we dismount closer to the dune."

Chintil and Barkav agreed. The main force moved ahead, rather slower now, to give the small group time to circle south and double back. It was a trick that would have worked well in darkness. At least the sun was dipping lower in the sky now. Anyone looking due west would be half-blinded by the slanting rays.

Kyra, Rustan, Ghasil, Chintil, and Ria rode south, then curved in a wide arc back toward the windward side of the dune. They could still see the main force; it was hard to miss that many people and horses, even miles away.

"Let us hope the guards do not have a scope," remarked Chintil.

"I doubt it," said Ghasil. "Making a scope requires the use of science."

"So does making a gun, no matter how primitive," said Chintil.

They approached the dune in silence. Off to the left, the main force was still almost half a mile away. The evening sun cast its slanted rays on the dune, turning it orange and gold.

"Now," said Chintil, halting near a small clump of desiccated trees. "This is as good a place to leave our horses as any."

They dismounted and proceeded on foot. Ria darted ahead of them, melting into the foreground until they could no longer distinguish her from the dune that towered before them.

At the base of the dune Ghasil paused, and his eyes turned inward with concentration. "Twelve men," he whispered. "Too many for me to compel at once, but perhaps we can do this together?"

Chintil shook her head. "I cannot sense them yet, and I doubt the others can." She withdrew her blade and it glowed blue in the evening light. "Save your strength, Elder. Let us use our kataris as they are meant to be used."

Ria reappeared beside them, her face tense. "They are on the other side," she whispered. "Two with guns, just as we were told. They are focused on the others right now. Five are on the ground, including one gun, and the rest halfway up the dune."

"Good," said Chintil. "Kyra, Rustan, and I will take the ones on top, if you and Elder Ghasil deal with the ones on the ground." She turned to Ghasil. "Do you agree?"

"It would be my pleasure," said Ghasil, stroking his mustache and showing his teeth.

Kyra and Rustan followed Chintil up the dune, their feet sinking into the soft sand. It was a difficult climb, made more so by their boots, and at last Kyra indicated that they should stop, and she removed her boots. Rustan followed suit. Chintil shook her head, but she took hers off too. The going was much easier after that. The sand felt soft and warm on Kyra's bare feet. It was almost peaceful.

Then all hell broke loose on the other side of the dune. Two ear-shattering shots rang out in quick succession. "Come on!" shouted Chintil. She raced up the remaining slope and disappeared on the other side. Kyra's heart pounded as she and Rustan followed, cresting the slope and sliding down until they spied their would-be attackers.

Three men lay on the ground, bleeding from grievous chest and throat wounds. The two with guns had taken cover, fleeing along the side of the dune. The remaining seven were halfway up the slope, aiming down at Ghasil. Ria, thankfully, was not visible. One of the men with a gun fired and a bullet threw up dust near Ghasil's feet.

Rustan swore under his breath. "Trust him not to wait for us," he muttered before letting fly his katari. It buried itself in the armed man's back, and the desert fell mercifully silent.

Kyra aimed her katari at one of the archers and struck him on the neck. She called her blade to return, urgent, as the men below twisted around and beheld them, their faces contorted in anger and fear.

Then Chintil was upon them with a roar, her blade dancing in the sun's last rays, slashing throats and ripping chests. Three men fell before her, stunned looks on their dying faces.

The remaining two—one archer and another armed with a lance—dropped their weapons and scrabbled to get away, but

Kyra and Rustan were faster. They tackled one each, falling into the dance of Empty Hands. Kyra punched her target on his chin, hearing the satisfying crack of a breaking jaw, and Rustan kicked his on the head, knocking him out.

"Stop!" screamed a man from below. "Or I'll kill him."

Chintil, Rustan, and Kyra froze. The man with the second gun had sneaked up behind Ghasil and now held the barrel of his gun to the elder's head.

"Why doesn't he use the Inner Speech?" whispered Chintil.

"Enjoying himself too much," said Rustan, a touch disapprovingly.

Indeed, Ghasil was grinning, his teeth shining white in his dark brown face, reminding Kyra of a wolf. He summoned the Inner Speech, and the face of the man behind him went slack. Then, unmistakably, the hand holding the gun turned so it was aimed at his own face.

Kyra began to turn away in horror, but at that very moment, the gun fired with a deafening roar, and the man's face flew apart in bits of flesh and teeth and blood.

Ria reappeared next to Ghasil. She looked as sick as Kyra felt. Even Ghasil appeared surprised as he beheld the remains of what had once been the head of a man.

"We will have to ensure all these weapons are collected and destroyed," said Chintil grimly. "Kai Tau has brought a disease into our world, and it will not be easy eradicating it."

Kyra knew what Chintil meant. Even if they isolated the kalashiks and destroyed all the imitation guns, they would still need to seek out and modify the minds of those who had worked to forge these weapons. This was dangerous knowledge that could not be allowed to spread.

Ria had stabbed the one remaining guard, so all twelve men

were now dead or incapacitated. Under Chintil's directions, they kicked the weapons into a heap and covered them with sand. Kyra picked up a small round metal ball and examined it. It was still hot to the touch. Chintil peered over her shoulder.

"Their bullets are crude," said the Mistress of Hatha-kala. "Not like the kalashiks. But they can still injure someone almost as badly."

"Good thing they only fire once before they must be reloaded," said Kyra.

Chintil indicated the dead man lying nearby, his shattered face an abomination. "Once is enough," she said. "The poor fool. Guns will turn on those who wield them."

"Elder, next time we would appreciate your waiting for us," said Rustan to the Master of Mental Arts.

"It wasn't my fault," protested Ghasil. "It was this young Markswoman. Utterly bloodthirsty," he added in admiring tones, and Ria reddened, looking annoyed.

Kyra knew that Ria was too disciplined to act in haste. Whatever she may have said was cut off, though, because horse hooves signaled that the rest of their company was close by.

Ria and Rustan backtracked to fetch their horses, and Kyra, Chintil, and Ghasil went ahead to meet their little army. Kyra felt a glow of pride as she beheld them, Marksmen and Markswomen riding together with clansfolk, as one people with one aim.

The horses came to a halt in front of them, and Chintil explained briefly to the Maji-khan and Navroz what had transpired, and how the guns seemed to work.

Navroz frowned. "I don't like this. They have warning of our arrival now and will be well prepared. How do we defend ourselves from bullets?"

"By letting me go first," said Kyra. "If Elder Ghasil will ride behind me, I will be able to protect him, and we should be able to mentally incapacitate those who hold guns."

Chintil shook her head. "There are five thousand fighters—far too many for us to bind with the Inner Speech. And you are needed to lead the attack into the heart of Kai Tau's camp. We must trust our shields and take our chances. Once we're close enough to use our blades and our voices, we will prevail."

Kyra was loath to let her friends and teachers ride into danger, but she knew the elder was right. "We are but two miles from Jethwa," she said. "Perhaps the healers can make camp here?"

Navroz agreed, and together with Elena, Nineth, Akassa, and a couple of apprentices from Khur, she set down her supplies, well away from the bodies that littered the desert floor. Two of the Marksmen checked the bodies and buried the dead ones under mounds of sand as best they could. Others dragged the few who still lived to where the healers had set up their station. Inner Speech would ensure their compliance when they woke.

They did not build a fire, but used a small, smokeless lamp. Elena arrayed bunches of roots and herbs around the lamp, and a sweet, familiar smell stole into the air.

"Time to go," said the Maji-khan.

Kyra went to Elena and Nineth, and they wrapped their arms around each other in a fierce embrace. "Come back," said Elena. "Promise us."

"I promise," said Kyra, but the words stuck in her throat, and she wondered if she would ever see them again.

CHAPTER 42

THE BATTLE OF
THE THAR

They approached Jethwa as the sun was sinking below the horizon. Far in the distance, gray-brown shapes blurred the line between desert and sky. Kyra couldn't make out what they were in the fading light, but she could guess. Barkav pulled out a small cylinder from his robe and peered through it. A scope? Kyra watched him, agog. At last he passed it to her, his mouth set in a grim line. She looked through it with one eye, closing the other with a hand, as she had seen him do.

A line of camels curved north to south, as far as she could see through the scope. Atop each camel was a warrior, some of them armed with the long, dark barrels she had seen in the hands of the two guards a mile back. Her gut clenched. There were so *many* of them. How could they possibly defeat such a huge army? She passed the scope to Chintil and said, "Their first circle of defense?"

Chintil looked through the scope before answering. "Spears,

bows, and guns. We cannot venture too close to them. Our horses are well trained, but a few might shy at the sight and smell of camels. We will keep to our original plan and lead two forces north and south to flank them." She passed the scope to Rustan.

"You will be spread very thin," Kyra pointed out.

"And you, Mahimata, will be smashing into them," said Chintil. She leaned sideways and, to Kyra's surprise, hugged her. Kyra hugged her back, overcome. The Mistress of Hatha-kala had never embraced her before. Then Kyra realized her teacher may well be riding to her death, and a lump rose in her throat. "We will defeat Kai Tau," she said fiercely.

The Maji-khan smiled a terrible smile. "Of course we will. Lead the way, Mahimata. I am anxious to get started."

They divided into the three prearranged groups. Chintil and Mumuksu led the biggest contingent south, and Ghasil and Felda led a slightly smaller one north. The smallest group stayed with Kyra and Rustan.

"Stay back until I give the word," Ghasil told Kyra and the Maji-khan. "We will unhinge them with the Inner Speech, soften them up for you a bit."

Then they were off. Up ahead, a bugle sounded the alarm. Their movements had been spotted. The Maji-khan looked through his scope. "One minute to engagement," he reported in a calm voice.

Rustan squeezed Kyra's hand, his face tense. "I'll be right beside you," he said.

"*Behind* me," she corrected. "You will stay five horse lengths behind me." Not that it would make any difference if a bullet found its way into his heart. Kyra resolutely pushed that thought away.

Shots rang out in the distance, echoing in the flat land. "Their line wavers, but it still holds," said the Maji-khan. "They are well trained."

"What about our side?" said Kyra, anxious. "Anyone down?"

"I cannot tell," said Barkav. He put the scope away. "It is almost time. Prepare yourselves."

Kyra took a deep breath. She turned and addressed the Markswomen and Marksmen clustered behind her. "You know your positions; hold to them, no matter what. Above all, do not try to overtake me. I am the only one impervious to bullets of any kind."

"Your head is unprotected," said Ria. "Should you not have at least worn a helmet like us?"

"I have something much more appropriate," said Kyra. She reached for the mask of Kali, which she had tied behind her, and unwrapped it. The Markswomen gasped in recognition as she brought it up to her face. The Marksmen and clansfolk stared, uncomprehending, at the terrible visage of Kali in her warrior aspect.

"I gave myself to the Goddess when I joined the Order of Kali," said Kyra. "But today, the Goddess gives herself to me." She donned the fearsome mask, tying it securely behind her head.

The first time she had worn the mask during her initiation, she had not felt any different. But this time, a jolt of awareness ran through her, as if someone watched her from a great distance with rising interest—as Kyra herself might look at an ant trying to climb onto her lap, holding out a crumb as an offering.

The faces before her changed to alarm, confusion, and fear. Even Rustan was looking at her as if he had never seen her before in his life. "Kyra?" he whispered. "Where are you?"

"Here," said Kyra, in a voice she did not fully recognize as her own. "And I am going to lead you to the bloodiest, most glorious battle of all your lives. Come, children. It is time to prove yourselves worthy of your blades."

She wheeled Rinna around. In a small part of her mind—the one untouched by the Goddess—Ghasil's warning sounded. *Ride now.*

"Go, Rinna!" shouted Kyra, and the mare snorted and set off across the sandy plain at a full gallop. Behind her, she sensed Rustan alongside the Maji-khan, five horse lengths behind, as she had instructed. Behind them, in a tight V, fanned out the rest of her small company, flanked by the clan warriors.

Live long and die well, she thought to them.

Then the enemy was in sight, and the first bullets whistled above her head. Kyra laughed, possessed by a strength and a confidence she had never felt before.

Part of it was the blessing of the Goddess and the indestruct-ibility of her armor, but it was more than that. It was as if her whole life had been leading up to this moment, this fierce charge against the evil that beset her world. Blood would flow today.

The camelry was in some disarray, but their lines still held. Those who had guns reloaded them. Others nocked arrows or held spears in readiness, their faces fearful but determined. The blast of Inner Speech from Ghasil and the others must have affected them enough to inspire fear and doubt, but not much more. As Kyra had suspected, the Orders were spread far too thin to make a decisive or bloodless end to the battle. She could no longer sense the first two forces; they must have flowed past the northern and southern flanks, taking care to stay out of accurate gun range. Unless there was a kalashik somewhere in the outer ranks. A kalashik knew the heart of its master, just the way a katari did.

A Tau warrior called out a command, and a forest of arrows flew toward them.

"Shields up," shouted the Maji-khan.

Kyra didn't have a shield—she did not need one. The arrows flew past her, one close enough that she felt the breeze of its passing. Behind her, others were not so fortunate. Several arrows clanged against the shields of the company, and there was a muffled cry as one found its way into flesh.

Noor Sialbi. Kyra's mind sought her out. She was injured but she still rode, her wounded leg gripping her horse, her thoughts fierce. She would hold. Kyra released her breath and focused on the enemy ahead. She did not know how deep the lines ran. She knew only that she must destroy them.

Hold the Inner Speech until we are closer, thought Kyra to them all, and it was hard, so hard to hold back when arrows rained down on them, but it was the right thing to do.

At last, as the men readied their guns on their shoulders for a second shot, Kyra thought: *Now.*

They blasted the men with the Inner Speech, their combined voices a wave of silent command that rolled over the enemy lines, tearing through their mental defenses like paper:

DROP YOUR WEAPONS.

FLEE.

FORGET WHO YOU ARE.

The simplest commands were the most effective, especially when voices joined together to amplify them. And it had the desired effect. Men dropped their weapons and clutched their heads. Dozens dismounted and ran away, across the twilit desert, as if demons were after them. Still more fled on camelback, opening up a space for Kyra and her followers to plow through. Some of the camels bolted even though their riders tried to stop them. They were not as well trained or used to combat as the horses the Orders were using.

Not all of Kai Tau's soldiers were equally affected, of course. And the Marksmen and Markswomen could not keep up this level of mental pressure without it impacting their own abilities. As Kyra approached the gap, a man aimed his gun at her, his face split in a snarl.

Kyra's katari was out without her even giving a thought to it. She spun it toward the man, and it buried itself in his unprotected throat. He slid off his camel, the gun falling from his hand. Other blades flew past her, finding similar targets.

Now the enemy was truly in disarray. Kyra called her blade back, and as it landed in her outstretched palm, she arrived at the chaos of the outermost line and galloped through it. Far in the distance, to the left and the right, she sensed the faint echo of the Inner Speech from Ghasil, Chintil, and the others as it broke down the enemy's resolve, driving them inward or causing them to flee.

But she had no thoughts to spare for them right now. Behind the camelry was a second line, men and women on horseback, armed with spears and fire lances. But it was not their primitive weapons that made Kyra's blood run cold. Her gaze went to a man clad in black, camouflaged so he almost blended in with the oncoming night, and to the long, smooth barrel held trained in his hand. *Kalashik.* She could smell the cold evil that emanated from it.

Stay back, she ordered the rest. They had their hands full containing the hundreds of fighters around them anyway. She could see, from her mind's eye, Rustan driving a spear into a man who had tried to shoot at them with a fire lance. Beside him, the Maji-khan roared in savage delight as he plucked a man from his saddle and broke his neck, before throwing him aside like a rag doll. Behind them, Noor Sialbi smashed her shield into the face of a man who had grabbed her injured leg. Ria Farad stood in her stirrups, barely visible on her horse, throwing her katari with deadly accuracy and calling it back with far greater speed than any of them. Kyra's heart swelled with pride and love for them all. They were her people and she would protect them.

Then she roared, "Victory to Kali," and the voice that emerged was not her own, but amplified through the mask, as if the Goddess herself spoke from the heavens. The second line stumbled back; horses reared in fright, toppling riders.

But the man with the kalashik was unmoved. Perhaps he had been held in the grip of his weapon for too long, and it had eaten his mind. He fired, and the bullet shot toward her heart.

"Keep going, Rinna!" said Kyra, and she closed her eyes. *You cannot hurt me*, she thought.

A small clang against her armor and a punch, as of someone kicking her in the chest, followed by another and another in quick succession. Kyra gasped and opened her eyes. The bullets could not pierce her shield, but they *did* hurt. Time to put this kalashik out of action. She flung her blade at the man in black. It penetrated his face shield, splitting his skull in half. He fell back in slow motion, the kalashik slipping from his fingers.

Other fighters tried to pick up the kalashik from the ground, but Kyra felled them with the Inner Speech. She bent down sideways from her horse and, counting on the kalishium armor to protect her, grabbed the gun with her bare hand. She slipped it into the bag slung across her saddle, her heart thudding. No dark voices came to her. As she had hoped, the weapons could not harm her while she wore kalishium.

The death of the kalashik-bearer and the loss of his weapon unnerved the fighters around them. Kyra and her company were through the second line in a matter of moments. It was pitch-dark now save for the fires that dotted the landscape, most started by the fire lances. Not too far distant, a cluster of tents burned, flames licking the sky. Kyra smiled grimly. When this was over, there wouldn't be much of Jethwa left to salvage.

Kyra reined in Rinna and wheeled her around to take a quick tally. Her eyes swept over her small but deadly group as they cantered up to her. Rustan was the first by her side, his eyes flashing with the light of battle. Noor had tied the wound in her leg with a scarf. None were missing—except the most formidable of them all.

"Where is the Maji-khan?" asked Kyra, a cold fist opening in her chest.

Ria jerked her head back. "In the middle of a knot of a hundred men, breaking necks and ruining minds." Her tone was admiring, but a current of fear shot through Kyra.

"Then we must extricate him," she said, spurring Rinna back. "How could you leave him behind?"

Rustan reached forward and gripped her arm, stopping her. "No. Kyra, we must move ahead. The Maji-khan can take care of himself. He has some of the clan warriors with him. He will keep Kai's soldiers busy, and they will not follow us."

Behind them, Barkav roared in anger, and there were several screams of pain.

"See what I mean?" Rustan released her. "He has bought us precious time. Do not waste it."

Kyra swallowed. "Fall into the wedge," she cried. "And let us destroy their last defenses."

They followed her across the desert, their horses' hooves thudding against the ground, kicking up sand that obscured them, so that they looked like a dark-moving cloud of fury.

In the distance, Kyra could see nothing of note: no mounted warriors, no flaming pits, not even a sentry. There was nothing but darkness and silence. This absence set off alarm bells in her head.

Be wary, Kyra thought to her group. *There will be traps, this close to the heart of Tau command.*

"Watch out!" shouted Rustan. But his warning came too late. The ground seemed to rise up in front of Kyra. Rinna stumbled and fell, trapping Kyra beneath her body. Kyra bit back a scream as the weight of her horse threatened to crush her leg. A heavy metallic net fell on her face, blurring her vision.

No. She freed her hands, pushing away the net, heedless of the barbs tearing the skin of her palms. At least the mask had protected her face. Wordlessly she soothed Rinna, who was terrified and hurt.

Behind her, Kyra sensed many of her group similarly caught, although Rustan, she was relieved to see, had evaded the trap. He danced away on his horse and cantered back toward her, murder in his eyes.

Dozens of fighters rose from the ground and rushed toward Rustan, throwing a net on his horse, forcing him to a stop. Rustan's horse bucked and screamed as the metal tore its flesh.

At last Kyra threw the net aside and faced her attackers

as they bore down on her. She tried to summon the Inner Speech, but in the darkness and confusion of the moment, it refused to come. She sent her blade into the heart of one of the men rushing toward her, but it was not enough; she needed a *hundred* blades, and she needed to protect those who were down, unable to reach for their weapons. She grabbed the spears strapped to her back and crossed them in front of her, deflecting a lance, sending it spinning back into the midst of her attackers.

And then she flowed into the Dance of Spears. Did not the Goddess herself kill demons with spear and sword? Kyra sent up a wordless prayer and fell upon her attackers with a hideous shriek that echoed across the desert and made them stumble back, hands over their ears, horror on their faces. The twin spears whirled before her, taking on a life of their own, piercing throats and spilling guts. A red mist came before her eyes. She could no longer see or think clearly. But she didn't need to see or think. She could feel the strength and fury of the Goddess within her, and it drove her on, cutting down the men who had dared attack her company. She threw one of her spears, stabbed with the other, retrieved a sword from where it had fallen to the ground, recalled her katari back into her palm. She fought with whatever she had, and she didn't miss once.

Around her, the others rallied, freeing themselves and their horses from the nets, joining their blades and their voices to battle, until not a single foe was left standing.

It's all right, Kyra. Stop. Rustan's voice penetrated the fog that had descended on her.

Kyra came to a halt, and a sword fell from her hand. A wounded man crawled away from her, blubbering in fear and pain. She undid the mask and blinked at the scene of carnage before them. Sweat trickled down her face. She felt cold and sick and weak. There was a taste of ash in her mouth.

The rest were staring at her as if they didn't know who she was or where she had come from. "We need to keep going," she said, putting as much strength as she could into her voice.

"We cannot ride," said Ria. Her face was bloodstained, and she had lost her helmet. "Most of the horses are too injured. They need to return to the healers."

"We cannot go back," said Rustan. "We must leave them here, and trust that we will find them later."

"Not alone," said Kyra. Her eyes sought four of the six remaining clan warriors. "Please stay with the horses and protect them as best you can."

"I doubt they will be targeted," said Ria. "They are not a threat and will probably be ignored."

Kyra nodded and started walking, although it was hard; her legs trembled, as if they could no longer support her weight. As if she would crash to the ground and let the blackness swallow her.

But not yet. Oh, not yet. Kai Tau waited for her at the end of this deadly dance.

The others fell into place behind Kyra. She sensed at least three serious injuries. One of the Marksmen could barely walk, and Ria's breath came short and ragged. But they would keep going until they died or she commanded them to stop.

It happened without warning, a little later. One moment they were walking in silence punctuated by distant screams, and the next moment they were surrounded by armed men. *Two kalashiks.* Weakened by the battle, they had not sensed the approach of the dark weapons. Kyra barely had time to process the horror of it, when the guns began to speak. Bullets punched against her armor, making her stagger back.

Behind Kyra everyone threw themselves on the ground. But the injured Marksman was not fast enough. A bullet tore into his face and he collapsed, soaked in blood. More bullets pierced the two remaining clan warriors, killing them instantly.

"PUT DOWN YOUR WEAPONS AND LIE FACEDOWN WITH YOUR HANDS BEHIND YOUR HEAD."

The powerful voice rolled across the dark plain and into Kyra's skull. Although she knew the command was not directed at her, she was almost impelled to the ground herself. It was a voice that could not be ignored, that could only be obeyed without question.

Before her eyes, the men who had come to kill her and her companions dropped their weapons and lay down. A few remained standing, struggling against the order, but Kyra could have told them it was no use. The voice repeated the command, even more strongly, and those who were still standing fell back, eyes rolling up in their skulls, the two kalashiks falling uselessly away.

This was Mental Arts at its greatest. And in her heart, she knew who it was, even before he rode up to them and the starlight fell on his face. Older, more serious, harder than she remembered, but Shurik, all the same. Did she not know his voice, more intimately than she had ever wanted to? He had used that voice to compel her once.

And he had used it now to save them.

Shurik dismounted near the fallen Marksman and bent over to check him. But the Marksman was dead, would have died at once, like the two clan warriors beside him. Shurik's face tightened with grief. He rose and went to Rustan, who embraced him.

"Ishtul," murmured Rustan.

"I know," said Shurik, his voice bleak. "I sensed it, but I was too far away, too late to help."

"So was I," said Rustan, releasing him. "But today we avenge his death." His gaze went to the fallen Marksman and darkened. "And Varun's."

One by one, everyone picked themselves up off the ground. Shurik greeted the remaining Marksmen. Kyra checked her Markswomen; no one else appeared to have been hit by the bullets, a miracle in itself.

At last, Shurik walked up to Kyra. "Are you all right?" he asked.

"Shurik," she said, and swallowed. "How?"

"Later," he said, his voice emotionless. "Let's kill Kai Tau first." He paused and glanced at the mask dangling from her hand, and added, "Interesting face," sounding almost like the Shurik of old.

Kyra held up the mask. "It represents the Goddess; it has power. And I'm going to need every bit of power I possess to defeat him today."

"I'm with you," said Shurik, "with whatever I have to offer." A flash of pain passed across his face. "I'm sorry for what I did to you."

"I know," said Kyra. "And I forgive you. Come, we have work to do."

A shot rang out, not too far from them. Worry crossed Ria's face. "We'd better hurry," she said.

"In a moment," said Kyra. She went to where the kalashiks lay, gleaming darkly beside their twitching handlers, and picked them up. She wrapped them in a discarded cloak and tied the bundle to her belt. One more burden, but it was not one she could allow anyone else to share.

Shurik went among the twenty-odd men who lay facedown on the ground, reinforcing his command not to move or touch their weapons. When he returned, his face had taken on a ghostly pallor. Even for Shurik, this was too much. It was going to cost him. She could not rely on him to repeat this feat, or it may well kill him.

Kyra cast an assessing look at her company. "Stay behind me in the wedge," she commanded. "Shurik, you will be abreast with Rustan. Let's go."

She set off across the desert, the sounds of fighting far distant and almost unreal. They were in the eye of a storm. All around them, shields clashed; men and women swore and screamed and died. But here was only a silence that waited for them, opening its mouth wider to welcome them in.

CHAPTER 43

BEHIND THE LINES

Nineth had wanted so badly to go with Kyra and the others into Jethwa. Instead she was stuck more than a mile away with Navroz, Akassa, Elena, and three young boys from the Order of Khur, who looked as if they should be home with their mothers. Navroz was explaining the basics of healing and first aid to them, while Elena was making herbal poultices in preparation for the wounded who were sure to come thick and fast when the fighting began.

Nineth imagined Kyra fighting for her life, surrounded on all sides by the enemy, and her stomach clenched. If only she was a Markswoman and not a mere apprentice. If only she had earned the right to fight by Kyra's side.

But she would have had to kill someone to be initiated as a Markswoman. And Nineth had not been ready to do that—at least, not before today.

Akassa touched her arm. "I know what you're thinking," she

said. "But Kyra did right, leaving us here. You never know, we might get attacked and have to defend Eldest and those little boys from murderous outlaws."

"Little boys!" said one of them, a boy called Darius, indignantly. "I'm almost fourteen."

Akassa rolled her eyes. "Could have fooled me," she remarked. "I was going to ask where your milk bottle was."

"Enough," said Navroz sharply. "I hear the galloping of horses. Akassa, Darius, check who it is. Nineth, conceal yourself and be ready with your blade."

There wasn't really any good place to hide, but Nineth flattened herself against the rock wall, trusting the shadows that pooled beneath it. Her heart beat fast with excitement. Was this the attack that would give her a chance to prove herself?

But it was only a dozen injured men and women and their poor horses, arrows stuck in their flanks, snorting and trembling in fear. Navroz was at their side in an instant, talking soothingly, finding the most severely wounded, and barking instructions to her temporary assistants.

Nineth put aside her anxiety and got to work with the rest. This was important too. What they did here could mean the difference between life and death for so many. She cleaned wounds, applied salves, and did her best to reduce their pain through some mild Inner Speech. Elena took care of the horses; Akassa and the boys helped Navroz, fetching whatever she needed, boiling water, and grinding lilac leaves for fresh antiseptic.

The injured men and women were from the Kushan clan, part of the force that had been led north by Ghasil.

"It goes hard for us," gasped a woman who had been speared in the leg and was in obvious pain, though she tried to control it. "The Khur elder is truly gifted, but his voice weakens. There are too many of the Tau vermin for us to hold back. We have been retreating for the last half hour. There are several among us who have fallen and will never rise again."

Nineth's heart sank. Was Kyra in trouble too?

"Never fear," said Navroz in a strong, reassuring voice. "The Valavians will join the battle soon, and they will lend their strength to ours. Rest, child. You have done the best you could. Sleep." The last command was spoken with a trace of the Inner Speech, and the woman's eyes fluttered closed, and she relaxed at last.

Nineth squared her shoulders. "You should let Akassa and me join them," she said to Navroz. "Two more kataris will help."

"No," said Navroz firmly. "I need you both here. Go boil some water. More wounded will arrive soon."

Nineth rose, seething. Boil water, indeed. Elena caught her gaze and grinned. Her face was flushed, and her eyes sparkled. She had dealt with all the wounded horses and was now supervising the apprentices from Khur. Elena was in her element. There was no other place she would rather be than here, the healing post. This was where she belonged.

Nineth wondered if she could simply take one of the horses and sneak off. It wouldn't be hard to do; they were all so busy, even Akassa. No one would bother trying to follow her.

She waited until Navroz was bent over a man who seemed to be missing half his face, then snuck away, deeper into the shadows. She wasn't exactly proud of what she was doing; she told herself she would only circle the perimeter of the cliff, make sure everything was all right, maybe take the horse for a wider circle. Of course, no telling what she might see once she was on horseback. It wouldn't be her fault if something demanded her intervention and she had to gallop away.

And so it was that when the assailants inched silently down the side of the dune, brandishing crossbows, swords, and spears, Nineth was the only one they did not see—and the only one who saw them. She was hidden by an overhang of the cliff, on the verge of slipping away, when she looked up and spied the dark shapes in the starlight creeping down the cliff.

For a moment she was confused, but the next moment her confusion vanished, replaced by dread, and then with cold certainty, she knew what to do, and so did her blade. It was in her hand without her remembering she had unsheathed it. The leader of the pack halted halfway down the dune and aimed a barrel-shaped weapon at Eldest. Navroz should have sensed something amiss, but she was bent over the wounded man, too absorbed by the severity of the injury that required her care.

Nineth had never thrown her katari at such an angle before, and she knew she wouldn't get a second chance. She slid her forefinger down the hilt, drew back her arm, said a brief prayer to Kali, and threw, spinning the blade up the dune so it resembled a blue shooting star. The man grunted in surprise and pain as the blade buried itself in his side.

It was enough. Navroz looked up in alarm and sprang to her feet. "Scattered defense!" she cried, and summoned the Inner Speech, felling two men before drawing her blade and flinging it into the attackers' midst.

"Scattered defense" was one of the code words of Hatha-kala, and it was an order to scatter as widely as possible while still retaining the ability to both protect oneself and others. Akassa and Elena instantly dropped their bandages and poultices and ran to opposite ends of the valley, melting into the shadows cast by the cliff walls. The Khur apprentices were quick to follow suit.

Nineth tried to call her blade back, but it refused to budge. Arrows rained down into the valley, some of them piercing the already wounded warriors who lay on the ground. Nineth swore and heaved herself up the cliffside, determined to get her blade back. She grabbed at the rocks and pulled herself up, thanking the Goddess she had regained some of her strength in the past few weeks.

Above was darkness and confusion and screams of pain as kataris found their way unerringly into human flesh. One man blundered down the cliff directly in front of Nineth and almost slammed into her. She sidestepped him and delivered a hard kick to his ribs that sent him tumbling down the rocks with a most gratifying crunch of bone.

Intent on the targets below, the men did not notice Nineth's arrival until she was upon them. She delivered a backfist punch into the neck of the man nearest her, the one who held the metal barrel, and followed it with a knife-hand strike to his head. He crumpled without a sound, but Nineth barely had time to feel triumph or register the pain in her hand, when she was surrounded by three attackers. A man thrust his sword at her, and she stumbled back, narrowly avoiding its swinging blade, only to feel a sharp, shooting pain in her lower back. She had been stabbed. A man holding a dagger stood behind her. He raised it again, his face intent.

Nineth fell to the ground in a feint. It was only half pretense; her body screamed in agony, and it was all she could do to stay conscious. As the men loomed over her, raising their swords to hack her to bits, she thought, *Now would be a great time for you to return.*

Smoothly, the katari slid into her hand, as if it had always been there. As if it were she who had made the mistake of not noticing it. *Thank you*, she thought, and thrust the katari up into the chest of the dagger-holder. She rolled away, avoiding the thrust of the second man's sword, and gripped the booted feet of the third, dragging him down.

And then Eldest was there, dispatching them one by one, her face full of cold fury and yet completely calm. When she was done, all fifteen attackers lay dead. Nineth's last thought, before she blacked out, was not the question of how many she herself had killed, or that she had never seen Eldest look so bloodthirsty and terrible, or even if Elena and Akassa and those silly boys were unhurt. It was the thought of Kyra, and how proud she would have been of her friend.

Chapter 44

THE SHAPE OF A MAN

As Kyra and her little group advanced into Jethwa, a scene of devastation met their eyes. Huts had been demolished and the ground leveled as if a storm had hit the village.

"Over there," said Rustan quietly from behind her. "Do you see the wall?"

She could, just barely. In the distance, a barrier rose up in the air, made of stones, bricks, brambles, and whatever else the builders had been able to lay their hands on. Including, if her senses were right, human bodies. Kyra forced herself not to retch. She represented the Goddess Kali, and to Kali all death was an offering. The souls that had been trapped by those poor bodies were free. It was all just organic matter now, which would soon return to the earth.

Still, it was hard to look upon the desecration and not feel sick. "Why?" she whispered.

"To put fear and doubt into us," said Rustan. "Do not let

them succeed." He squeezed her hand. "Also, perhaps as an offering to their kalashiks. The dark weapons thirst for death and cannot be denied."

How do you know? she wanted to ask, but didn't. Rustan had been touched by a kalashik. This close to them, he must feel their evil even more acutely than she did.

"It's a trap," muttered Ria. "Men with kalashiks hide behind the wall. They wait for us to come into sight. I am the only one who can safely move ahead."

"No," said Kyra. "That would be me. Once you used your katari or the Inner Speech, you would reveal your presence. Here I must go forward alone."

She ignored the sounds of protest. "Do not follow me," she warned. "Stay close to the ground to avoid being hit. This I order as your Mahimata, upon pain of exile. Until I call for you. Do you understand?"

The Markswomen assented; they had no choice, as they were oath-bound to obey her. The Marksmen were another matter. Rustan and Shurik were staring at her with mulish, set faces. "If you try to follow me," she told them, "you risk my life, because you will divide my attention. I am protected by my armor; you are not. If I spare even a fraction of my energy worrying about you, I'm probably going to die."

"You want us to just *wait* here?" snapped Rustan. "Suppose you do get struck by a bullet. What do you want us to do?"

"Retrieve me if you can," said Kyra. "I'm still the best chance we have against Kai Tau. If not . . . retreat."

Shurik opened his mouth to argue, but she raised a hand to cut him off. "I will not fail," she promised. "And I will call you when it is time."

Rustan exhaled. "Stay alive," he said, and she felt a sense of déjà vu. She was walking toward the door of death, hoping it would stay closed, and Rustan stood behind her, ready to follow her through that door if necessary.

Their eyes met, and the tenderness of his gaze pierced Kyra's heart. *I will be fine*, she thought to him. Then she donned her mask. They stepped away from her, a gap opening between her and the others, as if by wearing it she changed who she was. And perhaps she *did* change, for as before, wearing it gave her a sense of power and confidence. She felt untouchable, even if she was not. She tried to curb that feeling; it was dangerous to think you were invincible when you were but flesh and blood.

She raised a palm to the others. *Wait for my signal.* Then she turned and ran toward the barrier, blade in hand, feet thudding on the soft earth in time to the beating of her heart.

Five steps. Ten. Fifteen and the kalashiks found her. The firing began. One gun or five, did it make any difference? They could fire eternally, taking strength and sustenance from those who held them in the mistaken belief that they somehow owned the weapons, when in reality the guns owned *them*.

The bullets whizzed past her, most of them missing, the kalishium acting as a repellent. She hoped everyone else was lying low as she had instructed. Enough of the bullets hit to make her stagger and gasp with pain. It was like being punched multiple times, unable to hit back. She would be covered with bruises when this was over.

It was tempting to summon the Inner Speech, but she knew it would be hard to compel those who were in the thrall of their weapons. She didn't have Shurik's or Ghasil's skill in the Mental Arts, and she wasn't close enough. Only when she was almost at the barrier did she unleash the Inner Speech, targeting the man directly in front of her until she felt his mental defenses crumple and the gun drop from his hand. There were two more men on either side of him, and she blasted them with all her strength.

She dropped to her hands and knees, panting with effort. The barrier opened, and men poured out, armed with wicked-looking swords and machetes.

Come to me, she called to her friends, but it was hopeless, they were too far away, and the men were almost upon her. She raised her blade, determined to give herself up dearly.

And then Ria was there, shimmering into view, her blade flying into the throat of one of the leaders, her voice compelling those behind him. Kyra found her strength and lunged for the man closest to her, driving her blade into his heart and withdrawing it to stab another.

Rustan arrived, the others close at his heels. They fought with single-minded fury, even though they were outnumbered almost ten to one, and several were wounded. Many of their attackers lay dead or dying on the ground; several dropped their weapons and ran, chased away by the Inner Speech.

But there were far too many of them. Selene and Tonar were wounded by the more primitive guns; Kyra waded into the onslaught, stabbing and piercing, looking for the decisive thrust that would end this battle.

"Go, Mahimata!" shouted Tonar. "Find Kai Tau and kill him."

Kyra was loath to leave her Markswomen, but Shurik grabbed hold of her arm, his face almost unrecognizable in its battle fury. "We'll hold them back," he said urgently. "You and Rustan go ahead."

So Kyra and Rustan ran past the ruined barrier, into the heart of Tau command, while behind them their friends fought for their lives, fought to break the last circle of Tau defense.

A lone concrete building rose before them with a wraparound porch and a single lantern hanging at its entrance. Its appearance was absurdly ordinary in that hellish landscape of blood, screams, and death. But it filled Kyra's heart with fear.

"The council house," said Rustan. "This is where Kai Tau stays. But all the buildings around it are gone."

"So there can be no mistaking where I have to go," said Kyra. She handed her mask to Rustan and untied the bundled-up kalashiks from her belt. "Here I must go alone," she told him. "And I must go only as myself."

He took the mask from her in confusion. "Why?"

"Because only a daughter of Veer may kill Kai Tau," she answered. She smiled at him. Rustan, her beloved. What greater joy than to see his face before confronting her worst enemy?

He seemed to understand. He tilted her chin up and kissed her tenderly. It was a kiss of hope and desire and life, and it made Kyra want to put her arms around him and never let go. Instead, she disengaged herself and pressed a palm against his cheek.

"The Goddess watch over you," she said.

"She already does," he said, and smiled with such sadness that she was on the verge of asking him what he meant. But she didn't, and she would remember this later and regret it.

She walked toward the council house, concentrating on the dim light of the lantern, letting the sounds of battle fade behind her. She climbed the steps up to the porch and paused before the door.

A simple, innocuous door, and yet it filled her with foreboding. *Come in*, it said. *You have waited to open me your whole life.*

"Victory to Kali," whispered Kyra, but her words sounded hollow now, the name of the Goddess a mere word without any power. She closed her eyes and summoned her inner strength. She thought of Shirin Mam, of her parents and sisters. All those whom she had loved and lost, all the ghosts that peopled her dreams and waited for her on the other side.

Then she placed her hand upon the door and pushed it open.

Inside was a single oil lamp on the floor. Twisted shadows danced on the walls—strange shapes that had no basis in reality. Mutterings rose in the air, washed over her, drenching her with fear.

And from the far corner of the room, a man kneeling on the ground stirred and spoke:

"Welcome, daughter."

It was a deep, gravelly voice that put her in mind of seabeds and ancient mines full of darkness. She held on to the door to steady herself, but her head swam.

Behind her, Rustan's voice: *Stay strong, my love. I am with you.*

Kyra swallowed and entered the shadowy room. The door swung shut behind her, and she was alone with the man who had assaulted her mother and killed her family.

"I knew you would come one day," he said. "I have been waiting for you."

"To kill you?" She put as much contempt as she could into her voice, although she could barely speak. "Do you not have the guts to do the job yourself?"

He laughed, a high, crazy sound at odds with the rest of his speech. That laugh set her teeth on edge. It was the sound of a man on the far edge of sanity.

"You are wrong, daughter," he said.

"Don't call me that!" She gripped her blade so hard it bit her hands. "I am no daughter of yours."

"But you could have been," he said. "You might well be. After all, you have my gifts."

"The gifts you threw away," she said. Why was she talking to him? She should fling her blade into his heart and be done with it.

"But you won't," he said. "You want to know why I did it, don't you?"

Kyra opened her mouth to deny it, then snapped it shut again. He could hear her thoughts, sense her emotions. How, unless he was still bonded to his kalishium blade?

"I have gone beyond kalishium," he said. He shifted away from the shadows and into the pool of light cast by the lamp. "See?"

Kyra looked at him and almost fainted.

The thing that sat before her was still in the shape of a man, but it was no longer quite human. Where the forearms should be, two gleaming black barrels melded with the elbows, pointing straight at her. He wore a sleeveless deerskin coat, and she could see that the skin of his upper arms, face, and neck was covered by a network of thin metallic lines. His eyes were gray and cold as a winter sky. Stringy hair hung like rats' tails around his damaged face.

"What *are* you?" she whispered.

He grinned—a ghastly sight, because the inside of his mouth was a nightmare. The tongue was black, the teeth filed into points. "I have become my weapons," he said. "The result of loving them too long. The hardest thing will be keeping you alive long enough to have a little chat."

Kyra didn't need to hear or see more. She threw her blade with accuracy, straight into Kai Tau's heart. To her shock, the blade clanged against his chest and skittered away across the floor. Its light extinguished. She tried to call it back, but it would not move. She could not reach it with her mind. Panic took hold of her. She fought it down.

Kai Tau shook his head. "Your puny katari is no match for me," he said, sounding almost sad. His forearms rose, and Kyra stared at the barrels in fascinated horror. He pushed them down again, grimacing with effort. "Not now," he whispered. "Not yet, my darlings."

Kyra recoiled. He was *speaking* to them. Speaking to the guns fused to his arms as if they were beloved children.

He raised his head and locked eyes with her. It was like looking into a well of madness. "I kept these two with me always. I ate with them, slept with them. One day I woke, and they were joined to my arms, and my katari had vanished. I tried to cut them off, but it didn't work. My arms had hardened like the kalashiks themselves." He raised them up again for her to see. "Look, the one on the left killed your mother, the one on the right, the woman who bore my eldest son. Maidul, whom *you* killed."

Kyra flinched at the mention of her mother and her first mark.

"I wonder," he mused, "which one will kill you. I can never tell, you see. They take turns, but there is nothing linear about their thinking. Sometimes I cannot follow it. Sometimes they punish me."

Punish? Her confusion must have shown on her face, because Kai Tau gave a chilling smile. "Daughter, I am sorry. You have waited so many years to have your revenge. But there is nothing you can do to me. My guns will take your head off before you take one step forward. And even if I manage to stop them from shooting you, you cannot hurt me. You have come all this way and risked all these lives for nothing."

Kyra swallowed. "Even now, the Orders are defeating your soldiers. You will lose."

He gave a contemptuous shrug. "Soldiers are like cattle. I will get more, and train them better. The time of the Kanun is gone from Asiana. It is time for chaos. And what better king for such a time than the man who has become one with the weapons of chaos?" He slid one of the barrels up to his face and stroked it with his cheek.

"You have not told me," said Kyra, making her voice flat and calm, "why you did it."

"Ah, I thought you would come to that," said Kai. He rested both guns on his lap, as if he were crossing his arms. A contemplative look came onto his metal-scarred face. "It would be nice to have some sort of reason for you to pack away and take to your death. Let me see if I can think of one for you."

"I want the truth," said Kyra, anger giving her courage. "Don't lie for my benefit."

He threw his head back and laughed. "But I can lie for mine, can I not?" he said, still sounding amused, as if she was a child, or something to be toyed with. When she did not answer, he resumed speaking, his voice slowing, the shadows on the walls taking on even more tortured shapes, as if they sought to ferret out the last bit of sanity in the room and strangle it.

"It was twenty years ago," said Kai. "And still I remember it like yesterday. I saw a girl in a marketplace and fell deeply in love with her. The kind of love that happens in an instant, without regard for who or what you are. It takes you by storm, blinds you to everything but your goal—the pursuit and possession of the beloved."

"That's not love," said Kyra, her blood turning cold. "That's infatuation."

"What difference does it make what name you give to it?" he countered. "I loved her, and I persuaded her to run away with me."

"You compelled her," said Kyra, shaking with fury. "You used the Inner Speech to fog her mind."

"True," he said. "That is how it began. But that is not the way it continued. I reduced the pressure on her gradually. By the third day, she could have left me if she wanted to. She did not. She stayed with me, even singing to me in her beautiful voice as we rode over the highlands. She had fallen in love with me as deeply as I with her."

"You're lying to yourself," Kyra spat out. "You kidnapped an innocent girl and assaulted her. If she was too frightened or brainwashed to leave you, I do not blame her."

"You will never know," he said. "She is dead by my hand." He looked down at the guns fused to his arms and gave another crazed laugh. "*Literally* dead by my hand."

"Why did you kill her?" Kyra's voice rose in desperation despite herself. "*Why?*"

"Because she lied," snarled Kai. "She lied to protect herself. She betrayed me. If I could not have her, I vowed that no one else would." He paused and considered. "Besides, Astinsai told me before I left Khur that I would die by the hand of Fidan's daughter. I had to give you a reason to seek me out, did I not?"

Her mind reeled. "That doesn't make any sense."

"No," said Kai. "Foretellings rarely do. I think we've talked enough. My weapons thirst." His face twitched; he raised his arms and fired.

The sound was deafening in the enclosed space of the

council house. Bullets thudded against Kyra's chest, and she stumbled back with the force of the impact. She raised her arms to protect her face. She could scarcely breathe. Fear threatened to overwhelm her. This wasn't how it was supposed to go. She should have been able to kill him with her katari. How long could she survive this onslaught? Her blade—where was it when she needed it most?

A katari flew through the air, shining blue in the dim light, and lodged itself in Kai Tau's throat. *Rustan.* Momentarily, the blade appeared to confuse Kai Tau. He stopped firing and dropped his arms, stretching his neck. In the silence that followed, Kyra allowed herself to hope that he had been injured. But to her horror, the blade in his throat melted, and then clattered to the floor. This was impossible. Nothing could touch kalishium. Behind her, she sensed Rustan make a small sound of pain at the fate of his blade. *Go,* she thought to him frantically. *Leave!*

Kai Tau gave a hideous grin. "Someone you love," he said. "How perfect. I could not have hoped for better." And he raised his arm and shot Rustan. A single bullet.

Time slowed. Kyra whirled in an agony of fear. She tracked the bullet, threw herself in its path. It whistled past her head; she felt the small breath of its passing in her hair. And the soft, sickening thud as it found its mark.

A dreadful scream split the shadows on the walls, sending them scurrying into the corners of the council house. Kyra froze, realized the scream was her own, and ran to Rustan, her heart in a million pieces.

He lay in a heap at the entrance to the room, blood soaking his shirt. His face had gone gray. But his eyes, as they regarded her, were calm.

"Stay alive, Rustan," she whispered. "Navroz can heal you."

He opened his mouth to speak, and she bent closer to hear his words.

"Take. Shirin's blade," he rasped. "Finish him."

His eyes closed. But his chest rose and fell; his breath came in irregular gasps. He was still alive. And while there was breath in her body, she would do whatever it took to protect him.

She withdrew Shirin Mam's blade from the black metal scabbard at his waist, willing her hands not to shake. Then she turned and faced the killer who stood waiting for her, a smile playing on his lips. Standing, he towered over her. His arms hung loosely by his sides, the weapons gleaming wetly, as if they had drunk Rustan's blood.

"Another katari?" he said, sounding disappointed. "Is that all you have to offer me, daughter?"

"I. Am. Not. Your. Daughter," she hissed, and with every word she took a deliberate step toward him, even though she was shaking inwardly with fear and grief and rage. With every step she took, he took one forward as well, as if they were in a dance.

He expected her to throw the blade or stab him with it. She did neither. She made a sudden feint with her blade hand, pivoted sideways when he raised his arm to deflect her, and smashed her foot into his chest in a hard side kick.

It was like trying to smash a rock. Her foot felt as though it had broken in two. But it worked; Kai Tau stumbled back and fell. Quick as a fox she leaped on him, straddling his chest and pinning both arms down with her legs. She pushed aside her revulsion at the touch of the dark weapons. They could not hurt her any more than they already had.

She sent a quick prayer to Kali and thrust Shirin Mam's ancient blade into Kai Tau's chest.

The blade did not break, but it could not penetrate Kai Tau's skin. It was as if he wore armor of his own, impervious to kalishium. She gritted her teeth and kept up the pressure.

Beneath her, Kai Tau stopped struggling. "Twist the blade and find the chink," he said urgently.

Kyra glared with hatred into his eyes. "You want to die," she rasped. "You *want* me to kill you."

His body spasmed. "Quick," he said through gritted teeth. "I can't hold them back much longer."

He threw his head back and moaned. His eyes rolled in their sockets. The guns began to beat on the floor, a staccato rhythm. *Kill, kill, kill,* they sang.

Kyra closed her eyes and gave herself up to Shirin Mam's katari. She let her hands feel the blade, feel the small twist to position the edge just so, in that infinitesimal space between the metal fibers that protected Kai Tau's flesh. When she found the tiny chink, she did not even have to press down. The blade sank into his flesh and blood seeped out.

Kai Tau thrashed and fought beneath her, or maybe his weapons fought—was there any difference? Kyra hung on grimly until the thrashing slowed and then stopped. Kai Tau's head lolled to one side. His arms stilled. Blood frothed from his mouth.

Kyra withdrew Shirin Mam's blade, exhaling. She rose and made herself examine the body. There was no pulse in his throat.

Kai Tau was dead.

Her stomach heaved, and she stumbled away from the body. But she controlled herself. Rustan needed her. She pushed down her nausea, sheathed Shirin Mam's katari, and went to where Rustan lay unmoving by the entrance.

She licked a finger and put it to his nostrils. Still breathing. But he was so cold now, so clammy to the touch. He needed healing, fast.

Help me, she thought to Shurik and Ria and the others. *Please.*

She stroked Rustan's forehead, smoothed his tangled hair. He had let it grow out. After a while she realized that tears were falling from her eyes onto his cheeks, and she wiped her face with her sleeve.

Shurik and Ria arrived a minute later, along with some of the others. Not all were present. She couldn't remember who was missing. It was important, she knew, but she pushed it away, pushed everything away so she wouldn't have to feel.

Shurik brought horses and they slung Rustan over one of them, taking care not to touch his wound. They saw Kai Tau's body and asked her questions in urgent tones, but she could not make herself understand or answer them. She went back inside and retrieved both of the damaged blades, hoping that Rustan's might still have a spark of life. She could feel the pulse of a bond from her own. But Rustan's blade was cold and sterile, the tip twisted where it had melted. Even so, she slid it back into the scabbard at Rustan's belt. That was where it belonged.

Shurik picked up the bundle of kalashiks she had dropped in front of the council house and tied them to his saddle. The mask he handed over to Kyra. She took it without a word, unable to meet his gaze.

"Wait here," she said in a hollow voice. "Something I must do."

Something she needed the mask of Kali to do. She slipped on the mask, feeling the power of the Goddess surge through her blood and strengthen her for the loathsome task ahead.

No, not loathsome. Necessary. Best to do it now, while the body was still warm. She withdrew her blade and turned back to the council house.

"What are you doing, Kyra? We need to move," said Shurik from behind her.

"Removing his guns," said Kyra, and willed him to stay silent, stay outside.

Shurik, Ria, and the others did not follow her back in, for which she was grateful. She did not want them to witness what she had to do.

Inside the council house, the shadows on the walls went into a frenzy at her return. Kai Tau's body seemed to have moved to a different position, but how was that possible? Kyra gripped her blade and advanced on him. His eyes stared sightlessly at her.

We knew you would return to us. Take us for your own.

The cold, caressing voice startled her. Kai Tau's arms moved feebly, and bile rose in her throat. She swallowed her revulsion. The guns were still alive, even if the man they were fused to was dead. But they had no power over her, not while she wore kalishium, and not while she wore the mask.

"How right you are," she said tightly. "I have come to take you for my own."

And she brought her blade down on his upper arms, sawing through the metal and flesh and bone with sickening crunches. "For you, Mother," she muttered, as she perspired beneath her mask, not knowing which mother she meant: the one who had given birth to her, the one who had raised her, or the one whose mask she now wore.

When it was done, she picked up the two vile objects, still dripping with blood, and strode out of the council house. Ria averted her eyes and Shurik inhaled sharply, but she ignored them. She wrapped them in Ria's saddlebag and hung them on her mount.

At last they rode away. Distantly, Kyra could make out the sounds of battle; the fighting continued around them. Ria told her the Valavians had arrived and the Taus were in full retreat.

All that mattered was getting Rustan to Navroz in time.

It seemed to take hours. As they rode in and out of firelight, weaving between burning tents and broken bodies, it came to Kyra that she had come to conquer and kill, wearing the face of Kali. But the Goddess had extracted a heavy price for her victory—if it could be called such.

Kyra looked at Rustan, slumped over the saddle of his horse, and willed him not to die.

CHAPTER 45

ICE MOTHER

With the dawn came clouds, rare in the Thar Desert, as if the sun itself could not bear to look upon the carnage in Jethwa. Thousands of men and women lay dead or injured—among them villagers of the Thar Desert, who had been forced to join Kai Tau's army at gunpoint, and clansfolk loyal to the Orders, who had fought by their side and paid for it with their lives.

Tonar Kalam was dead. So was Noor Sialbi. Kyra was too stunned to take it in. They had fallen holding back Kai's men from the council house. Felda and Ghasil were missing, as were a number of other Marksmen and Markswomen. Chintil and the Maji-khan were badly injured.

Healers from the Order of Valavan picked their way through the bodies, reviving those they could, marking for the pyre those who were beyond their power to save. The elders of Khur led the search for kalashiks, directing the Marksmen to return them to the Order of Kali, with strict injunctions not to lay a hand upon the dark weapons.

The aftermath would hang over the Thar Desert for years. The dead would burn in mass funeral pyres, but the injured would take months to recover and return to a semblance of normalcy. Orphaned children had to be put into the care of relatives or foster families. The weapons had to be destroyed, as well as the forges that had been used to build them. The Order of Mat-su would be invoked to help deal with the psychological fallout from the loss of so many people in the region.

Kyra leaned against the wall of the cliff near the healer's post, her cloak wrapped around her shoulders in a futile effort to stave off the dawn chill. She had removed her armor and placed it with the mask of Kali in a saddlebag for Mumuksu. Her part in the battle was over, for good or ill. She had led the charge; she had killed the outlaw chief. *Like father, like daughter*, taunted an inner voice, but she ignored it.

She should be with the others in Jethwa, sifting through the weapons, checking the bodies, directing relief measures, and thought-shaping the survivors. But Faran Lashail, the head of the Order of Valavan, had stepped in to lead the cleanup. Navroz had told Kyra to stay with them, "where I can keep my eye on you."

It was not hard to obey Eldest. All of Kyra's thoughts were concentrated on the still form that lay before Navroz, covered with a blanket. As long as she could look at him, Rustan would stay alive. He would not leave her. She wouldn't *let* him. *Stay alive, Rustan.*

Navroz had explained to Kyra that she had removed the bullet from Rustan's chest and staunched the bleeding, but she could do nothing about the internal injury. Even now, black lines of poison crept over his skin. Unless they stopped, the best they could do for Rustan was keep him warm and pain-free until the inevitable end—perhaps no more than three days away.

Elena and Akassa tended to the others who had been wounded. But they came up to her now and then, to squeeze her hand or sit with her. She knew they meant well, but she wished they would leave her alone. She could not bring herself to speak, and the depth of the worry in their eyes made her feel guilty.

Nineth, who had been wounded, sat near Kyra, her face bleak. She had taken down her first mark, killed with her blade. So had Akassa. Kyra could sense the conflict in Nineth's thoughts. She had realized, as they all did sooner or later, how little glory there was in killing.

Shurik sat a little way away from them, his gaze also on Rustan. His eyes were exhausted, his face pale. He had expended too much of himself last night, and Eldest had told him gravely that he might never recover his powers in the Mental Arts. He had looked at her blankly, then bowed his head and said that it did not matter.

And how could it matter, how could anything matter, when Rustan's life ebbed away in front of their eyes?

Kyra tried to reach him with her thoughts, not caring who might overhear. *Wake up, beloved. Fight the poison. Stay with me.*

His eyes fluttered open and his head turned toward her. His mouth shaped her name: *Kyra.* Navroz beckoned her.

Kyra sprang up and rushed to his side, Shurik and Nineth close behind her. "Rustan," she said, bending over him, trying to smile. "How are you feeling?" She knew even as she said it how inane her words were. *How are you feeling after being shot with a dark weapon, its poison spreading through your body?*

"Kyra," said Rustan, his words clear although his voice was weak, "I must go to Kunlun Shan."

Her heart constricted. He was delirious. "We are taking you to the Order of Kali first," she said. "Navroz and I will take care of you. When you are well . . ."

His hand slipped out from under the blanket and caught hers. "I must go now," he said, his eyes fever-bright. "If you want to save me, take me there."

Confusion welled up in her. "I don't understand," she said. "How will going to Kunlun Shan save you?" His hand in hers was hot. He was burning up from inside.

"On the roof of the world, you will see and understand everything," said Rustan, and he closed his eyes, falling back into unconsciousness.

"We need to take him there," said Shurik grimly. "Those monks of his must have some sort of healing power."

Kyra started. She had forgotten his presence behind her. She had told him and Nineth about the monastery and the monks Rustan had talked about.

Navroz frowned. "He is in no shape to travel," she said. "We should take him to the caves of Kali."

Kyra swallowed, torn. "But, Eldest, you said you cannot do anything about the poison in his body," she finally said. "Perhaps there is something in the monastery that will heal him."

"Or perhaps he simply wants to go there and die," said Navroz quietly. "Do not get your hopes up."

Kyra's vision blurred. Eldest was most likely right. But she had to try. If there was the smallest chance that going to Kunlun Shan might restore Rustan to health, then she would do everything in her power to get him there.

"I'll go with you," said Shurik. "You'll need someone to help you carry him."

"And I," said Nineth firmly. "You're not leaving me behind this time."

"You're hurt—" began Kyra.

But Nineth interrupted: "A flesh wound. I will not slow you down, I promise."

"We'll take horses," said Kyra, and her heart began to lift. Despite Eldest's bleak words, hope stirred within her.

Navroz nodded, her face tight. "If your mind is made up, you should go now. I will inform the Maji-khan. And I will give you potions for him for the journey, to ease his pain." She looked up at Elena, who hovered behind them, her face taut. "I'm afraid we need you here, Elena. I can spare Nineth, but not you."

Nineth muttered something under her breath about being a spare, and Kyra could not help but smile. Elena had told her about the attack on the healer's post, and how Nineth had saved them all.

"When we return," she told Nineth, "we will have your initiation ceremony, as well as Akassa's."

Rustan stirred and moaned, spurring them into action. They saddled their horses, Shurik propping up Rustan in front of him with some effort. Navroz gave Rustan a brew to drink for strength, but it was obvious that he was in deep pain. Kyra's heart smote her whenever she looked at his drawn face, his tired eyes. *Soon, my love*, she thought. *Soon you will be free from suffering.*

Nineth packed provisions, and Elena gave them salves and analgesics. As the sun rose in the sky, they started toward Jhelmil, fifty miles away. They would take the door to the Deccan Hub, and then the door to Kunlun Shan. With luck, they could be in Kunlun Shan by early evening.

As they rode, they came across grim reminders of the battle they had fought the night before. Broken bodies littered the desert; people wept over them, searching for relatives. A group of stunned-looking children were being herded briskly by one of the Valavian Markswomen.

Kyra's eyes stung. It was a battle that had to be fought, and yet how she wished there had been no need for it. All because of one madman and the dark weapons he had stolen, which had in turn stolen all humanity from him. Once Rustan was all right, she was going to fulfill her vow and get rid of them, the only way she knew how.

They arrived at the Jhelmil door without incident. The little town was in upheaval, filled with refugees and survivors from Jethwa. Nineth and Kyra kept them away with the Inner Speech, although it was hard because both were spent from the fighting. Shurik could not summon the Inner Speech at all, although he tried. Even without it, he had a persuasive voice.

To one group of men and women who blocked their way to the door and demanded answers, explanations, and healing, he said in an exasperated tone that the able-bodied among them should go to Jethwa and help the less fortunate. He added the news that had been spreading like wildfire, but that none of them had believed: Kai Tau was dead, and the dark weapons were safe with the Orders once again.

Their faces cleared, and they bowed and stepped back. Kyra was grateful for Shurik's intervention. She knew it was not their fault, but she was impatient to get Rustan to the monastery, and anyone who stood in their way seemed nothing more than another obstacle to be overcome.

The Deccan Hub was busy, filled with the comings and goings of the Valavians and the clansfolk who had volunteered to help in Jethwa. They called out greetings to Kyra and cast curious glances at Rustan, but no one asked where they were headed, for which Kyra was grateful.

Their luck held; Kyra had been nervous about the door to Kunlun Shan, remembering how it had tricked her the first time she had tried to use it, how it had thrown her into the future and then into the past. But it worked like an ordinary door this time, and the four of them emerged into the dense forest of oak and pine at the base of Kunlun Shan, Nineth leading their horses, Rustan leaning on Shurik. Behind them, the door closed, the outline almost disappearing into the bark of the ancient tree.

Nineth inhaled deeply and gazed around in awe. Even Shurik seemed stricken into silence. Rustan, in contrast, perked up for the first time that day.

"Thank you," he said hoarsely, every word costing him effort. "If we start now, we might make it by midnight."

"It's already almost evening," said Kyra with regret. "We can camp here tonight and start at dawn. It will be dangerous trying to climb in the dark." She knew the perils of the forest and the icy slopes; Nineth and Shurik did not. Much as she wanted to get Rustan to the monastery as soon as possible, she could not risk the safety of her friends.

"How about we go partway and stop before the light fails?" asked Shurik.

Kyra agreed. They mounted their horses and Kyra led the way, Rustan stopping her from time to time to point out an easier path.

At dusk, they halted and made a small camp below the spreading branches of an oak.

You will lose someone you hold dear, the wyr-wolf had said. *But you will find them again. A bargain, is it not?*

Surely those words meant that Rustan would heal from his wound. Surely they must.

Nineth brewed tea and made Kyra drink it. They settled Rustan as best they could, wrapping him in warm blankets after spooning Navroz Lan's potion into his mouth to help him sleep. The lines of poison had spread; they extended from the wound on his chest up his neck, like the branching of a dark and terrible river. Kyra could not bear to look at them.

She took first watch, and Shurik the second. The horses they had tethered to the tree were calm and relaxed. No beast came to them that night, nor had Kyra expected it to. She had confronted it once; she had earned the right to be here. And you had to be alone to encounter it. But still there was that feeling of being watched, of being judged and found wanting. She could not escape the fear that she had missed an important piece of the puzzle, that her efforts were in vain.

And so she stayed awake, her eyes fixed on Rustan, even though Shurik tried to get her to rest. She could not sleep, not while Rustan twisted and moaned, talking in an incomprehensible language, words she could not understand. Perhaps he was talking to his monks. She hoped with all her heart that they could hear him, that they waited in their old monastery, ready to heal him with their mystic powers.

At dawn they set off after a meager breakfast of tea and dried fruit, Kyra once more taking the lead. The trees thinned, and they emerged above the tree line into the rocky splendor of the Kunlun Shan Range. The sun shone down, melting the ice on the paths. Peaks towered above them, seeming to touch the sky.

Rustan pointed to the highest mountain of all. "Ice Mother," he said, his voice breaking with exhaustion. "That is where I need to go. We will have to leave the horses tethered somewhere safe."

Kyra squinted, shading her eyes against the glare of the sun. "That is not where the monastery is," she said. "The monastery is halfway up a different rock face." Not that she could see it from here, but she remembered where it was.

Rustan hesitated. "I know. But I need to go to another building, on top of that peak. Trust me, the Sahirus are there."

Kyra frowned, calculating. It would take several hours to climb the highest peak, and Rustan was in bad shape. Why couldn't the monks have been waiting in the monastery?

"We have to climb *that*?" said Nineth in disbelief. "How?"

"I can go alone from here," said Rustan earnestly. "I will crawl, if necessary."

"Oh yes, you will crawl, and we will happily gallop back home on our horses," snapped Nineth. "Like that's happening. We may as well move along. If I die on the way, maybe you can all resuscitate me with whatever magical potions you find on top."

Shurik laughed—the first time Kyra had heard him laugh since they had parted ways. But Rustan looked troubled. *What are you not telling me?* she thought, but he did not answer, only sent her a wave of love and reassurance. With that she had to be content.

They climbed, their mounts picking their way delicately through moss-covered rocks and stones slippery with ice-melt. In the shelter of an overhang, near an outcropping of grass, they dismounted and tied the horses. While the horses grazed, they took a short break to eat and drink, then continued on without them. Kyra hoped the horses would be safe from bears and wolves, but there was no way they could take them any farther. The way ahead was too narrow and steep.

The path grew treacherous, as Kyra had known it would, and they were forced to proceed in single file. Rustan led the way, seeming to gain new strength the higher they climbed. Perhaps it was the proximity of the monastery that helped him. Kyra sensed when their path diverged from it, winding steeply up the side of the mountain.

Shurik was right behind Rustan, ready to support him in case he stumbled. Then came Nineth, red-faced and panting, but with a grim expression on her face that meant she was going to do this, no matter what. Kyra was last; she still had the feeling of being watched and followed, although she could hear and see nothing. Well, whatever it was, it would have to go through her to reach her friends.

At last, when Kyra's limbs were trembling with fatigue, and Nineth had actually begun to groan as she heaved herself up, one step at a time, Rustan said, "We are here," his voice breaking with emotion. And then he stumbled, and Kyra's heart jumped in alarm, but Shurik caught him in time, and helped him up the last few feet.

The ground leveled off, and Kyra blinked, unable to process what she was seeing.

Nineth whistled, and Shurik said, "What in the sands is *that*?"

They stood on the highest peak of the mountain range. All around, as far as the eye could see, snow-covered peaks stabbed the dark blue sky. The air was sharp and cold. Kyra took several deep breaths, trying to orient herself. Far below them, the thick green forest of Kunlun Shan hid the door that had brought them here. In the distance, a thin blue river snaked through a valley carved by glaciers.

But it was what loomed right in front of them, on the flat summit of the peak, that took away the breath, that made the mind stutter to a halt and think: *No*.

A massive oblong building with smooth, silver walls glinted in the afternoon sun. Several times larger than the Ferghana Hub, it was like no building Kyra had ever seen in Asiana. But in *Anant-kal*, the world beyond time, a structure similar to this had hung unsupported from the sky. *Like a strange moon*, she had thought then. The shape and size of the objects were somewhat different, but they were the same *kind* of thing. They evoked feelings of awe and fear in equal parts.

Rustan started toward the building, and dread seized hold of Kyra. She caught his arm. "Don't, please. It's too dangerous." Realizing, as she said it, that this had been his destination all along.

Rustan pulled her to him and grasped her shoulders. His hands were fever-hot, and his entire body shook. His eyes burned into hers, and she blinked back tears. The black lines of poison had begun to spread on his face. "I love you, Kyra," he said, touching her cheek with his fingertips, his voice raw with pain. "But this is where we must part. It's not safe for you here. Once I go into that building, anything might happen. Promise me you will leave."

"You said the monks would be here," said Kyra, hating the tremor in her voice. "You said they would heal you." *You said, you promised*. She wanted to cry. Because he had promised her nothing and she had *known*, known ever since she met the wyr-wolf, that she would lose someone she held dear. But had that stopped her? Had anything stopped her? She had done what she had to, and now she would pay the price.

"The monks *are* here," said Rustan. "Just not in the way you imagine. And I will be healed—at least, I think so. But as to what will happen after, I cannot say."

"It's a Hub, isn't it?" said Shurik, sounding troubled.

Rustan shook his head. "Not a Hub, no. But it is an artifact of the Ones. I don't know more than that, only what I am meant to do. And that you cannot follow me inside."

Kyra's hands curled into fists. "I'm going with you," she said fiercely. "You cannot stop me."

"No," said Rustan, exhaustion in every word, every line of his face. "But I can ask you to trust me. Only a Sahiru may enter this building. It is sealed to everyone else. I cannot go inside if you are with me. I have very little time left. Let me go, Kyra Veer. Let me go so that we may find each other again."

Kyra started. Rustan's words, so close to that of the wyr-wolf's, robbed her of all anger, leaving only a heartrending sadness. "Will you return?" she asked against the sting of tears. She could wait days, months, years even, if only she knew he was coming back.

"I don't think so," he said softly. "But wherever I go, I will wait for you. Will you come find me?"

Her stomach constricted. "You're talking of the door to death," she whispered.

His hand tightened over her arm. "I am not going to die," he said. "Doors can take us many places. Death is just one of them."

Shurik cleared his throat. "No doors here that I can see," he remarked, pointedly not looking at them.

Nineth muttered, "Idiot," and he shot her an annoyed look.

But Rustan didn't turn his attention away from Kyra. "Some doors are put there for us, and some we have to make," he said. "They go where we need them to. This is what I learned from the Sahirus."

He bent down and kissed her forehead, his lips warm against her cool skin. When he raised his face, it was damp with tears. And to Kyra's horror, the black lines of poison had reached his eyes, darkening his irises, cracking his pupils. He was falling apart, and she was selfishly preventing him from doing the one thing that might save him.

"Go," she said, pushing him gently, although every nerve in her screamed to hold on to him, to die with him, if that was what it took to be together. "Do what you must. I will find you again."

He stepped away from her, and it was like a chasm opening up at her feet, threatening to engulf her. Black spots danced before her eyes and she swayed, but Nineth was by her side, holding her up.

Rustan stumbled to the building, and every step he took away from her was like a punch in the gut. She wanted to double over and scream, but she didn't. She stayed upright, stayed silent, for his sake as well as her own. Nineth stood on one side of her, and Shurik on the other, and she gripped their hands, but it still felt as if she was drowning.

⚜

Time slowed. Every step seemed to last forever. It seemed to Rustan, as he drew one pain-filled breath after another, that he had detached from his damaged body. He watched himself approach the building, staggering as if he was drunk, his face nearly unrecognizable.

But superimposed on that pitiful image were other, pleasanter ones.

With the first step, he saw Shirin Mam. She held a baby in

her arms, and her face was full of wonder and joy. "I love you so much," she said, and kissed the top of the baby's head. Then she looked up into his eyes. Her expression became tender. "I love the person you will become even more," she said. "Go with my blessing."

Rustan's eyes stung. And he took the second step.

Now it was the Maji-khan, standing next to a gangly thirteen-year-old boy, beaming with delight. "Today we welcome a new apprentice of Khur," he announced. "Rustan, you have earned your katari at last." Cheers broke out among the assembled Marksmen. Barkav turned to face him. "You have worn it well," he said somberly. "Ishtul would have been proud."

Rustan swallowed the lump in his throat. And he took the third step.

And now it was a man he did not recognize, had never seen. But the contours of the face were familiar, and the lean, muscled body could almost have been his own. *Rubathar.* "My son," he said, and broke into a sad smile. "You are everything a father could wish for. Everything I myself could not be. My only regret is that I died before you were born. Please forgive me." He raised his curved sword in farewell, and Rustan took a fourth step.

He was kissing Kyra. Her hand tangled in his hair; his mouth was on her throat. Their first kiss, back in Kashgar, two days before her duel in Sikandra. Kyra broke away from the kiss and turned her smouldering gaze on him. "I thought I loved you then," she said. "But I was wrong. It was but a shadow of what I feel for you now."

Rustan's vision blurred. He thought he wouldn't be able to take another step, but she blew him a kiss and waved him on, even though tears gathered in her eyes.

At the last, it was the Sahirus who stood, tiny and indomitable, waiting for him to come to them. *How can he bear it?* asked the Younger Sahiru. *He has finally embraced life*, replied the Elder. *And now he will conquer death.* He turned his wizened face to Rustan and broke into a toothless grin. *Come.*

When Rustan reached the building, he laid his palm upon it, and it *glowed*. A wordless cry escaped Nineth's throat, but Kyra just watched, numb, as the door glimmered into existence. The door that would open only for him. The door that would take him away from her.

Rustan turned around, and for an instant stood framed by the open door. Kyra caught a brief glimpse of a vast, white hall. Then Rustan raised his hand in farewell. Kyra smiled, although it cut her heart in two, and blew him a kiss, as if he was going on a mission for his Order and would return in a week or two.

Then he stepped inside, and the door closed over him. The building shimmered and winked in the sun, as if it were waking up. Kyra's knees buckled, and she sank into the snow. A keening sound split the air: her own grief made audible at last.

Nineth slipped an arm around her shoulder, trying to soothe her, but Kyra could not hear what she was saying. Shurik frowned at the building and said something in an urgent tone. A look of alarm came on Nineth's face as she too gazed at the building. She tried to pull Kyra up, but Kyra didn't want to move from that spot. As long as she was still there, she could imagine, however hopelessly, that Rustan might emerge at any moment, healthy and alive.

Then, even through her anguish, she felt it: a tremor in the earth, vibrating her body.

The building was shaking, blurring at the edges. *No.*

Nineth was screaming now, still trying to pull her to her feet.

Rustan had said it was not safe. He had asked her to leave. She didn't care what happened to her right now—but through the fog of her pain, she realized she could not risk Nineth and Shurik.

Somehow, Kyra got to her feet and backed away quickly, her friends stumbling before her. Near the edge of the summit was a large rock, jutting out of the snowfield, and they dived behind it. There was no time to make a descent, and besides, whatever was happening might destabilize the snow and ice on the slopes and bury them in a landslide. They would have to wait this out.

The ground began to thrum. They held on to one another, held on to the rock, which was the one stable thing in the blurry landscape. The Order of Kali had lived through an earthquake in the Ferghana Valley when Kyra was ten, but this didn't feel quite like that. More as if something was shaking the earth, rather than the other way around.

The building came to life, lines and symbols dancing over its smooth walls. Kyra stared at it, and it seemed to stare back. Rustan was inside; she had let him go into that thing. *I am not going to die*, he had said, but how could he have known that for certain? She rose from behind the rock, with no clear idea of what she was going to do. Touch the building and see if it would open for her, maybe. Nineth and Shurik both tried to pull her back, but she shrugged them off and began walking, her steps unsteady, her heart hammering.

That was when it happened.

The structure vibrated, gave a final flicker of violet light, and *vanished*. One moment it was there, and the next gone, just like that. Kyra froze.

Silence returned to the summit of Kunlun Shan, and with it a sense of emptiness. A vast presence had examined her, found her wanting, and moved on, taking with it the man she loved. Or maybe it only felt that way to her. Maybe it wasn't personal at all.

"What?" Shurik sounded as stunned as she felt. "What?"

Kyra ignored him; she willed herself to walk to the space the building had occupied. She knelt on the ground, at the edge of the oblong-shaped crater. Heat emanated from the earth; it hadn't been a trick or an illusion. Something had been here, and now it wasn't.

"Kyra?" Nineth's voice was shaky but calm. "We can camp here tonight. Maybe he'll come back."

Kyra's eyes blurred. "He's not coming back," she said. "I'll have to go find him."

"We should return to our Orders," said Shurik, his voice rough with emotion. "Maybe the elders will know what to do."

Kyra didn't say anything; they all knew that the elders would not be able to help them. Shurik was grasping at straws. Perhaps he meant to comfort her. His own face was tight with suppressed grief. Rustan had been his closest friend.

Finally, she raised her eyes to his. Whatever he saw in them made him flinch. But she rearranged her expression, made herself smile, and took his hand. "The elders won't know what to do," she said. "But I will."

CHAPTER 46

THE COST OF VICTORY

By the time they returned to the caves of Kali, many of the Markswomen and some of the injured Marksmen had arrived there too. The rest were still in the Thar Desert, working with the Order of Valavan to repair the fabric of life torn apart by war and years of suppression under Kai Tau's rule.

The cost of victory had been high. Apart from the numberless casualties on Kai Tau's side, hundreds of loyal clansfolk had been killed or wounded. The central cavern of Kali had been converted into a sick bay. Those who hovered on the knife-edge between life and death had been given individual cells.

Felda Seshur, the Order's beloved mathematician, was dead. Kyra received the news, but was too numb to react. Her heart felt as if it were being squeezed in a cruel fist. Any moment now, she thought, she would see the scowling face of her favorite elder, and all would be as it was.

But nothing would ever be the same for any of them. Ghasil, the Master of Mental Arts, was dead too—not from bullets or swords, but from overextending himself on the night of the battle. He had incapacitated hundreds of Kai Tau's soldiers, saving countless lives in the process, but had lost his own.

Chintil had been shot by a kalashik. It had shattered her right arm, and Navroz had amputated it to prevent the poison spreading to the rest of Chintil's body. Now she lay gray-faced and still on a pallet in her cell, drifting in and out of consciousness, the stump on her shoulder wrapped in a blood-soaked bandage. If she survived, the Mistress of Hatha-kala would never again wield Double Katari or Empty Hands with the same level of skill. She would have to learn how to fight without her blade hand.

The Maji-khan had suffered hundreds of wounds on his body and had lost a great deal of blood. Samant, the Master of Meditation, sat by his side, spooning medicine into his mouth, assisted by the Marksman Aram.

The Valavians too had taken heavy losses in the fighting. Six of their number had been killed, and several wounded, among them Derla Siyal.

Kyra put aside her own grief and threw herself into helping the others. Navroz had summoned medicine women from miles around, but she still needed every bit of assistance she could get. There were far too many wounded for her and Elena to take care of. Navroz assigned Kyra to Chintil. Shurik was put to work changing bandages and thought-shaping the injured clan warriors who lay in the central cavern moaning in agony. He had recovered a small fraction of his powers, enough to alleviate the pain of those who suffered most.

Nineth supervised the novices, brewing potions and preparing salves. Tarshana sent for her own cousins to help in the kitchen, preparing healthful soups for those who could eat.

How much time passed? It was difficult to say. Weeks, perhaps, or months. One day blurred into another, with little sleep and less rest, marked only by the last rites of those who were gone forever from their midst.

One by one, clansfolk came to collect their surviving kin, to take care of them in their own homes. At last Chintil was able to sit up and snap at Kyra to stop hovering around her with a face like death, she was quite all right, thank you very much, and go take care of the others. Kyra smiled for the first time since her return as she left Chintil's cell. It felt strange, as if her facial muscles had forgotten how to smile.

She went to the Maji-khan, who had recovered enough to be able to sit outside under the mulberry tree, meditating with Samant, Aram standing guard behind them. The Maji-khan had been reduced to a mere shadow of his once-powerful self. His robes hung on his skeletal frame and his face was that of a much older man who had seen and suffered much. But his eyes were as deep and compelling as ever. Kyra exhaled and knelt before him.

It was hard to tell him about Rustan's fate, hard to add to the suffering in that face. But Kyra made herself do it, leaving nothing out.

When she was done, there was silence but for the sound of the wind in the branches of the mulberry tree. The last days of autumn, and soon winter would be upon them. Before that, Kyra would leave.

As if he had read her thoughts, Barkav said, "Your Order needs you."

Kyra bowed her head. "They have each other," she said. "And Rustan needs me too."

"Are you sure?" asked the Maji-khan, his voice soft. "Perhaps he has gone to a place you cannot follow."

"I have to try," she said. "He said he would wait for me. Perhaps my path is different from his, but our destination is the same."

"So be it," said Barkav, and sadness passed across his face. "Go with my blessing, Kyra Veer. May you find what you are looking for."

She rose and bowed to him, not trusting herself to speak.

The Marksmen left a few days later, along with their clansfolk. They would stay in Kashgar until the Maji-khan was well enough to travel to Khur. Shurik came to say goodbye to Kyra, but when the moment to part came, they were both tongue-tied. Odd, how much he seemed to have become a part of Kyra's own Order in the past few weeks. At last he gave her a brief, fierce hug, and told her to punch Rustan for him when she finally found him, which made her laugh through her tears.

With the Marksmen and clansfolk gone, the caves of Kali returned to their old quiet. Akassa and Nineth were initiated as Markswomen—Elena too, in a special ceremony that recognized her gift and her tireless efforts to heal the war-wounded. Helen passed her coming-of-age ritual and was made apprentice. Ria Farad was inducted as an elder into the council.

Slowly, classes resumed. Two new novices—twin sisters from Nineth's clan—found their way to the Order, and this so heartened the elders that they almost began to resemble their old selves.

Every evening, Kyra sat with the elders in the central cavern, discussing how the Orders might best survive the changes that had been wrought on their world by time and war. She brought up the incident of Akassa's first mark, and Navroz agreed that the woman had needed healing more than punishment. They constructed a decision tree on a roll of parchment that would help them resolve such situations in future.

She also finally confessed to her crime of Compulsion, telling the elders how she had used the Mental Arts to subjugate Rustan and steal the kalishium from the monastery. They were silent as she poured out the whole story to them, but when she asked for a penance, the words sounded hollow even to her own ears. They did not have to tell her that any penance they could devise would be as nothing compared to how she had already been punished. But under Mumuksu's guidance, she meditated every day, scraping out from her soul every last bit of influence that still lingered from Tamsyn's blade. The day she achieved the third level of meditation, she knew she had succeeded at last.

Felda's absence was an aching wound that became duller with time, but never quite healed. Mumuksu took up some of Felda's work, poring over her old books with Kyra, trying to decipher the mathematician's notes.

It would have been easy to slip back into this new routine, to forget what she had vowed to do.

But one full-moon night, a howl sounded outside the caves of Kali. Kyra awoke, her heart thudding. Her hand went to the tiny wyr-wolf image she kept hidden under her pillow, and she knew. It was time to deliver it.

She dragged on a cloak and stumbled out of her cell, clutching the image. Mumuksu, Ria, and Navroz strode into the cavern, their faces anxious, but Kyra deflected them. "It's a friend," she reassured them. "Someone I must meet."

Outside, the full moon bathed the landscape in silver light, transforming it so it looked unreal. And in the middle of the grassy hollow just beyond the caves, half hidden by the rushes that swayed in the chilly wind, was Kyra's visitor: Sudali, the alpha female of the Vulon pack.

Kyra went up to her and bowed. "Greetings, Sudali," she whispered. "I . . . I have what Menadin asked for."

She held out her palm, proffering the kalishium image. Sudali's eyes glowed and she dipped her massive head toward Kyra's hand. Kyra felt the wyr-wolf's warm breath, and then the image disappeared from her palm into Sudali's mouth.

The wyr-wolf reared back, snorting and gasping, and Kyra stepped back in alarm. The fearsome wolf shape twisted and elongated, replaced by a tall, strapping woman with golden eyes and long black hair streaked with silver. Her naked skin shone in the moonlight. She was both beautiful and terrifying to look upon. Kyra blinked, her mouth dry, and resisted the impulse to flee.

The woman held up her hands and laughed in delight. "I remember," she said in a rich, throaty voice. She touched her own cheek in wonder.

"What—what do you remember?" asked Kyra.

"Everything," said the woman, who was also Sudali. "The Ones made us—did you know that? They made us in the shape of one of their favorite images."

"I don't understand," said Kyra, her stunned mind trying to process what Sudali was telling her.

Sudali smiled. "They were—they *are*—shape-shifters themselves."

"What do they *truly* look like?" asked Kyra eagerly.

Sudali shook her head. "That they did not reveal, not to us. Perhaps not to any humans. Easier, you see, to take the shapes they found here." She squeezed Kyra's shoulder. "I must return to my pack and tell them what I have seen. I must share the kalishium, so they too can remember."

Kyra nodded numbly, trying to take in what she had learned.

Sudali's shape hunched and twisted back into a wyr-wolf. Watching the reverse transformation was somehow more alarming, but Kyra knew it was an honor to have been allowed to witness it, and she bowed in thanks.

Sudali gave a small whuff and touched Kyra's shoulder with her snout before turning away. When she had reached the edge of the hollow, the wyr-wolf turned and gave Kyra a last look.

It is time.

And she left, moving with silent grace, becoming one with the night.

⚜

Kyra returned to the cavern with leaden feet. Navroz sat on a bench, waiting for her.

"Eldest . . ." she said, a plea in her voice.

"You're going away," said Navroz flatly.

Kyra swallowed. "I have vowed to rid Asiana of the dark weapons. There is only one way I know how."

"And if that way takes you from us, is it worth it?" said Navroz, rising from the bench and coming up to her, gripping her arm hard.

"Never again," said Kyra. "Never again in Asiana will those kalashiks work their evil. Yes, it's worth it, and you know it, Eldest."

Navroz let go of her arm and leaned against the wall, closing her eyes. Kyra wanted to hug her, to tell her she was sorry, that she would stay after all, but she couldn't. So she hardened herself. If she weakened now, it would all be for nothing. Another Kai Tau would rise up, and the dark weapons would find a way to kill again. "Did you gather the weapons, as I asked?" she said instead.

Navroz nodded. "We stashed them in the funerary chamber," she said in a dead voice. "By the feet of the Goddess. To dampen their power."

"What about"—Kyra made herself say it—"what about the ones that were fused with Kai Tau?"

"With the rest of them," said Navroz. "All twelve kalashiks stolen by Kai Tau are accounted for. We have eight and the remaining four are with the Valavians."

Those twelve kalashiks had killed her entire clan. "Never again," repeated Kyra fiercely.

Navroz exhaled. "What about the ones in the Temple of Valavan?"

"I will get them tomorrow," said Kyra. "Faran Lashail will give them to me."

Navroz nodded. "Mumuksu and I will accompany you," she said. "You should have an escort for such a task."

"Thank you, Eldest," said Kyra, and this time she did hug Navroz, and took comfort from the warmth of her embrace. Her heart lifted, as if she had been released from a burden that had weighed her down for the past several weeks. And hadn't she? An unfulfilled vow was the heaviest yoke of all. Better the weight of the dark weapons on her back. Better the door that beckoned, saying, *Come, it is time.*

What had Rustan said? *Some doors are put there for us, and some we have to make. They go where we need them to.*

CHAPTER 47

INTO THE DARK

Half the Order of Valavan was still in the Thar Desert, working with the villagers to rebuild burned homes and broken lives. Derla Siyal, Kyra was glad to hear, had recovered from her wounds and been made a council elder. She had returned to the Thar to direct relief efforts. But Faran Lashail was in the temple, waiting for Kyra. Had been waiting, she told Kyra, for weeks.

"What is this way you've found to remove the dark weapons from Asiana?" she asked once the greetings were over and steaming hot cinnamon tea had been served. They sat in a small chamber down a passage off the Hall of Reflection. As they had crossed the hall, Kyra hadn't been able to help glancing at the mirrors, remembering the mishmash of images she had last seen.

But to her surprise, she saw just herself this time; the only bit that reminded her of Shirin Mam was the black robe, which had once belonged to her old teacher. Navroz and Mumuksu, she noted, studiously avoided looking into the mirrors.

Kyra set aside her cup and considered what to tell Faran Lashail. "I have found a door in a secret Hub," she said at last. "A door that leads out of Asiana."

Faran Lashail raised her eyebrows. "And it goes . . . where?"

She shook her head. "I don't know. It feels like an abyss. But it feels also as if I am meant to take that door. I have dreamed of it since my childhood."

"You are needed here," said Faran, echoing the words of the Maji-khan and the doubts in Kyra's own heart.

"The Mahimata will do what she must," said Navroz. "If this is the destiny she chooses, then so be it. But we will not anoint another, not during her natural life-span." She turned to Kyra. "We will wait for you. Try to return to us, if you can."

Kyra's eyes stung. Eldest's words of support and love cut deeper than any recriminations would have. "I will try," she promised.

They did not stay long after that. Faran ordered two of her elders to fetch the death-sticks from the underground vault where they were hidden. They were brought forth, wrapped in a thin kalishium shroud: thirteen of them, Faran said, the last remnants of the weapons of the Great War.

Kyra fashioned a sledge for herself with the help of the Valavians, using a narrow wooden pallet and a rope to drag the load. Mumuksu and Navroz lashed the kalashiks to the sledge, but Kyra would not let them pull it. This was her burden, and hers alone. The less the elders touched it, the easier it would go for them. The only tricky part was bringing it down the stairs to the Hub of Valavan, but Kyra managed it without breaking the sledge, which was a blessing.

And so they left the Temple of Valavan, Faran standing at the top of the steps that led down to the Hub, her hand raised in farewell, her face tight with sorrow. "Till we meet again, Kyra Veer," she called, as the Transport door closed behind them.

∽❦∾

The hardest part was saying goodbye to Elena and Nineth. They could not understand why Kyra had to go, why the kalashiks could not simply remain in the Temple of Valavan. Again and again she tried to explain it to them, but at last she had no more reasons left, and cried instead, the language of tears accomplishing what words could not. She gathered them in her arms, their individual griefs becoming one, enveloping them until she did not know where she ended and they began.

She left early the next day, deflecting their entreaties to stay longer. It would only get more difficult to leave with time, not easier. The kalishium armor, the mask of Kali, and Shirin Mam's blade she left in Mumuksu's care; they would stay in the funerary chamber until needed again. The Goddess willing, they would not be needed for many, many years. She took nothing but her own katari with her.

The entire Order came out to bid Kyra farewell. She turned to look at them one last time, the small knot of women under the mulberry tree. So few in number, so strong in heart. Akassa stood straight and proud, a fierce glare on her face, as if daring the tears to touch her cheeks. She nodded and gave Kyra an encouraging smile. *Go on now, do what you have to. Don't worry about us.*

The novices gathered around Mumuksu, the emotions evident on their young faces. Nineth stood with Elena a little way away from the others, the only one crying openly. Kyra's heart clenched. But she would not worry about Nineth. Nineth had Elena, after all, and all the others.

But what of Navroz? Eldest looked close to the door of death, her face ashen, her cheeks hollow. *Goodbye, Kyra*, she sent to her, and Kyra knew, in that moment, she would never see Eldest alive again.

She almost went running back to them. Was it worth it? How could anything be worth this? It wasn't fair.

Her katari burned with a quiet urgency, and with a start she remembered the dreadful burden she must drag all the way to Yashmin-Gah. And, remembering, she was barely able to stay upright.

She had a task to do, the most important task that had ever befallen a Markswoman, and she would do it even though every step she took away from her home was a knife through her heart.

Goodbye, Eldest, she sent to Navroz, holding her grief at bay. She would not disgrace her teachers and break down, but it was hard, oh so hard.

Elena moved away from Nineth and went to stand with Navroz. She put an arm around the elder, supporting her. Akassa and Nineth came and stood on the other side of the elder. And it seemed to Kyra that Navroz stood a little straighter, a little stronger. *Thank you, my dear friends, for everything*, thought Kyra. *The Goddess be with you till we meet again.*

She turned to go, feeling their gazes on her back, their longing pulling at her.

A long, drawn-out howl split the air. Far in the distance, Kyra made out several large shapes cresting a hill and loping downward.

Her spirits lifted slightly. The wyr-wolves were coming . . .

to send her off, perhaps? Make sure she did as she had promised Menadin and rid their world of the death-sticks?

The wyr-wolves—ten of them, all from Menadin's pack, Kyra guessed, led by Sudali—circled her once, then split into two lines, padding to her left and right.

Behind Kyra came gasps and tiny suppressed cries. This time, Kyra was able to smile as she set off across the grassy meadows between the hills. She had an honor guard to be proud of. The sun rose in the sky and stabbed her with its first rays, so that, for a moment, she could not see.

Then she saw, and the sight brought wonder to her heart, for the mountains looked as if they were on fire, and all around, flowers were unfurling pink and scarlet petals in the sun.

❧

How long did she walk across the valley? It could have been hours, or days. The wyr-wolves never once left her side, and for this she was grateful; otherwise she may have faltered. When she reached the base of Yashmin-Gah, it was dusk, and they loped ahead of her, showing her the way up the hill.

She dragged the sledge up the steep path, one weary step at a time. Thrice she slipped on the stones and fell, scratching her hands and knees, but she barely felt the cuts. She was like an observer, watching herself as she trudged up the hill, heedless of the pain in her back and legs.

At last, she arrived at the little pool of water. The moon rose, fat and silver, nestled against the starry sky. Kyra shrugged the rope from her burning shoulders and bent to drink from the shimmering pool. *I am drinking the moon*, she thought, splashing water on her face.

Exhaustion hit her, and she collapsed on the bed of rushes that edged the pool. It was soft here, and comfortable, and she would dearly have liked to rest. But she was cold, so cold.

Warm bodies pressed around her, giving her their heat, nudging her away from the pool. Kyra's eyes flew open. The wyr-wolves bent their hideous faces toward her, and multiple forked tongues caressed her cheeks. She sat up abruptly, her tiredness gone.

"Thank you," she said. "Yes, I'm leaving. I will keep my promise, if it's the last thing I do."

Before she could lose her temporary strength, Kyra crawled to the place where she knew the door was hidden and pushed away the spiky undergrowth.

And there was the door, just like before. She inserted the tip of her blade into the slot, and the door swung open. *Welcome*, it said. *I have been waiting for you a long time.*

Kyra pushed down her fear. "Well, here I am at last," she said. "I hope the wait was worth it."

She pushed the sledge with its repulsive load into the passage. It landed with a sickening thud, as if the Hub knew what it contained and was horrified by it. She turned to bid farewell to the wyr-wolves. They had retreated to the edges of the forest around the pool, but she knew they were there, all the same.

"Goodbye," she said. "Thank you for everything. I hope we meet again."

Then she squeezed herself into the passage. The door swung closed behind her, and she was once more in the womb of the secret Hub. She had escaped it once, only to return a second time, a willing victim.

As the passage broadened, Kyra stood, dragging the weapons

behind her. Nothing to be gained in delaying this any longer. The quicker she did it, the less chance of her panicking.

First door, second door, and . . . third door.

She stood before it awhile, letting the strangeness seep into her, become one with her. If she laid her palm on it, would she sense the world end the way she had last time?

But nothing happened when she touched the door. Only when she slipped the tip of her blade into the slot did a numbered screen slide out. She tapped in the third code from Felda's pyramid, and the door slid open to reveal an ordinary Transport Chamber. She entered, and pale blue lights came on in the circular room with seats melded to the floor. She sat down on one to wait, and still no vision came to her, no sense of anything amiss.

Several minutes passed, and Kyra sensed the spinning room slow down and then stop. She swallowed hard and stood. It was time.

She walked to the Transport door and pushed it open. A rush of breath escaped her lips, and she staggered back, her heart pumping.

There was nothing beyond the door. Just darkness. Not the darkness of a new-moon night, for that is softened by stars, nor the darkness of a Transport corridor, which is lined by the glowing slots of Transport doors.

This was the complete and utter absence of light.

But wasn't that also the definition of the Goddess Kali? Kali the *dark* one, she who came before light itself, before time itself.

Then what was there to fear about the dark?

Kyra gripped the rope of her sledge and steadied herself. She gathered her courage and shouted, "I'm coming, Mother!"

And then, before she could think about what she was doing, Kyra ran through the door and leaped.

And

she

fell.

She tried to hold on to the rope of her sledge, but it slipped from her, as did so much else. The first thing to go was her name. She tried to remember it as she fell, tried to remember why it was important. Something about a clan, a mother and a father who had been taken from her. But she could not remember them, could not recall what had happened, who had taken them, and why.

The next to go were her senses. There was nothing to see, to touch, to hear in the endless dark. As her memories vanished, one by one, there was nothing left to feel.

Except, she had loved someone once. Loved so much it hurt.

In every heart there was a blade, and . . .

Stay alive, Kyra.

The blade within her twisted and feeling came back in a rush of pain and fear. She would have screamed, if she had a voice left to scream with. She would have struggled, if she still had limbs.

Kyra, she thought. *That is who I am. Kyra of the clan of Veer and the Order of Kali.* She held on to her name like a talisman.

And still she fell, for an eternity or a moment—it was impossible to know. But now it was like falling *up*, as if this nothingness had a destination. Slowly, the rest of her senses returned to her. Coldness on her skin, a rush of wind in her hair, and in the darkness, far distant, a speck of violet light, almost unbearable after the pitch-black.

She opened her mouth, heard herself gasp in great lungfuls of the cold air. And still that speck of light grew larger, brighter, as if to say: *Look, there is still a world, if only you could reach it.*

Kyra sobbed and prayed, *Oh, Kali, let me live or let me die.*

She fell toward the light even faster, as if it had a gravity of its own. She thought it might be a door, but the light spread as far as the eye could see above her. *Like a lilac sky.* And with that thought she hit the ground, landing on her hands and knees in what appeared to be stiff purple grass.

She pushed herself up, trying to breathe normally and failing. The twilit air was sharp and cool, scented with unfamiliar odors, with a tinge, oddly, of raspberries. A red sun shone low in the sky. On the opposite horizon were two gibbous moons. It should have given her pause, made her examine her surroundings more closely. Made her wonder why she felt lighter than she was.

But she had eyes only for the man who stood facing her, facing the Hub she had tumbled out of. A tall man with dark hair, broad-shouldered and lean. A mind she recognized, and a heart that had called out to her across time and space, drawing her to him. A face that was older than she remembered, but with the same slate-blue eyes, the same tender smile. Free of the poison that had nearly killed him.

She opened her mouth to say his name but could not. Her breath hitched, and tears gathered in her eyes.

He opened his arms, and she took one step toward him. Then another. And then she was flying toward him, running so hard she almost knocked him over. He gave a low laugh against her hair and locked his arms around her. "Kyra," he said, and it was his voice, his pulse that beat with hers, his lips against her lips.

She laughed, cried, then laughed again. It was a long while before she could shape coherent thoughts. It was a long while before he released her. Then, and only then, did she step away from him and turn her gaze to the lilac sky.

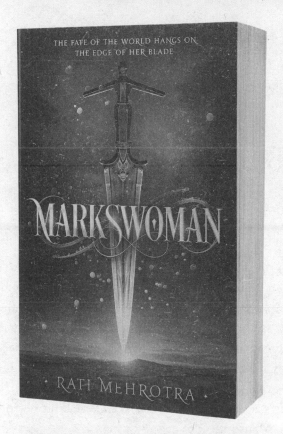

ABOUT THE AUTHOR

Born and raised in India, Rati Mehrotra currently makes her home in Toronto, Canada. When not working on her Asiana books, she writes short fiction and blogs at ratiwrites.com. Her short stories have appeared in Apex Magazine, AE: The Canadian Science Fiction Review, Abyss & Apex, IGMS, and many other publications, and have also been featured on the podcasts *Podcastle* and *Cast of Wonders*. Find her on Twitter @Rati_Mehrotra.